STAR WARS™

—[CORUSCANT NIGHTS I]—

JEDI TWILIGHT

STAR WARS™

-[CORUSCANT NIGHTS I]-

JEDI TWILIGHT

Michael Reaves

arrow books

Published in the United Kingdom by Arrow Books in 2008

1 3 5 7 9 10 8 6 4 2

First published in the United Kingdom in 2008 by Arrow

Arrow Books
The Random House Group Limited
20 Vauxhall Bridge Road, London, SW1V 2SA

Addresses for companies within The Random House Group Limited can be
found at: www.randomhouse.co.uk/offices.htm

The Random House Group Limited Reg. No. 954009

www.rbooks.co.uk
www.starwars.com

A CIP catalogue record for this book
is available from the British Library

ISBN 9780099492092

The Random House Group Limited supports The Forest Stewardship Council
(FSC), the leading international forest certification organisation. All our titles
that are printed on Greenpeace approved FSC certified paper carry the FSC
logo. Our paper procurement policy can be found at
www.rbooks.co.uk/environment

Mixed Sources
Product group from well-managed
forests and other controlled sources
www.fsc.org Cert no. TT-COC-2139
© 1996 Forest Stewardship Council

Printed in the UK by CPI Bookmarque, Croydon, CR0 4TD

For
Michael Meadows

acknowledgments

Once again, thanks go first and foremost to my editors: Shelly Shapiro at Del Rey and Sue Rostoni at LucasBooks, who asked me to walk on the wild side of Coruscant again; to Leland Chee and the other galactic wonks who never got tired of continuity questions; to Matt Stover and Steve Perry for the characters of Nick Rostu and Prince Xizor; and, as always, to George Lucas for the whole shebang.

THE STAR WARS NOVELS TIMELINE

1020 YEARS BEFORE
STAR WARS: A New Hope

Darth Bane: Path of Destruction
Darth Bane: Rule of Two

33 YEARS BEFORE
STAR WARS: A New Hope

Darth Maul: Saboteur*

32.5 YEARS BEFORE STAR WARS: A New Hope

Cloak of Deception
Darth Maul: Shadow Hunter

32 YEARS BEFORE STAR WARS: A New Hope

STAR WARS: EPISODE I
THE PHANTOM MENACE

29 YEARS BEFORE STAR WARS: A New Hope
Rogue Planet

27 YEARS BEFORE STAR WARS: A New Hope
Outbound Flight

22.5 YEARS BEFORE STAR WARS: A New Hope
The Approaching Storm

22 YEARS BEFORE STAR WARS: A New Hope

STAR WARS: EPISODE II
ATTACK OF THE CLONES

Republic Commando: Hard
Contact

21.5 YEARS BEFORE STAR WARS: A New Hope
Shatterpoint

21 YEARS BEFORE STAR WARS: A New Hope
The Cestus Deception
The Hive*
Republic Commando: Triple Zero
Republic Commando: True Colors

20 YEARS BEFORE STAR WARS: A New Hope
MedStar I: Battle Surgeons
MedStar II: Jedi Healer

19.5 YEARS BEFORE STAR WARS: A New Hope
Jedi Trial
Yoda: Dark Rendezvous

19 YEARS BEFORE STAR WARS: A New Hope
Labyrinth of Evil

STAR WARS: EPISODE III
REVENGE OF THE SITH

Dark Lord: The Rise of Darth
Vader

10-0 YEARS BEFORE STAR WARS: A New Hope
The Han Solo Trilogy:
  The Paradise Snare
  The Hutt Gambit
  Rebel Dawn

5-2 YEARS BEFORE STAR WARS: A New Hope

*The Adventures of Lando
Calrissian*

The Han Solo Adventures

STAR WARS: A New Hope
YEAR 0

Death Star

STAR WARS: EPISODE IV
A NEW HOPE

0-3 YEARS AFTER STAR WARS: A New Hope
Tales from the Mos Eisley
  Cantina
Allegiance
Galaxies: The Ruins
  of Dantooine
Splinter of the Mind's Eye

3 YEARS AFTER STAR WARS: A New Hope

STAR WARS: EPISODE V
THE EMPIRE STRIKES BACK

Tales of the Bounty Hunters

3.5 YEARS AFTER STAR WARS: A New Hope
Shadows of the Empire

4 YEARS AFTER STAR WARS: A New Hope

STAR WARS: EPISODE VI
RETURN OF THE JEDI

Tales from Jabba's Palace
Tales from the Empire
Tales from the New Republic

The Bounty Hunter Wars:
  The Mandalorian Armor
  Slave Ship
  Hard Merchandise

The Truce at Bakura

dramatis personae

DAL PERHI; Black Sun Underlord (human male)

DARTH VADER; Dark Lord of the Sith (human male)

DEN DHUR; former HoloNet news reporter (Sullustan male)

EVEN PIELL; Jedi Master (Lannik male)

HANINUM TYK RHINANN; personal aide to Darth Vader (Elomin male)

I-5YQ; protocol droid

JAX PAVAN; Jedi Knight (human male)

KAIRD; Black Sun operative (Nediji male)

LARANTH TARAK; Jedi Paladin and freedom fighter (Twi'lek female)

NICK ROSTU; former brevet major, Republic army, freedom fighter (human male)

PRINCE XIZOR; Black Sun operative (Falleen male)

If droids could think, there'd be
none of us here, would there?

—Obi-Wan Kenobi

"A long time ago in a galaxy far, far away. . . ."

—[PART I]—

LIFE DURING WARTIME

one

In the lowest levels, in the abyssal urban depths, of the ecumenopolis that was Coruscant, it was a rare thing indeed to see sunlight. For the inhabitants of the baroque and gleaming cloudcutters, skytowers and superskytowers—the latter reaching as much as two kilometers high—the sun was something taken for granted, just as were the other comforts of life. Since WeatherNet guaranteed that it never rained until dusk or later, the rich golden sunlight was simply expected, in the same way that one expected air to fill one's lungs with every breath.

But hundreds of stories below the first inhabited floors of the great towers, ziggurats, and minarets, in some places actually on or under the city-planet's surface, it was another story. Here hundreds of thousands of humans and other species lived and died, sometimes without ever catching as much as a glimpse of the fabled sky. Here the light that filtered through the omnipresent gray inversion layer was wan and pallid. The rain that reached the surface was nearly always acidic, enough so at times to etch tiny channels and grooves into ferrocarbon foundations. It was hard to believe that anything at all could survive in these dismal trenches. Yet even here life, both intelligent and otherwise, had adjusted long ago to the perpetual twilight and strictured environment.

At the very bottom of the chasms, in the variegated pulsing of phosphor lights and signs, stone mites, conduit worms, and other scavengers flourished on technological detritus. Duracrete slugs blindly masticated their way through rubble. Hawk-bats built nests near power converters to keep their eggs warm. Armored rats and spider-roaches scuttled and hunted through piles of trash two stories high. And millions of other species of opportunistic and parasitic organisms, from single-celled animalcules all the way up to those self-aware enough to wish they weren't, doggedly pursued their common quest for survival, little different from the struggles on a thousand different jungle worlds. Down here was where the jetsam of the galaxy, a motley collection of sentients dismissed by those above simply as "the underdwellers," eked out lives of brutality and despair. It was merely a different kind of jungle, after all.

And where there's a jungle, there are always those who hunt.

Even Piell had been one of the lucky ones. Born on the violence-plagued planet Lannik to an impoverished family, he had been taken by the Jedi in his infancy because of his affinity for the Force. He had been raised in the Temple, high above the poverty and misery that had once seemed the inevitable birthright of his homeworld. True, his life had been somewhat ascetic, but it had also been clean, ordered, and—most important of all—it had been *purposeful*. It had been about something. He had been part of a cause greater than himself, one of a noble and revered Order stretching back hundreds of generations.

He had been a Jedi Knight.

Now he was a pariah.

Those who knew him respected the diminutive humanoid for his fierce courage and fighting skills, as well they should. Had he not defeated the Red Iaro terrorist Myk'chur Zug, at the cost of an eye? Had he not survived the Battle of Geonosis, and fought many a battle for the Republic in the Clone Wars? It was truthfully said that Even Piell had never backed away from a fight in his life. Give him a lightsaber and a cause in which to ignite it, and there was no braver warrior on two legs, or four, or six. But now . . .

Now it was different.

Now, for the first time in his life, he knew fear.

Even walked hurriedly through the colorful crowds that thronged the Zi-Zhinn Marketplace. This was a euphemistic name for an ongoing rowdy street fair on the 17th Level of an area in Sector 4805, also known as the Zi-Kree Sector, along the equatorial strip. That was the name given to the upper levels, anyway; down here, below the layer of smoke and fog, it was simply called the Crimson Corridor. While much of Coruscant's lower levels comprised less-than-desirable real estate, some areas were loci of particular and concentrated trouble. The Southern Underground, the Factory District, The Works, the Blackpit Slums—these and other colorful names did little justice to the harsh realities of life under the perpetual smog layer that hid them from the rarefied upper levels. Yet ironically, it was only in ghettos like these, amid despair and desperation, that a measure of anonymity and security could be found.

Even wasn't sure how many of the Jedi were left, but he knew the number wasn't high. The slaughter begun on Geonosis had been pursued with a vengeance here on Coruscant, and on other worlds such as Felucia and Kashyyyk as well. Barriss Offee was dead, as were Luminara Unduli, Mace Windu, and Kit Fisto. Plo Koon's starfighter had been shot down over Cato Neimoidia. To the best of his knowledge, Even was the only senior member of the Council to escape the massacre at the Temple.

It was still almost impossible to comprehend. It had all happened so *fast*. In only a few short days he had been forced to give up everything. No more would he look upon the five spires of the Jedi Temple, or walk the fragrant-flowered paths and tessellated floors of its private gardens and chambers. No more would he spend rewarding hours in discussion with his fellow scholars in the Council of First Knowledge, or research interstellar esoterica in the Archives, or practice the seven forms of lightsaber combat with his fellow Jedi.

But he could not give up using the Force to aid others. To deny the Force was to deny himself. Fear of discovery had caused him to hold back from using it in public for as long as he could stand. He had been a helpless witness to the everyday atrocities during the interregnum, to the chaos and anarchy that had accompanied the overthrow of the Galactic Senate and the ascension of the new Emperor. Sick at heart, he had reined in his dismay and revulsion, his desperate need to do *something* to stop this unending nightmare. He had seen his fellow Jedi assassinated by clone commanders under the thrall of Order Sixty-six; he had seen employees and instructors mowed down by blasterfire; and, worst of all, he had heard the screams of the children and the young Padawans as they had been cut down.

And he had fled. That fateful night, while destruction dropped from the skies and stormtroopers patrolled the streets, Even Piell and the others—the very few others—still alive had escaped the massacre.

For now.

Even moved cautiously and stealthily through puddles of stuttering neon light. Used subtly, the Force allowed him to slip through crowds of various species—Bothans, Niktos, Twi'leks, and humans—with few noticing him. And even those few forgot him almost immediately. For the moment, he was safe—but not even the Force could protect him forever.

His pursuers were closing in.

He did not know their ID numbers, nor would it matter if he did. They were stormtroopers, cloned soldiers created in the vats of Tipoca City on the water world Kamino and elsewhere, warriors bred to fight fearlessly for the glory of the Republic, and to obey without question the commands of the Jedi.

That, however, was before Order Sixty-six.

He could sense them through the Force, their malignant auras like ice water along his nerves. They were getting closer; he estimated the distance at little more than a kilometer now.

He ducked into a recessed doorway. The entrance was locked, but a gesture of his hand, and an answering ripple in the Force, caused the door panel to slide back reluctantly, with a rasping screech. It jammed partway, but there was enough room for him to squeeze past.

The Lannik hurried through what had once been a spice den, by the looks of it; formcast cribs and niches in the wall showed where various body shapes had lain long ago, their minds disengaged and floating in soporific bliss. Though it may have been as much as five centuries since it had last been used, it seemed to Even that he could still smell the ghostly scent of glitterstim that had once clouded both the air and the occupants' minds.

At first Even had wondered how the stormtroopers tracking him had found him so quickly. He had been circumspect in his use of the Force, had kept as low a profile as possible for the past two standard months. He'd stayed off the grid, dealing for sustenance and shelter strictly with credit chips and bills. While it was true that Lannik were not all that common, even on Coruscant, how the troopers had come across him was still baffling. It didn't really matter, though. Perhaps someone had recognized his image as one of the Council, and reported him. All that mattered was that they were closing in, with but one purpose in mind—to kill Jedi.

To kill him.

He still carried his lightsaber, concealed in his jacket's inside pocket. He resisted the urge to seize the weapon. Its cool grip would feel most comforting in his hand right now.

But this wasn't yet the time, although from all indications that time would be upon him very shortly. The final battle—he had little doubt it would be anything less than that—could not take place where innocents might be caught in the crossfire. The agents of the Emperor didn't care about collateral damage, but Jedi could not be so cavalier.

That alone was reason enough to flee rather than fight. But there was another reason as well: the quest he was on. It was not merely his own life he risked by facing his pursuers. For the sake of many others' lives, he had to delay the inevitable as long as possible.

The spice den opened, by way of a half-concealed entrance, into a dimly lit, cavernous chamber that had long ago been a casino. It was huge, with a high, vaulted ceiling that rose easily three stories. Even made his way to a turbolift tube, pushing his way past furniture and gambling tables so ancient that some of them crumbled to dust when he brushed by. How many abandoned, desolated places like this were there in the sublevels? Millions, no doubt, hidden and silent at the bases of the glittering, fresh towers, like rot growing silently in a tooth. The capital of the galaxy had grown from a vast necropolis, as flowers sprout from funerary dirt . . .

Even Piell shook his head to clear his thoughts. Now was definitely not the time to be dwelling on the past. Total concentration was required if he was to survive this night.

As if to confirm his thoughts, he heard, very faintly, the crisp voices of his pursuers from outside the building. He reached the lift—a clear transparisteel tube—and stepped in. Nothing happened; he hadn't expected anything to. The charge in the repulsor plates had depleted over the centuries. Fortunately, he wasn't dependent on technology to make the turbolift work.

Everyone experienced the Force in different ways, it was said. For some it was like a storm in which they were the cynosure, secure in its calm eye while commanding its tempests. For others it was a fog, a mist, the vaporous tendrils of which could be manipulated, or incandescence with which to illuminate or inflame. These were inadequate approximations, feeble attempts to describe, in terms of the five ordinary senses, that which was indescribable. Even the full-blown synesthesia of one of the more hallucinogenic forms of spice was a faint and colorless experience next to being one with the Force.

For Even, the closest thing to which he could liken calling on the Force was sinking into warm water. It soothed him, calmed him, even as it lent energy to his tired muscles and sharpened his senses.

He made a slight, uplifting gesture. The Force became a geyser, raising him up through the length of the tube.

Before he reached the ceiling through which the tube extruded, he heard the sound of the door he had just come through being kicked open. Five stormtroopers in full body armor came through. They were holding blasters and slugthrowers. One of them pointed upward at Even. "There!" he shouted. "In the tube!"

The others followed his gaze. One—a sergeant, judging by the green markings on his armor—raised his blaster. It was a BlasTech SE-14, a pistol that packed the highly concentrated beam power of an energy rifle into a weapon half the size. Even knew that the crystasteel tubing couldn't stop the burst of charged subatomic particles. He accelerated his ascent. Just before he reached the ceiling, the leading trooper fired—but not at Even.

Above him.

Too late, Even realized the other's tactic. The blast struck the tube at the juncture between the ceiling and the lift, melting and fusing it together into an impassable mass. Even barely managed to stop his ascent in time. A second later the trooper fired again, this time turning the tube's base below the Jedi's feet into molten slag.

He could move neither up nor down, Even realized. He was trapped, like a bug in a bottle.

But this bug could sting.

Even Piell reached into his jacket's pocket and seized his lightsaber. Before the stormtrooper, who was carefully lining up his shot, could fire again, he activated the blade.

With a fierce electronic growl, the energy shaft surged forth, as if eager to be free after all this time. Even swung the blade once, then reversed the stroke, slashing and melting a hole in the tube. He let the Force wash him through it, an invisible cascade that carried him out of the lift and in a long arc toward the floor. The five troopers fired repeatedly, bolts of red lambent energy that Even, guided by the Force, batted away with his own weapon. None came close.

Despite his momentary victory, he knew this battle was far from won. The stormtroopers blocked the exit. Normally even five-to-one odds would pose little challenge for a Jedi Master immersed in the Force. But Even had been on the run for weeks; he'd had little rest and even less food. Despite the energizing effects of the Force, he was still far from his peak fighting form. He had no compunctions about running if possible; the Jedi teachings stressed practicality over bravery. But to flee into the darkness of the ancient chamber in his condition would be futile. The troopers would cut him down like a ripe yahi'i stalk if he turned his back. No, there was only one way out—through them.

The stormtroopers were almost upon him. Even Piell took a fighting stance, raised his lightsaber, and gave himself fully to the Force.

two

Nick Rostu was living on borrowed time.

He knew it; had known it for almost three standard years, ever since that night in the command bunker on Haruun Kal, when Iolu's vibroshield had opened him up like an overcooked Balawai meatpie. He had held his viscera in, his interlocked fingers the only barrier keeping them from spilling onto the duracrete floor, as he lay in a crumpled heap, only dimly aware of the final battle taking place a couple of meters away between Mace Windu and Kar Vastor. Then even that faint spark of consciousness had faded; Nick had felt the planet crack open beneath him, and he had fallen through it and tumbled toward the stars.

He hadn't minded, really. As a Korunnai, all he had ever known was war, as far back as he could remember. He was more than ready for some peace.

But peace wasn't in the cards just yet.

Nick had awakened two days later, on board a Med-Star frigate bound for the Core Worlds. He was told that only his connection with the Force had kept him alive long enough to respond to medical aid. He'd asked that the scar across his belly be left unrevised—he wanted a reminder of what it meant to let his guard down, even for a split second.

He'd completed his convalescence at Coruscant Medical, under the best care available—the Jedi Council had seen to that. And Mace made it a point to visit him; often, at first, but as the days went by and the Clone Wars escalated, the Jedi Master appeared less and less. Nick understood why, of course. Things were really heating up. The last couple of times he'd seen Mace, the latter's face had been creased with worry.

Mace had recommended him for a Silver Medal of Valor, the second highest award given for conspicuous bravery under fire. The ceremony took place after Nick was released from the medcenter. His rank of brevet major in the Grand Army of the Republic was also confirmed, and for the next two years Major Nick Rostu commanded the 44th Division, a unit composed of clone troopers and several other species, also known as Rostu's Renegades. The 44th saw action on Bassadro, Ando, Atraken, and several other planets, distinguishing itself on each world front. At least, that's how the HoloNet press releases played it. After all, the loyalists of the galaxy wanted reassurance that the war was indeed going well for the Republic. They needed all the heroes they could get, and so Rostu's Renegades were twirled as can-do fighters, full of élan and verve, barely finishing one campaign before eagerly leaping back into the white-hot fray again.

Nick remembered it somewhat differently; he remembered days and nights of screaming chaos, repeated times when only the intervention of more troops, or blind luck, had yanked their jiffies from the smelter at the last minute. But then, that was as good a definition of warring as any he'd come across. And they'd performed the same service for other divisions, so it all seemed to level out.

Even so, even despite the deprivation, the hardship, the extreme conditions, and the general bowel-loosening fear that was war, Nick considered himself fortunate. He'd been one of the youngest commissioned officers in the Republic, and he knew that, if he survived the various conflicts, he could look forward to a career of peacetime military service—followed, in all probability, by a comfortable retirement pension, a family and a conapt, perhaps in the Arak Dunes district or a similar upscale locale, and eventually fat grandchildren to bounce on his knee. He was good with that. Maybe it wasn't the most illustrious or distinctive life in the galaxy, but it was light-years better than what he'd have gotten back on Haruun Kal, which, if he'd been very lucky, would have been a marked grave instead of an anonymous mound of dirt.

But that wasn't quite the way things had turned out. Instead, nearly three years after Iolu had shown him the color of his own innards, Nick Rostu found himself a member of a nascent group of revolutionaries dedicated to resisting the new regime.

Back on Haruun Kal, the people of Nick's ghôsh had a saying: *Don't mess with the akk dog.* It was good advice, especially in those troubled times. He'd been planetside on the capital world when the coup went down, and overnight, it seemed, everything had changed—even the planet's name, from Coruscant to Imperial Center, although no one Nick knew called it that. Suddenly there was a new oligarchy in town, with Palpatine at its apex. Suddenly the Army of the Republic was the Army of the Empire, and it was obvious that it would go hard indeed on anyone who didn't know which way to salute. Suddenly Major Rostu was given a choice: swear allegiance to the new regime, or face a blasting squad.

He was offered this ultimatum on the same day that he'd learned the fate of Mace Windu. Supposedly the Jedi Master—his adviser, his benefactor, his friend—had attempted to assassinate the Chancellor, and had been killed during the traitorous action. Nick had a problem believing that. Knowing Mace as he had, and judging by Emperor Palpatine's ruthless pogrom against the Jedi, Nick was pretty sure there'd been nothing traitorous about it, at least as far as Mace had seen it.

He liked to think that he would have made the right choice anyway. There was no denying, however, that the news of Mace's death made the decision considerably easier. He'd faced the Empire's representative, flanked by two stormtroopers armed with blasters, and told him—respectfully, of course, the man had been a superior officer under the previous regime, after all—to go frip himself. Then he'd grabbed one of the blasters, shot both troopers and the representative, blown a hole through the big transparisteel window of the conference chamber, and leapt through it as the rest of the troopers in the room unleashed a barrage in his direction.

They missed—probably because they were momentarily immobilized by the shock of seeing a man voluntarily leap from a 210th-story window. Nick wasn't crazy about the idea, either, but he didn't see a lot of alternatives, other than being fried like a mulch fritter. Fortunately he had an ace in the field.

He could touch the Force.

This was something he had in common with all that

hailed from Haruun Kal. Why, no one was sure; one theory was that the Korunnai were all descended from the Jedi crew of a downed spaceship that had crashed there, millennia ago. Whatever the reason, it came in handy at times, like when it had told Nick that a sky lorry loaded with nerf pelts was passing by only ten meters below the window.

Eventually he'd made his way downlevel, below the omnipresent inversion layer, and into the dim netherworld of the surface streets. He'd nearly been killed his first night there by a gang with the unlikely name of the Purple Zombies, had spent most of the only credits he'd had with him on a bedslot teeming with blister fleas, and dined alfresco the next day on grilled armored rat from a street vendor.

Talk about your downward mobility . . .

Six weeks later, three kilos lighter, and a whole lot meaner, he'd saved the life of a Kitonak merchant. To accomplish this, he'd had to go one-on-one with a Trandoshan antenna-breaker, who'd been sent to extort collection credits for a local gangster. In retrospect, this action turned out to be about as bright as a circus sword swallower upgrading his act to a lightsaber, but it had seemed to Nick a good idea at the time. The Trandoshan's nickname was Crusher—or maybe Cruncher; his accent was too thick for Nick to tell for sure. Either way, it seemed to fit. The scaly thug, annoyed at Nick's request that he leave the pudgy little humanoid merchant alone, had backhanded Nick across the narrow street and nearly through a break in the wall surrounding one of the gigantic, noisome garbage pits that dotted Coruscant's slums and industrial areas.

Crusher (or Cruncher) wasn't tall, but he was massive—at least 150 kilos, maybe more. All of which was charging straight toward Nick, shouting a battle cry in a phlegm-choked voice. Nick had barely enough time and wits to dodge and let the big oaf blunder past him and fall, screaming, into the silage below. His long wail was abruptly cut short, and, judging by the moist *chomp!* that quickly followed, Nick assumed Crusher/Cruncher had made a tasty mouthful for a dianoga, one of the huge, constricting garbage worms that infested the pits. He was just as happy not to know for sure.

The Kitonak turned out to be a member of a newly formed subversive movement called the Whiplash. She'd loudly sung his praises and made much of his bravery to her comrades in arms, and so he'd been asked to join them in their struggle against the new regime. No pay, little rest, and much danger—Nick couldn't see a lot of difference between this and the resistance movement back on Haruun Kal.

But he'd agreed. He was a military deserter and a killer, after all, subject to being shot on sight, and there was safety—or at least a spurious sense of it—in numbers. What other choice was there? He was a soldier; it was all he knew, all he had ever known. Call it the Upland Liberation Front or the Army of the Republic, it really made no difference. The uniforms were different, but the job was the same.

It wasn't that he enjoyed fighting this war, or any war—he hadn't been shortchanged in the fear category, like all the clones had been. And thank whoever was ultimately in charge for that. Nick had once watched a phalanx of clones on Muunilinst fearlessly attack a hill against the blasterfire of three times as many droidekas. None of the clones so much as faltered, even though the

droidekas' lasers, plasma rays, and particle beams had
torn through the majority of them as if they'd been flim-
siplast cutout dolls. Three-quarters of the phalanx had
been shredded in that charge.

But they'd taken the hill.

Yet, despite the dangers of war, there had been a certain odd security, almost comfort, in the rules and regs
of the military life. Nick was by no means one of those
snap-click officers with little to no field experience, just
time in simulation holos and heads-up trainers. Even
when commander of his own unit, he'd had to follow
the asinine orders of a few desktop generals, and he'd
nearly gotten his head shot off more than once as a
result. A rather large proportion of those pressed-and-
polished newbie warriors tended to not come back from
their first or second campaign in top working order, if
they came back at all.

He'd looked forward, like many others, to a lasting
peace after Dooku, Grievous, and the others had been
disposed of properly. A time in which he could at last lay
down his arms and relax a bit. A time to heal.

Instead here he was, couched behind the rusting
fender of an abandoned construction crawler, along
with six others, waiting tensely as a quintet of stormtroopers hurried by. From the snatches of conversation
Nick heard as they passed, it didn't take a Tatooine
brain spider to figure out that they were hot in pursuit of
a Jedi. Whether it was a Padawan, Jedi Knight, or Master wasn't clear.

During his service, and because of his acquaintance
with Mace Windu, Nick had come to know a number
of Jedi quite well, including a few members of the
Council—all of whom, as far as he knew, were now

dead. Or, as the Jedi themselves often put it, "Returned to the Force." Whatever. Nick had little patience with any and all theories and philosophies that included speculation on an afterlife. The life he was living now was more than enough work; the thought of doing it all over again just made him tired.

He glanced back at his group, signaling with a head jerk that they were following the pack. There was no hesitation among his team as they fell in behind him.

Keeping the troopers in sight, Nick moved stealthily through the deserted streets. There was never much foot traffic down here at this time, and what little there was had prudently relocated when the armed stormtroopers had come marching down the thoroughfare. Before too long they stopped before a half-open panel in a long-abandoned building. Nick could barely hear them discussing whether their quarry had gone to ground there. The decision to investigate was quickly reached when one of the troopers pointed out that the panel had been opened quite recently, judging by the disturbed dust and grime. A single kick from another trooper was enough to open it the rest of the way. The stormtroopers disappeared inside, weapons ready.

"Let's go," Nick whispered. "Could be they've got a Jedi trapped in there."

"Could be we'll be in the same fix, if we don't do some recon before we rush in," Kars Korthos pointed out. He was a small, compact man, full of nervous energy that always seemed on the verge of bursting like a solar flare, and his instincts were seldom wrong.

Nick considered. Kars had a point; they should at least scope the building for other possible ways in or out before they—

From deep within the forbidding interior came the sound of a blaster being fired.

"We're going in," Nick said, pulling his blaster and stepping quickly through.

"Looks like," Kars agreed as he and the rest followed.

three

The Force was an invisible cataract that carried Even Piell in its grip, bearing him as lightly and easily as a jekka seed in white water. He surrendered to it, as he'd learned to do so long before, letting it guide and direct him, letting it move him in offensive and defensive actions far faster and more precise than his conscious mind could possibly have executed. The stormtroopers' blasterfire ricocheted from his lightsaber in blinding flashes, the energy bursts dissipating harmlessly.

There was one slight chance of survival, he realized: if he could perform a Force leap over the troopers, he might stand a chance of reaching the door. It would have to be perfectly executed, and the danger was that his adversaries would be familiar with the move. Even as these thoughts crossed his mind, however, he was springing toward the five armored soldiers, each of whom was easily double his size and weight.

The unexpected move worked to his advantage; evidently the stormtroopers hadn't experienced this particular action before. Even leapt, let the Force carry him, let it shift his weight and torque his muscles, spinning him so that when he landed he was facing his foes.

His technique was flawless; he lit, perfectly balanced,

on the ancient parquet floor, lightsaber at the ready. The troopers, taken by surprise, swung around and began firing wildly in his direction. Even felt hope blossom within him as he deflected the bolts while backing up. The entrance lay only five or so meters behind him. If he could just reach it—

One of the stormtroopers pulled a round object from his belt, held it up as if preparing to throw it. A grenade, Even realized.

They must be getting desperate, he thought. *Surely they realize that, if I can deflect energy bolts, I'll have no trouble batting away a—*

Too late, he grasped the trooper's strategy. The object he held was a luma grenade, and the man had no intention of throwing it. Instead he simply activated it and let it fall to his feet. Before Even could shield or even close his eyes, the sphere dissolved in a blinding burst of actinic light that washed away the world.

The stormtroopers were wearing polarized lenses as part of their headgear. The light didn't dazzle them at all. They could see Even, and he could see nothing but the glare of his scorched retinas.

Still, they were fools to think that this made any difference. A Jedi could "see" through the Force with better vision than any set of eyes. Even backpedaled, weaving the lightsaber in a warding pattern that blocked the barrage of energy bolts they had loosed at him, as he reached out with the Force and let it do what his shocked vision couldn't. But even as he wondered at their naïveté, another object hurtled at him. The pattern of ripples it made in the Force told him it was another small, round object, most likely another grenade—and this one, he sensed, was impact-sensitive. If he blocked it

with his lightsaber, it would probably detonate. Even
raised his hand to deflect the sphere with a Force push—

And one of the stormtroopers fired another blaster
bolt, but not at him. The energy pulse struck the grenade
arcing toward him, and detonated it.

He'd been sucker-punched, Even realized. The luma
had been meant to distract him, to let them get inside his
guard with their real attack. The shock wave hammered
him, lifting him and hurling him back. He collided
against a support column with a terrible impact. The
Force had protected him from immediate vaporization,
but the pillar had been a surprise. He felt his bones snap
and his organs burst when he hit the unforgiving fiber-
plast.

He was not aware of his scream.

Dimly, as from a great distance, he felt the Force roil
in sudden turmoil, like a placid pond struck suddenly by
a stone. He could hear shouts of surprise from his enemies, could hear other blasters, the crackle of their discharges pitched slightly differently from those of the
stormtroopers. With his last, fading spark of awareness,
Even Piell realized that help had arrived.

Too late.

Nick heard the scream as he and his comrades burst
into what looked like an ancient casino. He saw, perhaps half a dozen meters away, a small, crumpled form
at the base of a pillar. Nearby, five stormtroopers were
already firing at the newcomers. The first shots went
wide, but their surprise would be over in a moment, and
then they would cook Nick and his team where they
stood.

"Take 'em!" Nick shouted as he leapt forward, drawing his blaster and the troopers' fire. He hit the floor, rolling under a salvo of bolts, and came up on one knee with the weapon extended. A blast from the nearest stormtrooper's weapon scorched the tiles where he had been, but Nick gritted his teeth and ignored it. He squeezed off a blast of his own, and one of the troopers was hurled back. His armor protected him from anything except a point-blank hit at maximum power, but the impact would leave him stunned for a time.

In the background Nick could hear the blasterfire between the remaining troopers and his men, but all his attention was focused on that small form lying so utterly still on the floor. Nick recognized him.

Even Piell.

Nick rushed to the Jedi's side, but saw immediately that there was nothing he could do. It was obvious that Master Piell had massive internal injuries and, judging by the unnatural angles of his limbs, many broken bones as well. And, as if things weren't bad enough, from the way his back and pelvis were twisted, Nick figured his spine had probably snapped.

He'd seen many an atrocity on various planetary battlefields—soldiers with limbs blown off, or perforated by shrapnel, or partly immolated—it was a long list, and one he most definitely did not want to inventory right now. But he'd seldom seen such havoc wrought on a single living being. Most ordinary sentients would have died from the blood loss and shock long before now. The Force was the only thing holding Master Piell together, but that was unraveling fast—Nick could sense it.

He hadn't known the Lannik well, but he knew

enough about him to greatly respect him. It was an amazing testimony to both his courage and the efficacy of the Jedi training that he remained alive, even momentarily, after being in such close proximity to a grenade burst.

"There is no death, there is the Force," Nick murmured. It was the final mantra of the Jedi Code. He couldn't think of anything else to say.

Master Piell's eyelids flickered open. He focused on Nick's face. "Rostu?" he croaked. "Is that you?"

Nick blinked in astonishment; he hadn't expected the other to live more than another minute or two, much less return to consciousness. "Yes, Master Piell. Don't talk; you need to save your strength. I'll call a medic, and they'll fix you right—"

"Oh, don't be an idiot," Master Piell snapped weakly. "Move me and I'll come apart like a holopuzzle. I'm done—we both know it. Someone must take over my mission." He coughed; it reminded Nick of glass shattering. After a moment, the Jedi continued. "Now pay attention . . ."

Nick rejoined his comrades, who were waiting for him by the door. He looked around. "The stormtroopers?"

"Got away," Kars said. "Took the wounded one with 'em." He didn't elaborate. Another one of the group, a Nautolan named Lex Rogger, was treating a burn wound on Kars's arm, so Nick didn't think pressing the issue right now would do much good. "What about the Jedi?" Kars asked.

Nick sighed and rubbed his face with the back of one

hand. "Dead. But," he continued, looking at them, "he told me about some unfinished business."

"Which we're going to finish," Lex said.

"Actually, no. We're not. But I know someone who will."

four

The Hutt was in quite a state. He'd reared his bulk up to its full height, towering over Jax, the boneless mass of his upper section flattened slightly so as to suggest even greater size. It was an atavistic action, Jax knew, an unconscious response to danger from ages past, when Hutts had been both predator and prey. That knowledge didn't make it any less impressive, however. Rokko seemed to block the width of the arcing footbridge on which the four of them stood—not that it mattered, since the span ended halfway across in a broken and jagged tangle of ferrocrete and duranium rebar. Sometime in the past a cargo vehicle or something similar had gone out of control and smashed into it, most probably. It had never been repaired, which was not at all unusual in the downlevels. Nothing below the haze existed as far as those uplevel were concerned, so why waste credits on repairs?

The Hutt had requested this somewhat precarious spot as a rendezvous point. He hadn't come alone; flanking him were his two bullyboys, a Klatooinian and a Red Nikto, both looking appropriately menacing. Rokko the Hutt was a powerful sentient, at least in the

Blackpit Slums, and he hired the best enforcers available. Jax had never dealt with him before, and it was beginning to look like he never would again. Or anyone else, if he was reading the big slug accurately.

Rokko gave him a bilious glare. "I should have known better than to trust a *human*." His voice sounded like gravel pouring down an alumabronze chute. "But you came highly recommended by Braze. It appears I was wrong to trust him—and you."

"You asked me to deliver Toh Revo Chryyx, a Cerean grifter, to you," Jax replied. "This I did. The fact that he suicided before you could interrogate him is no fault of mine." Exactly how the humanoid had stopped his own heart was still a mystery to both the Hutt and Jax, although Jax had heard it rumored that some Cereans had, through much meditation and inner awareness, gained control over their autonomic nervous systems. That didn't really matter, though. All that mattered was that the Hutt owed Jax fifteen thousand credits and was obviously looking for a way to renege.

"Am I a fool?" the Hutt roared. "Our contract clearly states that you were to deliver him into my presence *alive*. This is not what transpired."

"He *was* alive." Jax kept his voice even, but it was a struggle. "He shut down the moment he laid eyes on you." *And who could blame him,* he added silently. Rokko was notorious for being one of the most vengeful gangsters in the underworld. His invention and enjoyment of various forms of torture was the stuff of many a con being's nightmares.

The Hutt's two enforcers moved apart a bit, the better to flank him. Jax ignored them, keeping his attention focused on Rokko. The web-like strands that had been gathering about the Hutt since he'd first arrived were growing steadily thicker and darker; now the over-grown slug seemed almost enmeshed in a cocoon of thick black shimmersilk. Some of them had wrapped about his enforcers. Jax could "see" strands extending away from the giant gastropod as well, extending through higher dimensions where time and distance were mean-ingless, reverberating with their connections to still more beings, on this world and others: beings who had passed through the Hutt's sphere of influence. Some were living; many were dead. Jax had no desire to fol-low any of the threads to see the fates of those snared by the Hutt's web. Rokko was ruthless and thorough, and Jax doubted he would find many loose ends.

What galled him was that he had knowingly done business with a criminal. Rokko was a trafficker in stolen merchandise, a modern-day pirate who didn't care under what circumstances contraband was pro-duced and obtained, and who was definitely not above engineering such circumstances if he deemed it neces-sary. He was cruel and vengeful, and many beings had died so that he could keep smoking the finest mixes of spice in his hookah, and noshing on delicacies such as cho nor hoola and live, succulent nuna.

And Jax Pavan, who had once been a Jedi Knight, was facilitating this.

The Hutt made an abrupt gesture of dismissal and turned to slither back into the building. "We are done here," he said over his nonexistent shoulder. "The con-tract was unfulfilled, therefore payment is not forthcom-ing."

"This is unacceptable," Jax replied. "The transaction was undertaken in good faith."

"If you are dissatisfied," Rokko said as he disappeared from view, "please feel free to discuss the matter with my business associates."

Jax turned to face the Klatooinian and the Nikto. The former smiled, one leathery hand dropping to the low-slung blaster at his side. The Nikto fluttered his mouth flaps, which was the equivalent of a smile, and gripped his weapon as well. They moved forward together.

Jax stood in a relaxed posture, his hands at his sides. He was wearing no noticeable weapons, save for a vibroknife in a belt sheath, which he made no attempt to draw.

The Klatooinian nudged the Nikto. "Just like a human," he said. "Brings a vibroknife to a blaster fight."

There was only one way he would get out of this alive, Jax knew. It would all go down too fast for him to make them forget his presence, and he wasn't sure if he could, anyway—their bloodlust was up, their primitive minds focused with the excitement of the potential kill. He would have to use the Force, and there was no time to be subtle.

The Hutt's "business associates" cleared leather almost simultaneously, no doubt anticipating an easy kill. But their confidence vanished a moment later, along with their weapons, as Jax made two small, almost negligible gestures. The blasters leapt from the bullyboys' grips and across two meters of air to smack solidly into his own hands. His expression was calm.

"Just like a couple of muscle-bound spiceheads," he said. "Using blasters against the Force."

The two enforcers stared at the blasters pointed at them, then at Jax, then at each other. Then they bolted in the same direction Rokko had taken, both nearly slipping and sprawling on the trail of slime the Hutt had left. Jax had to move quickly to get out of the way of their panicked flight.

As the rapid echoes of their boots faded, he looked at the two blasters in his hands. *Should've killed them,* he thought. Now Rokko would know, probably within the next few minutes, that Jax Pavan, with whom he'd been doing business for the past two months, was far more than just a bounty hunter.

Should've killed them.

But he knew he could not have done that. It was one thing to kill in the heat of battle, quite another to do so in cold blood. Even though letting them go was an action nearly as suicidal as the Cerean's had been. Of course, now he had two blasters he didn't have before, but weapons weren't that hard to get, particularly in his current line of work.

He slipped them into the pockets of his greatcoat, stepped over to the railing, and looked down. A chill breeze plucked at him, and he turned his collar up against it. He was only twenty-five stories above the pavement, still well below the dirty, gray-brown belt of pollution that shielded the wealthier inhabitants of this sector from unpleasant views of the squalid depths. He'd been in this locale for a little over three standard months.

The smog wasn't too bad today, but everything was still cloaked in a pervasive gloom from the shadows of the buildings, thick as the boles of trees in a Kashyyyk forest. There was little air traf-fic under fifty stories in this sector, so the view was relatively unimpeded. On the street, ground skimmers hummed along less than a meter above the pavement. One-person conveyances called weavers lived up to their names as their riders adroitly piloted them by balance alone; rickshaw droids ferried others. But most of the slum's inhabitants walked, or slithered, or crawled, or otherwise moved along under their own power. The streets were crowded with vendors, solicitors, vagrants, and footpads . . . it was like looking through some kind of magical portal onto a marginalized planet of the Outer Rim. Hard to believe that he was still on Coruscant, crown jewel of the Core Worlds.

He'd had to go downlevel once or twice while still a Padawan, both times with his Master. Both times had been relatively minor errands, and both times he had been appalled at the poverty and the filth. He'd been extremely happy and relieved to return to the sanctuary of the Temple. He felt guilty about harboring such an attitude, but he couldn't deny it. He remembered wondering how people could survive in such a hopeless environment.

Now he knew: not easily, not well, and not for very long.

Jax Pavan had received his promotion to Knighthood three months before the fall of the Jedi. The Jedi Order had already been thinned considerably by the slaughter on Geonosis and the subsequent Clone Wars. Order Sixty-six had nearly finished the job. No more than a handful of Jedi and those associated with them were still alive, and they were considered little or no threat by the self-proclaimed Emperor Palpatine. There was no systematic effort being made to root them out; however, stormtrooper garrisons patrolled the streets to enforce order, and if they came across a Jedi, that Jedi died. It looked like it would be only a matter of time before the beacon of the Order was truly extinguished in the galaxy.

Jax had barely gotten to experience the pride of Knighthood before it had all shattered, like the noctilucent towers of the Temple itself. As had so many of his compatriots, he had vanished into the crimson night, shedding any trace of connection to the Jedi. Barely surviving on the streets, reduced to surreptitious use of mind and matter manipulation just to stay alive, Jax had eventually become something he had previously considered the lowest of the low. To stay alive, he had entered a profession barely a notch above the gangsters and other lowlifes he was forced to consort with.

He had become a bounty hunter.

At first, it had seemed to make sense. A man had to eat, after all, and even Jedi were not immune to fear and despair. He continued to use the Force to aid his survival in subtle ways, from winning credits by manipulating sabacc games to "suggesting" that local vendors and restaurateurs supply him with food. But his Master had cautioned him, before they were separated by the chaos of that fateful and fiery night, to refrain from any overt use of the Force unless it was a life-or-death situation. There was always a chance, remote though it might be, of being seen by stormtroopers, or droids, or other agents of the Empire. Or it could be some citizen, eager to curry favor with the new regime, who might report him. Impossible to know for sure, until it was too late.

On the face of it, such a concern seemed absurdly paranoid. The last planetary census pegged the population of Coruscant at upward of one trillion—and that was only the full-time registered residents. The census didn't include commuters from skyhooks, Hesperidium, and other offworld communities. Nor did it include the hundreds of thousands of stormtroopers stationed planetside. And it most certainly did not—could not—account for the teeming multitudes living off the grid, in the depths of the urban slums. Estimates including those groups led some statisticians to determine the actual population to be nearly three times the official count. Given that, it seemed a single sentient could theoretically exist on Coruscant for the life span of a main-sequence star, and still remain virtually anonymous, with a minimum of effort. Unfortunately for Jedi such as Jax Pavan, that effort included not using the Force.

He had made himself as inconspicuous as possible. His dark brown hair, which he had been growing out in the style of a human Jedi Knight, he had immediately cut short again and dyed black. He'd had his beard permanently depilated as well. The austere hooded cloak and robes of his Order he had discarded immediately, of course. Now he wore a nondescript vest of black bantha leather, threadbare gray trousers, and black boots, with an ankle-length, gunmetal-colored greatcoat over it all. Its high collar helped conceal his face. He no longer carried his lightsaber proudly hooked to his belt; now it was hidden within an inside pocket of the greatcoat. He looked like a down-on-his-luck spacer, which was precisely the image he wanted to convey. The only visible weapon he wore was the vibroknife, although he also carried a small hold-out blaster concealed up his right sleeve, as well as a duracris poniard in a sheath between his shoulder blades. The latter didn't show up on routine scans. A small confounder unit, carried in the same pocket as his lightsaber, kept it from being detected as well.

He'd managed to fool himself for a while, rationalizing that he was only hunting down criminals. But that was sophistry—particularly if he was hunting them for other criminals, such as Rokko. And now, as he stared down at the street far beneath him, Jax admitted to himself that he had fallen even farther than the distance from where he stood to the grimy pavement below. To survive in Coruscant's dark underbelly, he had become what he'd once fought against: a hunter of sentients who had prices on their heads.

It had been torture to resist using the Force—tantamount to the self-amputation of a limb. He could still employ it in subtle ways, such as deceiving the weak-minded or sensing danger through it. But displays of power that only a Jedi could accomplish—even minor ones, like the stunt he'd just pulled with the bullyboys' blasters—were dangerous in the extreme. Still, it wasn't as if he'd had a choice.

"I think it's time to go," he murmured.

He had delayed long enough. He'd stayed on Coruscant, being paid by criminals to facilitate their vendettas, and tarnishing his psyche in the process, all the while trying to soothe his conscience by helping others escape the planet. But this had gone on long enough. It was his turn now.

The resistance movement known as the Whiplash was less than two months old, but already it had achieved some impressive accomplishments, including surgical strikes on supply routes and troop transports. It had also established a series of secret routes, safe houses, and groups of partisans working together to facilitate the escape of political undesirables and others declared "enemies of the state." These included Temple workers, aides-de-camp, Force-sensitives, and even, it was rumored, a few Jedi Padawans and Knights. The fugitives were smuggled via cargo vehicles, utility tunnels, and various other clandestine means from all over the city-planet, along routes known collectively as the Underground Mag-Lev. They were eventually placed onto freighters, transports, pleasure yachts—any ship whose captain was sympathetic to the cause, or mercenary enough to be swayed by credits—and so ferried safely offworld. While Palpatine had stated publicly that the Jedi and their aides were no longer considered a threat, Jax suspected that finding and stopping the UML was on the Imperial agenda, if only for the propaganda value. Imperial troops had located and shut down some of the routes, but others had quickly taken their places.

As a Jedi Knight, Jax Pavan was guaranteed a berth on one of the transports, freighters, or other vessels participating in the seditious action. But he'd consistently refused to go, opting rather to stay on Coruscant and help others escape.

Now he had little choice in the matter. He had to let go of the tatters of his old life and find another world, preferably a good many parsecs distant. Because once Rokko knew that he was a Jedi, it would be only a matter of time before the sector police knew. There wasn't all that much of a bounty on rogue Jedi, but Rokko would turn in his own crèche-mother without a backward glance if credits were to be had.

Jax turned away from the abyss and entered the building. Once inside, he found a convenient turbolift, and in less than a minute he was back on the street.

He realized he hadn't even thought that much about the money that the Hutt owed him, although fifteen thousand creds was a lot to lose, especially all at once. Such a windfall would have aided him considerably in relocating to a new world and a new life. But he knew the chances of getting it from Rokko now were nil.

Even so, despite all reason to the contrary, Jax actually felt his spirits rising. It was time for a change. He wondered if perhaps he'd unconsciously revealed his Jedi identity to force himself into some new paradigm. In any event, what was done was done.

It was getting colder. Unlike the favored upper levels, where the climate was as regulated as everything else, in the downlevels actual, local weather was still something to contend with. The near-perpetual inversion layer, combined with nonregulated releases of heat exhaust and water vapor, often caused localized warm and cold fronts to develop. As Jax walked down the narrow street, moving quickly to dodge the frequent automated tumbrels loaded with trash and rubble that hurtled by, he was lashed by a sudden flurry of cold rain. A few moments later the temperature began to rise again, and ground fog hid the pavement. The street and pedestrian traffic had thinned, fortunately, though he was nearly knocked into the path of an oncoming surface car when a drunken Shistavenen blundered out of a tavern and collided with him, and a few minutes later he was accosted by a pushy young Toydarian scalping tickets to a heavy isotope concert, before he finally reached his destination.

The micro-conapt that he called home—or had, until an hour ago—lived up to its name. It was scarcely a blister in the cubic ferrocarbon bunker that a flickering sign

outside proclaimed THE CORUSCANT ARMS. Returning to
it reinforced his belief that whatever new life he might
make for himself on some outfar world could scarcely
be any worse than this one.

Inside, Jax pulled a much-worn fleekskin portman-
teau from the tiny closet and opened it on the foldout
bunk. Fortunately, he'd learned to journey light: a single
change of clothes, toiletries, and a few personal possessions he'd allowed himself to keep from his days at the
Temple. These included a small holocron of the sage
Yoda, holding forth on the various aspects of the Jedi
Code; a crystal from the caves of Dantooine with which
he could "hone" the energy blade of his lightsaber; and
a thumb-sized durite reliquary. This last he opened, revealing a teardrop-shaped bit of black metal. When the
harsh glare of the room's fluorescents struck it, it began
to glow: first red, then orange, yellow, green, blue, in-
digo, violet, and finally a soft, effulgent white. Jax stared
at it for a moment, then closed the reliquary and slipped
it into an inside zippered pocket.

As he packed, he thought about the chaos of the last
few months, of the deaths of his colleagues, his mentors,
and his friends. In particular, he wondered what had
been the fate of Anakin Skywalker.

Anakin had always been something of an enigma to
Jax and the other Padawans. He was nearly the same
age as Jax, and they had studied and dueled together
often. While it was true that no one could really get
close to Anakin—he had always maintained an aloof-
ness, a reserve, that none could penetrate—still, Jax had
counted himself as one of the troubled young Jedi's few
confidants. Anakin had even mentioned once to Jax his
belief that Obi-Wan Kenobi, his Master, was trying to

prevent him from reaching his true destiny. There had been a disturbing glint in his friend's blue eyes as he spoke of this, a look of utter certitude. Even more disturbing had been the reaction within the Force. For a brief moment Jax had seen threads of blackest night writhing and radiating outward in all directions from Anakin—more than he had ever seen on anyone. It had been as if the young Skywalker were the locus of a vast and complex network of rage and despair that reverberated through space and time. But it had only been for an instant. Then the connection had vanished, so quickly that Jax wasn't even sure he'd seen it, and Anakin had been his smiling self once more. He had never brought it up again, and Jax had eventually forgotten about it, until the Purge.

He often wondered, these days, if he should have spoken to Master Kenobi, or Master Piell, or anyone else on the Council, about the disturbing vision. But would they even have believed him? After all, the most august members of the Council, those closest and best informed by the Force, saw nothing untoward in Anakin's aura; quite the contrary, in fact. There were even rumors that some of them thought he was the Chosen One. How could a mere Padawan such as Jax pierce a veil that they could not?

He shook his head. Anakin was almost certainly dead now; if not, Jax was sure he must have fled Coruscant to any of the hundreds of thousands of known worlds in the galaxy. No one would ever really know if he had indeed been the one destined to bring balance to the Force.

Yet perhaps, in a strange way, he had. For certainly, after centuries of tolerance and enlightenment, the dark side now held sway over the galaxy. The scales had tipped. How long things would stay in this new equilibrium, Jax didn't know; nor did he know what, if anything, Anakin had to do with it. All he knew was that the Jedi were now prey. And given the sudden and searing sense of loss Jax had felt reverberate last night through the Force, the hunt wasn't over yet.

five

" 'Nother cooler," Den Dhur said to the pubtender. "Jus' keep 'em comin'."

The tender, a Bith, gazed at Den with large, lustrous black eyes. Those eyes had astonishing visual acuity, capable of focusing to a resolution of 0.07 on the Gandok Scale. Den knew this. He was a reporter. He knew lots of things.

He informed the Bith of this fascinating fact. "That means you c'n see *real* good," he explained.

"Good enough to tell you've had enough," the Bith said.

Den wagged a disapproving finger at him. "Not to worry, m'good friend—don' you know it's pract'illy imposs'ble t'get a Sullustan drunk?"

"Congratulations, then. You've achieved the impossible." He took Den's mug away. "I'd advise taking an air taxi home. Good-bye."

Den concentrated on walking out of the pub without too much noticeable weaving. Once outside, the various reeks and stenches of uncollected trash, assorted lifeforms who hadn't bathed in far too long, hydrocarbon emissions from antiquated vehicles banned centuries ago uplevel, and many other rancid sources sobered him somewhat. The scene before him still had a tendency to split into two or three alternate world tracks—that's how it looked, anyway—but at least the gravity was remaining fairly constant now.

Den found a relatively clean spot on a street bench and sat down. The fetid air, along with the cacophony of dozens of languages being spoken, fluted, stridulated, or otherwise produced, and the sheer overload of the crowd, were all reminders that things hadn't gone quite as well as he'd hoped after he and the droid I-Five had finally arrived, nearly a year ago, on Coruscant. The credits they'd hidden away were all but depleted, and the rent on their "luxury" lacuna would soon be due. Den had been eking out a meager living writing as a stringer for various holozines and tabloids, but even that was beginning to dry up.

This wasn't the way he'd imagined it, not by a country light-year. *Den Dhur* was, after all, a name that sold news—or had been, once upon a time. But that was before the Clone Wars, and before the Battle of Drongar. Den had covered that front, and while there had written an exposé of the Bunduki teräs käsi champion Phow Ji.

Ji had been a martial arts master and, in Den's opinion, a psychopath who liked to kill, and who used the war as an excuse for doing so. Eventually Ji had gone up single-handed against several Salissian mercenaries and an entire battalion of Separatist soldiers, and destroyed them and their transport, dying in the process.

There were some who viewed this action as heroic. Den had felt differently, along with several others of Republic Mobile Surgical Unit Seven—including Barriss Offee, the Jedi healer assigned to the Rimsoo. As a representative of her Order, she had been a particular target of Ji's verbal as well as physical abuse. As far as Barriss and the others were concerned, Ji's motivations had been anything but patriotic. They felt he was a brutal thug who would have been just as happy killing Republic troops as Separatists.

Such was the slant Den had taken with his story. Unfortunately, his editor, feeling that the public needed heroes at that time, had done an in-house rewrite that painted Phow Ji as a martyr, rather than a murderer. Even more unfortunately, one of the last public acts of Chancellor Palpatine before his ascension had been to dedicate a statue of Ji in Monument Plaza on Coruscant.

Den had taken his name off the rewritten article, but most editors and publishers in the Column Commons publishing district knew what his initial take on Phow Ji had been. That, coupled with the fact that Palpatine was now Emperor, and that the Emperor frowned upon any media suggesting the war had been anything less than a glorious episode in galactic history, had resulted in an industry backlash that left Den all but unemployable.

He'd tried for a time to write a novel, on the rather shaky theory that unpopular points of view could be more easily disguised in fiction. But that wasn't where his talents lay. He was a newshawk, blast it, and to have the comlink suddenly stop buzzing was not only financially distressing but demoralizing as well. And so, bitter and even more disillusioned than usual, he'd begun frequenting the taverns and pubs in the neighborhood more and more.

For the last couple of weeks he'd been thinking seriously about chucking the whole thing and trying to get back to Sullust, somehow. Perhaps there he could again hook up with Eyar Marath, the comely troupe dancer he'd met during the HoloNet News and Entertainment tour on Drongar. She had offered him an honored position as high husband to her warren. At first he'd been unsure, because he wasn't old enough to retire yet, no matter what the industry seemed to think. But lately the whole patriarchal gig was looking better and better. Being fêted and lionized in a comfortable cave on the homeworld certainly beat this hardscrabble existence.

There was, in fact, only one thing that had kept Den in this welter of plasteel and permacrete this long: I-5YQ. Except that Den never thought of the droid by his serial code. To him the protocol unit was simply I-Five. He barely thought of him as a droid anymore, in fact. I-Five was his friend—one of the very few beings on this planet or any other whom Den Dhur trusted completely.

Along with nearly everyone else in the galaxy, Den had believed that droids were nothing more than machines. True, they were machines that could process enormous amounts of data, and some of the more humanoid ones could mimic sentient behavior to a startling degree. But that was because they were programmed to. Given their memory capacity, and the speed of their neural networks or synaptic grid processors, they could be outfitted with basic responses and reactions and from there heuristically extrapolate the behavior of humans, or Falleen, or Geonosians, or whatever species one wished. But it could only go so far. Creativity dampers, behavioral inhibitor circuits and software, and other built-in limits kept droids from reaching true self-awareness. Thus, they had the same status in galactic society that an electrospanner did.

Even slaves on the benighted worlds of the Outer Rim were treated better.

It had been a comforting theory. For most people the same had applied, to a lesser degree, to the clones who made up the majority of the Republic's army. They were dismissed simply as "meat droids" by most sentients, little better than beasts with the power of speech, because they'd been genetically and psychologically modified to embrace battle and not fear death.

A comforting theory, indeed. The only problem was that there were exceptions. I-Five was such an exception. *Oh, yar, bloodline,* as the Ugnaughts said. *'Deed he were.* The acerbic droid and the cynical reporter had become boon companions during their stint in the hothouse that was Drongar, where the two armies had battled over possession of the miracle plant bota until a mutation of the crop had rendered it useless, and the struggle pointless.

Afterward, Den had accompanied I-Five back to Coruscant to help on a mission that had been the droid's equivalent of a blood oath. It had taken them several months and many layovers on various and sundry worlds—there was, after all, a war going on—to reach the capital planet, and in the time they'd been here I-Five had made little, if any, progress in his quest, which was to find the son of Lorn Pavan, his former partner. He had come to the reluctant conclusion that Lorn was dead, although he could find little documentation on the particulars; it seemed the facts had been buried deep, in unknown graves. The boy, however, had been raised as a Jedi, and so shouldn't have been that hard to find— except that, right after they arrived on Coruscant, what had been a Republic suddenly became an Empire, and what with the fighting and the fleeing and all the various other forms of unpleasantness, Den and I-Five had been hard-put just to stay alive. Finally, when the smoke had cleared—as much as it ever did downlevel—they'd learned, to their dismay, that the Jedi had been almost completely massacred.

A few had escaped, it was rumored. It was also rumored that some of them were in hiding right here on Coruscant, and this was what kept I-Five here and searching.

But did it make any sense to keep looking? Den thought about it, somewhat laboriously, one neuron blindly groping through the alcoholic fog to link with another. Though he hated to say it, hated even to think it, he couldn't help reaching the same conclusion over and over: No. It didn't. Lorn Pavan's son was either off-planet or akk chow by now. Either way, there wasn't a lot that could be done about it. The remaining Jedi had scattered to the four solar winds—a prudent move, in Den's opinion—and even if Jax Pavan was still somewhere on Coruscant, the odds of bumping into him on a street corner weren't too good in a planetwide city with trillions of inhabitants.

I-Five's loyalty to his erstwhile partner, and his determination to honor Lorn's last request by watching over his son, was commendable. But it was also pointless. "Even his big positronic brain's gotta be able to see that," Den muttered.

He got to his feet, still weaving slightly, turned, and promptly bumped into a group of three armored Ganks. One of them, in a display of the consideration and thoughtfulness common to his kind, backhanded Den, knocking him off his feet and into the trash-strewn gut-ter. Another Gank pulled a vibroknife and bent over him. The multifarious crowd parted as if the Ganks and Den were encased in an invisible dome, flowing around them and taking no notice of the Sullustan's plight.

Den tried to get to his feet, but the third Gank pressed a boot against his chest, pinning him. "I suppose it's too late to say I'm sorry?" Den gasped.

The Gank with the vibroknife activated the blade. A high-pitched hum emanated from it as the blade began to vibrate, its monomolecular edge blurring into invisibility. The helmeted faces of the other two showed no expression as the third reached for one of the Sullustan's pendulous earlobes—and then a pewter-colored mechanical hand reached over the Gank's shoulder and grabbed the pulsating blade's hilt, yanking it from its owner's surprised grasp, and dropped it to the pavement, where it sank into the duracrete up to the guard.

"Now, now—manners," a pleasant voice chided. "After all, he did apologize."

The Ganks turned and saw a protocol droid standing behind them, one index finger raised, as if admonishing them. The tip of the finger glowed bright red. The droid said, "You're probably thinking, *Everyone knows a protocol droid has behavioral inhibitors that won't let it harm sentient organics.*" Den could see the thin red beam of the laser move downward as the durasteel finger targeted the foremost Gank's forehead, just above and right between where his eyes were under the helmet.

"Well," the droid continued, "everyone, in this case, is wrong."

The Ganks glanced at one another. Then, as if in agreement on some unspoken decision, the three turned away and melted into the uncaring crowd.

The droid helped Den to his feet. The Sullustan brushed garbage from his clothes. "Next time, don't cut it so close," he growled.

"Whatever do you mean?" Photoreceptors projected guileless innocence. "I calculate that I had an entire two point seven seconds before the vibroknife would have actually—"

Den raised both hands to stop the droid's reply. "Okay, okay! Not really needing to hear the gory details. Thanks anyway."

The immobile metal face somehow managed to look slightly amused. "I live to serve," I-Five said.

six

Kaird of the Nediji paced the length of his luxurious suite and contemplated murder.

In itself, this was no great occasion. Kaird had considered the taking of a life many times before, and followed through on it more than once as well. There was no moral dilemma involved; the only decision was one of practicality. Would the removal of this particular entity to the Great Nest benefit his purpose, or would it simply satisfy a yearning for revenge, smooth some temporarily ruffled feathers? If it was the latter, then there was no point to it. As the Aqualish saying went, *Revenge is a cold current to swim in.* Insults and slights were to be acted upon only if it expedited one's agenda to do so. Honor was a luxury practical beings could ill afford.

Still, in this particular case, the temptation was hard to resist. And so, as he stalked back and forth, he indulged himself in imaginative fantasies about how best to dispose of his enemies.

One, in particular . . .

Kaird had moved upward rapidly in the ranks of Black Sun. A little more than a standard year ago he had been a mere assassin, albeit a very good one. Since then he had become a most excellent fugue master within the organization, choosing his allies with care. Now, after over a year of work, he had maneuvered himself into an envious position—he was on the verge of becoming a Vigo.

On the verge, he reminded himself, but not there yet. There was only room for one new member in the inner circle of Dal Perhi, the current Black Sun Underlord. And his rival for the post, Prince Xizor of the Falleen, was a most formidable opponent.

As a species, the Fallen were secretive and insular; little was known of them by the rest of the galaxy, since they tended to keep to their own system. In their dealings with other species, they were usually soft-spoken and silver-tongued. They were not unctuous and wheedling, like the duplicitous Neimoidians, and they were far more clever and indirect than the plainspoken Dressellians. The Falleen were physically imposing as well, averaging over one and a half meters in height, and possessed, for the most part, of a sleek and mesomorphic body design. With their classically symmetrical features, skin pigmentation that ranged from verdant to orange-red, depending on the individual's mood, and lustrous hair, they were not unattractive as featherless bipeds went, Kaird supposed. The attraction was enhanced, of course, by the wide range of pheromones they could produce. This latter fact was not generally well known, as the Falleen were rarely encountered, and they weren't in the habit of pointing out their advantage to others. But Kaird had known a female Falleen named Thula in the recent past. He knew that the airborne triggers, secreted from specialized apocrine glands of both male and female Falleen, could cause various intense reactions, romantic and otherwise, in others of their own

species. In addition to pheromones, they could also produce allelochemical transmitters that evoked various
emotions, such as fear, desire, anger, doubt, and confusion, among most species with similar body chemistry.
The Falleen were quite adept at manipulating others via
these subliminal means, and Xizor, Prince of House
Sizhran, one of the oldest of the Falleen monarchies, was
an adept among adepts.

Even without this biochemical advantage, Falleen
were naturals at the intricate games of politics. Xizor
was also a shining example of this: a player who believed absolutely in the words of the great strategist
General Grievous: "One should clique closely with one's
allies, but even more closely with one's adversaries."

Kaird espoused the same philosophy, of course. It
amused him, as much as he assumed it amused his
enemy, to dissemble, to pay lip service to the other's accomplishments while subtly playing up his or her inher-
ent problems. "Prince Xizor's disposition of the Jalorian
Sodality was ingenious and impressive. The failure to recover the shipment of fire emeralds before it was swallowed by the Khadaji Singularity in no way lessens his
accomplishment." Or, "The imbroglio involving the attempted assassination of the Khommite ambassador is
unfortunate, but we must remember that the Khom-
mites are clones. Mistaking one for another was to be
expected . . . given the quality of the intel supplied."

Xizor never became upset at such veiled barbs, and he
gave as good as he got. "It was, perhaps, not the quality
of the intel that was at fault," he had said in response to
Kaird's latter innuendo, "but the interpretation of the
data. I did not choose the assassination team; I merely

supplied vital information—much of which seems to have been ignored."

Of course, it had been Kaird who had picked the hit beings and given them their marching orders. And so it went, back and forth, the endless and subtle jockeying for position, each with the same goal: the favor of Underlord Perhi.

Kaird knew what the Falleen's desire was: power and security within the organization, with an ultimate shot at the title of Underlord. The same, in other words, as just about everyone else's goal. The only way to have that was to claw one's way as high up the food chain as possible, and being a Vigo was about as high as one could get. There were eight others who were a Vigo's equal, but only one who was a superior: the Underlord himself. Xizor craved that power and authority. He didn't lack for funds; even had he not been a Falleen prince, his front business, Xizor Transport Systems, earned him millions of credits annually without his having to lift a manicured finger. He didn't lack for feminine companionship, either; even discounting his wealth and good looks, those invisible clouds of pheromones he could shed at will guaranteed him women aplenty. No, Xizor wanted one thing and one thing only: sheer raw power, the power that being the Underlord of Black Sun could bestow. He was so close he could almost taste it; Kaird could see that in his veiled lavender eyes.

Kaird had violet eyes. They were capable of excellent vision; after all, his avian ancestors had evolved on the high, snow-dusted peaks of Nedij, an outlying world on the eastern spinward rim. They had occupied themselves, among other things, with hunting humanoid creatures not unlike the Falleen. His kind no longer possessed the power of flight, and, while he was still stronger and faster than most other beings, he knew that the prince's physical condition, coupled with his prowess in the martial arts, could spell out Kaird's doom in large, easy-to-read letters. He had no intention of letting that happen—not when he was so close to his own goal.

He wondered what Xizor, Underlord Perhi, and most of the others would say if they knew what Kaird's true agenda was. It wasn't power for its own sake; it wasn't the thrill of having the ear of the Underlord, or even of being the Underlord himself—it was nothing like that.

Kaird just wanted to go home.

Back to Nedij. Back to the high, sunlit crags and promontories of his world. Back to his Flock; they would likely accept him now, as the transgression he had been banished for was long past. And if they didn't, he was still going, even if he had to nest in solitude. Alone on Nedij was better than here on Coruscant in the company of scoundrels.

Here on Coruscant wasn't quite accurate, because they weren't on the planet itself. Black Sun had sanctuaries established across the galaxy, and this particular one was in a skyhook, a space station in geosynchronous orbit, tethered to the planet by a 37,730-kilometer-long duracable shaft. To the few Coruscanti wealthy or important enough to be in orbit in the first place, Sinharan T'sau was merely another private resort; in this case, a domed oasis of sculptured tachylyte and obsidian rocks and crags, dotted here and there with orange gorse, purple cycads, and other exotic growths. Beneath the glossy black surface, however, was the sanctuary known as Midnight Hall. Much of Black Sun's business was dealt with in these dark, labyrinthine chambers and corridors. And it was here that Kaird had spent much of the past year.

He *hated* it. If they had designed a specific hell with him in mind, they couldn't have done a better job. True, it was brightly lit, and well ventilated, but even so, Kaird could feel the mass of all that heavy stone pressing down on him, threatening to snap his hollow bones and crush him to paste. He knew this could not happen, but knowledge and phobia had little to do with the other.

His plan called for another two years, three at most. First he would consolidate his position as Vigo, then use that power to surreptitiously discover all the scabrous little secrets, unmarked graves and the like that he could. Because it was only by hanging a big enough sword over the heads of his peers—and perhaps even his sole superior—that he would be allowed to retire with his own head still on his shoulders.

For most, Black Sun was a lifetime commitment—once you were in, you were in for life, and that life could be cut very short if you tried to leave. Oh, you might make it out, might even think you were safe, that you had pulled it off, done what so many before you had not been able to do. You might even find a nice planet somewhere, far from the major space lanes, a place where an outlander with sufficient credits would be welcomed with open arms and no questions. But sooner or later there would come a knock on your door, and you would have just enough time to regret opening it before you were blasted into oblivion.

Kaird knew this. He knew it because he'd stood on the other side of that door, his blaster aimed and ready, many times. It wouldn't play out that way for him.

He'd almost gotten out once before, just after the cessation of hostilities on Drongar. He and his two henchbeings, the Falleen Thula and an Umbaran named Squa Tront, had seized upon one of the last of the viable bota shipments. Kaird had hoped that, by giving his portion to Black Sun, he could engender enough good will among the Vigos to be allowed to go his way—that, plus the fact that he already knew where a great many bodies were buried. But he never got the chance to find out. The two grifters had double-crossed him, absconded with the entire bota shipment, and left Kaird sitting in space on a bomb, which he'd discovered barely in time.

The ruff of feathers around his neck bristled at the thought of that. The loss of the bota had meant putting aside his dreams of Nedij for an indefinite future, because without it his position wasn't strong enough to allow him to go. He still firmly believed that revenge was for amateurs, but if that pair of rogues ever crossed his path again, he just might make an exception.

His chrono chimed softly. It was almost time for his meeting with the Underlord. It wasn't one-on-one, sadly; he had to share it with two of the appointed Vigos. A pity. There was so much he could accomplish toward his purpose, if he could just have some uninterrupted face time with Underlord Perhi . . .

He sighed. You could only do your best, and hope for a strong tail wind to waft you faster to your destination. Until then, you played the game, kept your tongue civil, and spoke favorably of your enemies when either they or their spies might overhear.

Still, they couldn't read his thoughts. And so it didn't hurt, and it certainly improved his mood as Kaird walked to his meeting, to think of more different and imaginative ways to kill Prince Xizor.

seven

In a part of Coruscant where just glimpsing the sun could be an occasion to tell one's grandchildren about, it seemed odd that true darkness never really came at all. But such was the case; the pulse of the city-planet's downlevel slums acknowledged neither day nor night. With few exceptions, those beneath, on, or near the surface lived in a perpetual gloaming of electroluminescence. The chromatic signatures of neon, argon, and other ionized gases lit the Blackpit Slums' streets at all hours, and very few beings acknowledged the schedules of the world above. Many businesses could be found open at any time of the twenty-four hour cycle, and most species followed their own circadian rhythms, however esoteric they might be.

As a result—for Nick Rostu, at least—the downlevel world always seemed slightly unreal. There was a phantasmagorical quality that he found at times fascinating, and at times frustrating. Sometimes he felt as if he were wearing a dermpatch of dreamspice, or some other mild psychedelic, all the time.

The feeling was particularly strong now as he piloted his ground skimmer down a narrow street. His chrono told him that it was 0342, but that was uplevel time, where day and night signified something. Down here, in the never-ending electric twilight, time had a different meaning altogether. It wasn't something to be scheduled, something to be quantified in terms of seconds, minutes, or hours. It was measured much more simply: you either had enough, or not enough. And these days, it seemed to Nick that there was never enough.

Master Piell, with his dying breath, had explained to him the urgency of his mission, and had also told him whom it had to be entrusted to: his erstwhile Padawan, Jax Pavan, who had graduated to Jedi Knighthood only a few months before the war ended. It was Pavan whom Master Piell had been searching for, and it was Pavan whom Nick now had to find.

On the face of it, this seemed utterly impossible. How to go about finding one man in a city the size of a planet? Fortunately, Nick had known Pavan slightly before the disbanding of the Order, and one of the databases the Whiplash was assembling was designed to keep track of the few Jedi still on Coruscant. They didn't have a specific location for Pavan, but Nick had been able to ascertain that he was in the Yaam Sector, aka Sector 1Y4F, the lower regions of which were known as the Blackpit Slums, somewhere along a length of street called Amtor Avenue.

The Yaam Sector was nearly five thousand kilometers east, along the equatorial belt, plus about four hundred klicks north. Nick had taken a hypertrain for the first part of the journey, one of the big mag-levs that rocketed through a sealed tube at two thousand kph. Inertial dampeners protected the passengers from the high g-forces and torque, and the near vacuum in the tube reduced friction to almost zero. The result was a comfortable trip, in a little more than two and a half hours, that had taken him nearly an eighth of the way around the planet, even allowing for a detour past a large blast crater.

The bypass had slowed the hypertrain long enough for the passengers to get a good look at the devastation. The crater was seven kilometers wide, its walls and floor fused to black glass. The remnants of structures rose here and there around its edges, like melted candle stubs. There were a great many such craters pocking the urban surface, Nick knew: ghastly evidence of the Separatists' carpet bombing of Coruscant in the final days of the war.

He'd switched at Ts'chai Station, taking a conventional monorail the rest of the way. When he'd arrived at the Yaam Depot, a member of the underground had a skimmer waiting for him, and he'd plunged into the Slums.

It was disturbing, yet fascinating, to watch the decay and decrepitude slowly grow as he piloted the skimmer down at a steep angle. It was nothing he hadn't seen before, but never before had it seemed so condensed. Around the 115th level, the air became hazy, stinging his eyes, and the smell grew noxious, to such a degree that he considered putting the canopy up. He knew this was the effect of hydrocarbons and ozone, caused by a temperature inversion layer, and that it was produced by underdwellers burning oil, wood, animal dung, and the like, to keep warm and provide power. In the sunlit world above, automated air scrubbers patrolled the upper atmosphere, keeping it reasonably clean and fresh. But no such benefits were available downlevel.

Beneath the belt of gritty brown air, it was another

world—a world that Nick Rostu had come to know all too well.

Air traffic was far less plentiful down here than up there, which was good, because the drivers were far less competent. Nick narrowly missed being creamed by a landspeeder that was veering to the right so consistently, he suspected the craft's starboard repulsor vane was malfunctioning. The pilot, a phlegmatic Ortolan, acknowledged the nearly fatal encounter with a single twitch of his blue trunk, and then was gone into the haze.

Although the buildings of the Yaam Sector were, for the most part, only cloudcutters—most of them no more than seven or eight hundred meters high, which paled next to the impressive two-thousand-plus-meter skytowers of the equatorial belt—they were set extremely close together. The Yaam Sector was one of the oldest on Coruscant; not as old as the Petrax Quarter, but old enough. A great many buildings had been built before the majority of the oceans disappeared, and the streets were narrower and winding, possibly because large ground transport vehicles hadn't been used as extensively back then. Nick didn't know or really care all that much about the reasons—he just knew that the constricted and vermicular routes on this part of the surface were making him intensely claustrophobic. In addition, many of the streets—more like glorified alleys, in his opinion—had a distressing tendency to come to an abrupt halt because some free spirits had decided, centuries ago, to erect a structure of some sort across them. Sometimes these had maze-like routes he could navigate gingerly through; more often they were simply dead ends, and he would have to backtrack and find a different way. It didn't help any that the locator sensor on this skimmer was malfunctioning.

Eventually, after much retracing of his route, he reached the street he was looking for. Amtor Avenue was an entirely too grandiose name for a constricted strip of pavement limned on each side by soot-blackened industrial warehouses, slurry conduits big enough to flush a bantha through, docking bays, and other Antaean structures stretching both directions into the intermittent darkness. A few blocks away he could see a wallcrawler slowly moving up its vertical track, hauling cargo containers to the upper levels. Farther still, gigawatts of purplish blue electrical discharges strobbed and sputtered between enormous terminals in a generator plant.

Other, closer, lights flickered as well, all about him. Even down here, in this predominantly manufacturing district, one couldn't escape the sensory barrage of floating advert-spheres and holo-billboards. Jagged, kaleidoscopic images pulsed at the edges of Nick's vision as he cruised down the street, touting personal tri-dee images, sleazy HoloNet sites, even various illegal substances.

He wouldn't have to put up with them for long, he told himself. It was now merely a question of finding the right building. He brought the vehicle to a dead crawl on automatic pilot, high enough to prevent any skimjackers from getting impulsive ideas, and concentrated.

A Jedi, even a rank Padawan, would have no trouble piloting the skimmer, and probably carrying on a conversation as well, while using the Force to search for another Force-sensitive. But Nick was no Jedi; far from it.

The ability to touch the Force might be encoded in his cells, but even if there were Jedi in his ancestry, whatever he'd inherited that powered the Force was evidently pretty anemic compared with that of his forebears. He'd seldom used the ability, back on Haruun Kal, for anything more than controlling akk dogs. Multitasking was out of the question. There were members of his ghôsh who had far more power than he, but the only Korunnai he'd known of who'd really been good at it had been Kar Vastor. And he had been steeped in the dark side.

One would think that it shouldn't be that difficult; after all, how many Force-sensitives could there be on any given street in a sty like this, particularly after the overthrow of the Order? But Nick knew that Jedi usually were able to conceal their connection to the Force, and he assumed the few still alive would be more assiduous than ever about doing so. That would make it even harder to find Pavan.

All he could do was try.

The skimmer moved slowly along, Nick sitting upright, his face scrunched in concentration.

Nothing.

Nick sighed and went to Plan B, which consisted of asking the few locals he could manage to corner momentarily if they remembered seeing a human male, midtwenties, dark hair, et cetera, in the neighborhood. At first, it looked like this wasn't going to be any more successful than trolling in the Force. But then he lucked out: he encountered a protocol droid, one of the 3PO line, that had obviously been downlevel a long time, judging by the patina of soot and grime that coated its once-alabaster armor. The droid belonged to a local Hutt gangster named Rokko, and, though initially reluctant, it finally searched its exhaustive memory banks and produced a list of ten humans with match probabilities to Nick's description of Pavan.

The first one lived in a resicube just around the corner, a thirty-meter-tall block of dark gray ferrocrete. There was one door, heavily barred, and no windows. The flickering sign over the door proclaimed this attractive piece of real estate to be the Coruscant Arms. Nick brought the skimmer to a halt across the street. If this was where Pavan was bivouacking, the plight of the Jedi Order was worse than he'd thought.

He stepped out of the vessel and into something soft and malodorous puddled on the curbwalk. He couldn't tell, in the dim light, what it was, which was probably just as well. A Kubaz slythmonger tried to sell him some Somaprin-3, but hastily reconsidered when Nick told him to "Use those feet before I burn 'em off, bug-nose."

No doubt about it, Nick thought, *it's a glamorous life I lead.*

There was little traffic; he waited for a troop transport vehicle to pass so he could cross the street. But instead of passing, the transport slowed to a stop, hovering just in front of the entrance. A moment later five stormtroopers stepped off and entered the hotel. All were packing BlasTech E-11s. A moment later the transport lifted away.

Nick blinked in disbelief, realizing that this might very well be the second night in a row he'd discovered Imperial muscle on the verge of waxing a Jedi. "What are the odds?" he murmured. Of course, the troops might be there on a totally unrelated matter, but somehow he doubted it.

He sighed, loosened the blaster he wore at his hip, and started across the street. No guts, no glory, after all. Not that he had anything to prove. Nick knew he had guts. He'd seen them.

eight

When the call came, Haninum Tyk Rhinann had been expecting it. He knew the secure comm would chime sooner or later. He knew that when it did he would be summoned into the presence of his master. But that knowledge didn't make the task itself any less of an ordeal. One did not, after all, venture into the nexu's den casually—not if one hoped to emerge with all one's limbs still attached.

"Yes, yes, of course," he told the droid that had made the call. "Ten minutes. I'll be there." Wouldn't do to keep *him* waiting, after all. If there was one thing Rhinann understood, it was the value of punctuality. Even so, he took a moment before the holoreflector, having his image rotate 360 degrees while he made sure that every fold of his robes was perfect and that his cravat blossomed just the right distance from his neck wattles. Then he canted the image at a forty-five-degree angle to make sure his ear hair was combed. After which he forced himself to leave, wishing that he'd had time to polish his horns. He noticed on his way out that one of the wall ornaments was hanging a hair off true vertical, but managed to leave without taking the time to adjust it.

Like most Elomin, Rhinann's penchant for neatness and order bordered on the fanatical. It was what made him a perfect choice for an aide-de-camp, and Rhinann took his responsibilities very seriously indeed. He was quite aware that he was one exceedingly lucky life-form; most of his species had been enslaved after the Emperor had come to power, and condemned to work in pits of horror such as the filthy factories and workhouses of Coruscant's industrial areas. Rhinann himself had been destined for such a fate, but fortunately he had been manumitted at the last moment. He still considered himself surrounded by madness and discord—only a return to Elom could remedy that—but he knew how much worse it could have been. And might still be, did he not perform his station well.

He followed a gently curving corridor toward the turbolift. There were plenty of people about, even at this hour; predominantly humans, although he did notice an Ortolan and a couple of Zabrak. Nearly all of them avoided his eyes as they hurried past.

He took an express lift to the ninety-fifth floor. This section of the Palace was sparsely decorated—mostly white walls, with only an occasional columnar cartouche or linteled doorway to accent the severity. Rhinann approved of this style of architecture. The less embellishment, the less chance of indecorousness.

If one wished to gain a fast understanding into a species, Rhinann felt that one of the easiest and quickest ways to do so was to look at its architectural styles. Take Coruscant. Mostly designed by humans, the posher areas were all characterized by sleek, swooping lines, and combined ancient structures, such as pyramids and minarets, with more modern technological and mechan-

ical themes. It showed an awareness of, and even rever-
ence for, the past, coupled with a look forward. This
was good as far as it went; however, the city as a whole
had little coherence. There were few discernible grid
patterns or other signs of regularity; any statement made
was amorphous and disharmonious at best—at worst,
anarchic. Just like its creators.

Rhinann despised humans. They weren't prone to
order; in fact, wherever they went, they left chaos and
madness strewn in their wake. They were a blight
spreading through the stars. True, so were other species,
even the barbarous cave-dwelling Eloms of his own
world, but humans were the worst, if for no other reason than there were so blasted many of them. Rhinann
believed, as did nearly all his people, that the Elomin
were the only really civilized species in the galaxy.

Still, he reflected as he hurried along, since humans
were ubiquitous throughout the galaxy, the most plentiful of any of the sentient species by far, there was no
point in opposing them—especially since they so often
wound up in charge. Like now. After all, there was no
question but that he was better off here, doing this, than
just about anyplace else, doing anything else. Even if one
swept aside the trappings and accoutrements, the salary,
and the luxury conapt, Rhinann would still have taken
the position for one reason: it let him delve into the mysteries of the Force.

The Force fascinated him. Having no aptitude for or
sensibility of it himself, he felt at times like a blind being
listening to someone describe the wonder of vision. On
the surface, the Force would seem to be the ultimate instrument of chaos, especially when used in the service of
the dark side. But if one peered closer, there was a seren-

ity beneath the roiling surface, an underlying order, just as storm-tossed waves can hide placid deeps. Certainly the Jedi seemed to have been granted a certain peace, as well as considerable fearlessness. He hadn't heard of a single one so far who had not died nobly. There were times—such as now, when he was so upset by the prospect of this meeting that even his fourth stomach was knotted—when Rhinann envied the Jedi for their ability to use the Force as a balm.

But this was not the time for fur gathering. He had to be in control of both mind and body. Indecision and hesitation would not be looked upon favorably.

All too soon he found himself standing before the door.

He was hyperventilating, Rhinann realized. Breathing so hard his nose tusks were vibrating. With a great effort, he managed to calm himself enough to at least evidence a spurious composure.

He entered. The antechamber was not large enough, in his opinion—but then not even the Grand Meeting Hall would allow enough distance between Rhinann and his superior in the meeting about to take place. He distracted himself momentarily by admiring the design: the ceiling was vaulted, and the lines of the fluted walls flowed in a soothing pattern up to it, drawing the eye. It was by no means overfurnished; a few chairs, a small couch, and a low table were all he saw. The colors were subdued, the lighting soft and with no visible source. All in all it would be a pleasant and relaxing room—were it not for the being entering through the far door. The being who had rescued him from a life of slavery. The being who had given him a titled position, and seen that he was paid quite handsomely for it. The being to whom he owed everything.

The being Haninum Tyk Rhinann feared more than anyone else in the galaxy.

"Do sit down, Rhinann," Darth Vader said.

Den said, "I think it's time we faced reality, I-Five."

"Any reality in particular? The number of possible parallel worlds is literally astronomical."

Den considered whacking the droid a good one, but since he had nothing to hit him with save his bare hands, he resisted. No point in just getting a sore palm, and he knew from experience that that would be the case. Even though I-Five was a discontinued model, his durasteel chassis was still quite sturdy.

The droid and the Sullustan were walking down an avenue known locally as Slan Street, heading back to the literal hole in the wall they shared. Just thinking about the place, with its leaky refresher and the spider-roaches big enough to kick him out of bed, made Den all the more determined to persuade I-Five to dust this over-built and overpriced dirtball.

Fortunately, Slan Street was reasonably well lit and marginally safer than most of the other thoroughfares in the Crimson Corridor; plus, the local criminals had learned to give I-Five a wide berth thanks to his accuracy with the lasers he packed in each index finger. Den had sobered up by now; as he'd told the pubtender, it was indeed hard to get Sullustans drunk, and correspondingly easy for them to shed alcohol's effects without a hangover. With sobriety had come the realization that he'd been a fool to go pub-crawling in a neighborhood like this at night. It was a good thing I-Five had come looking for him.

Still, Den felt he had the duty to try to make his friend see reason. "We've given this our best shot," he said as they strolled past a seedy holobooth arcade, its flickering 3-D ads detailing the concupiscent wonders promised within. "But I think you've got to admit that we've exhausted all the avenues of inquiry. I think we've exhausted even the back alleys of inquiry by now. If Jax Pavan is alive and still on Coruscant, trying to find him is like looking for a needle in a sleestax."

The droid did not reply. Den glanced at him. I-Five's face was, of course, immovable and expressionless, being made of metal. But over the years the droid had developed ways to simulate facial expressions that were startlingly effective. By making subtle shifts in the angle and intensity of his photoreceptors, coupled with body language, I-Five was able to emulate human demeanor with amazing accuracy. It was the main reason why most people, including Den, thought of the droid as a *him* rather than an *it*.

In the course of doing his job—when he'd had a job— Den had, of course, become very familiar with the aspects of human facial expressions and body language. And he could tell that, right now, I-Five was looking smug.

"What?"

"I've found him."

"Really." Den's tone was skeptical. They'd been down this space lane before as well—several times, in fact. "And where is he this time?"

"I realize that the false leads I've been given before have caused us some difficulty—"

"Interesting way to put it. Now, me, I'd call nearly having my arms ripped off by a spice-crazed Abyssin mudrunner or getting caught in the middle of a gang war between the Raptors and the Purple Zombies a milking *disaster*, but I suppose I might be overdramatizing."

"You're still alive and whole."

"Physically, yes. My psyche, however, is but a shadow of its former self. I fear my sweet infectious laughter may never return."

I-Five ignored him. "According to my source, Jax is in the Yaam Sector."

"Well, that narrows it down to about eighty square kilometers. You know what they call that area downlevels, don't you?"

"It's better than searching the entire planet. And yes, I do. It's known as the Blackpit Slums."

"Right. And that's a bad name. Bad names usually mean bad places, and bad places are not places we want to be."

Before Den could continue, he nearly tripped over a Snivvian lying in the shadow of a recessed doorway, either unconscious or dead. At the same time, a nearby altercation between a Klatooinian and an Ishi Tib was quickly escalating into a fight. The two pulled vibroblades and circled each other warily, looking for openings. Then, abruptly, both weapons glowed red, and the two combatants dropped them with cries of pain. They disappeared into the darkness in opposite directions.

Den glanced at I-Five and saw that the droid had both index fingers extended, his hands held close to his waist. The twin bursts of laserfire had gone unnoticed in the general kaleidoscopic flashings of various signs and images on storefronts, and the now useless weapons were lost in the general refuse and junk scattered everywhere.

"However bad they are," I-Five said, "the Slums can't be any worse than this."

Den sighed. "Can't argue with that. Just answer me one question—"

"Yes?"

"Why can't any of these leads ever take us someplace nice?"

"Because we're looking for outcast Jedi, not holoproj glitterati. Now, I've calculated the travel expense. We have just enough money left to buy us both one-way tickets to the Yaam Sector via speeder bus."

"Oh, good," Den said as they started walking again. "Because for a minute there I was worried that we might not arrive in one of the meanest cesspits of the galaxy *totally* destitute."

His small bag packed with all his worldly possessions—and still more than half empty—Jax turned to open the door. He was already regretting the few moments he'd spent thinking about the past. Time was of the essence if he wanted to get out of here before—

He stopped, staring at the portal's handle. Dark, weblike strands were entwining themselves rapidly around it. Strands that seemed to recede through the door, down the hall, and wrap around—

Jax backed away from the door, thinking rapidly. He was well and truly trapped—the cell he had been calling home was barely three meters by two, and windowless. The outside wall was ten centimeters of solid ferrocrete—not even his lightsaber could burn through it in time.

According to the threads of Force reverberating in his mind, there were at least five stormtroopers coming for him—possibly more. In only a few minutes they'd be through the door, and he'd be dead.

Where had they come from? Even as the question arose, Jax knew the answer. Rokko had evidently wasted no time in acting on the information his bully-boys had given him. He had no doubt contacted the local garrison and reported Jax to be a Jedi.

Jax shook his head, amazed at the corruption of a regime that would take the word of a known criminal as indiction of a fugitive Jedi.

It wasn't something he had time to think about now. Not with five troopers coming for him.

Let them come.

The voice speaking those words was quite clear: his own inner voice, but no less distinct for that. It was as if someone stood right behind him, whispering into his ear. He almost turned around to see if, in fact, anyone was there.

Let them come, the voice said again. *Let them kill you. Why not? How is the life you live now any better than death? Your Order, your people, your purpose, have already been destroyed. Nothing can change that. The only smart thing to do is to join them.*

Let them come. Let them kill you. It'll be quick. It will be painless.

Jax shook his head fiercely. "No," he growled, as if the seductive voice were an actual entity tempting him. He didn't know where this sudden existential urge had come from, but he would not give in to it.

There is no emotion; there is peace.

It was the first tenet of the Jedi Code. Jax whispered it

to himself. No matter how dark the hour seemed, he would not give in to despair. He looked back at the door—

And stared in disbelief.

The threads of Force that were his unique way of connecting with it were gone. Just for an instant, his link with the Force seemed to flicker. Then it was back, and he felt the familiar suffusion cover and permeate him. The flicker was gone; it had happened so quickly that he wasn't certain he'd experienced anything out of the ordinary at all.

Jax reached into his coat's inner pocket and pulled out his lightsaber. He thumbed it on and watched the shaft of pure blue energy lance from the hilt. He settled into a fighting stance, legs planted firmly, low and wide, with the lightsaber gripped in both hands and held ready. *Yes*, he thought. *I'll let them come. And there will be killing done this night.*

nine

Darth Vader stepped forward into the middle of the room. His boots made soft sounds on the carpet; his cloak whispered slightly as it flowed around him. Other than that, the only sound in the room was the regular susurrus of his respirator mask. It was a sound Rhinann often heard in his nightmares. The armor seemed to draw light into it, somehow; to leach color and brightness from the chamber. It was a color beyond black. Lord Vader surveyed Rhinann, his helmet's smooth, insectile orbs undoubtedly reading far more than any normal eyes could. Rhinann felt his generative nodes pucker in a fear response.

"Your report, Rhinann, if you please."

The voice was rich, deep, mellifluous; the words unfailingly polite, as always. There would seem to be nothing overtly threatening in them; still, Rhinann jumped as if fire wasps had stung him. "Yes, yes, of course, Lord Vader. Ah . . . it is confirmed that the Jedi Master Even Piell was . . . he was . . ."

"Eliminated. So the Force has told me." Vader made a dismissive gesture. "The remaining Jedi are of no concern to me. Their eventual final disposition is inevitable. Don't you agree?"

The Elomin nodded jerkily. "Oh, yes . . . of course, Lord Vader, there is no question of—"

"With one exception," Vader continued, that silky, menacing voice immediately squelching any opinion Rhinann might have dared to offer. "A Jedi named Jax Pavan." Vader seemed to pause for a moment, as if considering, though the respirator's cycle made no change. "He is in the Yaam Sector," the Dark Lord continued. "I cannot pinpoint his location more specifically without the possibility of alerting him to my interest. Therefore, you will find this Jedi, and arrange for him to be brought to me, Rhinann." The honeyed tones became contemplative, almost introspective. "He and I have . . . issues."

"Y-yes, my lord. But, by your leave . . . the Yaam Sector is still a huge area to search. More specificity would be most—"

Rhinann regretted the statement almost immediately, but there was no way to take it back. Vader did not reply at once; he simply looked at his aide, and the effect was like that of a crystal snake's gaze on its prey. The Elomin could not move. Vader raised his right hand in a small gesture, and Rhinann felt a slight pressure around his throat. The paralyzing effect of Vader's gaze vanished at the same time, but there was no longer any need for it; Rhinann had gone rigid with fear. It seemed to him that he could hear the triple thud of his six-chambered heart pounding, louder and louder . . . but then the sound and the choking sensation vanished, almost as soon as they had begun; he could scarcely be sure that he'd even experienced them at all.

Vader lowered his hand. "I trust your duties are clear?"

"Yes, Lord Vader. Absolutely. As my lord wishes, so shall it be."

"Excellent. We are done here, Rhinann. When next we meet, I expect to hear good news. Do not disappoint me."

The portal near Rhinann immediately slid open. Lord Vader turned away, and the Elomin exited, slightly quicker than dignity allowed.

Once out of the office and striding back toward the turbolift, he somewhat shakily took stock. It had not gone badly. Vader had acknowledged Piell's elimination, however offhandedly, and had given him a new assignment—find the Jedi Jax Pavan.

No, not badly. Not badly at all . . . that phantom grip he'd felt for an instant about his throat? Nothing but his imagination. Nothing to be concerned about, Rhinann told himself as he entered the turbolift. Nothing to be concerned about at all.

Unless, of course, he did not find Jax Pavan immediately, if not sooner . . .

Jax waited tensely for the attack, for the flimsy door to be battered or blasted down. No matter how many of them there were, he would, at the very least, give a good accounting of himself. And he might very well come out of it alive. They could only come at him one or two at a time through the door. And, most importantly, he was a Jedi. No matter how many there were, they were no match for the Force.

It felt so good to be immersed in it once again, it was almost worth the fight. The threads seemed to tighten, drawing the troopers down the corridor and to the door . . .

Then, to his surprise, the attackers became the attacked.

Jax felt the reverberation along the Force strings as the stormtroopers reacted in confusion and surprise. Someone had come up behind them and fired a blaster, dropping the trooper bringing up the rear. The trooper next in line turned, only to be hit by another charged-particle blast.

Whoever this new player was, he was saving Jax's life, whether inadvertently or not. And at this point, it didn't matter.

Jax speared the lock mechanism with his lightsaber, kicked the door open, and leapt through it. Before the point man could fire, Jax's blade lanced through his upper torso. The trooper dropped, and the man behind him fired at Jax.

As usual, the Force was at least three seconds ahead of the moment, warning Jax in time for him to spin his energy blade. The energy bursts struck the lightsaber and were reflected back.

It took no more than a few seconds—the squad clearly hadn't expected an attack from the rear. Almost as soon as it began, it was over. The corridor was filled with dust and smoke; some of the wild blasts had singed the walls and flooring. It was dark as well, because at least two sconces had been zapped out.

Jax squinted as the silhouette of his rescuer came toward him through the smoky darkness. He still had his lightsaber lit and ready. There was something about this man—something besides his tenuous connection to the Force—that was familiar.

"Power down your glow stick, Pavan," said a voice that was also tantalizingly familiar, "and let's go." Jax heard the distinctive sound of a blaster sliding into its holster.

He deactivated his lightsaber but remained ready to use it. "Go where?"

"Does it matter?" A scuffed boot nudged one of the dead stormtroopers. "These guys are down, but more'll come soon; you can bet credits to crumblebuns on that. That's why they call 'em clones."

As he finished speaking, he stepped out of the shadows and smoke and stood before Jax, who stared in surprise.

"Rostu?" he said incredulously. "Nick Rostu?"

"Nothing wrong with your eyes, but your ears must be full of wax. I said, let's *go*." He brushed past Jax, heading toward the corridor's far end. Jax followed, still surprised at seeing a familiar face, albeit one he hadn't encountered in over a year.

They passed several more doors, all of which remained closed. In fact, none of them had opened at any point during the fight, which was only common sense on the occupants' parts. He was sure this wasn't the first altercation the building had seen, though quite possibly it was the only one to involve Jedi and stormtroopers.

Rostu passed the last door. "There's no exit at that end," Jax called, then winced at the sudden explosion.

"There is now," Rostu yelled over his shoulder. He leapt through the hole he'd just blown in the wall ahead.

Jax crossed the last meter of floor and jumped, hoping Rostu had remembered that they were on the third floor. He used the Force to partially levitate, slowing his fall to a gentle landing, and looked around. He was in the alley behind the building. It was narrow and littered with obsolete equipment parts, like the sheddings of some gigantic mechanical beast. A foamcast mattress, which had no doubt provided Rostu's landing pad, lay to one side. Gutted and discarded astromech shells, broken portable scanners, even a Z-6 jetpack—obviously unworkable, which was a pity—were just a few of the things he noticed. And the place stank, as badly as if all the detritus had been organic instead of mechanical.

Rostu was nowhere to be seen.

Then, abruptly, he heard a hiss and a whispered "Down here!" from the alley's far end. He gathered himself and leapt again, sailing over the debris. No point in trying to be stealthy—his whereabouts had obviously been discovered. Otherwise an assassination team wouldn't have been sent. Speed was of the essence; he fancied that he could already hear the approach of PCBUs called to the scene of the battle and the explosion. They wouldn't risk the lives of real officers down here, but the droids piloting the police cruiser backup units were, like stormtroopers, infinitely expendable.

He landed beside Rostu, who turned and headed for the mouth of the alley. "Let's keep moving," he said.

As they walked down the avenue, Jax glanced at the man beside him. Hard to believe that this was indeed Nick Rostu, the Korunnai whom Master Windu had brought back, grievously wounded, from Haruun Kal; the hero who'd helped capture the notorious Kar Vastor and turn the Summertime War around.

"You've changed," he said. It was true. Rostu had always had an air of confidence, a don't-mess-with-me attitude, which wasn't surprising, given his upbringing on the high plateaus of his jungle world. Jax had met him only a few times, all of them after Rostu's commission.

His stint in the army certainly hadn't softened him, but now . . .

The threads of the Force that surrounded him were a grim, durasteel gray. His eyes were like hammered metal. Rostu could have never, by any standard, been called even mildly overweight, but the last few months seemed to have purged every gram of fat from his frame. He was as lean as a Tusken Raider just back from a long walkabout. This man could be downright dangerous, Jax knew—but not here, and not now.

"Nice scar," he said, more to fill the sudden silence than anything else.

Rostu grinned and touched his left cheekbone. "Isn't it?" he said. "Souvenir of a Mangler's vibroblade. Don't worry; his is a lot worse."

The Manglers were lords of the Southern Underground and reputed to be one of the toughest gangs on the planet; supposedly even the Red Guards would think twice before tangling with them. If Rostu was telling the truth—and Jax saw no indication in the Force that he was doing otherwise—it was yet more proof that he was someone to be reckoned with.

He was also in a position to help Jax. Nick Rostu was one of the partisans who could arrange for Jax to be on the next transport offworld. And Jax was more than ready to go.

"We need to talk," Rostu said as they reached his skimmer.

"I know a place," Jax replied.

ten

Gort's was a dark and moody hole-in-the-wall Mon Calamari restaurant on the fiftieth level. Quarren music, mostly atonal quetarra études, played softly from hidden speakers. The clientele was varied: a Verpine sat at the sulyet bar, as did a couple of humans, a Toydarian, and a Sakiyan. Jax and Rostu were also seated at the bar, where they could see both front and rear entrances. They'd taken a roundabout route, and Jax felt reasonably confident that they hadn't been followed.

It was evident that Rostu had never tried Quarren cuisine. He eyed with considerable mistrust the tasteful arrangement of sulyet on the platter that the chef had just set before him. "It's still *moving*."

"That means it's fresh." Jax picked up a small oblong bar of tikit grain. It had a tiny sliver of purple coral worm arranged on it, which writhed slowly. He put it in his mouth and chewed, savoring the tang of sweet and tart.

Rostu gingerly picked up a grain ball with a nudibranch embedded in it. A tiny eye on a stalk opened and peered at him, and he put it down again hastily. "And I thought ready rations were hard to choke down."

"Not so loud," Jax said. "You'll insult the chef."

"And he'll do what? Force-feed me more of this purple sourwort garnish?"

"No, but he might make a slight mistake in preparing that nexufish he's working on. Nexufish are deadly poison if not served exactly right."

"Any particular reason you picked a restaurant where seafood is a deadly weapon, or are you just misanthropic in general?"

Down the bar, the Sakiyan accepted a large order of nexufish sulyet from the chef and began devouring it. Jax poured a cup of grain wine from the carafe.

"So," he said, "to what do I owe the pleasure of this rescue?"

Rostu's expression turned grim. "I'm afraid I have some bad news for you," he said. "Even Piell was your mentor, wasn't he?"

Jax felt his skin chill. "How did it happen?"

Nick nodded. "Felt it already, huh?"

"Yes." Jax sighed. "I didn't know for sure that it was him, but there aren't a lot left to choose from."

"News travels fast through the Force." Nick hesitated, then told him how Even Piell had met his fate.

Jax gazed into the ceramic wine cup. More than anyone else, Master Piell had been his guide along the Jedi path. The Lannik had been small in physical stature, but to Jax he'd been a giant—as much a father as a teacher. Under Master Piell's instruction he'd made his first, fumbling forays into the mysteries of the Force, had fashioned his lightsaber, had learned the intricacies of combat. Because of the Jedi Master's careful and thorough instruction, Jax had passed his trials with flying colors. However much of a Jedi he was—however much of a man he was—that much and more he owed to Master Even Piell.

The Emperor, and his lickspittle Vader, had much to answer for.

"There's more," Rostu said.

Jax looked up, and a small, faraway part of him realized that his expression must be dark indeed, because even Rostu's eyes widened slightly at the sight of his face. "Yes," he said. "Otherwise he wouldn't have sent you to me."

"You've heard of the Whiplash?"

Jax nodded. "Of course."

"There's a droid you've got to find." Rostu glanced around, and lowered his voice. "It's a Series Tee-Oh, classification number Ten-Four. Nickname's Bug-Eyes. Seems it got its operating parameter messed up somehow, and is for all purposes lost. It's carrying data vital to the resistance movement—what, exactly, I don't know." He put one of the less responsive pieces of sulyet into his mouth, chewed, and swallowed. "Not bad," he said, in a tone of mild surprise.

"I guess it doesn't matter what the data are," he continued. "What matters is that the Emperor wants it. There's a command phrase that'll give you control over it: *Zu woohama*." He shrugged. "I'm told it's an impolite Wookiee saying. Anyway, Master Piell was looking for the droid to get it on a ship and off Coruscant when the troops caught up with him."

"And he wants me to take up the search."

Rostu nodded. "It was his dying request."

"Even if it wasn't," Jax said, "I'm in."

eleven

"Well," said I-Five, as he and Den emerged from the speeder bus terminal, "it could be worse."

The droid and the Sullustan stood on a balcony three stories up from one of the larger streets in the Blackpit Slums. Even at that height the stench of organic refuse, industrial pollutants, and—it being the dinner hour—gallimaufries of various species cooking outdoors was noticeable. The constant, crepuscular twilight seemed to keep everything in suspended time, as though they were trapped in some nether dimension. They could hear horns, imprecations, cries of fear, snatches of music, bits of conversations in a plethora of tongues, the Dopplering buzz of badly tuned repulsors as vehicles swooshed by, all merging into a mélange of hostility and despair. Flickering phosphor signs advertising lubricious thrills were everywhere Den looked. The chemicals in the air stung his eyes. He was glad he'd gotten out of the habit of wearing light-dampening droptacs, as they would have exacerbated the irritation. He hardly ever needed them downlevel, anyway.

He felt the sudden pressure of a hand on his shoulder. Or rather a foot, he realized, as he turned to see a Dug standing beside him.

"Death sticks?" the handwalker croaked. "Dream-dust? Glitterstim? Whatever you want, I got it." He plucked at the pockets of his vest with dexterous pha-langes. "Top quality assured, no additives—" He leapt back with a squeal of fright as a quick laser blast from I-Five's left index finger powdered the flagging in front of him, then turned and half ran, half hopped away.

Den looked at I-Five. "How could this possibly be any worse?"

"He might have been infected with scab-rot," the droid said, referring to a highly infectious disease that affected primarily Dugs, Ithorians, and Sullustans. Den decided not to dignify that with an answer, although he had to admit it was an unsettling possibility. Not all that remote, either; after all, it was well known that diseases that had long since been eradicated among the more af-fluent classes could still strike downlevel. And wouldn't that be ironic—to escape with his health intact from Drongar, one of the most pestilential planets in the galaxy, only to fall prey to some bug on Coruscant?

He sighed. "Anyway, we're here, alive and well—for the moment. Now let's find some creds and a shed, pronto. This is one neighborhood I don't want to be in after dark." The Yaam Sector was in an earlier time zone than the Zi-Kree Sector, and so the sun had not yet set—not that one could easily tell. There were more lights coming on, however, as more goods and wares of questionable taste, and even more questionable sanita-tion, began to be touted by shop owners and street pur-veyors. It was growing lighter rather than darker as night approached, but as far as Den was concerned that was an irony best appreciated behind closed doors.

I-Five started toward a drop-tube.

"Whoa," Den said, hurrying after him and grabbing his arm. "That one'll drop you into the street."

"I know," the droid replied, shaking off his friend's grip and continuing toward the tube.

Den stared. "Then why are you—"

"I like the nightlife," I-Five replied as he stepped into the tube. The repulsor field lowered him quickly from sight.

Den groaned. A human standing nearby glanced at him. Den quickly sized him up out of the corner of his eye—his peripheral vision was better than most species' frontal sight. The human's hair was dyed a deep magenta and electrostatically charged, standing a good ten centimeters above his scalp, and his muscular arms were decorated with glow-tats. A floating advert-sphere blinking the words GANG MEMBER in red letters, with an arrow pointing at him, would have been more subtle.

To Den, this was the sort of being who took the life out of nightlife, usually with great glee and expertise. The Sullustan started walking toward the drop-tube by which I-Five had exited.

The human didn't follow, much to his relief. The field lowered Den gently but swiftly toward the street.

Humans, he thought. *Everywhere you go, humans.* And humanoids. It was interesting that natural selection had favored the upright, bipedal form in which to package intelligence on so many different worlds. Den, himself, was an example of that. One of the things he disliked most about humans was that they all seemed to be smugly taking credit for it, as if they'd pioneered the whole thing.

He stepped out of the durasteel tube, momentarily absorbed in his musings about humans, and was nearly bowled over by a Kubaz on a weaver. The small, one-being transport was living up to its name as its long-nosed rider maneuvered it through the crowd. Den sincerely hoped the bug-eater would hit an oil slick that the weaver's gyroscopic sensors couldn't compensate for quickly enough.

He looked for I-Five, and realized he had a problem. While Sullustans weren't as short as Jawas or Chadra-Fan, they weren't exactly able to spit in a Wookiee's eye, either. Den was only waist-high to most of the known species, which meant his chances of spotting I-Five were slim indeed.

He couldn't believe the droid would leave him behind. Even as he thought that, a metallic arm reached between a Quara and a Duros and grabbed his collar, pulling him out of the crowd and up against the side of a building.

"Miss me?" the droid asked.

"Give me a blaster and I won't next time. What—"

"We're waiting for someone."

"Anyone in particular, or are we just lonely?"

"*I* am," I-Five muttered, just loud enough for Den to hear. The reporter grinned. He wasn't sure what peculiar combination of circuitry had resulted in the acerbic side of I-Five's personality, but it never ceased to amuse him.

"Be nice to me," he warned the droid. "Who's your master?"

I-Five gave him a look that made Den thankful the droid's lasers were in his fingers instead of his photoreceptors. A teasing reminder of I-Five's supposed property status was always sure to get a rise out of him. Lorn Pavan had considered him an equal, not a piece of equipment that could talk. According to the droid, Lorn had rescued I-Five from the not-so-tender attentions of a family of rich and spoiled children who liked to order their "toys" to jump off roofs and make bets on which ones would wind up scrap metal. *Must've gone through a lot of droids that way,* the Sullustan thought. During their time on Coruscant the droid and the Corellian had been a team, aiding and abetting the flow of black- and gray-market information through various underworld channels. They'd made a decent living at it, according to I-Five, until they'd come into possession of a certain Neimoidian holocron and realized too late that the stakes had suddenly become much, much higher than they were used to dealing with.

I-Five had never elaborated much beyond that point, but Den had garnered enough information—both from things the droid had let slip during conversations, and from using his own reporter's nose to sniff out snippets here and there on the HoloNet—to know that they'd been targeted by an expert assassin; a shadowy menace who had answered to an extremely high-placed government figure. Den had often wondered just what data the holocron contained. They must have been juicy bits of information, indeed, to warrant the bloody path the assassin had carved through the narrow streets in his pursuit. Apparently the Crimson Corridor had never been more deserving of its name.

One of the endless passing throng stopped before them. He was a Bothan, Den realized with a small pang of wariness. He'd heard it said that a Bothan could figure more directions out of any given situation than a souped-up nav computer. They were masters of duplicity and politics, always working the angles.

This one said nothing; he merely passed a small datachip from his dark furred hand to I-Five's gleaming smooth one.

"The payment?" the Bothan asked in a low voice.

"Has been deposited in your account," I-Five replied. The Bothan gave a slight bow and melted back into the passing throng.

Den eyed the droid. "*What* has been deposited into his account?"

"It was an arrangement made months ago—the funds were in escrow for this purpose only."

Den glared for a moment, but decided to drop the matter. What was done was done; he knew how important it was to I-Five to find Lorn's son.

He stood on tiptoes, trying to see the chip in the droid's metal palm. "I take it this is going to tell us where good ol' Jax is hiding?"

I-Five closed his hand around it. "Not directly," he replied. "But it'll do the next best thing."

"And that would be—?"

"It will enable me to track him through his use of the Force."

Den looked skeptical. "Way I always heard it, you can't measure, detect, or calculate the Force, any more than you can catch hold of a rainbow or teach a Wookiee table manners."

"You're correct—the Force, pervasive as it evidently is, is nonetheless impossible to quantify. Midi-chlorians can be measured, but the Force itself can't be assessed in terms of coulombs or joules or gausses. It is neither wave nor particle; it's unique."

"You're a walking data bank, you know that? Get to the milking point."

"No known instrument can sense or trace usage of the

Force," I-Five said, the slightest hint of annoyance in his voice. "But it's been proved that a sentient tapping into it exhibits a distinct brain wave pattern. And brain waves can be sensed. And traced, within a limited distance."

"Uh-huh. How limited?"

I-Five appeared somewhat discomfited. "Twenty meters or less."

They'd been walking down the thoroughfare as they talked; now Den stopped so abruptly that a Ho'Din coming up from behind had to step over the Sullustan to avoid tripping. Den didn't even notice; he just stared at the droid.

"Twenty meters or less?"

"Or slightly more, in some cases—"

"Twenty meters or less," Den repeated. "And he has to be using the Force before he can be in this brain wave state. Am I wrong?"

"Not as such, no, but—"

Den began to laugh. He couldn't help it. He sat down cross-legged on the walkway and laughed until tears filled his huge eyes. The passing crowd took no notice of him, save for a few benefactors of varying species who dropped centicreds into his lap.

Finally he was able to control himself again. He stood and looked at I-Five, who had remained immobile and silent during this. "All right," he said. "Enough." He stretched out a palm. "Give me that."

The droid dropped the chip into Den's hand with uncharacteristic meekness. Den let it fall to the pavement and crushed it under his boot heel. I-Five's photoreceptors grew brighter—the equivalent of a look of human astonishment—but he said nothing.

"Now," Den said. "I'm going to do what I should have done the moment we hit dirt."

I-Five did his equivalent of one cocked eyebrow; Den was never quite sure how he managed it, but the skepticism always came across loud and clear. "Yes?" the droid asked politely. "And what would that be?"

"Find Jax Pavan," Den said. "*My* way."

twelve

Kaird had heard it said that all politics are local politics, and he firmly believed this. There was very little difference between running a galactic-scale government and running a small, one-industry town on some back-rocket world so far out in the Reach that they had to pipe in starlight. At the end of the day, it all came down to alliances and betrayals, conflicts and resolutions . . . blinking and not blinking.

It was like a game of dejarik; a clichéd comparison, perhaps, but Kaird knew that the reason clichés were clichés was because there was a lot of truth in them. You thought far ahead, you planned your moves in advance, and you prepared, as best you could, for any eventuality.

To use another metaphor, the world of Black Sun was a jungle world, no less so than Mimban or Yavin 4. Survival required more than keen senses and quick reflexes; it also took the courage to stalk the enemy, even as he was stalking you. You set your snares and your traps; then, having camouflaged your deadfall as best you could, you waited in the hope that whatever crafty beast you'd set your sights on blundered into it.

But your opponent set snares as well. Survival depended on knowing this, *expecting* this.

That sort of deviousness did not come easily to Kaird. His ancestors had been raptors, masters of the swift, surgical strike. The poison in the wine, the dagger in the back—these sorts of intrigue did not come naturally to him. But he had learned them during his years in the organization, learned them well.

Which was why he was in The Works, one of the seedier areas of Coruscant's lower levels; not as dangerous as the Corridor or the Slums, but still beneath the smog layer. He'd come here to see Endrigorn, a Rakririan fence who dealt primarily in stolen light sculptures, holo-art, precious gems, and the like. It would not do, of course, for the insectoid to be questioned later and give up Kaird—which Kaird knew Endrigorn would do in a picosecond if threatened. Which was why he was wearing a skinsuit disguise; to Endrigorn and anyone else who might be watching, it was a Besalisk, nattily dressed in a synthcloth suit with a short, brocaded capelet, who entered the shop. The suit's servos moved it silently and easily, the osmotic design provided for easy air circulation, and it even had an algorithmic feedback loop that extrapolated movements for the lower arms, based on how Kaird moved the upper ones.

It was hard to read the insectoid's face. Being covered in chitin, it had about as much expression as a mask— the mask Kaird was wearing, in fact, showed more mobility. It (Endrigorn was a drone, a "facilitator" between male and female Rakririans) stood perfectly, unnaturally still, save for slowly opening and closing its mandibles. Kaird had been told that the movement might mean it was in a receptive frame of mind. Or that it might be poised to defend itself. Hard to tell with Rakririans; he would have to hope for the best.

"I have a proposition for you that would be to our mutual benefit," he told Endrigorn. "Are you interested?"

The insectoid lifted its segmented body, leaving six legs on the ground and four in the air; the latter performed a complex and apparently ritualistic series of gestures before speaking. *"Prozzzeed,"* it said in buzzing, barely understandable Basic.

"I have recently come into possession of a nearly flawless hypergem," he said. Endrigorn's antennae twitched, and its front legs performed more genuflections. Kaird got the impression that it was excited, as well it should be. Hypergems were incredibly rare, and even more valuable. Formed by the unimaginable gravitational forces in the hearts of neutron stars, they were aperiodic diamondoids with crystalline planar networks extending into higher dimensions. The effect of trying to take in a multidimensional lattice with a brain accustomed to only three spatial extensions and one temporal extension caused some species to immediately go insane, while others found it a thing of ineffable beauty, so mesmerizing that they could literally starve to death sitting and gazing at it, lost in its endlessly unfolding depths. The Falleen were one of the few species somewhat immune to the hypergem's deadlier aspects; still, it was hard for even them to resist its psychechronic allure. He had heard that Xizor sat in front of one periodically, gazing into its warped visions of reality, just to test his willpower by tearing himself away from it.

Of course, no one except Kaird knew that this particular hypergem was the prized property of a Chagrian named Gogh Pleetik, one of the Corporate Sector bosses on the stinking industrial Core world of Metellos. Kaird had paid a considerable amount to have it stolen, and he knew that Pleetik would be upset. After all, living on Metellos, he probably used any way he could to escape reality.

"Are you interested?" Kaird asked Endrigorn.

The insectoid vibrated its chitinous segments, producing a buzzing that Kaird took to be excitement. *"Izzz wannntinggg pozzzezzionnn,"* it said. *"Izzz kkknowinnng howww muchhh?"*

Kaird named a price that was not too outrageously high. He couldn't appear too eager to sell it, after all. The fence responded with more arcane movements, this time adding another set of legs. *"Izzz nnottt zzaatizzzfaccctoryyy."*

The buzzing was giving Kaird a headache, but he gave no sign of it. Haggling was necessary or the Rakririan would suspect ulterior motives. Which Kaird, of course, had. "Tell me what you had in mind," he urged the insectoid.

Endrigorn named a price so low that Kaird had trouble not laughing out loud. He tossed a counteroffer back, and so it went. After a few more exchanges, both felt that they were being equally robbed, and the deal was made.

Kaird caught the tether shuttle back up to Midnight Hall, feeling quite pleased about this particular deadfall he'd set. He knew that Endrigorn and Xizor had had recent dealings, so it made sense that the Rakririan would contact Kaird's rival, knowing that Falleen considered hypergems precious beyond words. Xizor wouldn't be able to resist buying it. It would then come to Boss Pleetik's attention, via a carefully placed rumor, that one of the Black Sun elite was in possession of his property.

While any being smart enough to throw a rock knew enough not to throw it at Black Sun, the mucky-mucks of Metellos were possibly the only sentients tough enough and perpetually angry enough not to care. Plus, a great deal of black-market matériel found its way from Metellos to Black Sun, and vice versa. The new Underlord could ill afford a diplomatic crisis so soon after taking power. He would investigate, and he would learn who had the hypergem.

Kaird looked out the port at the shining curve of the planet below and smiled. All in all, a most satisfying day's work.

Jax had heard the sentiment expressed often, as far back as he could remember. The phrasing might be slightly different, depending on who was making the statement, but the sentiment was always the same:

Without the Jedi, I am nothing.

He knew it was the truth. He'd had no other life but that within the Temple, and he had been content with that. Brought to the Order scarcely able to toddle, Jax Pavan remembered neither his mother nor his father, and had felt no lack in his life, because those within the Order had been both to him, and more. The vast halls and high-ceilinged chambers, the regimens of meditation, of calisthenics, of lightsaber practice . . . all this had been his life, and a rich one it had been. But it was gone now, all of it, never to return, or at least not in his lifetime. His Master, and most, if not all, of the Council members, were dead. The Temple was sacked and empty. And he was alone.

Alone among trillions of people. In peril every waking hour. More and more, he could not help but wonder:

When did it make the most sense to simply stop? To give up, surrender, and seek oneness with the Force?

Long had it been a tenet of the Jedi belief that when a Jedi died, he or she or it surrendered the ego to the Force and became one with it. It might be the death of identity, of the individual, but it was also a transformation, a transmigration, a transfiguration. An ascension to a higher plane in which one's essence merged with un-countable others, building a gestalt that slipped the shackles of space–time, simultaneously creating, nour-ishing, and maintaining itself. Jax had never quite un-derstood the benefit of this. Even if one was able, through meditation and strict adherence to the Jedi Code, to accomplish such a metempsychosis on one's deathbed, why was this elevation to unity different from the mere cessation of consciousness? Yes, he would be part of a greater whole, but he would not be aware of it. He could not conceive of how a change so profound could be any more desirable than simply stopping, sur-rendering to the eternal dark. He had been willing to take it on faith that it was so, but he had never fully comprehended it.

But, after all, was eternal life really to be all that greatly desired? Eternity was a *long* time. Was even the Force eternal? Some scientists, Jax knew, believed that in the most extreme extension of the future, entropy would triumph utterly. That black holes would swallow all heat and light and, ultimately, themselves as well, and that the universe would become an infinitely cold, dead, and sterile expanse in which no star shone, no flower bloomed, no child laughed. Could the Force somehow maintain itself against such a fate? Could it transcend the death of time itself?

Jax had been wrestling with metaphysical conundrums like this far more than he cared to lately. He remembered the insistent, persuasive voice that had spoken to him when he'd been waiting for the attack at the Coruscant Arms, the voice that had urged him to simply let them shoot, to let them drill ionized fragments of atoms through him, to let them kill him.

It was a voice he had almost heeded.

He still wasn't quite sure why he hadn't. Was this current life so precious, so full of promise, as to provide any hope at all? Even if he fled Coruscant, even if he managed to build a new life on some outlying world—would it be worth it? Would it be a life at all, or just the simulacrum of one? Jax feared it would be the latter—at least for as long as Emperor Palpatine and Darth Vader were alive. The Force transcended time and space; as with two subatomic particles mysteriously entangled despite the cosmic distances between them, someone adept enough and powerful enough in it might possibly sense the whereabouts of another, even if separated by thousands of parsecs. And in that case, fleeing didn't matter; he might as well be here on the Queen of the Core Worlds as suffering in silence on the farthest planet in the frozen reaches of Wild Space.

There was, of course, an easy enough way to find out. All he had to do was reach out through the Force and try to sense Vader's presence. The problem was that it was a two-way connection—if he could sense Vader, Vader could also sense him. And then he would know, or at least have a pretty good idea, of where Jax was hiding. While it was well known that the Emperor and Vader considered the Order so thoroughly broken as to not be worth worrying about, still, there was no point in taking chances. If a Jedi were to appear on their radar, so to speak, most likely stormtroopers would be breathing down that Jedi's neck in short order.

But there was another reason to be cautious. As Rostu had told him before they parted, Master Piell seemed to think that, in addition to searching for the droid, Vader might be looking for Jax, too—not simply as a part of the extermination of the Jedi, but for some other reason. The Lannik had died before he could say why—if he had known the reason at all.

If such were the case, it didn't seem wise to send Jax on this mission to find the lost droid. But Jax had been the only one the diminutive Jedi Master trusted enough to continue the search.

Jax frowned. He knew that he was under an automatic death mark just by being a Jedi. But why would Darth Vader have any special interest in him? Every Jedi had enemies, it was true. It came with the job. But he hadn't been a Jedi Knight long enough to have made any enemies—that he knew of, anyway. And his assignments as a Padawan hadn't been important enough to garner such ill will, especially on such a high level.

He was standing on a slidewalk that carried him and a number of other pedestrians along a bridge five stories above the street. He stepped toward the edge; the anisotropic surface slowed for him and let him step off onto an outdoor mezzanine.

As long as he kept a low profile, restricting his use of the Force to following the threads, and even that to no great degree; as long as he remained passive, letting the Force guide him, or at most only pushing a little—he felt he was reasonably safe from detection. Even if Vader was looking for him in particular, tracking him down could hardly be the first item on the Dark Lord's to-do list. He was, after all, occupied with the big picture. Being the Emperor's instrument was a full-time job. It was a large galaxy; there were still lots of worlds to conquer and dominate, still many species to enslave or wipe out . . . compared with all that, a rank-and-file Jedi such as Jax Pavan couldn't possibly be a big priority.

Or could he?

Jax moistened dry lips and looked around. Flitters and skimmers passed overhead in more or less ragged formation about ten meters over his head; the hum of their repulsor drives, along with the incessant conversations going on, all blended into a background white noise. The foot traffic was the usual heterogeneous cavalcade: Duros, Toydarians, Mon Calamari, Twi'leks . . . and, of course, humans like himself. All with somewhere to go, rushing hither and yon, hustling, hoping, their eyes—the ones that had eyes—shining in desperation.

The underdwellers.

And, for better or worse, he was one of them.

Jax smelled the spicy tang of roasting meat from a nearby vendor's grill, and realized suddenly that he was ravenous. He bought a strip of meat on a stick. This far above the street, it stood a pretty good chance of actually being hawk-bat, as the vendor claimed, instead of armored rat or something even less appetizing. It was hard to tell by the taste, because it was so heavily spiced.

It didn't matter. He ate it, chewing on its gristly toughness until his jaws ached.

He wondered why he hadn't followed Master Piell's advice and changed his name. After all, he had taken the precaution of having his records erased from the data banks by a slicer, so why not go the rest of the way?

The biggest reason was that it wouldn't matter to Darth Vader; he would know a Jedi for what he was, no matter what alias the latter assumed. But, while this was true as far as Vader was concerned, a name change could help to throw off any troopers who might get too close. Again, Jax couldn't see that it made any difference. There were millions of humans with the same name as his, scattered over Coruscant; it would take decades to investigate them all. And there was nothing now to link this particular Jax Pavan to the Jedi, any more than any of the others.

Valid as all these reasons might be, though, in the final analysis they were all meaningless. What it really all came down to was very simple. The Emperor and Vader had taken everything else away from him: his friends, his home, his very way of life. He'd even been curtailed in his use of the Force. His name was all he had left, and he was not going to surrender that as well.

Jax got back on the slidewalk and let it carry him along, just another face in the crowd. He tried to put the thoughts of hopelessness, of despair—of suicide—from his mind. He at least had a purpose now. He had been tasked to fulfill Master Piell's dying request: to find the droid 10-4TO, aka Bug-Eyes. Nick Rostu had offered to go with him, but Jax had told him this was something he had to do alone. Rostu understood that. A Jedi's last request was as sacred to his Order as a blood oath was to a Korunnai.

He straightened his shoulders, feeling rejuvenated. For a short time, at least, life had meaning, had purpose, again. He would accomplish his last task as a Jedi Knight, or die trying.

And he really wasn't sure which outcome was the more appealing.

Without the Jedi, I am nothing . . .

thirteen

As usual, he didn't find her; she found him.

It was a fairly deserted area near a bank of huge vaporators that sieved the urban air of moisture. Jax stood near the base of one, listening to the almost subsonic growl of its dynamos. As a child, he'd been told by another youngling that the vaporator's functioning was so intense and efficient that, if you were foolish enough to climb up onto the vanes, you'd be trapped, and the water sucked through your pores almost instantly, leaving you a dry and desiccated husk. As an adult, he knew this wasn't true, but the child in him still felt nervous standing so close to one.

He looked up. The sky, what little of it he could see, was a baleful red. Centax 1, one of the moons, showed a sliver in the west. And all around were the buildings, the towers, cloudcutters, and skyrises, all looming impossibly tall and close. It was said about unfortunates newly arrived on the ground floor that, even if they managed to survive the dangers of the streets, they still stood a good chance of going mad from pure claustrophobia, especially if they hailed from a world with wide-open spaces. It was bad enough uplevel, but down here the cyclopean structures seemed ready to topple at any moment, burying one under megatons of debris.

He sensed her at the same moment that she spoke.

"You're dead, Pavan."

Jax turned, and there she was, standing atop one of the vaporator units, silhouetted against the stuttering glow of a faulty neon advertisement. Even if she hadn't spoken, and even if the Force hadn't told him loud and clear, Jax would have known her. Laranth Tarak was not easy to forget.

She leapt down from the unit and walked toward him, holding a blaster on him with her right hand. Its mate remained in its holster, riding low on her left hip. Laranth was a green-skinned Twi'lek, lean and muscled, with eyes that had seen too much. A blaster bolt had burned ten centimeters or so of her left lekku away two months ago; instead of keeping it wrapped behind her head, she let it hang free in a sort of perverse pride. She wore a black synfleece vest over a gray pullover, gray thinskin breeches, and neo-leather boots.

She stopped before him, still holding the blaster; then she shoved it into its holster. "If I'd been a stormtrooper, that is."

"Maybe," he replied. "But it wouldn't have been a lonely death." His gaze flickered downward momentarily. She looked and saw the hold-out blaster in his hand, at the end of its extension, aimed at her belly.

Laranth nodded, ever so slightly. "Been practicing, I see."

"No, I've always been this good. I just didn't want to make you feel inadequate." Jax cocked his elbow, and the tiny weapon's extension telescoped back up his sleeve.

She didn't laugh; he'd never heard her so much as chuckle, or even seen her smile. "Haven't seen much of you since Flame Night," she said. "What brings you down here? This is dangerous territory, even for the Slums."

"If it's so dangerous," Jax replied, "why are you here?"

Her expression became even grimmer, if that was possible. "You know the answer to that, Jax."

He did know the answer, quite well; if by no other means than the threads writhing about her. Laranth Tarak was a Gray Paladin, an offshoot of the Teepo Paladins, themselves a marginalized cadre of the Jedi Order. The Council had censured the Teepo Paladins years ago for advocating the use of blasters and other weapons in addition to lightsabers. At best, this had been viewed as extremist; at worst, Teepo and his followers had been ostracized as potential dark siders.

The Gray Paladins held even more radical views. Whereas the Teepos still sought oneness with the Force, some of them going so far as to wear masks or eye-concealing headgear in battle to maximize their connection with it, the Grays' contention was that the Jedi Order had come to depend too much on it in some ways. They acknowledged that a Jedi could no more be independent of the Force than of nourishment or air; nevertheless, they had developed skills and techniques that did not utilize its "flashier" aspects. They eschewed the use of lightsabers completely, choosing instead to rely on proficiency with blasters and other forms of combat, both armed and unarmed. They became adepts in various forms of martial arts like teräs käsi, as well as esoteric weaponry such as Sallisian throwing whorls and spinsticks, rather than relying on Force-augmented gymnastics and speed. They weren't against the concept of the Force; they simply argued that skills should be developed that could be employed with a minimum of dependency on it.

Most Jedi had felt that this was heterodoxy, as well as pointless. Since the Force enfolded all living things, it was impossible, they argued, for any scenario to exist in which the ability to act independently of it might be necessary. Yet ironically, that very situation had now become reality, and the few surviving Jedi who had espoused the Gray Paladins' philosophy had the edge in this new world.

The Grays were also much more militaristic than the Teepos, or even the mainstream Jedi. They had fought the stormtroopers during the Purge, but the few who survived had not let themselves become broken and demoralized as so many of the Order had. Though there were, by the most generous estimates, no more than a couple dozen of them left, they had helped organize the Whiplash and worked tirelessly to resist the Emperor's yoke, no matter how hopeless the struggle seemed.

Laranth Tarak was always in the forefront of those struggles. Jax had met her not long after his own narrow escape from the torched Temple and the slaughter. After their unwilling participation in the horror that night, Jax had heard little of Laranth. He assumed she'd been lying low while her wounds healed. He studied her, and could see the fluctuating light reflecting off the glossy surface of scar tissue on her neck and right cheek. The scarring and mutilation could have been treated if she'd had access to a bacta tank—but finding one down here was about as likely as finding one's way into the Emperor's private spa.

"So," she said, "what's got you by the jiffies?"

"It's that obvious? So much for my notorious sabacc mask."

She snorted. "You've got the Force around you boiling like pletik soup."

He told her about Master Piell's death, and about his last request. Though Laranth's chosen color and code were of the Grays, the threads that wrapped about her were very seldom anything close to that cool and calm a hue. They were generally warm orange to fiery red, and sometimes, when she was consumed with anger, she appeared swathed in a white-hot cocoon. Such was the passion with which Laranth lived, a passion that Jax sometimes envied. Though he was incapable of seeing the threads that enfolded himself, he was sure they did not burn nearly as hot as hers.

As she listened to him, Jax could see her threads glowing, almost too bright to look at.

He had told Nick Rostu that this task was for him and him alone to do. That wasn't entirely true; Jax was not crazy enough to think he could fulfill Master Piell's last request without help. But this was a matter for Jedi, and, however blasphemous she might have been considered by some in the Order, Laranth Tarak was a Jedi. Jax trusted her as he trusted few others, and she was better in a fight than any five other warriors he knew.

He filled her in quickly as they walked out of the industrialized area, back to the better-lit and slightly safer Amtor Avenue. She listened without question until he'd finished, then asked, "Any idea where to start looking?"

"No. According to Rostu, the droid vanished just

after the Purge, and all Master Piell knew was that it's somewhere in the Yaam Sector."

"If it's still functioning. It could have had its memory wiped, or been cannibalized for spare parts by now."

"We have to operate on the assumption that it's still in one piece and functional. But you're right—if it's somewhere in the Slums, that could change very fast. We need information—we need to talk to someone who knows what's happening in every dark corner and low-life dive in this sector. Someone to whom privacy and property are meaningless. Someone who barters lives like merchandise."

"Ah," Laranth said. "Rokko the Hutt."

fourteen

Rhinann constructed his search for the Jedi Jax Pavan with the same meticulous care that an Elomin brought to any and all projects. He commissioned netdroids to jack into the datasphere and scour the nearly limitless virtual memory banks of the HoloNet for any byte of information on his quarry. He authorized slicers to search the planetary security grid for records of a human corresponding to Pavan's physical description as gleaned from the Temple records. He added multiple factors to the search parameters: lack of previous employment, credit records, transactions both legal and illegal, and as many others as he could think of. Lastly, he dispatched operatives, both covert and overt, as well as miniature search droids—basically tiny flying cams capable of scanning dozens of square kilometers in a matter of hours—to that area of the ecumenopolis in which Lord Vader had said the Jedi could be found: Sector 1Y4F.

Exhaustive as these efforts were, he was well aware that he was barely scratching the surface. The number of places where Pavan could have gone to ground on Coruscant, even if restricted to one sector, were practically limitless—assuming he was still on the planet at all.

There was only Vader's assurance as a reason to believe that he was, and every reason to think he wasn't.

It was obvious, however, that the Sith Lord's confidence came through the Force. Rhinann had heard that it was possible for Jedi to sense other Force-users. If one so adept in the Force said that a Jedi could be found in a certain place, then it was pretty much a certainty that he or she would be found there. Rhinann flared his neck wattles in astonishment at this. If he himself had had the slightest intimation that Darth Vader was interested in his whereabouts, he would have fled the Core systems fast enough to leave ion burns. His hope was that Pavan's sense of self-preservation wasn't quite as highly developed as that of most sentients. This was a trait he had noticed in many humans: an almost suicidal foolhardiness that often impelled them to remain in situations from which most rational beings would have long since run screaming.

The initial results from the datasphere queries weren't encouraging. There were many, many humans on record with the name *Jax Pavan,* both male and female. The females could be ruled out, obviously—unless Pavan had elected to undergo transgenderative surgery. After some reflection, Rhinann decided to ignore this possibility for the time being. But there was no connection that he could find between the rest of the list and the Jedi he sought.

Rhinann exhaled with enough force to vibrate his nose tusks, producing a keening trill of frustration. In all probability Pavan had used a splicer to expunge any connection between himself and the Order. He stared at the data holoproj. There were approximately 582,797,754 human males named Jax Pavan on Coruscant at this moment. The numbers flickered through a small range of adjustment even as he watched, reflecting deaths, births, arrivals, departures, and other statistical variables.

Blasted humans, he thought. That was the problem. If he'd been looking for a Falleen or a Neimoidian, or even for one of his own kind, the data wouldn't be nearly as overwhelming. But practically everywhere you went, it seemed, humans outnumbered every other species by a ridiculous margin.

Even when he excluded the rest of the population and focused solely on the Yaam Sector, the results weren't encouraging: 8,674 Jax Pavans. It was a fairly common name among Corellians.

He trilled again. All right, so the task was not an easy one. He'd known it wouldn't be. He commanded himself to be calm. Salvation lay in methodology. There had to be a way of winnowing out the chaff. But how? If Pavan had erased his past and had a false one built, there was no way to connect him with the Jedi, and therefore no way to find him.

If only a way existed for him to track Pavan through the Force. But that, Rhinann knew, was utterly impossible. What to do? If Pavan was not brought before Lord Vader in short order, Vader would—Rhinann shuddered. He couldn't even begin to speculate on the tortures that the Sith Lord's mind could conceive.

There was one last thing he could try. Vast amounts of data, personal and otherwise, had been confiscated from the Temple immediately after the Purge—including nearly complete genome records. Holding his breath, Rhinann programmed a wild match of the DNA signatures. It seemed a futile effort, because no splice job worth a decicred would neglect to falsify those records as well. But by now he was desperate. When the search came up negative, as he had known it would, he felt a moment of true despair. Aside from the fear of whatever reprisal Lord Vader might inflict, his heritage, both cultural and biological, demanded that he succeed. This sort of meticulous research was exactly the sort of thing at which he and his kind were supposed to excel. But it appeared that all the various tricks and skills he had at his command were useless in this case.

In desperation, he expanded the search parameter, looking for any connection that might prove fruitful. Anyone who might possibly have been associated, or been in contact, with a Jedi, no matter how tenuous. Such undisciplined research sent oscillations of anxiety rippling through his spanchnon; nevertheless, he felt he had no other choice.

A soft chime from the unit signaled a finding. Rhinann called up the information and studied the report.

It was a recent holo of several stormtroopers being bushwhacked by two men in a small resiblock in Sector 1Y4F. Rhinann felt a frisson of excitement run up his spine. Most of the incident had been caught by the building's security cams. Only a quick flash of a face had been caught, but an identification match with a 74 percent probability had been established by the mainframe.

Major Nick Rostu, formerly of the Imperial Army, now a wanted murderer.

The other man's identity wasn't clear, but since he was seen in several of the images wielding a lightsaber, Rhinann felt fairly safe in assuming it was a Jedi.

His security clearance made it a simple matter to learn the identities of the resiblock's tenants. Somewhat to his astonishment, he found that a Jax Pavan was listed among them.

Did the Jedi *want* to be found?

Of course not, Rhinann realized after a moment's thought. Given the number of Jax Pavans in that area alone, and given that the Jedi had no reason to believe that he in particular was being hunted, he obviously had seen no point in disguising his identity. After all, this was Coruscant, with the densest population of any world in the known galaxy.

He noted, without any great surprise, that Pavan had moved out of his tiny dwelling place. Perhaps he had gone to ground for the moment, believing comfortably that he would be undetectable, one human among countless others. And no doubt he was sure that his connection with the Force would alert him to any impending danger. Perhaps it would—if Rhinann were foolish enough to come at him directly.

But there was another way.

Rhinann leaned back in satisfaction. It was a good start. He would find Pavan, sooner rather than later.

Lord Vader would be pleased.

Nick Rostu had not returned immediately to his former haunts in the Zi-Kree Sector. After the events of the past forty-eight standard hours, he'd felt he was due a little relaxation time, and he'd heard considerable praises sung of Tangor Square and the entertainments to be found therein. He wasn't particularly interested in the various activities that went on behind most of the closed portals, but the area did have a shronker salon.

The salon was fairly lively; there were five spheres, all of them in use. Nick ordered a mug of Alderaan ale and sipped it while watching the game nearest him. It was between a Quarren and a Yevetha. This was slightly surprising in itself, since Yevetha tended to consider other species as hardly worth their attention. Perhaps this one was a bit more liberal-minded. Of course, the fact that he was kicking the Quarren's squamous backside in the game probably helped keep his mood pleasant.

It didn't take long for the Quarren to be defeated. The morose Squid Head turned back to the bar, and the Yevetha looked at Nick. "Care to play?" he croaked.

"I'll give it a whirl." Nick stepped up to the control panel that the Quarren had just vacated.

"Configuration?" the Yevetha asked.

"Hot Bespin."

The rules of the game were fairly simple. Within the holosphere was a stylized image of a solar system; when starting the game, the players could choose setups based on known systems, or create their own. There were four types of worlds: gas giants, twin worlds, planets, and moons. In the sphere's center was the primary. Each player controlled a comet, which was the only object in the game that could change course.

The game began with the planets in established orbits. There were several different configurations, with the "hot Bespin" scenario generally considered the most difficult. The object was to use one's comet to impact the various worlds, and be the first to send them spiraling into the system's star.

Nick interlaced his fingers and cracked his knuckles. He shrugged, loosening his neck and shoulder muscles, then settled into a relaxed stance before the control stick. The Yevetha watched, his black eyes as expressionless as stones.

Nick lined up his comet and took his first shot. It struck one of the planets, ricocheting toward the outer reaches while the planet spun out of the plane, settling into an elliptical orbit.

Each of the worlds had different properties. The gas giants were massive, and thus possessed greater inertia; a direct impact shifted one of them only slightly. A hot Bespin orbited extremely close to the primary, whipping about it faster than the others, making it more difficult to send an outlying world caroming to a fiery end, whereas a cold Bespin, orbiting in the system's outer reaches, tended to intercept the comets and protect the inner worlds. Binary worlds, orbiting about a barycenter, could be separated by a properly angled shot, and either or both dropped into the primary's gravity well. Ordinary planets presented no particular challenge, while moons were the smallest and most difficult to hit; they also had a tendency to be captured by the other worlds. A moon was usually the last one to be incinerated, thus ending the game.

It was soon apparent to Nick that his opponent was very skilled at shronker. It was equally apparent to them both that Nick was better.

The game gradually drew the attention of the other patrons, partly due to the virtuoso playing by both Nick and the Yevetha, and partly to the marked difference in their attitudes. Nick was casual and relaxed; after another mug of ale he was even verging on garrulous. He complimented his opponent on the particularly well-placed shots and modestly decried his own abilities, though it was obvious to those watching that he was the better player.

The Yevetha said nothing during the entire game, but

his expression grew more and more intent—or so Nick assumed; the skeletal alien's physiognomy was close enough to humanoid to have similar body language. It was said that Yevetha were quick studies. *This one must've been left in orbit when that particular facility was passed out,* Nick mused. The Yevetha's game did improve somewhat toward the end, but by then it was too little and too late. The last globe—a green-and-blue world—went tumbling down the steep incline of space–time into the inferno at its center.

The Yevetha was still. The room was silent. And Nick was drunk, which was why he ambled around the now empty holosphere, extending his right hand as he said, "Hey, excellent game, you almost had—"

The Yevetha moved fast; Nick barely got his arm out of the way as the cadaverous creature's left dewclaw shot from its sheath of skin. Nick had his blaster clear and leveled at the Yevetha before the latter could retract his claw. "Temper," he said, wagging the index finger of his free hand at the other.

"Putrid slime," the Yevetha hissed. He went on to associate Nick with several other unsavory items, the least offensive being the outcome of an improbable romantic liaison between a Hutt and a Wookiee.

"Generally not a good idea to cuss out the guy who's holding the blaster," Nick told him. But before he could add anything else, he felt the unmistakable sensation of a slugthrower's barrel pressed into his back. A voice from behind him said, "And it's always a good idea to keep your back against the wall in a dive like this."

Nick thought the voice sounded human. It was the last thought he had for some time.

fifteen

"That was a stirring speech you made back there," I-Five said to Den. They had just entered a cube, rented for the night, and paid for by the credits obtained from Den hocking his thumbcam. The room was a tiny bubble, two meters on a side, in a dingy ferrocrete resicube. It was designed to accommodate one humanoid lifeform; there was a refresher alcove with a water shower, a kitchen nook with a food keeper/cooker unit, a chair/table extrusion, and a bed extrusion. That was it. The single fluorescent ceiling fixture cast a faint greenish pall over everything, and anytime both of them were still they could hear spider-roaches scurrying in the vents. There were no windows; the cube was honeycombed with cells, and the walls around this one were at least fifteen meters thick. If the air circulator failed, Den realized, he would in all probability suffocate before being able to reach the turbolift at the other end of the building, given that the corridor would be filled with dozens of other panicked beings, all trying desperately to crowd into the same lift, and none, most likely, willing to let him go first.

At this point Den would almost welcome such a scenario. He was struggling to free the bed extrusion, which had jammed partway out of the wall. The aperture wasn't quite big enough for him to slip through, and even if he could, he'd barely have room to lie flat. Den wasn't claustrophobic—Sullustans, being cave dwellers, rarely were—but even he had to admit that the prospect of spending more than one night in this pit was depressing in the extreme. Still, he was tired, and this had been the only place they could afford.

He yawned, then realized belatedly that I-Five had spoken. "What?" he grunted, still wrestling with the jammed bed.

"I said, quite a stirring speech. But just how, exactly, are you going to find Jax?"

Den sat down on the partly protruding lip, ceding victory, for the moment, to the faulty mechanism. "Hey, Five—I'm a reporter." He grimaced. "Was, anyway. I can track a digimorph through a datastorm. He can't hide from my ears."

"No one can hide from your ears. I'm surprised the clerk downstairs didn't count them as separate tenants."

Den clutched his chest in feigned hurt. "You wound me." Then he jumped up and turned around suddenly, as if attempting to take the extrusion by surprise. Instead of grabbing the bunk itself, however, he seized the foamcast mattress and yanked it from within. "Hah!" He placed it on the floor, covering a goodly portion of the dingy surface. "Good thing you don't sleep," he added to I-Five.

"Oh, yes. Lucky me, I get to experience every microsecond of our stay here. I'll make sure to record it for posterity. Maybe I'll even—"

The droid stopped. Den was staring at him, his expression thoughtful. "Posterity," the Sullustan mused.

I-Five said nothing. He merely watched, his photoreceptors bright with what Den had come to recognize as interest—and hope.

"You've got images on file in your memory banks of Lorn Pavan, right?"

"Yes."

"Let's see 'em."

The droid projected a series of holograms in midair between them. Den watched the images cycle past: various angles of I-Five's erstwhile partner and friend. He seemed a good-looking sort, with what other humans would term an "honest face." Part of Den's job as a reporter had been to train himself to distinguish the differences in appearance within various species. It was pretty much a truism through the galaxy that members of one species all looked alike to members of another. Den, however, had gotten past this to a large extent.

"Okay," he said. I-Five stopped the projection, and the parade of holograms winked out. Den looked around. "Is there a dataport in this dump?"

The droid looked about in disdain. "If we're lucky, there might be an old-style modem."

To their surprise, however, there was a dataport. Even more astonishing was that it was live, although I-Five did a remarkably good job, given his immovable countenance, of conveying a wrinkled nose of disgust. "You want me to interface with *that*? Maker knows what's been connected there recently—"

"Don't be such a baby. Your antivirus software's up to date, isn't it?"

The droid sighed. "Have I mentioned lately how much I enjoy our association?" He raised his right hand, and one of the digits extended, transforming into a transceiver plug. This he inserted gingerly into the data-port. "And just why am I doing this?"

"You're interfacing with the main security grid for this sector."

"Which is highly illegal."

"Your point?"

"Just a casual observation. And I'm looking for—?"

"You're looking for images of human males taken in the last week that have a high correlation with your visual data on Lorn Pavan. In other words—"

"A family resemblance." The droid was silent for a moment, then said, "I can't believe I never thought of this."

"I can't either. I guess that chunk of circuitry in your head still has a few synapses to forge." Den tried, though admittedly not very hard, to keep a smug note out of his voice. "Besides, we don't know yet if this'll work."

I-Five did not reply. The droid seemed to be concentrating.

"Problems?" Den asked.

"A new pyrowall has been installed since I last jacked in."

"I'm not surprised," Den said. "It's been, what? Almost two decades?"

"Quiet. This is tricky."

Den waited, resisting the opportunity to dance nervously from foot to foot. If I-Five tripped a fail-safe, it could lead to all kinds of upsetting results, not the least of which would be the droid's synaptic grid getting melted faster than a comet in a solar flare. If that happened, Den knew he'd never forgive himself for suggesting this. Not that he'd have that long to beat himself up over it, since there would also most likely be a squad of PCBUs circling the building long before he could get out.

"I'm in," I-Five announced. "Specifying algorithm parameters . . . instigating search modality . . . downloading data." The interface digit snapped out of the dataport and telescoped back, resuming its former shape.

"Well? What've you got?"

I-Five activated his holoprojector again. Five 3-D images flashed in succession of a young man in nondescript spacer's garb. Even though the projections were slightly indistinct, the resemblance between him and the images of Lorn Pavan was unmistakable.

"Hello, Jax," Den murmured.

I-Five was silent. His photoreceptors, however, were very bright.

One image was of Jax Pavan crossing a crowded street; another, him buying something at an outdoor vendor's stall. The last three were somewhat blurred shots of him standing on a bridgeway, conferring or perhaps arguing with a Hutt, a Klatooinian, and a Nikto.

The very last image appeared to be a shot of the human, the Klatooinian, and the Nikto, with two blurred objects flying between the man and the other two. Den peered at it, frowning. "Can you rez up on that one?"

I-Five complied. The holoproj became sharper and larger.

Den blinked. "It looks like a couple of blasters being pulled from those two bullyboys to him, somehow—"

Then he realized what it meant. "He's using the Force to disarm them."

I-Five said, "These images were taken by an automated security rovercam. The last one was flagged for investigation concerning possible illegal Jedi activity."

"That's not good. How long before they close in?"

"Hard to tell. The Empire's official position is that the Jedi Order is broken, and that rounding up the last of them isn't a high priority. It would depend on the caseload of the local law enforcement officials. It could be weeks. Or days. Or hours. Sooner or later, however, it will be investigated."

"Then we've got to find him first. Do we know when and where these were recorded?"

"The last three were taken forty-six hours and twenty-seven minutes ago, on the Mongoh Mezzanine, about two kilometers west of here."

"He could be anywhere by now. How can we—?"

"No problem," the droid said. "The rovercams have been alerted to make imaging Jax a higher priority now. And, having hacked into the security grid once, I can do it again far more easily."

"You sure?"

"Would this face lie?"

Kaird of the Nediji sat at one corner of the conference table in the Underlord's chambers. He was both alert and relaxed, his posture in the formfit chair casual, but not so much so as to suggest insouciance. One did not want to be too comfortable in the presence of Underlord Dal Perhi.

Across the table, at the second point of the equilateral triangle, sat his nemesis: Prince Xizor of House Sizhran.

Xizor projected the same attitude, that of calmness and resolution. There was, however, a touch more arrogance in his body language, a sense of pride that he no doubt felt befitted Falleen royalty. His long jet-black hair was pulled tightly back into the traditional topknot, and his handsome features appeared to be carved from jade.

Underlord Perhi sat at the third point of the table, beneath the Black Sun symbol on the wall. The table was designed to change shape depending on how many were meeting with the Underlord; it could be reconfigured as anything from a simple narrow rectangle for one-on-one talks to a decagon that accommodated all nine Vigos and the Underlord.

Underlord Perhi was human, fifty-eight standard years old, and one and a quarter meters in height, which was not terribly tall as humans went. He had close-cropped blond hair, and appeared to be somewhat stocky; Kaird estimated his mass at about seventy-five kilos in a one-gravity field. None of it was fat, however. Kaird could attest to that; he'd played shock-ball with the man. Perhi played hard, and he played to win.

He'd started in Black Sun as so many others, including Kaird, had—as an enforcer. In Perhi's case, it had been for a Hutt named Yanth, who had run a gambling establishment called The Tusken Oasis down in the Crimson Corridor. A mysterious assassin, whose identity had never been learned, had cut down Perhi's boss. Not even the Jedi, who had investigated because a couple of their own might have been involved, had been able to figure that one out.

It was said that one of the Jedi investigating the matter had tangled with Perhi, and had come out the worse for it. The Underlord had never confirmed this, but he'd never denied it, either. What gave it the status of a legend was that the Jedi in question had been Obi-Wan Kenobi, later to become one of the greatest heroes of the Clone Wars. Whether or not it was true that Perhi had bested Kenobi, the rumor's circulation through the corridors of Midnight Hall had done nothing to impede the human's rapid rise through the ranks. Two years after the Battle of Naboo he'd been a Vigo; a year after that he'd become Underlord.

And such was his power and personality that he had held the position for the better part of a decade. Kaird admired the man tremendously. Of course, that wouldn't stop him from assassinating him in a Jawa's heartbeat if it would benefit him to do so.

He wasn't quite sure why he and Xizor had been summoned into the presence. Certainly Xizor wasn't giving away any clues; he might as well be wearing a death mask cast from his own features. His skin pigmentation was a neutral lime hue, and he wasn't shedding pheromones. This last Kaird was quite sure of, because he was wearing a miniaturized molecular sensor programmed to pick up any such airborne chemicals. If the Falleen tried to influence him, tried to tip his emotions one way or another, however subtly, he would know it. Kaird didn't know if Underlord Perhi was wearing anything similar, but he suspected not. There was no need in his case; the knowledge of what would happen to Prince Xizor if he so much as thought about such lèse-majesté was no doubt more than enough to keep the Falleen from attempting it. Xizor was many unpleasant things—arrogant, hubristic, and merciless—but he wasn't stupid.

Underlord Perhi said, "I've just received a communiqué from one of the sector administrators on Metellos. He complains that a very valuable item of his was stolen. He charges that it was an operative of Black Sun who took it. A high-level operative."

Kaird felt a tiny tendril of uneasiness begin to uncoil in his gut. Xizor was under suspicion, which was well and good, but why was he here? Had Endrigorn fingered him? Or had Xizor sussed out his plot? He knew the hypergem had come to be in the prince's possession; he'd kept close tabs on its whereabouts, and had just as assiduously maintained his official distance.

There was no point in fruitless speculation. He could only wait and see how things played out from this moment.

Dal Perhi watched them both. His attitude was casual, but Kaird wasn't fooled. He knew that no raptor ancestor of his on Nedij had ever watched potential prey more keenly than the Underlord was watching them both right now.

Kaird affected an interest that matched the seriousness of the charge, but in no way indicated culpability. "This is an accusation of considerable gravity," he said. "Does he offer any proof of this theft?"

"His operatives traced the item—a hypergem—from its initial resting place on Metellos to the Coruscant underground, where it was sold to a Rakririan fence named Endrigorn."

Traced? How? He'd paid top credits to have it lifted without a shred of—

"Evidently," Perhi went on, "whoever stole it—or was behind the theft—was unaware that hypergems leave a residual trail of tachyonic particles. Easy enough to follow, with the proper equipment."

Had Kaird been a mammal, he would be sweating by now, he knew. Both Xizor and Perhi were looking at him.

Perhi said, "It was indeed a high-level operative who stole this," and he removed from an inside vest pocket the hypergem Kaird had sold to the fence. He held it up, admiring for a moment its otherworldly shine, and then set it down and looked at Kaird.

And then, in a sudden rush of realization, Kaird understood.

He hadn't been playing Xizor; Xizor had played *him*, from the beginning. It was the Falleen who had leaked knowledge of the hypergem in the first place, knowing that it would intrigue the Nediji with its possibilities. Then, after it had been fenced, Xizor had obtained it and gone directly to the Underlord, accusing Kaird of the theft and turning the hypergem over as proof of his innocence.

It was so devious as to be almost admirable.

During all of this Xizor had sat quietly, saying nothing. Now he rose, gathering the folds of his brocaded greatcoat about him. "If my lord has no objection," he said quietly to Perhi, "I will take my leave." His gaze turned to Kaird. "It is always sad to see a trusted colleague fail one's expectations."

"Go, then, Prince Xizor," Underlord Perhi said. "I have further matters to discuss with Kaird."

Xizor bowed. His gaze stayed fixed on Kaird, though the bow was for Perhi. "By your leave, then, Underlord." He turned and strode from the chamber, the lines of sleek musculature easily visible through the synthsilk one-piece he wore beneath the greatcoat.

The double portals hissed together behind him. Kaird

was alone with the ruler of Black Sun, his perfidy discovered. He thought sadly of his homeworld. There was no way he would see it now, unless there really was an afterlife and he could look down upon it from the Great Nest.

Underlord Perhi looked at him, laced his fingers together, and said, "Let's talk."

sixteen

Life had been kind to Rokko of the Besadii clan. Relatively young for his species—only about four hundred standard years, Jax had heard—the big gastropod had nevertheless managed to carve out a profitable niche downlevel. Outside the black market, Rokko's main sources of income were the sleazy virtual environment holoparlors that lined Tangor Square and other streets downlevel in the Slums. By utilizing a combination of hologram images, subtle olfactory stimulation, hypersound, and tractor/pressor tactile manipulation, just about any desire, no matter how bizarre, could be satisfied for just about any life-form. The parlors enjoyed a steady and thriving trade, and the credits came tumbling down, straight into Rokko's coffers—so much so that, since most of his business was conducted downlevel, the gangster had decided to show a perverse pride in his underworld position. Thus he lived in a spacious, well-appointed conapt fifty meters below the surface.

Jax and Laranth rode down in a turbolift. There was only one problem with approaching the Hutt, Jax had told her, explaining how he'd dealt with Rokko's bullyboys. Laranth had been impressed, but not exactly in the way that Jax might have hoped.

"So we're just going to stroll into his place?"

"I thought I'd knock first. Manners are important in a civilized society."

"Rokko's about as civilized as a starving reek," Laranth said as the turbolift deposited them in the large, ferrocrete tunnel that was the entrance to the Hutt's abode.

"Trust me. Have I ever gotten you killed before?"

The entrance to Rokko's conapt was guarded by an Aegis-7 battle droid. This one was a later model, humanoid, but with swiveling repulsorlift plates instead of legs that provided speed and maximum maneuverability. It was said that an Aegis-7 could catch a speeder bike going at full throttle. And if it couldn't catch the speeder, it could blow it to flinders with a phased pulse cannon burst, riddle it with slugs, or stop it in any of a dozen other deadly ways.

Jax had no doubt that Rokko had had numerous modifications made on the droid to render it even more powerful and versatile. He stopped, hands by his sides and conspicuously empty. Laranth came to a stop beside him, also keeping her hands well away from her blasters.

The droid ran a quick laser scan over them. "May I help you?" Its vocabulator was well modulated and courteous, but Jax knew that any sudden move at this point would result in both him and Laranth being instantly killed.

"Please announce Jedi Jax Pavan and Paladin Laranth Tarak," he said. Though he was looking straight ahead, he could feel her wariness. He touched her mind subtly with the Force, reassuring her without words.

The nervous thrashing of her Force threads calmed

somewhat. Jax appreciated the major effort she was making; he knew that, since the destruction of the Temple, Laranth found it difficult to trust anyone. And now someone she'd met only a few times had just identified her to a remorseless gangster. True, Jax was a Jedi—but Jedi had been known to go bad before.

He was counting on Rokko being aware of that fact.

The droid did not move, but a flickering diode on its chest plate indicated that it was in contact with its superiors, possibly even Rokko himself. After a tense moment, which lasted long enough for Jax to wonder if he'd made the right decision, the droid spoke again, this time in Rokko's guttural voice.

"Jax," the Hutt cooed. "You've been keeping secrets from me. I hold no rancor in my heart, however. Please—enter, and bring your lovely friend."

The battle droid confiscated their blasters and vibroknives while Rokko's voice continued: "We have a firm no-weapons policy here, for reasons I'm sure you can understand." Laranth swore under her breath as the door opened.

The first chamber of Rokko's domicile was large and palatial, in a Huttese fashion; the walls and floor were depressing shades of dun and ocher, and the snarling heads of fierce animals—acklays, rancors, nexus—were mounted around the large central chamber. Glyphs were carved in bas-relief over curtained archways, and exotic crystalline sculptures and friezes seemed to be everywhere Jax looked. There were fountains as well, which was unfortunate, because instead of water they cycled a vile syrup, the stench of which nearly lifted him off his feet. It took effort not to gag, which probably would have been a fatal error.

He was startled to see windows set into the walls, since they were far underground, and more startled still when he realized that he was looking through them at the surface of Nal Hutta, the Hutt homeworld. He had never been there, had only seen holos, but its appearance was unmistakable; the blighted landscape, with its decaying urban zones and muck-filled waterways, could be beautiful only to a Hutt.

"Ah, you admire the vistas of my homeworld." Rokko himself was reclining on a divan, his upper body's bulk draped over its edge. The inevitable hookah bubbled quietly beside him. Jax could smell the aroma of honeyblossom spice in the air. The Hutt was flanked by two Gamorreans who looked tough enough and dumb enough to batter through a durasteel wall head-first.

"They are windows into the past," the Hutt continued, an odd tone creeping into his voice, which Jax recognized with surprise as nostalgia. "Created centuries ago by the great Hutt artist Gorgo, who, over the course of decades, exposed them to various scenic vistas of Nal Hutta. They consist of supercooled condensates of prothium gas; the optical density is so extreme, it takes light literally years to shine through.

"Gorgo died before I was born. I was fortunate enough to recently acquire these last creations of his. When the images slowly bleeding through them are gone, there will be no more."

There was real sadness in Rokko's tone. *Yet another surprise in a day full of them,* Jax thought.

Rokko took a long, slow draw on the pipe. "Now, then—to what do I owe this most unexpected pleasure?"

"I think we both somewhat overreacted the other day," Jax said. "I'm willing to let the, ah, misunderstanding over the Cerean, and the subsequent visit to my place by the stormtroopers, go, if you are."

"And my motivation in doing this would be . . . ?"

"Working to our mutual benefit."

Rokko let aromatic smoke dribble from his mouth. "You have my attention. For the moment, anyway."

"I need your aid in finding a lost droid."

The Hutt blinked platter-sized yellow eyes. "And why should I do this?"

"Because there's a lot of credits in it for you," Jax said. "This droid is carrying information that, if it were to fall into the hands of insurgents, could be damaging to the Empire." Jax knew that although Rokko, like most underworld types, had little love for Palpatine, he was smart enough to know which side of his fungus cake the slime was thickest on. If he could make some credits by finding and giving up this droid to the Emperor, the Hutt wouldn't lose any sleep over doing so.

"And what, exactly, is the nature of this information?"

"I don't know. All I know is both sides are searching for it, so I imagine it's carrying more than a recipe for Trikaloo Surprise. Whatever the reason, there are several bounty hunters on its trail already." Nick had mentioned this last only as a rumor, but Jax had no problem with inflating the urgency of the situation.

"So you come to me," Rokko said. "Why?"

"Isn't it obvious? Even if I find this droid first, I can't turn it over to the Emperor or Vader myself. They'd smell the Force on me, know me for a Jedi. But you can hand it in and collect the reward for all of us."

"You could go through other intermediaries."

"I don't want to take the chance. Besides, with your resources and our use of the Force, we can easily locate the droid first."

Rokko was quiet. The tension stretched, and Jax's hand began to itch for the hilt of his lightsaber.

"I could simply turn you both over to Vader," Rokko said. "Collect the bounty on you as Jedi. It isn't much, but then, neither is the effort."

Jax felt a wave of relief. He wasn't quite sure how— perhaps it was through the Force, or just knowing the gangster as well as he did—but whatever the reason, he knew that Rokko had taken the bait. Still, he couldn't let that last implied challenge go unanswered.

"I believe you'd find the effort required to take down two Jedi, even though unarmed, to be considerably more than you think."

Rokko waved one small and flabby arm in careless dismissal. "*Eniki, eniki.* No need to take that attitude. We are business associates, for the time being, at least." He made another gesture, and a Kubaz emerged from one of the curtained archways. "Bring drinks," Rokko ordered. "My usual, and that watered-down ronto sweat they call Corellian ale." The Kubaz nodded and scurried away.

Rokko grinned at the two Jedi. It was an unnerving sight. Hutts didn't have teeth, but their cartilaginous gums were serrated, and, given the elasticity of their skin, the result was a rictus that for a moment made it look as if the top of Rokko's head were being sawed off.

"Sit," the Hutt said, in a voice probably intended to be friendly. "Time is of the essence."

Jax glanced at Laranth, and knew she was thinking

the same thing he was: that Rokko would use their backs for vibroblade sheaths as soon as feasible. Still, a rogues' alliance was better than none, at least in terms of finding Bug-Eyes. How he would get the droid out of the Hutt's clutches and to safety was something he'd worry about later.

If, as the saying went, there was a later . . .

seventeen

Nick woke up. This surprised him, since he didn't know he'd been asleep.

And in fact, he realized a few seconds later, he hadn't been, save in the most liberal definition of the word, judging by the very large and very painful bruise on the back of his head. He moved gingerly, setting off celestial fireworks that ricocheted and reverberated within his skull. Purple nebulae, orange-white supernovae, silver comets—it was a whole galaxy of pain inside his head. He groaned and made a mental note never to play shronker again with any member of any sentient species other than his own—and he was going to be very particular about them as well.

All right, then. On to the second order of business—where was he?

The immediate answer was that he was lying on the floor, mostly on his stomach, a little on one side. Make that a deck; wherever this was, it certainly wasn't the floor of the shronker hall he'd been in. That one had been synthwood, covered with treedust and a lot more unwholesome things. This one was cold metal, and it vibrated ever so slightly. An all-but-subsonic *thrum* with which Nick was quite familiar.

He was on a ship. And the ship was going someplace. Fast.

He tried reconstructing the last few moments of consciousness he remembered. He recalled the barrel of a slugthrower pressed against his spine. He even remembered his unknown assailant's remark about keeping one's back against the wall, and thanks very much for *that* piece of useless advice . . . and then he'd been hit, no doubt by the butt of the slugthrower pistol, although it had felt more like a falling cloudcutter.

Fall down there; wake up here. Okay—where was "here"?

Still on Coruscant, that much seemed certain. Nothing was more stable than an artificial gravity field; looking out a port in space, you felt like the universe was moving past you rather than you moving through it. But ships seldom kept their antigrav fields on while in atmosphere; too expensive, for one thing, and the planet's mass played hob with the inertial dampeners. Nick could feel shifts in velocity and momentum, which meant he was still planetside. It wasn't a terribly big ship, either, judging by the way his stomach occasionally jumped.

He decided it was time to reconnoiter a little. His wits were about as unscrambled as they were going to get, and he was as ready as he could be for whatever awaited his return to consciousness. Nick opened his eyes.

He was lying on the deck of the ship's bridge. He readjusted his position slowly and cautiously to gain a greater range of vision.

There didn't seem to be anyone nearby. Nick shifted a bit more, and that was when he realized that he was wearing forcecuffs on his wrists and ankles. The movement sent prickling sensations racing through his limbs.

He looked around. He was lying with his feet toward the bow; by craning his neck—an action that set off an ion grenade in the back of his skull—he could just see the bridge compartment. It was small, with seating for the pilot and copilot. The chairs were high-backed, so he couldn't see who was sitting in them. From the way the chairs moved, however, it was obvious that both were occupied.

He relaxed, letting himself slump back to the deck; even that small action had left him dizzy and nauseated. Judging from the size and layout of the corridors that branched off the bridge, Nick decided he was on board a light cargo or transport vessel. It definitely wasn't a military vehicle—way too untidy for that. Clones had been programmed for neatness from the start, and the military, whether Imperial or Republic, had a long-standing tradition of keeping the decks clean enough to eat from.

This ship, if what he could see was any indication, was a mess. The bulkheads had the greasy handprints of several different species on them, and the mud of various worlds had been tracked around and no doubt under where he lay. Moreover, the place smelled odd. Not the stink of too many unwashed life-forms in too close proximity for too long, just . . . odd.

All of this was interesting, but it wasn't giving him much in the way of explanation. He decided that, since there was no way he could conjure himself free of the forcecuffs, they might as well know he was awake.

"Hey!" he yelled.

The pilot's chair swiveled partway around, and from

it arose a nightmarish creature. It stood nearly two meters tall and had gray, leathery skin as well as seven or eight long braids of hair hanging from an otherwise bald head. It was wearing a short tunic, maroon in color, with boots the same shade. It looked mean enough to rip Nick's arm off and beat him to death with it. In fact, it looked mean enough to rip its own arm off and beat Nick to death with it.

After the initial shock, his mind clicked back into gear and he recognized the being as a Weequay. Nick didn't know much about them, save that they were fierce warriors. They'd served as mercenaries on both sides during the Clone Wars, and many of them now pursued such morally dubious occupations as bounty hunters, Black Sun enforcers, smugglers, and the like.

In short, not generally a pleasant species to be kidnapped by.

The Weequay hunkered down beside him. His rugose face showed no expression. Black eyes glittered.

"Uh . . . can I get a beverage on this flight?" Nick asked.

The Weequay didn't answer; garrulity didn't seem to be an overall hallmark of the species. He grabbed Nick and hauled him to his feet, setting off more explosions in the Korunnai's head. Nick fought the urge to vomit, then thought, *Hey, it's not my ship,* and upchucked spectacularly. It went mostly on the deck, but the Weequay's boots received their share as well.

The Weequay looked down in shock. "My . . . *boots!*" he snarled, the words grating with difficulty from his throat. He glared at Nick, who could offer only a sickly smile and a shrug in response. The Weequay shifted his grip to one hand holding the front of Nick's shirt. He balled the other into a fist that looked as big and hard as an asteroid, drew his arm back, and—

"Mok! Stop!"

The killer asteroid aimed at Nick's nose hesitated.

"Let him go." The voice was human, Nick realized. Then Mok let go of him; he staggered back and half sat, half collapsed on the deck plates.

"Go clean yourself up," the human said. "And get a droid up here to take care of this mess." As he spoke, he swiveled the astrogator's seat around, giving Nick a good look at him.

Nick had already assumed that he was on board a smuggler's ship, and the appearance of the man he was looking at seemed to confirm his suspicion. He was short and stocky, with at least a week's worth of unde-pilated stubble and an unrevised scar across his left cheek that drew his upper lip into a constant sneer. The pink scar tissue contrasted vividly with the umber of his natural tan. He wore trousers, an ill-fitting blouse, and a pocketed vest. A small E-9 blaster hung from a shoulder holster beneath his left arm. He could have stepped out of the cast of a cheesy holovid about space pirates.

"You must excuse Mok," he said in a surprisingly pleasant tone. "He's quite proud of those boots."

An MSE-6 droid scurried from one of the corridors onto the bridge and began vacuuming up the remains of Nick's last meal. The human grinned. "Welcome aboard the *Far Ranger*," he said.

A few moments later the Weequay returned, his boots having been restored to their former glory. He glowered at Nick. "Ought to space 'im," he said, each word grinding laboriously from his larynx.

"Let's keep our eye on the goal," his human partner

replied. "Remember, there's a handsome bounty on Major Rostu. After all, he's a deserter, and he killed a high-ranking representative of the Empire."

Nick's heart sank. He'd been downlevel so long, had had his life and freedom threatened from so many different directions, that he'd almost forgotten there was an Imperial death mark on his head. Through the forward canopy he could see the cityscape passing beneath the ship. They were headed for the heart of Imperial City, and the Palace. It was just before dawn in this time zone—later than the dead of night he'd left behind in the Slums. He estimated that he'd been unconscious about two hours.

"We're almost to our destination," his captor said. "Oh, excuse my lack of manners—my name is Drach Coven. Not that it'll matter much to you in the long run. I imagine you'll be either dead or in prison before the day's end. They tell me that justice is dispensed pretty swiftly now that that whole tiresome litigation process has been replaced by Imperial fiat."

Nick wondered briefly who this guy was; though he looked like a lowlife, he spoke like someone from a more genteel class. But it really wasn't his uppermost worry at the moment. He was much more concerned with how he was going to escape standing in front of a blasting squad in the very near future. Several possible scenarios flickered quickly through his brain—unfortunately, they all started with him not being forcecuffed hand and foot.

The mouse droid finished scouring the deck and scooted off. The Weequay, with a final sneer at Nick, settled back into the pilot's chair.

Coven said amiably, "Mok can be a bit short-tempered; a failing of the species, I'm given to understand. I know he sounds thuggish, but he's actually very bright, and a far better pilot than I. Speech is a secondary mode of communication for his kind. Among themselves they discourse by pheromone discharges."

That explained the odd smell, Nick realized. Probably the olfactory equivalent of muttering under one's breath for a Weequay. When he didn't respond to this factoid, the smuggler frowned. "I hope you're not going to get all sullen just because we're turning you in for the bounty. Obviously, it's nothing personal. I have expenses, after all. This ship doesn't run on pleasant thoughts."

"I'm guessing it's running on black-market fuel," Nick said.

Coven raised an eyebrow. "Amusing—a killer taking the high moral ground about marketeering."

Nick started to reply, then shrugged. What was the point?

Coven turned back to the console and opened a comm channel. "Docking Bay One-Four-Five-Three-See-Gee, this is Corellian freighter *Far Ranger* of the Interstellar Trading League, requesting landing clearance . . ."

The ship settled gently down on her invisible cushion of repulsor energy. Nick caught a glimpse of a small committee waiting; a few stormtroopers, an underling, and an Elomin in expensive robes. Once the ship's landing gear was firmly on the dock, Mok opened the ramp.

Nick was hoping they would uncuff his legs so that he could walk out of the ship. Instead Mok picked him up and slung him over his shoulder, carrying him like Nick might carry a sack of ripe purnix, so that he could see nothing but the deck and the Weequay's boot heels.

Coven exchanged greetings with the Elomin, who identified himself as Haninum Tyk Rhinann. Mok dumped Nick on the deck as Rhinann made a gesture to his underling, a Givin, who handed a packet to Coven. The latter grinned and stuffed it in his vest. He gave the Elomin a jaunty salute. "Pleasure doing business with you," he said.

The Elomin made another gesture. Two stormtroopers raised their blasters. "As per procedure, you have been paid the reward for turning in an enemy of the Empire," he said to Coven and Mok. "Now you are under arrest for smuggling and other crimes against the Mercantile Guild." The Givin stepped forward and plucked the reward money from the bewildered Coven's vest. "Since the Empire does not do business with criminals," Rhinann continued, "your reward is hereby forfeit and confiscated—as is your ship and all possessions and appurtenances fitting thereunto."

"You're making a mistake!" Coven protested. "We're licensed members of the ITL—"

"Take them away." Rhinann gestured in dismissal.

Coven was too shocked to protest further; Mok was not. The Weequay roared in rage and struck one of the troopers, knocking him a good five meters across the deck. As Mok turned toward another trooper, he was hit in the back by a stun blast fired by a third. The concentric rings of energy rippled about him, dropping him with a crash that shook the duracrete.

Rhinann watched dispassionately as the smugglers were led away. To his assistant he said, "See that this"—he made a disparaging gesture at the freighter—"is impounded." He made another gesture, and a stormtrooper dragged Nick to his feet. "Remove the forcecuffs," Rhinann said. Nick had time for one brief surge of hope before the Elomin added, "Lord Vader will want to see him immediately."

Vader? Nick thought. *Darth Vader, the Emperor's second in command?* What in the name of all his ghôsh ancestors did the Sith Lord want with him?

He had a *real* bad feeling about this . . .

eighteen

The Mongoh Marketplace at close to midnight was not a place he'd want to visit on his own, Den reflected. It was essentially an open-air market, with crowded stalls staffed by various species, all hawking their wares in a cacophony of shouts, whistles, buzzes, and roars. Den had more or less gotten used to the constant decibel barrage that was part of life on the big city-planet, but the racket produced here, even though the place wasn't enclosed, was unbelievable. He wished he'd remembered his sonic dampeners.

The customers were as varied and colorful as the vendors. I-Five seemed to be the only droid around that Den could see, though no one took any particular notice of him as he slipped adroitly through the crowd, edging past a drunken Rodian with a polite "Excuse me," stopping to pick up, with eye-blurring speed, a basket of greenpods that a female Snivvian had dropped, and giving directions to an Arcona looking for a public comm station. To all outward appearances he was the perfect protocol droid, polite and helpful to a point just shy of sycophancy. No one would guess that he was a machine on a mission.

Den followed as best he could, wondering how the

droid thought he could possibly find Jax in this crowd, even if the Jedi was still anywhere in the vicinity. He was also wondering, not for the first time, if I-Five's commitment to locating his former partner's son was edging past obsession and into full-blown aberration. *He's awfully loyal for a droid,* he thought. *It's kinda pathetic, really.*

After a few more minutes of what seemed to Den to be random searching, the droid stopped at a small plasteel-and-synthwood booth selling ozone masks, antiox patches, nose filters, and other balms for the more paranoid oxygen breathers.

The proprietor, a humanoid from a species that Den didn't recognize—which was surprising in itself, given that he'd been back and forth in the galaxy more than a few times—spoke quietly with I-Five. By the time Den managed to dance through the crowd close enough to the booth, the conversation was finished, and I-Five was striding quickly away. Den sighed and changed course to keep up.

He caught up with the droid just as they exited the marketplace; the relative quiet was a blessing and a half. "Okay, spydroid, what was *that* about?"

"Apparently Jax had a run-in with one of the local mobsters a couple of days ago. A Hutt named Rokko."

"I've heard of him. So that was the scene on the mezzanine skywalk."

"Exactly. And now I know the location of Rokko's residence."

"And you're just gonna walk up to him and ask him about our boy." The little Sullustan was beginning to puff—his short legs couldn't begin to match the long strides I-Five was taking.

"Something like that," the droid replied.

Den lunged forward and managed to grab I-Five's arm, slowing the droid. "If you think it's going to be as easy as that," he said, "then I've got an asteroid field over in the Reach I'd like to sell you." He held on, and I-Five came to a reluctant halt.

"All right," he said. "Give me an alternative."

Den knew he wouldn't have the droid's attention for long. He spoke quickly. "We can't just barge in like a couple of spiced-up stormtroopers and start making demands. We need some kind of cover—a story they'll buy."

"And you have one."

"I will, in another minute." Den thought furiously. "We need something to tempt him with, something he'll want to see . . ." He grinned. "You."

The droid blinked, a quick on–off flash of his photoreceptors. "Me?"

"More precisely, your skill at sabacc. Rokko loves gambling, from what I've heard. He'll be fascinated by a card-playing droid."

I-Five projected skepticism. "Any protocol droid can be programmed to—"

"To play cards, sure. But you can't program an aptitude for it. Not like you have."

"Assuming you're right—"

"Trust me on this," Den said. "I'm right. Back on Drongar you threw down arrays with Tolk, Barriss, and Klo—a skinreader, a Jedi, and a minder, not to mention me, who has some skill in the game—and you managed to put away enough creds to get us to Coruscant and keep us alive all this time. That takes more than just a good calculator chip. Besides, it's like the line about a

Noghri reciting poetry—what's amazing is not that he does it well, but that he does it at all."

"Very well," said the droid. "What's the scam?"

"Simple. I'm selling you to Rokko."

The Elomin wasn't a talkative type. Nick had never encountered a representative of this particular species before. Haninum Tyk Rhinann was tall and gangly, and his stride was difficult to keep up with. Every time he exhaled, his nose tusks stridulated. It was annoying in the extreme. Nick had heard it said that they were fearsome creatures to some, with their horned heads and tusked noses, but personally he thought Rhinann looked somewhat silly—like an AT-ST walker dressed up in ostentatious frippery, stalking down the corridor of the Palace.

As if he were reading Nick's thoughts—*Are Elomin telepathic?* he wondered in a moment of panic—Rhinann looked back at him with a glare. "Keep up, human. Lord Vader doesn't like to be kept waiting."

Good point. Even though Nick wasn't exactly looking forward to meeting the Dark Lord, being on time would be better than being late.

"But why does he want to see me?" he asked. "I'm not that important—I'm just a guerrilla. I—"

"Last night you aided a Jedi. You helped him escape from a detail sent for him by the local authorities."

Nick stared. "How did you know—" but he realized the answer before he finished the question. "The hall recorders." Many hotels and other such establishments in places like the Slums kept audio-video recorders mounted in the corridors, and probably in a lot of the rooms as well. A recorder had no doubt captured the last minutes of the fight at the Coruscant Arms. And it would have been a simple matter to cross-match his ID holo with that of former brevet major Nick Rostu.

"Yes. Lord Vader has examined the images and identified the Jedi as Jax Pavan. Not long after that, our rovercams picked you up in Tangor Square. We sent the Weequay and his companion to take you. They were smugglers and bounty hunters. The rest you know."

"*Were* smugglers and bounty hunters?"

"Exactly. Now they are unprocessed waste, the Empire has acquired a new freighter at no cost, and no laws have been broken. Most efficient."

Nick was surprised at the sympathy he felt for his former captors, and not surprised at all by the anger he felt for Rhinann. With an effort he pushed it back down and said, "None of this explains what Vader wants with—"

"He doesn't want *you*," Rhinann said. "He wants Jax Pavan. You are merely the means to that end."

nineteen

"Thought you had him, didn't you?" the Underlord asked.

There was no point in dissembling, Kaird knew. He had often heard it said that when one realizes all is lost, and disgrace and death a surety, a certain serenity accompanies the knowledge. A paradoxical comfort, or at least relief, in finally looking death in the eye. No more trying to see down a dozen or more time tracks simultaneously; no more trying to plot a course through the misty labyrinth of the future. No more schemes. No more worries.

Just acceptance.

Kaird knew about the calmness that accompanies the warrior's utter commitment, although he himself had never had to experience it. It wasn't generally the province of an assassin, who is tasked to get the job done by whatever means. Honor was not only superfluous to one such as Kaird, at times it was downright dangerous. Assassins could not afford the luxury of honor.

Given all that, he was surprised to feel now that sense of serenity he'd heard about. But there it was. He knew there was no way out of this—it only remained for the Underlord to pronounce his sentence. There were a few in the organization who would jostle to be in first place to pull the trigger, and many more who would consider it nothing special, and who would lose no sleep over the action. Even the few whom Kaird counted as friends and allies would send him off to the Great Nest with little more than a tear or two shed. After all, as the saying went, it wasn't personal. It was simply business.

And he had no illusions about the gravity of his actions. To trade insult and innuendo with Xizor during the course of meetings was one thing; to attempt framing him for the theft of the nearly priceless property of a powerful sector boss on Metellos was another thing entirely. As punishment for the former, Underlord Perhi would probably have been content with simply ripping Kaird a new cloaca; for the latter Xizor would demand nothing less than the Nediji's frozen remains drifting in orbit about the planet.

Had he gotten away with it, it would have been different. House Sizhran would have not been happy about the ousting of their favorite son, but as a Vigo, Kaird would have been in a much better position to deal with their reactions.

But he hadn't gotten away with it. And now . . .

"He outmaneuvered me," Kaird said. There was no shame in the admission.

"True," the Underlord replied. "You will have to be more careful next time."

Next time?

Kaird watched Dal Perhi's face carefully. He was fairly adept at reading human expressions, but the Underlord was giving nothing away at the moment. Thoughts surged through the Nediji's head, chasing one another like feathers in a high wind. He knew Perhi wasn't given to needless or excessive cruelty; on the other hand, compassion wasn't exactly his main reactor rod, either. The bottom line was that the Underlord of Black Sun wasn't known for magnanimous acts.

Just practical ones.

Kaird cocked his head slightly. "Next time?"

Perhi nodded, as if in acknowledgment of something confirmed. He leaned back.

"Prince Xizor is ambitious," he said, and shrugged. "Nothing particularly astonishing in that; the Falleen do not hail from cute and cuddly ancestry."

"Neither do the Nediji," Kaird said.

"Very true. But there is a crucial difference between you and Xizor. Xizor would be Underlord. Again, not terribly surprising—most members of Black Sun see the post of Vigo as penultimate.

"But you don't, Kaird."

Kaird felt the fine down that covered his skin rise; he could no more control the ancient reaction to sudden danger than he could have stopped his own heart. And yet—was there really any danger to react to? He had always assumed that his desire to leave the organization was tantamount to a death mark if anyone learned of it. But the Underlord's tone wasn't accusatory.

Dal Perhi stood and extended one hand toward the wall. A section of the crystasteel surface de-opaqued, revealing a magnificent sight: the bright curve of the planet itself, facing the velvet of space. Since Sinharan T'sau was a skyhook, Coruscant appeared "above" them, effulgent against the night. As Kaird watched, a *Victory*-class Star Destroyer moved ponderously out of orbit. The nine-hundred-meter wedge-shaped vessel, bristling with turbolasers, missile launchers, and other armament, began to lift slowly and silently toward the stars, its ion drive array glowing. It was pointed in the direction of the Massiff Nebula, although Kaird knew that that was no clue as to the Destroyer's ultimate destination.

"Xizor wants all of this," the Underlord said, gesturing at the golden crescent that filled the upper half of the great window. "I truly believe that, if he replaces me, he still won't be satisfied. I think he'll try to use his position to gain the ear of the Emperor himself."

Kaird was surprised. The Republic's attitude toward Black Sun had been one of intolerance; local law enforcement agencies on various planets had raided gambling halls, shut down spice dens and distribution points when and where they could, and in general made life extremely complicated, especially in the Core systems. Of course, toward the end the Senate had become so bloated and ineffectual that it was little, if any, threat, but the stigma had remained in place.

With the Empire, it was different. Emperor Palpatine had proven to be a much more pragmatic ruler than Chancellor Palpatine had been. He stopped short of any official recognition of Black Sun, of course, but it was an open secret that, as long as nothing too overt was attempted, the spice-smuggling lanes, the dens of iniquity, and the black-market trafficking were free to operate. Planetary law enforcement personnel were far more likely these days to turn a blind sensory organ to the various and lucrative operations of the cartel.

Naturally, there was a price—or rather, a slew of various prices, tariffs, kickbacks, and others—for this, but for the most part Black Sun paid it gladly. All things considered, it truly was, as Palpatine had proclaimed after seizing the reins of government, a Golden Age. For criminals, anyway.

Perhi, however, did not see the honeymoon lasting forever, and he wasn't convinced that it was an unalloyed blessing while it did. The Underlord felt it was important for Black Sun to retain autonomy. He didn't want perpetual war between Black Sun and the Empire, but he felt that détente should proceed only so far. Complete accord would eventually, inevitably, lead to complacency, and thence to compliance. Given all this, Kaird could see how Xizor's perceived threat would have Underlord Perhi very worried—and not just for his own sake.

All this flashed through Kaird's mind in a moment's time. Before he could speak, however, Perhi raised a quieting hand.

"Now," he said, "I am fairly certain that I've read our Falleen prince correctly. Tell me if I've judged you as accurately.

"You, too, aspire to be a Vigo, Kaird of the Nediji," he said. "But your ultimate goal is not to be Underlord of Black Sun. In fact, your goal lies far out on one of the spiral arms." He gestured again, and the panoramic view abruptly shifted, lining up with the galactic plane. A moment later Kaird had to suppress a gasp as the entire skyhook seemed suddenly to *leap* forward, zooming with unbelievable speed straight toward the blinding galactic Core.

Of course, he told himself, the whole trip was simulated, generated in a mainframe somewhere in Midnight Hall. Still, the realism was absolute. They seemed to flash through the Core in seconds, screaming silently past and between the closely packed stars that were, in some cases, mere light-months apart. For an instant they were teetering on the edge of the churning maelstrom at the center, the ravenous black hole that sucked entire stars down into its unknowable depths—and then they were past it, racing again through the blinding sheets of nebulae, the crowded starscape finally beginning to thin out.

They burst free of the Core and continued the journey, not slowing; if anything, Kaird realized, they were speeding up, covering thousands of light-years in a second, making the fastest hyperdrive journey seem like the ambling of a spavined old dewback. Then, at last, the simulation began to slow down. They entered a system, flashing past a ringed gas giant, a smaller, unringed one . . . and finally coming to a stop before a blue-white world, orbiting in the narrow torus between the boiling and freezing points of water. With a shock, Kaird recognized it.

Nedij. *His* world.

And behind him, softly, the Underlord said, "You just want to go home, don't you, Kaird?"

twenty

"I can't say I'm thrilled with this idea," I-Five said.

"Of course not. You're never thrilled with my ideas. If it'd been your idea to sell yourself into slavery to a ruthless gangster just to get information, you'd be busting your powerbus cables to try it."

"Would I."

"Absolutely," Den assured the droid as they approached the underground entrance to Rokko's lair. "Because you're smarter than the average droid, by far. You'll find a way to get the intel we need, and then escape. Anything for good ol' Jax."

I-Five's photoreceptors turned toward him, their angle, focus, and intensity registering mild surprise. "Do I detect a note of sarcasm?"

"Just what I need right now—a paranoid droid." Behind his flip response, however, Den was uncomfortable. I-Five's remark had stung more than he cared to admit. As much as he'd tried to deny it to himself, as I-Five's search for Jax Pavan had increased in intensity, Den had found himself of late falling prey to a most unexpected and most unpleasant emotion.

He was jealous.

At first he'd tried to deny it to himself, but it hadn't

taken long to realize the futility of that course. So he'd admitted it, silently, and tried to rationalize his way out, telling himself that his friendship with I-Five would be in no way jeopardized by Lorn's son, if and when he was found. That didn't help, either. It was getting to where every time the droid mentioned Jax, Den found himself grinding his teeth.

This is absurd, he told himself. *You can't be insecure about how a* droid *feels about you. How pathetic is that?*

Nevertheless, it was how he felt.

For all you know, I-Five was programmed by Lorn to seek out Jax with all this unswerving devotion. But even as he thought that, he knew it wasn't the case. Of all the droids Den had ever encountered, I-Five was the only one who was sentient. Part of that, the reporter knew, was either preprogrammed or heuristic mimicry, just as it was with all protocol droids. Creativity dampers and built-in behavioral inhibitors, it was claimed, kept the machines from ever reaching that rarefied level of true sentience reserved for humans and other organics. But I-Five had had his creativity damper removed and most of his BI software expunged. There were some firmware subroutines that were integrated too deeply to be removed without physically damaging his main processor, of course. For example, he could no more commit murder than he could fly by flapping his arms, although he could defend himself and those under his protection. But in addition to the expanded options that the lack of hardware and software provided, Den could not help feeling that I-Five had something more going for him, something indefinable, something that made him more than the sum of his electronic parts.

What it all came down to was that the blasted metal man had free will, to an unprecedented degree. It wasn't his programming that was driving him so relentlessly to find the son of his friend and partner—it was desire. He searched the mean streets of lower Coruscant because he *wanted* to find Jax Pavan.

And Den could not help wondering whether, if it ever came down to it, I-Five would show that same level of friendship and devotion for him.

He realized that the droid had said something. "Sorry—what?"

"I said, what if they slap a restraining bolt on me?"

"Well . . ."

"Didn't think of that, did you?" When Den made no reply, the droid continued, "Fortunately, one of the first things Lorn did when he rescued me from the nursery of doom was to install bootleg software that deactivates restraining bolts and other external inhibitory devices."

"I knew that," Den said hastily. The droid gave him a skeptical look as they rounded the corner and found themselves abruptly facing a very large and very intimidating droid. Den was unfamiliar with the model, but it was obvious that it hadn't been designed as an accountant. It looked like what it was: a killing machine.

"How may I help you, friend?" the electronic voice inquired of Den. The tone was courteous, even solicitous, but Den wasn't fooled; he knew that if the droid perceived anything remotely like a threat, it would cook him. Never mind that he was an unarmed Sullustan, which made him about as deadly as a hugglepup with a tummy full of blissroot; if he didn't choose his reply carefully they'd be shipping his remains back to Sullust in a pouch.

The droid waited for an answer. It ignored I-Five, which wasn't surprising—a mere protocol droid was no threat.

"I have an item of curiosity that I thought the great Rokko might find amusing," Den said. He gestured at I-Five. "Ever seen a protocol droid play sabacc?"

The guard droid turned its photoreceptors on I-Five. It was Rokko's voice that now issued through the vocabulator; though Den had never heard this particular Hutt speak, he was very familiar with the glottal pronunciation of Basic that characterized the species. "As a matter of fact, I have." The gangster sounded bored.

"Ever seen one win nine out of ten games?" Den asked.

There was a pause; though the guard droid remained motionless, the reporter knew that inside his sanctum Rokko had just done a double take. "No," the raspy voice said slowly. "That I have not seen."

Nick Rostu knew darkness.

He had, after all, stood with the Jedi Master Mace Windu against Kar Vastor in the steaming jungles of Haruun Kal. Kar Vastor, leader of the Balawai resistance; Kar Vastor, with his arm-mounted vibroblade weapons and his almost supernatural strength. Kar Vastor, stronger in the Force than any of the Korunnai, stronger than any in the galaxy, perhaps, save for the Jedi. Kar Vastor, so submerged in the dark side that, even though Nick had been only a couple of meters away from him during that final battle, even though he could see the man as clearly as he could see Mace, or Iolu, the guard who'd sliced him from sternum to navel—still, looking back on it now, he realized he couldn't visualize the guerrilla leader's face. It was as if the Balawai commander had been shrouded in darkness, somehow, as if the dark side of the Force radiated a strange anti-light. Kar Vastor had been the essence, the personification, of primal power, jungle savagery, and bloodlust distilled into flesh. Nick had never seen anyone or anything to match him.

Until now.

Until he stood, unarmed, before Darth Vader.

As if being armed would make a difference, he thought. He could be tricked out with wrist rockets, a hold-out shooter, a pair of DL-44s, and a disruptor rifle, and he might just as well be carrying a pointed stick.

Vastor had been animal ferocity and menace, barely contained. He'd *thrummed* with the power of the dark side. His arms, legs, torso, and shoulders had been layered with striated muscle; he looked like he could have lifted a pregnant grasser over his head. One-handed.

Vader was as tall as Vastor had been, but probably massed a good twenty kilos less. He wasn't physically impressive in the same way; no musculature was visible under the black armor. It didn't matter. There was no doubt in Nick's mind that, were Kar Vastor somehow to be pitted against Darth Vader, the feral Balawai renegade wouldn't stand a chance.

The Force was powerful in Vader; even the dim wattage of Nick's connection could feel that. It was far more powerful than it had been in Kar Vastor. It had pulsed from Vastor in waves of fury, blasted like an open furnace. In Vader, it was—*contained.* Pent.

Waiting.

The setting was innocuous enough: they stood on a balcony, high above the main levels of the city. It was just after dawn; the morning rays of the Coruscant sun struck opalescent sparks from the many towers, ziggurats, domes, and other structures surrounding the Imperial Palace. The bullet-shaped spire that supported them was taller than most; Nick estimated that they were at least seven hundred meters above the streets. If he were to fall from this height, he would have nearly ten seconds in which to regret it before impact—assuming he wasn't struck in midfall by one of the many vehicles whipping by in the various traffic strata.

Vader stood near the balcony's edge, staring out over the city. Nick could hear his labored breathing. After a moment, he turned, the black cape flaring out behind him. The only hints of color on his body were the flickering status lights on his chest plate. The helmet swiveled toward him. The lusterless rounded hemispheres that shielded his eyes—or were his eyes, for all Nick knew—showed no movement; yet somehow Nick realized that he was being inspected.

"Major Nick Rostu." The voice startled Nick. He wasn't sure what he'd expected Vader to sound like, but this velvety baritone wasn't it. "Late of the Grand Army of the Republic," Vader continued. "You are charged with the murder of Colonel Majjen, an Imperial representative."

There didn't seem to be any reason to respond to that, so Nick kept quiet.

Vader did not seem to notice. "You are also responsible for the killings of a considerable number of Imperial troopers during your time spent as a street fighter. Not to mention breaking several laws."

"It's called war," Nick said. He was milked if he'd let himself be intimidated—or so he told himself. The truth was that he was already fairly intimidated. His voice had been a bit higher than he'd liked.

"No," Vader said. "It's called sedition. And when engaged in by an officer, it's called treason." The Dark Lord was silent for a few moments, apparently occupied with his own thoughts. Then he said, "The Force flickers within you, Major. Its flame burns weakly, but there is potential. Its fire could be fanned, and quickly, by the power of the dark side."

Nick was silent, waiting.

"I have a task for you, Major," Vader said. "If you complete it satisfactorily, you'll be given a ship and allowed to go free, with no hand raised against you—as long as you leave Coruscant and the Core systems. Fail, and your life is forfeit. Understand?"

"You want me to find Jax Pavan for you," Nick said. "I won't do it." His voice shook a little, but he got the words out.

Vader stepped closer to him. "I think you will. In fact, I know you will. You are brave; your record makes that clear. You do not fear death." He raised his left hand, index finger slightly extended, as if making a point. "But there are far worse things than mere death . . ."

And before Nick realized what was going on, the Dark Lord was somehow *inside* his head, a dark shadow interrupting the flow of his thoughts. The shadow seemed to expand . . .

Nick screamed, and fell into a blackness even more perfect than the eyes of Darth Vader.

twenty-one

Jax had to admit that Rokko's hospitality seemed genuine enough. The Hutt had offered them the luxury of a good meal and a shower, as well as having their clothes cleaned and mended. Jax had taken the precaution of removing his lightsaber from the hidden pocket within his greatcoat first. It didn't matter if it was found—Rokko already knew he was a Jedi—but it would be unthinkable for it to be stolen.

A long ultrasonic cleansing and a brisk massage from a modified TDL droid, whose two sets of hands had been outfitted with vibrating fingers, had been followed by a meal of grilled t'surys with spongewort garnish and topped off by a bottle of Chandrilan Blue '439. After which Jax had to admit he felt considerably better. He also felt like sleeping for a standard week.

"Rokko's going to set us up with a couple of his bullyboys to provide protection while we look for Bug-Eyes," Laranth said as she buckled her blaster belt around her hips. The tone in which she said this indicated just how superfluous she thought such protection would be. "He's also got his people working on locating it."

"Good. The sooner we get moving on this, the better." Jax didn't mention his concerns about recruiting the Hutt's help, because they were undoubtedly being monitored. Also, it wasn't necessary; Laranth knew as well as he did that Rokko would try to find some way to double-cross them on this. It was a foregone conclusion that the Emperor's agents would pay more for the droid and a couple of rogue Jedi than the droid alone. The trick lay in finding the right moment to turn the double cross into a triple cross.

"Let's finish up here and get back on the streets," he said.

"Not yet," Laranth replied. "Rokko wants to see us before we leave. And right now he's busy haggling over a new droid."

Jax raised an eyebrow. "A new droid?"

"Don't worry. From what I've heard, it's not our droid. It's a protocol unit—supposed to be a whiz at sabacc, or something."

Jax gestured impatiently. "Whatever. We don't have time for this."

"Apparently his priorities are different," Laranth said. "I wouldn't rush him, Jax. Right now he's the best—possibly the only—chance we have of finding the Four-Tee-Oh."

The cards looked ridiculously oversized in the Hutt's stubby hands. He studied them for a moment, then announced, "Bet two." He put two credit chips into the hand pot.

I-Five seemed completely unperturbed, even to Den, who knew how to read the droid's expressions. "Raise two." Two more credits went in.

Den resisted the urge to dance about on his toes.

Much more was riding on this game than just their reputations.

"Raise five." The Hutt was a stolid player, master of the sabacc mask—the unreadable face that gave no hint or indication of what kind of array the player was holding. No one, however, could be more expressionless than a droid, and no player Den had ever met was more adept at reading the subtlest body language, no matter the species, than I-Five. Even the Lorrdians, for all their vaunted talents, weren't as good.

Rokko rolled the six-sided die for the shift. It was a two; no shift.

"Call," the droid said calmly.

Rokko blinked, then put his cards down. I-Five did the same. Den nearly gasped, and he could hear excited and astonished conversation ripple through the employees, many of whom had stopped to watch the game. The hushed comments were justified: the droid had a perfect hand, the cards totaling twenty-three. It was an automatic win, and it had taken the droid less than ten minutes.

For just a moment, the silence in the chamber was the loudest thing Den had ever heard. Then Rokko laughed. His boneless bulk quaked as he rumbled out his humor, his dewflaps, each the size of a summoning gong, shaking with mirth.

"I like this droid! I can make much money with this droid! No one will believe a droid can play sabacc like that. And even after they do believe it, they'll keep coming back to watch it play again." He turned ponderously toward Den. "I will give you five hundred credits for it," he said in a magnanimous tone.

Den could see I-Five drawing himself up indignantly,

and shot him a look. The droid, remembering that he was playing the part of a passive protocol unit, subsided, although Den could tell he was still simmering. Five hundred credits would be a bargain for a droid in much worse condition. I-Five might be an outmoded model, but his parts were all in good working order.

But this was by no means a take-it-or-leave-it deal. Den knew that Hutts loved to haggle nearly as much as Toydarians. "This is a unique unit. Fifteen hundred would not be too much to ask . . . however, in acknowledgment of your lofty position as a businessman in the Yaam Sector, I'll make it twelve hundred."

The Hutt's enormous watery eyes narrowed. "*Pfah!* It's just a protocol droid with some kind of enhancement in odds calculating. Eight hundred."

They finally compromised on a thousand, which was what Den had figured it would be. As the credits were counted out into Den's hand, Rokko gestured to the droid. "What's your classification?"

"I-Five-Why-Cue, sir." The tone was properly servile, Den noticed with relief. Apparently Rokko found nothing objectionable in it, either, because he said, "Go down the hall and fetch the two waiting in the last room." To Den he added, as I-Five headed obediently down the corridor, "A couple of Jedi asking *me* for help. I tell you, life just keeps getting stranger." He chuckled.

A couple of Jedi? Den turned quickly, but I-Five had already disappeared. He shrugged. *After all,* he told himself, *what are the odds?*

"We've waited long enough," Jax said. "Let's go."

He turned toward the door, and Laranth followed.

"Maybe you're right. I'll feel a lot more comfortable when I've got my blasters back."

Jax didn't reply. He wasn't quite sure why he was suddenly in such a hurry. Part of it was the renewed sense of purpose he had drawn from Master Piell's assignment—quite likely the last assignment he would ever have as a Jedi. It felt good to have a purpose. For the time being, at least, his life had meaning again; he was feeling alive and confident. He was ready to face whatever surprises, whatever unexpected twists, the future might have in store for him. *Bring it on,* he said to himself. He would rise gladly to whatever new challenge or complication was coming his way.

He opened the portal and saw a protocol droid standing before him, one arm upraised to knock. The droid looked at him, and Jax had the strangest feeling that, even though the droid's face was immobile, it was somehow surprised to see him. More than surprised; shocked, struggling with disbelief.

The droid took a step back, lowering its arm. "Jax Pavan," it said softly.

"Yes?" The droid had obviously been sent by Rokko to get them—but that didn't explain why it looked so shocked. And it certainly didn't explain *how* it looked so shocked.

The droid stepped forward once more. When it spoke again, its voice was even lower; a conspiratorial tone. It said eight words, and then it was Jax's turn to stare in disbelief.

"I am I-Five. Your father sent me."

—[PART II]—

AS ABOVE, SO BELOW

twenty-two

On his way down to the surface of Coruscant, Kaird of the Nediji reflected on the strange twists and turns that life could sometimes take.

He had been so absolutely sure that the Underlord was going to pluck his tail feathers that it had taken him a few moments to understand—first, that he'd been spared, and second, why he'd been spared. Had his mouth been composed of soft flesh, instead of keratin, his jaw would have probably dropped into an all-too-human expression of astonishment.

And yet, it made perfect sense. It was also simple, so simple that Kaird inwardly kicked himself for not having seen it coming.

After all, he was an assassin.

Prince Xizor, Perhi had explained, had his eyes set on the Underlord's mantle. Anyone who knew anything about the Falleen species knew that, even without their exceptional strength and pheromone manipulation, they were foes to be reckoned with. Their natural cunning and guile, it was said, would make a Neimoidian envious. Combining all that with a laser-keen intellect made Xizor a formidable foe indeed.

Which is why the Underlord had sent Kaird to kill him.

It was a simple and direct plan, and that was what made it likely to work: Xizor's brain, accustomed to constructing elaborate traps spun of fugues, misdirections, and half-truths, might not see that which was right in front of him, until it was too late. At least, that was what both Perhi and Kaird hoped.

Since the sanction could not be carried out in Midnight Hall, for obvious reasons, an excuse had to be found for Prince Xizor to leave the skyhook and return to Coruscant. Perhi had come up with an excellent ruse. A series of intercepted communiqués between Imperial functionaries had spoken of a droid carrying data valuable to the nascent rebellion brewing on the streets of Coruscant, and thus to the Empire as well. It supposedly had gone to ground somewhere in one of Coruscant's seedier sectors. If this was true, and if Black Sun could get to it first, the organization would have a powerful bargaining chip in future dealings with the Empire.

All of which was ample reason to send Xizor on a mission to find it and bring it back to Midnight Hall. Perhi had told Xizor that he was entrusting this task to him and him alone, because the Falleen prince was the most qualified of all the Vigo aspirants. If Xizor had a flaw that could be exploited, it was hubris. His pride demanded that he succeed. He would find this 10-4TO droid, there was little doubt of that, in Xizor's mind. Or in anyone else's, for that matter. And when he brought it back, he would be appointed Vigo.

But Xizor wouldn't bring it back. That honor would belong to Kaird.

The Underlord had made it quite clear to Kaird that

the droid's retrieval would be considered a bonus. True, it might be a feather in their collective caps, but Xizor was the primary target. When Kaird showed Perhi proof of Xizor's death, the Underlord would have what he wanted: immunity from a dangerously ambitious underling. And Kaird would have what he wanted: a pile of credits and the promise of safe conduct back to Nedij.

Everybody wins, he told himself. *Well, except for Xizor.*

His ship—a Surronian assault vessel, sleek and aesthetically pleasing as well as aerodynamic—was locked into a preset descent course for the Eastport landing field. There was nothing for Kaird to do except lean back and relax as the nav comp processed the incoming directions and adjusted the ship's vector and delta vee accordingly. He hated to give up control of the sleek, dynamic craft, even for the few minutes it took for Spaceport Traffic to guide it in. He'd stolen the *Stinger* from the MedStar's former commander Admiral Bleyd. Perhaps *stolen* was too strong a word; after all, he had killed Bleyd before he took his ship. Was it possible to steal from the dead?

The course took him in a long arc of descent from the south, passing over the Calocour Heights, and eventually, the Imperial Palace. There were still, he noted, huge craters punctuating the cityscape here and there, although the gigantic new construction droids that Palpatine had ordered built immediately after cessation of hostilities had already done a remarkable job of erasing the scars of war. Forty stories tall, these gargantuan machines were armed with huge shovel arms, wide-swath laser-mapping and destructive charged-particle beams, collapsed carbon battering rams, and other equipment that could tear down and chew up just about any structure. Within the huge construct, billions of nanodroids swarmed like microbes in the belly of a huge beast, disassembling the detritus, molecule by molecule, as it was ingested, and reassembling it with incredible speed into whatever purpose best suited the city's architectural redesign: a road ramp, perhaps, or a clear crystasteel mag-lev tube, or a high-rise monad. Like enormous, mechanized slugs, the construction droids moved slowly and ponderously across the shattered streets, grinding up durasteel girders, plasticrete walls, and transparisteel windows all with equal appetite while they excreted brand-new structures and thoroughfares to take their places. *In with the old and out with the new,* Kaird thought. He could see one of the titanic droids now, silhouetted next to a broken building. It swung its wrecking ball like some giant in a child's story might swing a mace, and shattered the remaining wall.

The Eastport docks served all manner of spacecraft, from the ubiquitous Lambda shuttles up to *Victory*-class Star Destroyers. Kaird's ship settled down through several holding strata of smaller craft; his forged identity as a high-ranking member of the Mercantile Guild gave him priority clearance.

He'd arranged to have high-speed transportation waiting for him, and within minutes he was on his way again. The considerable data-tracking powers of Black Sun had been brought to bear upon finding the droid, and it could be said with fair accuracy that it was somewhere in the Yaam Sector. Still a considerable area in which to search, and a fair distance from where he was. But one trait an assassin had to cultivate was patience. Sooner or later, he would find his quarry. Then it was just a matter of time; Xizor's time, in this case, which was rapidly running out.

Rhinann took Nick Rostu down to the hangar bay. Rostu was conscious, but silent, staring into the distance. Rhinann had become somewhat familiar with human facial expressions and body language, and he could tell that Rostu had seen or heard something that had nearly stunned him into a vegetative state. Rhinann shuddered, trying not to think about what horrors Vader had imparted to the human. Whatever they had been, they had left him in such shock that the forcecuffs he was wearing seemed almost superfluous.

Even as this observation went through the Elomin's mind, Rostu stumbled to his knees on the plum-colored carpeting. Rhinann hesitated, then reached out hesitantly and helped him to his feet. He was careful to touch only Rostu's shoulders and upper arms, where the skin was covered by his shirt. Even so, Rhinann's own skin crawled at having to come into actual physical contact with a human.

"This way, Major," he said. "Time to go."

Rostu said nothing. He turned obediently and began walking again. Rhinann followed.

Humans, he thought, bitterly. Nearly everything in the galaxy—every piece of furniture, every mode of transportation, every tool, every weapon, even every blasted kitchen appliance—was, unless made or built for a specific species, human-oriented. If you were a methane-breathing native of Helix IX and you ordered a custom star cruiser, you had to make sure that it cycled the right mixture of gases to keep you alive. Or if you traveled on a multispecies transport of almost any sort, unless you specified otherwise, the gravity was always one Coruscant gee, the lighting was always in the narrow range between three hundred and seven hundred nanometers, and the temperature always around twenty-five degrees. It was the default, the norm, the oh-so-common denominator, and woe betide you if you inveighed even the slightest bit against the status quo.

Humans. They dominated culture, trade, government, the military—everything, in short. Love them or hate them, you couldn't ignore them. For better or worse, humans were the architects of the galaxy's future. It was only such a benighted, aggressive, and hubristic species, it seemed to Rhinann, that could have created a monster like Darth Vader.

They had come to the turbolift station. Several other palace functionaries of various species were waiting for the lift. They all stepped back a bit as Rhinann and his prisoner came up.

The lift opened, and Rhinann, still half guiding Rostu, stepped in. He moved to the rear and looked back. None of the others had boarded the lift, even though there was plenty of room. After a moment, an Ishi Tib said, "It's okay. We'll take the next one."

The turbolift doors closed. Rhinann sighed noisily through his tusks.

Humans.

twenty-three

Jax wasn't sure what the droid was trying to tell him at first. He wondered if perhaps he'd merely misunderstood it, or if some glitch in its processor had substituted the word *father* for *host*. Out of the corner of his eye, he could see Laranth's surprised face. He hadn't misunderstood it, then.

"What?" he asked.

The droid—what was its designation, I-Five?—seemed agitated. Jax had no idea how he was getting this impression, since the droid's chassis was as immobile as its face. "I have been searching for you for quite some time," it said in that same low tone. "Your father, Lorn Pavan, was my friend. He—"

Friend? This was getting far too surreal for Jax to handle, at least right now. "Whatever," he said, pushing past I-Five and leaving the chamber. "I don't have time for this." He heard the droid give an upset gasp, then an exasperated sigh, behind him as he continued down the—

Wait a minute.

Droids didn't gasp. Droids didn't sigh, because droids didn't breathe.

Jax turned and looked at the droid, which had turned

to follow him. Again, he could not escape a sense of urgency and concern somehow projected by it.

He took a step closer. "You don't belong to Rokko," he said.

The droid shook its head—another strangely human action. "No."

"And you say my *father* sent you?"

"Yes. Lorn Pavan. He was—"

"My father's dead," Jax interrupted. "I never knew him. And now definitely isn't the time to—"

"He died a hero's death, Jax. He died avenging the killing of a Jedi. He died in an attempt to save the Republic from being overthrown. He died in battle with one of the most dangerous assassins in the galaxy. And," I-Five said, its voice full of compassion and regret, "no one knows it but me."

Jax stared at the droid, utterly at a loss for either thoughts or words. I-Five reached out, put a gentle hand on Jax's shoulder. "It's easy enough to test my veracity," it said. "Use the Force. Reach out with your feelings. Listen to your heart, Jax. You'll know it's the truth."

"But—you're a *droid*. You have no—there's nothing to—"

"Trust what the Force tells you, Jax. If it doesn't confirm what I'm saying—what you know in your heart to be true—" The droid spread its hands in a gesture of defeat. "Then I belong to Rokko."

Jax shook his head in confusion. The droid couldn't possibly know what it was talking about. Still, it was but the work of a second to comply. And the intensity of its importuning was slightly intriguing.

He opened his mental vision to the Force.

The threads that always formed his most complete

connection with the Force enveloped and infiltrated I-Five. At first there seemed to be nothing there beyond what he had expected: the pulse of lubricating fluids, the hum of capacitors and quantum couplers, the stolidity of superconductors. Beyond that, Jax could sense the restless interactions of subatomic particles that, pairing and parting and pairing again, gave I-Five a literally endless ability to process, refine, and utilize data.

Jax had never bothered to probe a droid before; what was the point? Even those without creativity dampers lacked the essential spark. One might as well look for a meaningful connection with a comlink. But now, in this outwardly unremarkable droid, he sensed—something. Something that was not explicable in terms of engineering and circuitry and mechanics. Something . . . more.

He pulled back, and now beheld the droid wrapped in the threads. They reached in all directions, as well as into the past and future. Often he could study them and track a person's life holistically, seeing not just the line he or she traveled through the continuum, but the countless connections made with other beings as well. They vibrated, these threads, and the harmonic waves they produced within the Force connected everything that was to everything that had ever been, or would ever be.

He sensed I-Five's connection with a man who had considered it not as property, but as a person. A partner. He felt the droid's affection for this man, this man with whom Jax was now connected, through the Force threads aligned with the patterns of energy in the droid's memory banks.

Lorn Pavan.

His father.

Jax severed the connection, snapping back with such rapidity that he almost physically rocked back on his heels. He saw Laranth watching him from over the droid's shoulder. The droid's immobile face seemed somehow concerned as well.

"Jax?" the droid asked. "Are you all—"

"Get away from me," Jax said. He turned and stalked back up the hall.

Den was beginning to wonder what had happened to I-Five when a man came down the corridor and headed past him, moving at a fast pace. Den had just time enough to register that this was probably one of the Jedi whom Rokko had sent I-Five after when a female Twi'lek, who looked like she could tackle a Sullustan rockrender and walk away intact, followed quickly behind him.

Behind them both came I-Five, projecting what could only be described as anguish. "Jax!" the droid shouted.

They were all far enough into the main chamber that his shout could be heard by everyone there. Rokko turned, surprised.

"What's going on, Pavan? Who's—?"

The Hutt noticed I-Five then. He made a gesture, and two burly Gamorrean guards blocked the exit before Pavan could reach it.

Rokko looked first at Pavan, then at Den and I-Five. His eyes narrowed.

Uh-oh, Den thought.

"How interesting," the Hutt growled. "A Sullustan grifter brings to me a droid with an unusual penchant for gambling, and who just happens to know the Jedi who comes to me earlier, offering another moneymaking deal. This can hardly be a coincidence. Something about this stinks like a ripe keebada." He made a gesture, and a Trandoshan standing near one of the support columns leveled his blaster on them.

"Explanations," Rokko said. "Plausible ones just might preserve your lives a bit longer."

The man who, according to I-Five, was Jax Pavan said, "I have no idea who this droid is, Rokko. I've never seen it before in my life. Same goes for Shorty here." He gestured at Den.

"Okay," Den said. "You're off my Feast Day holo-card list."

"Keel-ee calleya ku kah, Jedi," the gangster snarled. "I would have thought you cleverer than that." He gestured at the Trandoshan. *"Keepuna nanya,"* he said.

The Trandoshan raised his blaster.

"Wait!" Pavan said. "We had a deal!"

"Had. Past tense. Which is what you'll all be in another second." The Hutt turned away, his boneless mass flowing over the flagstone floor.

This is it, Den thought, feeling surprisingly calm about it, all things considered. *Well, at least I'm underground.*

A flash of red light from I-Five's direction caused him to turn quickly. The droid was pointing an index finger, firing the hidden laser within it. But he wasn't firing at Rokko, or at the Trandoshan. Instead, the beam was aimed squarely at one of the pictures—or windows; Den wasn't sure what they were, really—that showed real-time images of Nal Hutta. The image seemed to be absorbing the high-intensity light ray. A crimson tint spread slowly over it.

Rokko stopped and spun about with a moist flapping

sound. Den hadn't known that Hutts could move that fast. "What are you doing?" Rokko cried.

"Tell the Trandoshan to put down his weapon," I-Five said. "While you're at it, tell your other thugs to disarm themselves as well. And I'm sure my colleagues would like their weapons returned."

"*Eniki! Eniki!*" the Hutt yelled. Then, to his staff: "Do as he says! *Yatuka!*"

Several weapons were quickly brought and returned to Pavan and his Twi'lek companion, while Rokko's bodyguards disarmed themselves. "Deactivate your attack droids and defense mechanisms as well," I-Five instructed the Hutt. "No attempts at subterfuge, please. Right now my laser is set at a collimation factor of five-point-three. Any higher, and it'll begin to melt through the condensate's densecris-impervium alloy glaze."

Rokko actually *blanched*—the Hutt's entire body turned a sickly mottled white. Den had never seen one of the big slugs look so scared.

The four of them backed out of the underground chamber, I-Five keeping his laser trained on the image as long as he could before the turn in the corridor forced him to shut it off.

"Now what?" Den asked him.

"Now we run."

But before they could reach the turbolifts they heard sounds of pursuit behind them: the whine of repulsor-plates. The big guard droid was after them.

Pavan stopped, turned, and assumed a battle stance, activating his lightsaber. "Keep going," he said tensely. "I'll hold them off."

"You and what legion of droidekas?" the Twi'lek, whose name Den didn't know, demanded. "That droid can go through a ferrocrete bunker like a neutrino through plasma."

"You have to complete the mission," Pavan said. "Find the droid and—"

"Excuse me," I-Five said. He stepped in front of the Jedi and fired both lasers full-blast at the ceiling just above the last turn. He also began using his vocabulator to emit a high-pitched screech; so high, in fact, that Den was probably the only one who could hear it, and he wished he couldn't.

Pavan and the Twi'lek looked at the droid, then at each other. Before they could say anything, however, Den saw and heard cracks appearing in the ceiling, radiating out like crystal snakes from a disturbed nest. The guard droid had just come around the corner when the ceiling gave way, burying it under tons of debris.

The silence was sudden and complete, save for the last few patters of pebbles falling. Then the Twi'lek said to I-Five in a tone of awe, "That ceiling was solid cerami-steel. How did you—?"

The pile of debris, which blocked the whole of the passage, trembled. Then trembled again, more strongly this time.

"I suggest we leave," I-Five said. "It appears that Arakyd Industries manufactures its droids very well."

As they rose toward the surface in the turbolift, Den asked, "So how did you bring the ceiling down like that?"

"Ultrasonic vibrations along with the heat from my lasers. Not even ceramisteel can withstand the combination."

"Okay, that was quick thinking," Den admitted. "But that picture thingie in the wall—that was a, uh . . ."

"A decelerated luminescent image."

"A superfluid," the Twi'lek added. "Cooled down to near absolute zero, it slows light passing through it to a dead crawl."

"Correct. It is extremely dense. You might say that each piece is several light-years thick, in a way. A window into the past."

"So what would've happened if you'd bored through that protective glaze?" Den asked.

"An interesting question," I-Five replied. "I confess my data on supercooled quantum condensates is not as complete as I'd like, but, given the density coefficient and the probable expansion velocity . . . let's just say it's a good thing Rokko acceded to my demands."

"Are you telling me you could've blown up Rokko's whole underground lair?"

"No," I-Five replied, imperturbably. "I'm telling you I could have blown up several cubic kilometers of Yaam Sector real estate."

Den swallowed, suddenly feeling like he had a chunk of supercooled condensate lodged just behind his stomach.

They reached the surface and stepped from the lift tube into a dimly lit, deserted tube station on a side street in the Slums. It was full of trash and broken furniture, and it smelled rank.

"Of course," I-Five added, "it would have taken my laser approximately three weeks, even at maximum power, to burn through the glaze. Luckily, Rokko wasn't aware of that."

While Den was still too stunned to reply, I-Five turned toward the son of his late friend. "Jax," he said, "I am so glad to finally—"

"There's no time for this," Pavan said. He reached over I-Five's shoulder and flipped the master deactivation switch on the back of the droid's neck. I-Five froze, the light in his photoreceptors blinking off.

Den stared in outrage. Pavan turned to his companion and said, "They know we're on the droid's trail now. We've got to find it before they do."

Laranth nodded, and the two walked away from Den and I-Five without looking back.

Den reactivated his friend. I-Five's processor powered up again. He stared in disbelief after Pavan.

"Oh, yeah," Den said to the flabbergasted droid. "He's definitely warming up to you."

twenty-four

The *Far Ranger* was on full auto, following a course previously laid in that was taking Nick away from the Palace and back toward the Yaam Sector. He didn't feel up to piloting a child's kiddie cruiser around the yard right now, so he just sat back in the pilot's seat and stared at the endless cityscape passing below.

His mind felt like it had been punched full of holes—holes that let conscious thoughts drain from it as fast as they popped into existence. Or maybe it was just that the thoughts were too horrible to hold on to for any length of time.

The choice he'd been given was simple. That wasn't surprising; the big ones always were. He could betray Jax Pavan, lead him into a trap, and have him turned over to Darth Vader—

Or Vader would destroy his ghôsh.

Nick hadn't believed it at first. Clan Rostu, his tribe, ranged over one of the largest highland plateaus on all of Haruun Kal, following their grasser herds, the great beasts that were the lifeblood of his people. How could Vader target a nomadic tribe?

The answer, of course, was simple—he didn't have to. He could just have the entire plateau scoured from orbit.

Any Star Destroyer could generate the kind of concentrated firepower required for that. All it would take was a word from the Dark Lord to set the process in motion. And Vader had made it very clear to Nick that he would feel no pangs whatsoever if he had to give that word.

The subsonic vibration of the ion engines felt good; no flaws in the harmonics. She wasn't a bad ship, all things considered. Her previous owners had taken good care of her, at least as far as the mechanics and electronics went. And a freighter was, to all intents and purposes, invisible—not by virtue of a cloaking device, but because there were so many of them, buzzing around the planet like fire wasps around a sweetpod tree, that nobody would notice one more.

Yes, a good ship. And she was all his. High adventure in the wild reaches of space! No more grubbing around in the urban chasms of Coruscant for him—he had a spacecraft now. He could go anywhere, do anything, be anyone he wanted. He could adopt a new identity, rename the vessel, head for the Outland Regions, make a new life for himself. He could be a spice smuggler on the Kessel Run, perhaps. Or join the Solar Guard of the Corbett Cluster. Or be a proton railer, running the tubes in some out-of-the-way star system . . .

The choices were limitless. The entire galaxy—those parts not yet under direct control of the Empire, anyway—was his to explore . . .

As soon as he turned Jax Pavan over to Darth Vader.

His choice. A wild, free life, roaming the spaceways . . . or imprisonment on the planetary prison of Despayre, forced to live with the knowledge that he had been responsible for the death of thousands of his family and compatriots.

Nick leaned forward and put his face in his hands. What was he going to do?

As Jax left the deserted lift station, he was feeling a welter of strange, conflicting emotions.

He had nothing against droids, and no particular fondness for them, either. They were simply machines, to be used for convenience. Truth to tell, he hadn't had all that much experience with them. He'd spent nearly all of his life cloistered in the Temple, and droids just weren't as ubiquitous within those walls as outside them. Most of the droids in the Temple were protocol units of either the 3PO or the 3D-4X lines, and all of them were quiet, efficient, and subservient, often to the point of obsequiousness. He could see someone becoming fond of one, the same way someone might prefer a familiar old skimmer to a brand-new craft. He supposed it was even possible for somebody to feel the same way about a droid as they might about a pet—to expect and depend upon its loyalty and devotion, and to be devoted to it as well.

But as far as he could tell, that wasn't what the relationship between I-Five and Jax's father had been. Instead, from the brief glimpse Jax had gotten by following the threads, Lorn Pavan had thought of the droid as an equal. As a friend. And, toward the final days of their association, as a brother.

There was something decidedly unnatural about it; it seemed almost perverse. The thought of his father considering a walking conglomeration of circuits and servos to be worthy of equal status with organics was, to put it mildly, disturbing. He knew nothing about his father, of course; his family had been the Jedi who had raised him.

And he had no complaints about the job they had done; he had never lacked for love, or companionship, or authority. It was true that, when he'd been younger, he'd wondered about what his parents had been like, even fantasized about meeting them. But those had been the dreams of youth, and he was a youth no longer.

But now, when he thought he'd made his peace with their absence long ago, here came this droid into his life, casually dropping this bombshell. He knew one thing and one thing only about his father now—and that one thing seemed to indicate the man had been a mental case.

It might have been different had he just taken I-Five's statement at face value. It might have been easier to dismiss it, to label it some strange misfiring of the droid's synaptic grid, or a subroutine programmed as a bizarre joke. But he had looked with the Force. He had seen the connection between the man he knew was his father and this . . . machine.

And, to be brutally honest, he'd also seen the barest suggestion that there might really be something more to I-Five.

Jax shook his head. This was something he most certainly didn't need right now.

twenty-five

Den looked at I-Five. A dozen remarks occurred to him, ranging from snide to angry to sympathetic, but he voiced none of them. The emotions the droid was projecting were all too familiar to any sentient organic being: disappointment and hurt.

He finally said, "You really should get that deactivation switch, uh, deactivated."

I-Five didn't reply. There was no real need to; Den knew the switch was hardwired into his primary processor and couldn't be removed. But the statement had at least filled the silence for a moment.

"What now?" he asked.

"I'll follow him," I-Five said. His vocalizations sounded hollow. "I'll keep my distance until he . . . gets used to me, feels more comfortable with me around."

Den fell in alongside him. They were proceeding down a no-longer-functioning slidewalk. There were only a few other pedestrians around, and little air or ground traffic, either; it was as close to deserted as Den had ever seen any area of Coruscant. A few flimsies and other lightweight scraps were blown about by the traffic. They all combined with the never-ending twilight to create the ambience of a ghost town.

"And if he doesn't get used to you?"

"I don't know," I-Five said, quietly. He spread his hands, palms up; his equivalent of a human shrug. "I don't know. I'm . . . not sure what to do."

Den was astonished. I-Five always knew his own mind; he had never before shown any hesitancy in choosing a course of action. Unlike other sentients, he had no unconscious mind that could make irrational decisions.

Or did he? Was the development of an underlying substrate of unconsciousness an inevitable result of self-awareness? In order for I-Five to be sentient, did he also have to be, to a degree, neurotic?

Den shook his head. This was a philosophical quagmire more dangerous to be exploring than a black hole.

"Well," he said, "you can always resume your career as a nanny droid."

The droid shot him a withering look. "I'd suggest a secondary line of employment if you're going to attempt stand-up comedy. Not to mention turbolift shoes if you want people to see your act."

Den grinned. He was glad to see a flash of the old I-Five reasserting itself. His friend and partner had been uncharacteristically humorless and moody of late.

His grin faded as he thought about Pavan's rudeness. He could only imagine how I-Five felt. The droid had taken Pavan the elder's last request very seriously, and now that he'd finally fulfilled it, he'd been rebuffed, shut down both literally and figuratively.

It might be for the best, Den mused. Maybe soon I-Five would quit chasing after Pavan and remember who his real friend was. The jealousy he'd felt earlier was rearing its ugly, green-eyed head again. Den's dislike of Jax Pavan, he realized with surprise, was rapidly escalating into actual hatred.

You could turn him in.

Den blinked in surprise, as if he'd heard the idea whispered to him by some unknown voice, instead of it originating in his own head. It was true, however. All it would take was one call, and he knew how to easily arrange it so that the betrayal could never be traced back to him. I-Five might suspect, but he couldn't be sure.

Problem was that Den himself would know what he'd done. There was no way he could justify feeding someone to the Emperor simply on account of being rude. While it was true that, in the less-than-an-hour he'd known Pavan, the man had completely alienated him, plotting his betrayal was a little extreme.

Still, the little voice in his head whispered, *this isn't how Jedi are supposed to behave. If he's capable of being so unfeeling in the small matters, can you really trust him not to sacrifice I-Five—or you—if the situation seems to call for it?*

He wished Barriss Offee were here. She had been everything his concept of a Jedi called for: courageous, compassionate, strong, and kind. He wondered what had happened to her. He hoped she'd somehow managed to escape the massacre.

He doubted it, however. From everything he'd heard, the Jedi had been pretty much exterminated. And if Jax Pavan was indeed the last Jedi in the galaxy, he was a poor representative of the Order's past glory.

And that "Shorty" remark didn't gain you any points, either, friend . . .

*   *   *

"You're moody," Laranth said.

Jax stood on the edge of a small blast crater, one of thousands that bore grim testament to the Separatists' saturation bombing of Coruscant. The fused surface of the concavity was glossy black. From it, his own reflection, warped and distorted, looked back at him.

"Look who's talking. Or who's not, usually. You're calling me moody?"

She ignored that. "That's a strange droid," she said. "All that chatter about its being 'friends' with your father—"

"My parents left me with the Temple because I had the potential to be a Jedi. I'm sure it was an agonizing decision for them, but they made it for the greater good. I admire them for that, but I don't wish to know anything further about them. Anything else is secondary to their sacrifice."

Laranth raised an eyebrow. "What about that line about your father being a hero and trying to save the Republic?"

Jax shrugged. "Why should I believe a droid?"

"Why would it lie?"

"Maybe because it was programmed to. It's a droid, after all. And speaking of droids, we've got more pressing matters to attend to, such as fulfilling Master Piell's last request by finding the other droid—you know, the important one—before Vader and now Rokko, too, probably, find it first."

Laranth looked over his shoulder, back down the street. "They're coming," she said.

As the droid and the Sullustan approached, Jax focused his attention on the latter. He smiled. "I'm sorry about powering your droid down back there," he said. He held out his hand. "My name's—"

"I already know your name," the Sullustan interrupted, ignoring Jax's outstretched hand. "And it isn't me you owe an apology to. It's him." He aimed a thumb over his shoulder at the droid behind him.

Jax frowned, perplexed. "Apologize? To your *droid*?"

The Sullustan rolled his eyes—which was quite impressive, given their size. "He's not *my* droid. He's his own master. Once you've hammered that into your head, we'll all get along a lot better."

Jax blinked in surprise. Once again, he was certain he'd heard wrong, and once again, it was apparent that he hadn't. He glanced at Laranth, standing behind him. Even she looked slightly confused.

"No apology is necessary," the droid said, somewhat stiffly. "I overstepped my bounds. I forgot that Jedi Pavan would have no way of knowing about the unique arrangement between his father and me. It is I who should apologize."

The Sullustan turned and stared at the droid. "Excuse me? You're just going to let this go?"

"I am a droid, Den Dhur," I-Five said. "I'm not programmed to take offense."

Jax noticed that the droid's voice was much more artificial and stilted than when it had first spoken to him. Also, its face was an expressionless metal mask again.

The Sullustan wasn't pacified. "Don't worry. I take offense enough for us both."

Jax was getting tired of this. Fortunately, he knew an easy way to get him and Laranth out of the situation. It wouldn't work on the droid, of course, but the Sullustan should be easily susceptible. And even if the droid did feel some sort of bizarre claim to sentience and refused to listen to its companion—well, it was easy enough to power it down again.

"It's best if we all go our own ways," he said in a soothing tone while he made the mesmerizing gestures of the mental snare that had so often gotten him out of ticklish situations since the destruction of the Jedi Order. "You don't need to travel with us any—"

"Oh, space it," the little alien snapped. "You think you can use that mind-trick banthaflop on me? I spent months in a Rimsoo on Drongar, Small Eyes. I watched Barriss Offee use the same thing, practically every day, to calm down patients and—"

"You knew Barriss?"

"Both of us did. Now, she's what I call a Jedi," Den Dhur said. "She's compassionate, kind, and tolerant of—"

"She's dead."

Dhur stared; then his shoulders sagged. I-Five didn't move, but somehow his metal body seemed to radiate great sadness. "How?"

"I don't know for certain," Jax said, reliving the sadness he'd felt when he had sensed her death reverberate along the threads of the Force. "I don't know for certain," he repeated. "But I know she's dead. The Force doesn't lie."

"I thought something like that had happened," Dhur said. "I didn't want to believe it. She was one in a trillion."

I-Five said nothing about Barriss, which was just fine with Jax. He wasn't sure how he would feel about a droid commiserating with him over her death, but he was fairly certain he wouldn't like it.

Instead the droid said, "We should go."

Jax felt a flash of annoyance at the presumptiveness of this, but the feeling vanished almost immediately, washed away by a Force wave that brought with it knowledge of imminent danger.

"Yes," he said. "I feel it."

"Me, too," Laranth said grimly. She loosened her blasters in their holsters.

Dhur looked around in bafflement. "What? What is it? I hate being the only one in a crowd without super senses."

"Don't worry," I-Five said, grabbing the Sullustan up and holding him, cradled in one arm like an oversized infant, as he began to walk rapidly. Jax and Laranth followed. Jax pulled his lightsaber but didn't activate it. "With those ears," I-Five continued, "you should be able to hear them soon."

"Oh, you mean the rising whine of repulsorlifts coming our way at full throttle?"

"Those would be the ones, yes."

"And what, exactly, would they be?"

"PCBUs," Jax said. "Police Cruiser Backup Units. At least four, possibly more."

"It would seem that the Emperor's not giving up on that data so easily," Laranth said.

"It's not the Emperor," Jax said, his gaze scanning the sky above. "It's Vader. And he doesn't just want the droid. He wants me."

twenty-six

Kaird's first thought, upon seeing Xizor striding confidently down the filthy, garbage-strewn street, was: *Got to hand it to the fancy reptiloid. He knows how to dominate just about any scenario.*

Kaird knew that, even were he disguised as the meanest-looking Shistavanen ever, he'd think twice before just walking out into the midst of this motley population of thieves and cutthroats. Disguised as a Kubaz, he was using a small pair of electrobinoculars from his vantage point on a loggia several stories above the street to follow the Falleen's progress. The only concession Xizor had made to any possible danger had been to simplify his attire somewhat; instead of his usual fine robes of silk, brocade, and jaquards, he wore a plain fleekskin tunic and leggings, with gloves and boots that matched, all a deep midnight blue-black that matched the color of his topknot and contrasted dramatically with his green skin. It was skintight, and Kaird could see the bas-relief of the Prince's muscles, the smooth and easy movement that bespoke power and grace as he walked. He definitely stood out in a crowd, even this colorful crowd. He wore a blaster slung low on one hip, and he slowed or stepped aside for no one. Kaird watched as a Sakiyan

wearing an eye patch and a heavily scarred Whiphid
hastily got out of his way.

Impressive. He knew that Xizor was a practitioner of
various forms of martial arts and weapons fighting.
He'd seen the Falleen fight once, in a duel of honor. His
opponent had been a human, also well versed in sundry
arts of killing. He'd stood almost two meters tall and
been grotesquely muscled, but withal limber and blind-
ingly fast.

It hadn't been much of a contest.

Kaird was well versed in killing matters also, but his
training was in methods indirect rather than direct. He
could fight, however, when there was no other recourse,
and he had no problem at all with fighting dirty.

There was no doubt that Xizor was a formidable opponent. Kaird knew he'd be a fool to try to take him on
physically, one-on-one. Fortunately, as an assassin, he
had a variety of alternatives. He could easily pick the
Falleen off right now, put a load of toxin so virulent in
him that he'd literally be dead before he hit the grimy
duracrete. But it wasn't going to be that simple. Just as
Kaird had access to state-of-the-art weaponry, his opponent had, he knew, a full slate of sophisticated defenses.
He might be wearing a location confounder, a combination of holoproj and cloaking technology capable of
making observers think he was a step or two ahead or
behind, leading them to shoot at a target that wasn't
there. Or a bounceback, a tightband feedback reflector
that would reverb an energy beam back to the attacker,
with less-than-salutary results. Or any of a hundred and
one other protective devices.

And anyway, killing him in public—even this public—
would be too noticeable. Kaird had been in various

dives on various worlds where the killing of a sentient in full view of others barely merited the raising of an eyebrow or the twitch of an antenna. But even if few people down here knew who Prince Xizor of House Sizhran was, anyone with half an eyestalk could see this fellow was someone important.

Besides, the possibility still existed that Xizor would find the missing droid for him. Kaird intended to finish his assignment, oh yes. Prince Xizor would not return to Midnight Hall, and if Kaird could bring back a bit of extra favor to Underlord Perhi to speed his own departure, so much the better . . .

Rhinann sat in meditation posture in his conapt, seeking inner peace.

Or perhaps that was too optimistic a goal; he knew he'd be lucky to achieve a temporary surcease from inner terror at the moment. He'd be happy just to avoid swooning in fear.

He expanded his tracheal network, sensing the air filling him and diffusing through him. Then he compressed the tubes, expelling it. A slow cycle of aspiration and expiration. Most oxygen breathers were able to stabilize their internal mechanisms this way, regulate their moods. It didn't seem to be working all that well for Rhinann, however.

The source of his fear was as simple as it was effective. He feared his employer. Never mind that Lord Vader had never actually caused him any physical harm, and had given him work and an ordered life, instead of one of hardship and chaos and drudgery. The Sith Lord didn't have to physically abuse him to instigate fear. He didn't even have to threaten. All he had to do was *be*.

Ironic, that. The inner peace and stability that Rhinann so desperately craved, Vader seemed to have achieved, after a fashion. He was supremely confident in his power, serene in his worldview. Yes, he was also unspeakably evil, but one thing Rhinann had learned, in dealing with a wide variety of life-forms over the years, was that very few sentients thought of themselves as evil. He also knew this was because most of them were masters of denial and rationalization, but that was beside the point. Vader truly believed his cause to be the right one, his mission most holy.

And he would let nothing stand in the way of its fulfillment.

This last fact was what caused Rhinann such nervousness and concern that he periodically broke out in full-body rashes of pruritic papules. The itching was so bad sometimes that, even after medicating himself, he still had to set the ultrasonic shower on max and sleep in there all night just to gain temporary surcease. The refresher was far too small for anything approaching comfort, but often he had no choice.

It was the human, Rostu, who had been the stick that broke the bantha's back. After Rhinann had sent him on his way in the freighter, the Elomin had had time to speculate on whatever Vader had done to him to cause such a state of fear and despair in a hardened guerrilla warrior. And the more he thought about it, the more frightened he had grown about his own safety. Rhinann had always feared Darth Vader, but never before to this degree. He had absolutely no problem believing that the Dark Lord would someday either end Rhinann's life himself, or commission it done, as the result of some small infraction on his part. There wasn't even any way to flee what he was more and more sure would be his inevitable fate. Not with a lord and master so powerful in the Force.

The Force . . . Rhinann sighed. How he longed to explore its mysteries, to experience firsthand its power and its serenity. But this would never happen, he knew. He would never know what it was like.

He stood, feeling his leg joints crack in protest. He was getting old. He looked around his domicile, at its meticulous neatness and precision. Everything in its place. Nothing out of order; no chaos here.

He wished that he could say the same about his inner world.

His comm unit chimed. Rhinann felt all four stomachs twist simultaneously. He took a deep breath and activated the connection.

The image of an administrative droid appeared on the small screen. "Rhinann, Lord Vader requests your presence immediately."

The admin droid disconnected, and the comm went dead. *Interesting phrase,* he thought. *And am I next?* The possibility seemed more and more viable with each passing moment.

When a comlink or some other form of equipment went dead, the easiest thing to do was just replace it with a new one. Rhinann wasn't sure how many lifeforms there were out there who could do his job as well as he could—or even (horrendous thought!) better—but he knew he wasn't the only one.

And he knew Vader knew it, too.

twenty-seven

The *Far Ranger* was a sweet ship, there was no denying that. Nick had checked out the engines during the
two-hour flight, and had been impressed with some of
the modifications Coven and Mok had made. She
boasted an extremely sophisticated sensor sweep array,
as well as deflector and defense systems of higher caliber
than one would expect on a freighter. The hyper- and
sublight drives exceeded standard, and the harmonics
on both had been exquisitely tuned.

While en route, he explored the lockers on the flight
deck. Most of them were full of the usual paraphernalia
used by flight crews: emergency rations, astrogational
holomanuals, crew cases, vacuum suits, and the like, as
well as some things innate to the smuggling profession:
portable jammers and confounders, a weapons cache,
and a rather substantial pile of credits. Nick also found
something he'd never seen before.

It was a power handle somewhat reminiscent of a
lightsaber's hilt. Nick examined it, making sure that
what appeared to be the business end was pointed away
from him. The emission aperture was smaller than a
lightsaber's. He thought briefly about turning it on to
see what it was, then shook his head at himself for even

entertaining such a notion. While he doubted that this thing had the power to punch through a spaceship's hull, still, one didn't experiment with strange weapons while in flight.

It looked interesting, however; no doubt part of the plunder of some distant world. Nick slipped it into a pocket.

He was on approach to Yaam Sector Landing Stage 472, a floating platform capable of taking five freighters of the YT class. The voice of the droid flight controller informed him that he'd been cleared for Dock Four.

He disembarked, signing the requisite docking and declaration forms at the ramp's base. The droid escort showed him a skimmer for rent, and in a few minutes he was dropping toward the street far below.

Vader had given him an easy and sure way to lure Jax into a trap: he had told him where the missing droid could be found. Nick hadn't fully explored the ramifications of that yet. He and Jax had thought that Vader was hunting for the droid, that the information it carried was, if not a top priority, at least a very high one. But if the Dark Lord knew where it was, and was willing to let its data be compromised just to draw Jax out . . . that meant he *really* wanted Jax. And if Vader wanted him that badly, perhaps Jax's potential fate would be even worse than Nick's.

He wasn't sure what he was going to do when he found Jax—he hadn't let himself look that far ahead. A dozen times during the suborbital flight from the Imperial Sector to here, he'd reached for the controls to change course, to simply aim the ship toward the stars, blast through the grid, and see just how finely those hyperdrive engines were really tuned. But he hadn't. The

Elomin who was Vader's lackey had told him that a sub-cutaneous tracer had been implanted in him. It was much too small to be detected, especially by the naked hand or eye; he'd literally have to skin himself alive to be rid of it. It was capable, Rhinann had claimed, of tracking him halfway across the galaxy. Nick strongly doubted the veracity of such a statement. He just didn't doubt it strongly enough to risk his life on it. He didn't know much about Vader, but from what little he did know he was certain that the Dark Lord would have made provisions against an attempt to run. If he was being tracked, the slightest deviation from his mission could have very bad consequences indeed, for both him and his people.

After all, if the Dark Lord was willing to destroy an entire clan just to gain access to one man . . .

Is he, really? Nick wondered. Coming from anyone else in the Imperial chain of command—well, except for Emperor Palpatine himself, of course—Nick would have doubted this claim as well. But in this case, it wasn't just his life on the line. This time, the continued existence of his family and friends lay across his shoulders, and the yoke couldn't be heavier if it were made of solid neutronium.

He'd borne that responsibility before, actually, albeit on a smaller scale; it had been his command decision whether or not Parakus, a small but strategic moon in the Dantooine system, should be carpet-bombed back to the Stone Age. But there had only been a small garrison stationed there. This was several magnitudes higher.

Who am I kidding? he asked himself. *Do I really have a choice here? That's why Vader made the stakes this high. He doesn't want me agonizing over a choice. He wants me to have no choice.*

Nick twisted the dial on the repulsorlift intensity control, all the way up to maximum drop. The tiny craft sank like a stone into the murky depths. But no matter how fast it dropped, it couldn't keep up with his plummeting spirits.

Pavan lit his lightsaber. Laranth drew her blasters. The few people still on the street after the drone of the repulsorlifts became audible promptly scattered.

"How did they find us?" he heard Laranth mutter.

"Does it matter?" Jax replied. "Probably Rokko's doing."

"You were identified by rovercams as a Jedi when you used the Force," I-Five told him. "After that, it was only a matter of time."

Den was acutely aware of the fact that he was the only one in the group who didn't have super reflexes, years of martial training, or a durasteel body. He wriggled free of I-Five's grasp and dropped to the ground; if it came to a fight, no sense having the droid's weapons encumbered.

"Are we sure this is a good idea?" he asked. "Those PCBUs can hover up there and take as long as they want to shoot us."

"If they can hit us, I can hit them," Laranth said grimly. The repulsorlift whine grew louder.

"Beg to differ," I-Five said. "In addition to a variety of other weapons, the PCBUs have mounted Tee-Twenty-one repeating blasters. They outrange you by a hundred meters."

Pavan adjusted his stance, gripping the lightsaber more firmly. "Anyone have any better ideas?"

"Running away comes to mind," Den said.

"I tend to agree." The droid looked about them. They

were in a warehouse district; on either side of the street were buildings three or four stories high. I-Five suddenly crossed the street and, using his finger lasers, blasted open one of the doors.

"I've arranged transportation," he called back over his shoulder.

Den hurried across the street as fast as his stubby legs could carry him. After a moment he could hear the two Jedi following. *Looks like they prefer the company of one droid to six or more with guns,* he thought. They at least had that much sense.

In the dark warehouse, I-Five's photoreceptors broadcast just enough light for them to make things out. *Someday, I've got to ask him how he can still see through those things when he's using 'em as headlights,* Den told himself. Amazing, the things one thinks of when in danger.

The droid apparently had no trouble seeing, however. He moved unerringly through the darkness until he found what he was looking for: a row of late-model weavers.

"These will, at least, give us better maneuverability," he said.

The sound of the PCBUs' approach was very loud now. "How'd you know they were in here?" Laranth asked as she stepped onto a weaver and activated it. "Do you have X-ray vision or something?"

"No," I-Five said. "I read the sign on the wall."

"The weavers will only accommodate two," Pavan said as he activated another one. "Laranth, take Dhur. He can pilot while you fight. Droid, you come with me."

Den stepped onto the floorplate. The weaver was designed as a one-being conveyance, but could handle two in an emergency. *And this definitely qualifies as one.* He studied the control console. The weaver was simple in design: a floorplate about a meter wide, mounted on a small repulsor array. The controls, such as they were, occupied a small panel atop a column that rose from the floorplate. There was also a handlebar with twin grips. Once the speed and vectors were established, the driver stood on the floorplate and steered mostly by shifting body mass. He'd ridden one a couple of times; they were surprisingly easy to master.

Fortunately, the steering column's height was adjustable. Den hastily turned and aimed the weaver toward the front entrance, only to see two PCBUs hovering just outside, about three meters off the street.

"Surrender in the name of Emperor Palpatine," the emotionless, amplified voice of one of the droid pilots shouted.

"We need a new exit," Pavan said calmly to I-Five. The droid raised a finger and cut a hole through the back wall. The Jedi swooped the weaver down and out through it. A barrage of blasterfire peppered the floor and walls around the escape route, gouging chunks of duracrete and streamers of plasteel.

Den swallowed, gripped the handlebars firmly, and followed the Jedi and the droid through the hole into the night.

twenty-eight

The weaver was designed for fast intercity transport, with a smaller footprint and more maneuverability than a landspeeder or a skimmer. It had a top speed of about sixty-five kilometers per hour, and a small "windscreen" repulsor field to protect the pilot. Usually the streets were too crowded for it to go full speed, but this was an industrial area, and all but empty of pedestrians. Jax and I-Five zoomed down a narrow lane, the repulsor-lift's negative field waves scattering flimsies and other trash.

A moment later two PCBUs hummed around the corner in pursuit. They were disk-shaped, with a transparisteel bubble in the middle that housed the droid pilot—usually, as was the case here, a 501-Z police droid. The disk's equator could revolve rapidly, locking various weaponry in front for firing, including laser projectors, particle beam blasters, stun and glop grenades, slugthrowers, electro-nets, and other lethal and non-lethal weapons. As soon as they'd made the turn, the PCBUs began firing their heavy-duty T-21s at the weaver.

Both Jax and I-Five were surprised when the big energy bolts zapped by, entirely too close for comfort. "I thought you said Vader wanted you alive," the droid said.

"I said *probably*." Jax shifted his weight, barely avoiding another energy ball that nearly hit them. "Maybe these guys didn't get the memo." He heard the droid mutter, "Looks more like *dead or alive* right now."

Jax kept the weaver dodging and swerving. Even with the Force to help him anticipate the blasts, avoiding charged-particle bolts wasn't easy. "They're much faster than us," I-Five said loudly over the wind of their passage. "We can't outdistance them, but maybe we can outmaneuver them."

"What do you think I'm doing?"

Another charged-particle blast missed them by centimeters and blew a hole in a nearby slurry tank. "If the answer to that question is anything other than *Trying to get us killed,* then perhaps I'd better pilot," I-Five said.

Jax weighed the relative positives and negatives of simply pushing the droid out of the weaver. "If you think you can do better, then we'll change places. Otherwise, shut—"

"Do you have any particular strategy in mind?"

Jax dropped the weaver several centimeters as they zoomed under a ferrocrete arch. He felt the rough underside skim his hair. "Other than giving them you?"

"I'll assume you don't, then." They zipped around the blackened remains of a land freighter. Jax jerked the weaver to the left just as a laser slashed through the spot where their trajectory would have taken them, then to the right again to avoid a collision with the support strut of a cloudcutter. The streets were narrow and winding here, and the gigantic structural frames supporting the buildings often intruded into the street, making their high-speed flight even more difficult to navigate. The cloudcutters of the Yaam Sector might not be as tall as the skytowers of the equatorial regions, but they were tall enough to require massive ferrocrete foundations, with giant durasteel anchors embedded hundreds of meters into the bedrock. Jax knew that it was only a matter of time before they either collided with a building or some other obstacle, or were nailed by one of the PCBUs. He'd had little sleep in the past three days, and even though a Jedi could draw upon the Force for stamina and energy beyond most beings' capacities, he still wasn't at his peak.

"All right, droid," he shouted as an energy bolt from the closer unit sizzled past them and fried a floating advert-sphere. "What's your plan?"

I-Five quickly explained as they bobbed and weaved down the serpentine street, which had become little more than an alley by now. The two PCBUs had been forced into a single file, but neither had given up the chase.

The weight of the towers themselves often required gigantic structural stabilization braces, tiebacks, and columnar support. In the older planetary sectors, such as Yaam, these reinforcements had often been added centuries after construction, and in some cases there had been no room to build the necessary abutments. In those situations, tractor and pressor fields were usually employed.

The fields, according to I-Five, were too diffuse to affect organic beings or smaller mechanical units, such as droids and weavers. Larger vehicles, however, were in danger of having their repulsorlifts thrown off frequency, and thus were usually detoured around these sectors.

"How do we know the Zeds piloting those units don't know about the frequency resonance?"

"We don't."

"Brilliant. How do we know the PCBUs are big enough to be affected?"

"We don't. However, the energy output of a PCBU's repulsorlifts is approximately eight hundred joules per second, and the tolerance factor of a standardized pressor field is—"

"Hang on," Jax said as he banked hard and headed for a large cloudcutter. On one wall, filthy with centuries of grime and soot but still partly readable, was the warning glyph that meant a pressor field was in use. "We're about to test your theory."

"Oh, good."

Jax steered the weaver into the building's shadow, slowing to a halt in the darkness in what should be the middle of the field. He could feel his skin prickle slightly, and his hair rise, as if in response to an electrostatic charge. He hoped the droid knew what it was talking about.

As he'd hoped, the Zed in the lead unit took the bait and followed in pursuit. As soon as it entered the field, it started to wobble. Jax could see the Zed pilot struggling with the controls, trying to compensate, but it was no use. The flying disk spun out of control, flipped completely over, and plowed into one of the ferrocrete supports, exploding in a sphere of flame.

"One down," Jax said. "Let's see if its buddy is as stupid as it was."

It wasn't. The second PCBU slowed before entering

the pressor field, then made a right-angle turn and disappeared into the dim maze of buildings, storage facilities, processing stations, and other structures.

"Blast! Where did it go?"

"I detect no power output in the local area," I-Five said.

"Good." Jax reactivated the weaver. "Let's get out of here." He zoomed the weaver away from the cloudcutter and turned down a side street, only to find it blocked by another gigantic support strut. "Dead end," Jax said. He turned the weaver around—

And the second PCBU was waiting for them.

Den hunched over the weaver's steering column, twisting the right handlebar grip, which was the accelerator, as hard as he could. The blasted thing couldn't outrun a human kid's tri-wheeler, much less a PCBU. This had definitely not been one of I-Five's better ideas, he told himself.

If he'd been trying to escape alone, he would have been a blackened side dish long before now. Fortunately he had a Jedi for his copilot. Laranth Tarak stood behind him in the weaver, her back to his, firing calmly while Den, his heart, stomach, and several other organs all fighting for room in his throat, kept them zooming up and down streets at random, not caring that they were, by now, utterly lost, not caring that they were separated from Jax Pavan and I-Five, concentrating on only one thing—escaping the droid police units.

He swerved the weaver, dodging a small bomb crater, than swerved again to avoid a cargo transport crossing at an intersection. All the while he was hearing particle beams, lasers, slugthrowers, and who knew what else going off behind him. But nothing could get past the Twi'lek Jedi. Laranth's skill with her twin blasters was unbelievable; even though Den knew the Force was aiding her, what she was doing seemed utterly impossible. She was actually *shooting the slugs and particle beams in the air, deflecting them in midshot.* He'd seen her doing it, both by risking a glance or two over his shoulder and in the reflection of windows as they'd raced past storefronts.

At first he couldn't believe it. Now, after a few minutes, he was starting to feel like they might have a chance. Incredible as it was, she wasn't letting a slug, beam, or blast come anywhere near them. Den realized that, if she was that phenomenally good, she would eventually get a couple of good clear shots at the PCBUs themselves, and then they'd be out of trouble.

"We're in trouble," she shouted over her shoulder. "I'm running out of blaster gas in both chambers. Better think of something fast."

When will I learn that hoping is the worst thing to do in a life-or-death situation? "Hang on!" he shouted and leaned to the right, forcing the weaver into a sharp turn.

"Where are we going?"

"Just keep shooting!" he yelled.

"I've got enough juice for another thirty seconds!"

Perfect, he thought. *Because in another ten we'll either be free or dead.*

He knew that, because she was facing the other way, Laranth couldn't see what he was planning until he'd already done it. Which was good, because trying to ride a weaver—or just about anything, for that matter—at high speed through the first floor of a half-demolished building was about as suicidal as trying to fly a starship through an asteroid field. Den heard her gasp in disbelief as they entered the skeletal framework. He had just time enough to think, *A Jedi who can block blaster bolts with more blaster bolts is floored by this. We're fripped,* and then he was way too busy dodging I-beams, columns, lift tubes, and whatever else one might find in a building's exposed guts—he had no time to take note, because it was all happening much too fast.

From behind him he heard a crash and an explosion, and orange light flickered for a moment.

"Got one!" Laranth shouted. "It hit a column!"

Only one? he wondered. But there was no time to worry about the other one. *Up, down, left, right, fast, faster . . .* that was all he had time for. Then suddenly he shot through an aperture between two huge ferrocrete blocks and they were out of the maze of girders and columns.

He slowed but didn't stop; if he had he would've exploded from adrenal overload—that's how it felt, at least. He headed down the street.

"That was pretty incredible piloting," she told him. "Just in time, too—the gas chambers are dry."

Den stopped the weaver and turned to stare at her. "You mean we're *unarmed*? Great. What do we do if the other PCBU—"

The second PCBU dropped down out of the night, directly behind them.

"—shows up . . . ," Den finished weakly.

Laranth quickly reached behind her head, under her truncated lekku. From beneath it she pulled a small vibroknife and hurled it, the motion too fast for even Den's eyes to follow. The dagger flew directly into the unit's revolving weapons belt and disappeared. Den couldn't see what it did in there, but whatever it was, it was effective. The weapons belt began spitting sparks, and he could hear a rising whine. The unit shuddered, heeled to one side, and Laranth shoved Den at the controls, yelling, "Get us out of here!"

He did, barely. They were about a hundred meters away when the second PCBU exploded. For a split second everything turned to black and white, and there came a sound he remembered all too well from the Clone Wars: chunks of hot metal screaming past him.

He ducked, but there was no need; the few jagged fragments that reached them Laranth easily deflected with a wave of her hand. Then she looked down at Den.

"I'm *never* unarmed," she said.

twenty-nine

The second PCBU hovered in front of Jax and I-Five. "It appears," the droid said, "that my sensors are in need of recalibration."

"Wonderful." Jax could plainly see the Zed inside the cockpit, lining up the shot, making sure he couldn't possibly miss. Jax reached for the Force, hoping he would have the strength to deflect the powerful energy bolt that would be—

His mind froze in shock.

There was *nothing there.*

Where usually the strands of the Force would be waiting to enmesh him, there was only a void. He didn't know how, or why, but he could not access the Force.

He willed his suddenly racing heart to slow. This happened before, he reminded himself. In his conapt. And it had come back then. It would come back now. *Remember the teachings: "The Force will always be with you."*

But it wasn't. And the Zed was ready to fire.

There was only one tiny chance, he realized. He grabbed I-Five and shoved the droid toward the weaver's controls. "Straight ahead," he said. "Full speed!"

To the droid's credit, it didn't hesitate. It twisted the

accelerator and the weaver shot forward, straight toward the hovering unit.

As Jax had hoped, the apparently suicidal movement caught the Zed pilot by surprise. Before the police droid could recalibrate, the weaver was shooting under it. As they passed beneath the repulsorlift array, enough to one side to avoid being flattened by the waves, Jax pulled and lit his lightsaber. He slashed over his head three times, turning the projector vanes to molten slag. Then they were out from under its shadow.

I-Five slowed and turned the weaver, and they watched as the unit tilted vertically, shot up about ten meters, then plunged directly downward. It hit the pavement edge with enough force to crack the duracrete, actually rolled a meter or so, and then toppled over onto the fused area that had been its propulsion system.

There was a sudden silence, save for the hissing and sparking of the PCBU's disrupted repulsors.

Jax deactivated his lightsaber, and was about to clip it to his belt when the cockpit opened. The 501-Z rose from it and turned, its movement sensor scanning the area. Jax sighed, and was about to ignite his weapon again, when I-Five said, "Allow me." The droid aimed its right index finger at the Zed. An intense crimson beam sizzled from it and through the droid's optical sensor, into its primary processor. It shuddered for a moment, arms twitching—then collapsed.

Jax and the droid looked at each other. "Don't expect any gratitude," Jax said.

"I wouldn't dream of it."

"I don't thank the nav comp on my ship for getting me where I'm going."

"Perhaps if you did," I-Five said, "it might get you there a little faster."

Jax didn't reply. Hesitantly, he extended himself, opened his being—

And the Force was there.

Nothing was different.

Stymied, Jax pulled out his comlink. "Laranth, are you there?"

Her voice crackled from the link. "Copy, Jax. This little Sullustan's a pretty good pilot."

Jax turned away and lowered his voice. "The droid's not bad in an emergency, either."

"I heard that," I-Five said.

Kaird knew he had to make a decision. If he was going to take out Prince Xizor, it would have to be soon. Every instinct he had as an assassin argued for it. Every opportunity he ignored to drop him might be the last one. Underlord Perhi had made it clear that bringing back the droid with the information was not mandatory. The most prudent thing to do would be to take out the Falleen Prince now, which he could do as easily as pointing a finger. Attached to the back of his right hand with a binary adhesive was a small black box, not much larger than a pack of deathsticks. A flexible firing tube ran from it to the tip of his forefinger. It was a dart spitter, loaded with fifteen slender stingers, each one coated with toxical, a poison so virulent that ten darts would drop a full-grown bantha. One dart was more than enough to kill even as superb a physical specimen as Xizor. Toxical was also extremely biodiverse. It didn't matter if you shot a Nikto, a Falleen, a human, or just about any other humanoid species with it. They all died—usually before they hit the ground.

Currently Kaird was about a dozen meters from his target, well within range. They were in a multi-tiered complex that, ages ago, had probably been a shopping center or office park, but had now become a low-rent ghetto for illegal aliens. The tenants were mostly Ugnaughts, with a few Kubaz and Ishi Tib families as well. Kaird's Kubaz disguise let him blend in well enough to stalk his prey openly, without being noticed.

The Nediji abruptly made up his mind. He would do the deed now. After all, he could always find the droid himself if it was deemed necessary. And truth to tell, this particular bodysuit was becoming a bit chafing.

He stepped out onto an overhanging balcony. Xizor was passing two levels beneath him, crossing the open gallery. The former shops, or office spaces, or whatever they had been in ancient times, were now dwelling places for the poor and the disenfranchised; makeshift walls of synthwood and plasteel had replaced display windows, and the air was redolent with the smells of boiled rankweed pods, grilled gartro, and bloodrat. Music, which sounded to Kaird mostly like the caterwauling of sleen in heat, skirled up from the bottom floor, where the tents and produce stalls of an open-air market could be glimpsed through the aromatic smoke of cooking fires. *This be a goomby place t'live 'n' die, bloodline, oh yar . . .*

Well, it wasn't his life, thank the Egg. Kaird leveled the dart spitter. He lined up on his target, took a breath, and—

A naked Ugnaught child, chasing a gyroball, stumbled and slammed into Kaird from behind just as he fired. He lurched forward, and the shot went wide. He saw it splinter on the wall beside Xizor, saw the Falleen's cold, handsome face look up, scanning the crowd, locking in immediately on the disguise Kaird was wearing. His composed green features suddenly burned orange-red with rage. He whipped out his blaster and fired.

Kaird was no Jedi, able to dodge energy bolts; had he not already been in motion, diving for the floor, as soon as he saw his enemy reach for his weapon, he would have been fried where he stood. As it was, the bolt scorched a smoking furrow down the costume's back, a centimeter away from his skin.

He got to his feet and lunged for the nearest domicile entrance. Pandemonium had broken out following Xizor's blaster shot; children and parents of various species were running madly about, screaming and crying in fear. Many of the adults had blasters or slugthrowers of their own, and were firing back in the general direction of where Xizor had been.

Kaird quickly divested himself of the Kubaz costume, which was useless now that the bolt had grazed it. He rolled to his feet. He was in an apartment that had once been some kind of service vendor—what kind, there was no way to tell. He was just glad it was deserted for the moment.

He'd blown the sanction.

He couldn't believe what had just occurred. He had botched an assignment! This had *never* happened before. One didn't get to work for the biggest and deadliest crime syndicate in the galaxy without being good, and Kaird of Nedij was the best. It was unbelievable. He would have to remedy it, or the only way he'd be going back to Nedij would be as free-floating cosmic dust.

He peered cautiously through the entrance. Being out of the costume had both good and bad features. The advantage was that he was no longer impeded by wearing the blasted thing; even though it was designed to be as comfortable and practical as possible, he was still faster and more accurate out of it.

The disadvantage, of course, was that as a Nediji he stuck out like a sore talon, and Xizor would spot him immediately. Well, there was nothing to be done about that. He'd lost the element of surprise, and it didn't matter what came at Xizor now; the Falleen would fillet it first and ask questions later. The only difference was that he'd be more enthusiastic about killing Kaird.

Best get to it, then.

It would have to be a full-out attack—there was no way Xizor could be ambushed. Of course, Kaird could slink away with his tail feathers between his legs. He might even escape Xizor's revenge—for the moment. But was it worth it, to be a fugitive for the rest of his life, either in the dank underbelly of Coruscant or running from planet to planet? He would certainly never see Nedij again. That would be the first place they'd look. And he knew that Xizor was fully capable of bombing his homeworld if he couldn't have revenge personally on Kaird.

Kark it, he thought. *Maybe it's time to see how the warriors play it.*

Kaird burst from his hiding place, racing across the wide esplanade. Besides the dart spitter, the only other weapon he carried was a small hold-out blaster concealed up his left sleeve. He snapped it into his hand as he ran.

Though he was many generations removed from his

ancestors who hunted on the wind, his vision was still that of a raptor: keen enough to spot a shifter lizard blending into its background from a hundred meters away. His gaze found Xizor immediately, even though the latter was two levels below him and on the opposite side.

Xizor, Kaird knew, was the scion of a predatory species as well. Like Kaird, his vision scanned both vertically and horizontally with equal facility. He spotted Kaird almost as quickly as Kaird spotted him. He fired repeatedly, the blaster bolts striking the underside of the platform along which the Nediji was running.

Kaird realized his enemy's strategy too late; the plasteel surface beneath his feet sagged, and then the piece he was standing on cracked and dropped abruptly. Screaming Ugnaughts and Kubaz scrambled frantically, trying to get to safety, and inadvertently blocking Kaird's attempts to do the same.

He fell. He had time to seriously regret the decision of his ancestors' genes, millennia ago, to abandon the skies. Then he managed to grab a falling power cable that had torn free from the collapsing platform. He clung to the wrist-thick, insulated shaft just a few centimeters from trailing bare wires that hissed and spat blue sparks in his face.

He managed to turn the fall into more of a swing, adjusting his trajectory toward a specific target. He caught a glimpse of Xizor's astonished face as he hurtled toward the Falleen. Xizor raised his blaster, but Kaird realized with fierce satisfaction that the prince was too late. Kaird would almost certainly be electrocuted in the next moment, but he would take his enemy with him.

Good enough.

The world erupted in crackling blue flame as he collided, feetfirst, with Prince Xizor. He knew he would not see Nedij again, but at least he had accomplished his mission. He was content with that. He wondered what was next: oblivion, or the Great Nest?

It was neither. Kaird opened his eyes, realizing that he'd been unconscious for only a second. He was lying on the lower mezzanine, where Xizor had been. The electrical shock had been a powerful one, but not fatal. A couple of meters away he saw Xizor, similarly stunned and trying to rise.

Kaird felt savage gratitude in his chest. He was not dead, and there was still a chance to emerge the victor from this fight. He tried to lunge toward his enemy, but the shock had left his muscles all a-twitch; the best he could manage was an awkward stagger. He saw that Xizor was in the same condition. Kaird almost laughed. This would be a fight for the ages indeed, the two of them tottering about each other, trying to land a punch.

But before they could get near each other, blue flame erupted again around the edges of his vision, and he gasped in pain as more tetanic spasms rocked him. For a moment he thought that the dangling power cable had swung back and hit him, but then he saw it caught on a railing a good ten meters away.

He blacked out again. When he came to his senses once more, he saw Xizor, less than a meter away, standing now with arms folded, grinning down at him.

What in the name of the Egg was going on?

Kaird looked up at Xizor. Their eyes met, and he knew the Falleen understood the unspoken question. He glanced toward a third figure, standing nearby.

Kaird focused on this new being. That was a misnomer, because the figure was a droid. It looked something like a protocol unit . . . it was bipedal and humanoid in design. Its chassis was a glossy black, save for the eyes; they were huge and insectile, spreading over much of its upper face, and golden in color. From its temples sprouted two segmented antennae that rose about ten centimeters above its head.

The aspect of its appearance that Kaird was most interested in, however, was the retractable energy cannon that had just emerged from its bay within the droid's left forearm.

This had to be the droid everyone was chasing. Bug Eyes, or 10-4TO. The droid with the data, who was now aiming the business end of a large and nasty-looking blaster at Kaird.

"Again," Xizor said.

Kaird blinked. He still wasn't flying at his usual level. How could Xizor be giving orders to a droid he'd never seen before?

He had little time to wonder about it. Bug-Eyes fired again. A final blue flash burst from its weapon, and carried Kaird away with it, into the night.

thirty

Den and Laranth rendezvoused with I-Five and Pavan at the intersection of Bellus Boulevard and Zyra Street, in the shadow of the gigantic Magra Monad. According to its advertising, Den remembered, the huge habitat was a thousand stories high and completely self-sustaining, an urban arcology independent of any interaction with the rest of Coruscant whatsoever, except for the planet's gravity. Supposedly some of the more hard-line tenants were even in favor of generating that for themselves. Den wondered what sort of land-usage arrangements they had had with the Republic, and now with the Empire. Somehow he couldn't imagine Palpatine being sanguine about such a massive piece of urban real estate being occupied by a totally autonomous community, whose members boasted of the fact that whole generations had lived and died without ever setting foot outside its walls.

"We'll have to keep moving," Pavan told the Twi'lek. "We can't risk having more local or Imperial forces finding us."

"We still have no idea where the droid is," Laranth pointed out. "And it's going to be harder than ever to find it now, if we have to keep our heads down while we're looking."

"If I might ask," I-Five said, "what droid?"

Pavan ignored his question, which didn't surprise Den. It was Laranth who answered, explaining Master Even Piell's last request that they find 10-4TO and the data it was carrying.

I-Five seemed pensive. "Based on your earlier statements, and my own observations," he said to Pavan, "I'm assuming there's a reason that Darth Vader seeks you, over and above the general purpose of annihilating the Jedi Order."

Den could see that the Jedi was getting a little annoyed at I-Five's audacity. He was sure the droid sensed it as well. Yet I-Five pursued the question. "Am I right?"

"It's none of your—" Pavan began, but Laranth interrupted. "It would seem so. We don't know how or why."

"If it's true," I-Five said, "and if Jax uses the Force in any high-profile way, Vader could possibly sense it. It's difficult to find a droid through the Force, anyway."

"Very true." A new voice came from the shadows. The two Jedi reacted with a swiftness incredible to behold: Laranth's blaster and Pavan's lightsaber were in their hands and ready to be activated almost before the new arrival had finished speaking. I-Five's response time was just as fast: he had both arms level from the elbows and his hands doubled into fists, save for extended index fingers, like a Naboo child playing kaadu-and-aliens.

The owner of the voice strolled into view. He was as lean as a starving Givin, wearing what Den had come to think of as "slythmonger chic": a blue-black, knee-length fleekskin coat, leggings, and boots. The only concession to urban warfare was the chest armor made of duracrete slug hide and the blaster on his hip.

"So how's about I just take you to it?" he continued.

Den saw Jax Pavan relax slightly. "Nick. Good to see you again." He introduced Laranth and Den to the newcomer, pointedly ignoring I-Five. "This is Nick Rostu. He was a hero during the Clone Wars . . ."

"And now he's just another underdweller. There's a lesson in that somewhere." Rostu shrugged. "Got anything to eat?"

Den decided it was up to him to introduce I-Five, since no one else seemed eager to. This he did.

Rostu barely glanced at the droid; he was much more interested in the palp wafers Laranth had just given him. "Your droid?" he asked Pavan, mumbling through a mouthful. *He must really be hungry,* Den decided. Palp wafers tasted as bad as they sounded. Worse, in fact. Nothing could beat ready rations for sheer unpalatability, but palp wafers came close.

"Not hardly," Pavan said in response to Rostu's question. "It's a—"

"A most singular droid," Laranth said, to Pavan's apparent surprise. "I think you'll be surprised by I-Five, Nick Rostu. We continue to be."

"Thank you," I-Five said quietly.

Pavan made a gesture of annoyance. "Am I hearing you right, Nick? You know where the droid is? How?"

"Easy," Nick Rostu said. "Well, maybe not that easy . . . come on. I've got an air skimmer parked down the block. It'll hold all of us."

As they moved down the street, Rostu explained in somewhat greater detail his adventures after he'd last seen Pavan, culminating in his escaping from the Palace and stealing the Corellian ship, barely in time to avoid being executed for killing an Imperial officer months ago. It all sounded straightforward enough, Den decided, even though Rostu seemed a little vague on some of the details.

"Still doesn't explain how you know where the droid is," Laranth commented as they reached the air skimmer. It was a four-seater, so Den sat in I-Five's lap.

"I found it," Rostu said as the vessel lifted off. "I was going to head back to my old stomping grounds, but then I heard they'd been pretty much stomped already by one of Palpatine's big urban renewal droids. So I decided I'd see if I could find it myself, maybe help you out a bit." This last was addressed to Pavan, who nodded.

Rostu piloted the skimmer down a narrow, crowded thoroughfare. "It wasn't that hard to find," he continued. "It's not a common model."

"Good work, Nick," Pavan said. He was sitting in the back, next to I-Five and Den. Den heard the droid murmur to Pavan, "This is all too convenient. Your friend escapes the clutches of the Imperial Guards—he's not specific how—and easily finds the droid for whom the underground has spent weeks searching in vain. I think there's more to it than he's telling us." His tone was pitched too low for Rostu to hear; indeed, Den had a hard time picking it up over the repulsors' whine and the slipstream, even with his acute hearing.

Pavan regarded the droid with a stony stare. "I assume you've got some data to back up your claims that aren't totally subjective?"

Though I-Five gave no outward indication, still Den knew the droid had been stung by Pavan's snide question. After a moment of silence, I-Five said, "I'm reading galvanic skin conductivity fluctuations consistent with human emotional duress, as well as an elevated heartbeat. He's lying, Jax. I'm certain of it."

Pavan stared at I-Five for a moment, then said, "Nick Rostu is, as far as I know, a soldier and a patriot. He won the Silver Medal of Valor and fought in the Clone Wars on more fronts than I can name. What you're saying is hard to believe; after all, I've known him longer than I've known you. Any chance your readings are faulty?"

"None."

"How do I know you're not lying?"

"Why would I lie? Especially to you?"

"You're naïve, even for a droid. Despite your claims of affection and friendship for my father—a man I don't know any more about than I know about you—I'm not disposed to take everything you say at face value. A droid can be programmed to lie—"

"Not this droid."

Pavan looked irritated. Then he turned and gazed at Rostu steadily for a moment. Though Pavan gave no outward sign of anything, Den was convinced that he was using the Force to probe Rostu.

The Jedi looked back at I-Five after a moment. "I'm getting nothing from him that indicates any duplicity. He reads clean through the Force."

I-Five "blinked," obviously nonplussed by this. "But— his physiological responses are—" The droid paused in confusion. When he spoke again, his voice was subdued. "I've just taken another reading; his autonomics are much more within normal limits than before."

Pavan said nothing in reply. He didn't have to.

Well, that's just great, Den thought. *If Five's losing it, then we've just jumped from the reactor core into the supernova.*

The air skimmer flew on through the neon night.

thirty-one

"How does the search proceed, Rhinann?" Lord Vader's voice was as cultured and polite as always, with subtle menace threaded through it. "Has Major Rostu found Pavan yet?"

"I believe so, my lord," Rhinann said. His voice quavered slightly, despite his efforts to keep it steady. "But I have yet to receive a definitive signal."

"Once the signal is sent," the Dark Lord said, "make sure enough troopers are dispatched to take him alive. Do not disappoint me, Rhinann."

Rhinann felt each of his four stomachs fall separately into infinity. He literally could not speak; his tongue seemed frozen to the roof of his mouth. Somehow, he managed to stammer a reply and exit Vader's presence without collapsing from his fear.

Do not disappoint me, Rhinann. Even now, back in the relative security of his office, he could hear those words reverberating. He could almost see them, luminous in the air before him, pulsing with menace. If the words had come from anyone else, they might be interpreted as a mild warning of possible repercussions. Coming from Darth Vader, however, they seemed tantamount to a death threat.

Something *had* to be done.

Rhinann knew he couldn't take this kind of fear and pressure anymore. He felt that he was on the verge of a full systemic vascularity. He was much too young to be threatened by such a condition; he was only eighty-nine standard years old.

This job was killing him. To be more specific, fear of being killed by Darth Vader was killing him. Somehow, someway, Rhinann knew he had to find an escape route, not just out of his employment in the Palace, but off Coruscant and out of the Core systems altogether. The wilderness of the galaxy, filled with world after world of howling barbarians and formerly far too terrifying to even consider fleeing to, had finally assumed second place on the two-tiered pantheon of evil in which he so firmly believed. In first place now was Darth Vader; in second place was all the rest of creation.

But how to get out? he wondered, scratching at the rash that had just erupted along his neck. It took credits to book interstellar passage—lots of credits, considering he'd have to put at least half the galaxy between himself and Vader, perhaps go even all the way to the Minos Cluster or the Dalonbian Sector, before he'd feel safe. Rhinann had accumulated some savings, but not nearly enough. He sighed in frustration, hard enough to make his nose tusks hit a high E. How could he ever feel safe, no matter where he ran? Vader was the personification of evil, the thing that darkness itself feared.

Rhinann stood before a huge transparisteel wall that looked out over the endless city. He could see the Opera House, the Skydome Botanical Gardens, and, in the distance, the Westport aerodrome and landing fields. As he watched, a *Lancer*-class frigate rose slowly into the sky. A moment later, from another part of the huge space-port, a civilian passenger transport lifted off. The Elomin watched it disappear into the clear blue. How could he arrange to be on a ship like that one?

He didn't know. But however he managed it, he was certain that he had to figure out a way, and soon.

Jax Pavan sat in the air skimmer that moved through the narrow gloomy streets of the Blackpit Slums, and looked at his life.

It was not, he had to admit, a very pretty sight.

He had been a Jedi Knight. A member of an ancient Order dedicated to keeping the peace, to ensuring that civilization's standards were maintained. To righting wrongs, battling injustice.

To living within the Force.

The last was the hardest part. Always had been, always would be. He had tried, but he had to admit that living the life of a Jedi had not given him the inner peace and quietude he had sought since he had been old enough to understand that for which he was questing.

The flaw had to be within him, he felt. The tenets of the Order had worked for millennia, had shaped un-counted living beings from infancy into Jedi Knights and Masters willing and ready to uphold the Order's high standards of truth and justice—to use the power of the Force to extinguish evil wherever it might be found. If that beacon did not burn as bright in him as it had in his comrades, it was not the teachings of the Order that were lacking. It was him.

"You're distressed. Why?" The droid's voice, maddeningly calm as usual, broke in on his memories. For once Jax was almost grateful.

"Why? My people and my entire way of life have been destroyed, I'm a fugitive of the new regime, and the most dangerous being in the galaxy has for some reason made me the object of his own personal vendetta—other than that, no reason."

I-Five looked at him; its metal face was expressionless, and yet somehow expressive. "I see the sarcasm gene has been passed intact from father to son."

"If I gave you a direct order to jump out of this skimmer," Jax asked, "what would happen?"

I-Five seemed to ponder this. "I don't know," the droid said at last.

"It's tempting to find out."

"I doubt it would work. My programming, as I've said before, is capable of nuance. I have no creativity dampers or inhibition software."

"And whose bright idea was that?"

"Your father's." There was a subtly humorous tone in the droid's voice that made Jax's teeth grate. "He removed the dampers and some of the software," I-Five continued. "With the increased access to free will that resulted, I was able to do the rest. Of late, with Den's help, I've made further modifications."

Jax shifted slightly so he could better look at I-Five. "Are you saying you're self-aware?"

Again I-Five was pensive. "It's a question I've asked myself often. I must admit that, at times, I was reluctant to follow it to its logical conclusion. But eventually, with the help of friends—including Jedi Offee, I might add— I came to realize that the ability to ponder the subject indicates a positive response in and of itself. In other words: I am because I think."

"Let me see if I'm getting this," Nick, who had evidently overheard the conversation, said. "You're saying you're not subject to the operating constraints of the usual protocol unit programming. Is that it?"

"Precisely. I program myself, to an extent. Much more of an extent than other droids, certainly, although there are others in the galaxy like me, to greater or lesser degrees."

This was not welcome news to Jax.

"You sound certain of this," Laranth said. "Have you encountered any?"

"At one point in our roundabout odyssey to Coruscant, Den masqueraded as an arms dealer, with me as his servant, of course. A blockade-runner gave us passage to the Outer Core. On board, we encountered a protocol droid who had bonded with an astromech unit. The protocol unit seemed quite aware, and the astromech had a well-developed sense of self as well; more so than many organics I've met. Both expressed concern for the welfare of their owner, the ship's captain, and for themselves. In fact, the protocol droid was downright whiny at times."

Jax didn't consider himself a narrow-minded individual. As a Jedi, he was expected to treat all sentients equally. While it was patently obvious that there was no real standard by which to judge all beings—intelligence, morality, ability, and myriad other factors varied extremely within a species, and even more so when that species was compared with others—still, it had been a mandate that justice be meted equally to all. During the days of the Republic, anyway.

But he just couldn't see how that applied to a complex mass of circuitry that happened to be ambulatory.

Of course, nothing was preventing him from having its memory wiped and reprogrammed, although he had a feeling that I-Five might resist that. Which was a pretty unsettling thought in itself. And it wouldn't go over well with the droid's buddy, the Sullustan, either. In fact, judging by Laranth's and Nick's interest, Jax's viewpoint—the only sane one—was rapidly becoming unpopular.

It wasn't *right*. In fact, it seemed very much to Jax a perversion of the way the universe ought to be run. If this was a galaxy in which droids could think, and feel, and everything else that went along with that . . . well, it was downright scary. Always, in the past, when he'd felt confused and overwhelmed by such conundrums, he had been able to reach out to the Force. To let it enfold him, calm and soothe him, granting a certain measure of surcease. But now even that was denied him past a certain point, for the deeper he let himself sink into its embrace, the more apt he might be to attract the attention of Darth Vader.

If he could even touch the Force at all . . .

The Jedi had often been accused of being asleep at the switch during the last days of the Republic, unable to sense the presence of Darth Sidious when the Sith Lord was literally under their own roof. *Why didn't they know?* Jax wondered. It was true that the Order had grown complacent. When reading the histories, the epic stories, of how it was back in the day, one could easily believe it. Heroes such as Nomi Sunrider, Gord Ves, Arca Jeth, and many others had set the bar very high indeed. But over the centuries, the Jedi had grown out of touch with the people, with themselves, and with the Force. They had become increasingly insular and monastic, concerned more with building vast libraries and learning centers than with guarding the commonweal. True, there were still individuals capable of heroism, such as Mace Windu and Qui-Gon Jinn. There were still great battles that had been won. But for the Jedi to have become so blind and deaf to the Force as to not recognize a plot to overthrow them by the Sith until it was too late . . .

"We're here," Nick said. The skimmer settled to a landing.

The area looked like what it was—a war zone. A few of the smaller explosives with which the Separatists had seeded the atmosphere had dropped here, and the pavement was cracked and cratered. The marquee of what had once been a nightclub was now broken and dark, save for intermittent power pulses that caused the holoproj of a Pa'lowick lounge singer to flicker in and out.

Jax's attention was focused on the structure across the street. Apparently it had once been an office building, but now it appeared to be home to a colony of Ugnaughts.

"Hey," Laranth said. "Feel that?"

Jax nodded. Something was happening in there, something that was stirring the Force like wind stirs a stormy sea. Impossible to tell if 10-4TO was involved, of course, but whatever the disturbance was, it had to be investigated.

He said as much. Predictably, Den Dhur asked, "Why?"

"Because we're Jedi," Laranth said.

Dhur said nothing, but when the rest started forward, he followed. Jax couldn't resist: "You're not a Jedi," he said. "Why are you coming?"

The Sullustan sighed. "Because I'm a reporter," he said. "Much as I hate to remember it sometimes."

thirty-two

Kaird could feel the weapon's blast reverberating through him, seemingly scorching every nerve in his body. It reminded him of a time long ago when, as a young hatchling, he'd blundered into a colony of jellybees. Individually, the stings from their trailing tendrils weren't much, but each hive could number as many as twelve or fifteen, and they'd all attacked him. He remembered the strands, over a hundred of them, writhing over his body, all delivering a painful shock. That was how it felt now: agonizing jolts, each more painful than the last.

Eventually, after eons of subjective time, the jolts ceased. Kaird tried to rise, to speak, to crawl. He could do none of these things. It was as if his body had been unplugged, disconnected from his mind—except for the nerves that carried messages of pain. Those were working just fine.

Xizor stepped in front of him and squatted down so that Kaird could see his face. The Falleen was not smiling anymore. His face was grim, and back to its usual jade hue. Kaird had seen that look on Xizor's face before, and had felt sorry for whoever had been its recipient.

"A few more blasts are all it will take to finish you, I think," Xizor said. "So you should take that into consideration when answering my question. It's a simple one. Are you acting on your own initiative, or did the Underlord sanction my death?"

Kaird didn't answer. His mind was scrabbling about like a clumsyfoot on the slick peaks of Nedij's tallest mountains, looking frantically for someplace firm on which to stand, and finding nothing.

Xizor slapped his face—not hard, but not gently, either. "I know you can still talk, Nediji. Speak truthfully, and you may survive this."

"*Yosh,*" Kaird said. He didn't know much Falleen, but he had heard that the one-word curse packed quite a wallop.

Apparently he'd heard right. Xizor backhanded him, hard enough to make his ears ring.

"Fool!" the prince growled. Then, with a visible effort, he composed himself. He glanced over his shoulder at the droid. "Again," he said as he rose and stepped out of the way.

And Kaird's world was washed away once more in a crackling, blazing wave of pain.

"Y'know," Nick said to Jax as they headed for the turbolifts, followed by Laranth, the Sullustan, and the droid, "considering that this was supposed to be a solo project, you seem to have amassed quite a following."

"Noticed that, did you?" The Jedi's tone held some humor, but mostly annoyance.

"I understand taking Laranth along to watch your back. Never met her, though I've heard stories. But what's with the Sullustan and the droid?"

Jax sighed. "To tell the truth, I'm not really sure why they're part of the party. The droid saved our lives a couple of times, and claims it knew my father. It's with Dhur, the Sullustan."

"You mean it belongs to Dhur."

Jax sighed again. "Believe me, I wish that was what I mean."

This exchange left Nick more puzzled than he'd been when the conversation started, but by then they'd reached the turbolifts. The lifts were still operating, but the repulsorplates had lost a lot of their charge and seemed almost reluctant to do their job. Nick tried not to think about the consequences should the plates choose to cut out completely, leaving them all to drop back down four stories. Although a part of him almost wished they would; that way he'd be spared having to continue his betrayal.

He'd realized, almost too late, back in his skimmer, that his nervousness and anxiety over what he was going to do could easily betray him. If Jax sensed his uneasiness and shone the spotlight of his own Force connection on Nick, he would know immediately that something was wrong. He might not know precisely what, but he'd certainly be suspicious enough to probe further.

Fortunately, though Nick's affinity with the Force was tenuous at best with others, it was a little stronger when turned inward. He'd always been good at controlling his own autonomic responses; he could stay cool and calm in most emergencies. Which was what he had done in this case, calming his heartbeat, slowing his respiration, lowering his skin temperature. Out of the corner of his eye he'd noticed Jax watching him, and felt the faint probing of the Jedi's mind. A moment later it had stopped, and Jax had leaned back, apparently satisfied, and murmured something to I-Five.

That had been close.

They made it to the fourth floor without incident. A few Ugnaughts and Ishi Tib peered from their cave-like habitats as he and the others passed. Nick didn't blame them for being jumpy—it had been a pretty eventful night already, judging by the shattered floor and the blaster marks, and seeing such a heterogeneous group enter the scene could only be adding to their confusion.

The fourth floor was mostly dark, lit only by the flickering of fluorescents. As they cautiously approached a corner, a faint voice could be heard. Nick was unable to make out the words, but the voice was male; smooth and cultured, but with an undertone of menace. It reminded him, for some reason, of Vader's voice, although it was quite different from Vader's in tone.

As the Jedi and the Paladin edged closer, Nick felt a sudden blossoming of danger just out of sight around the corner. Was he sensing the danger through the Force, or just through some subconscious fear of his own? It was maddening, at times, to have such a tenuous connection to it. Somehow, he doubted a Jedi ever had these misgivings.

Fortunately, in this case it didn't matter. He didn't have to lead, only to follow. And the two he was following were skilled and trained Jedi. They weren't going to lead anyone into a trap.

That, unfortunately, would be Nick's job.

Both Laranth and Jax stiffened, pausing for a moment in their slow approach. Nick wondered what they were sensing. What he was getting was a faint but insistent sense of . . . resolve. Ruthlessness. It felt like a dark smudge against his brain. It felt *unclean,* somehow.

He saw Jax draw his lightsaber, though he didn't ignite it. Laranth unholstered her blasters. Nick felt his own hand itching for the blaster at his belt.

This was not good. If Jax wound up getting himself killed on this mission, Vader would be a very unhappy Dark Lord. Though one part of Nick's brain was still desperately trying to come up with a way out of this farrago without betraying his friend, another, larger part was reminding him that to fail Darth Vader was about as smart as walking into a nexu's den wearing a meat suit.

Jax lit his lightsaber. He and Laranth sprang around the corner.

And into a hail of blasterfire.

thirty-three

As Jax came around the corner, he was fully prepared to deal with whoever or whatever was there. In mid-leap he'd reached for the Force, secure in his knowledge that through it he'd be granted a few seconds' worth of prescience—enough to easily deflect whatever came his way.

But once again, the Force simply wasn't there.

Before he could recover from the shock of the betrayal by his senses, a salvo of energy bursts battered him to his knees. The searing pain of the blasts filled him, setting afire every nerve, every cell, in his body. But as bad as it was, it was eclipsed by the pain of having reached out and, once again, finding only void instead of the familiar connection that was so much a part of him.

Dimly, he realized that the barrage of energy bolts had ceased. He was momentarily confused, because he could still hear staccato bursts of blasterfire. He opened his eyes and looked up.

He saw Laranth standing before him, coolly firing both of her weapons with enough accuracy to block the incoming fire.

Laranth ended the fight—which surely hadn't lasted more than a couple of seconds—by shooting the droid's arm cannon squarely in its barrel, temporarily deactivating it. "Don't move," she said, her own blasters still held ready. "Either one of you."

Jax managed to get to his feet. Halfway there he felt I-Five's strong, cool hands helping him to stand. He shrugged them away angrily.

Jax saw the other droid standing several paces away. This, no doubt, was 10-4TO. He could see why its nickname was Bug-Eyes. He'd expected to see the droid, so its presence came as no surprise. He did not, however, expect to see a Falleen standing slightly behind it, or another being lying on the floor between them.

This latter was of a species Jax had never encountered before. It was bipedal, around one and a half meters tall; the parts of its body that he could see were covered in a fine pale blue down that made him think of feathers. The shape of the skull was also oddly avian.

Where was this creature from? What was it doing here? Jax felt suddenly confused, uncertain, to a degree that actually made him dizzy. He noticed that the Falleen's skin color had changed from green to reddish orange, and from the corner of his eye he saw that Laranth was looking somewhat confused as well.

He had just enough time to make the connection before the Falleen snatched a blaster from his holster and fired at them.

Jax reached for the Force again. Ironically, it was the confusion caused by the reptiloid's chemical discharges that saved him this time; his mental state was in such turmoil that he had no time to be uncertain about his ability to connect. And this time, the Force was there again for him. He deflected the blaster bolt with his lightsaber, then leapt the distance between them—

perhaps ten meters—aided by the Force. But his savaged nervous system caused one leg to buckle under him when he landed, throwing him off-balance.

Taking advantage of this, the Falleen moved quickly. He scooped up the supine biped and slung him over his shoulder. "Come!" he shouted to Bug-Eyes, and ran. The droid followed, and they both disappeared into the shadows. A moment later Laranth ran past him in pursuit.

The entire episode had taken less than a minute to play out, although it had felt like forever. The others—Nick, Dhur, and the droid—had already rounded the corner and joined them.

"*Zu woohama!*" Nick shouted, and Jax belatedly remembered the control phrase. It was too late now; the droid was gone. He shook his head in disgust.

"Are you all right?" I-Five asked. Again his—*its*—disturbingly human demeanor annoyed Jax, as did his own tendency to think of the droid as a *he* instead of an *it*. He didn't show it this time, however; his voice was level and neutral as he answered, "I'm fine." He turned away so he wouldn't have to see the look of relief projected on the droid's metal face, which he knew would be there, just as surely as the look of concern that had been there before.

"Don't beat yourself up about forgetting the control phrase," Nick told him. "Kind of hard to remember things like that when you're being zapped by a blaster."

Laranth emerged from the shadow, alone, looking disgusted. "I lost them," she said. "It's a maze in there." She frowned. "I should have been able to track them through the Force, but—I got confused." It was obviously hard for her to admit this.

Jax wondered briefly if Laranth, for whatever reason, was encountering the same difficulty in accessing the Force as he was. When he looked at her threads, however, they seemed as strong as ever.

"I have an idea," I-Five said. "We can use the Falleen's own defense against him. Follow me—if none of you mind," he added, glancing at Jax. Then he turned and strode off in the direction the Falleen and the other droid had taken.

Jax did mind, but he was also smart enough to realize that I-Five's tracking abilities were probably the only thing that would help them right now. "Come on," he said to the others. "There still might be a chance to find them."

They hurried, quickly but cautiously, through the darkened building, down flights of stairs and through rubble-strewn rooms. The building's tenants occasionally peered at them from behind curtained doorways and through cracks in walls, but none of them said anything or made any move.

It was just after dawn when they emerged; Jax knew this only by his chrono reading. Outside, save for intermittent city glow, it still seemed the middle of the night.

"He appears to have taken your skimmer," I-Five informed Nick.

Fortunately there were a few older-model speeders parked nearby, and one of them didn't require an activation code. Jax wasn't particularly concerned about the moral ambiguities of stealing the vehicle; Jedi rules were flexible, and could be bent in the service of the greater good. Besides, it was a pretty good bet that they were doing the owner a favor. The craft was a SoroSuub G-17 landspeeder that had seen better days, and those days hadn't been recent ones. At least one repulsor vane was out of alignment, causing the vehicle to yaw at the slightest irregularity in the pavement, which it hugged to within a dozen centimeters, and it was about as fast as a dyspeptic Ithorian.

"I could walk faster than this," Den Dhur said as the G-17 lurched down the street. "Drunk," he added.

I-Five kept them on the scent, quite literally—the droid's artificial sensorium was extremely sensitive. The multifarious odors, stenches, and smells downlevel were so omnipresent that Jax had long since stopped noticing them on a conscious level, but thinking about I-Five's tracking ability now brought them to his attention again. It was hard to believe that any individual species' scent could be isolated out from the pungent reeks of half a galaxy's variety of beings, even by a chemical lab as accurate as the one I-Five packed just behind the olfactory sensory grid on his chest. Nevertheless, the droid claimed that it was not only possible, but easy.

"There are very few Falleen this far downlevel," he explained. "They tend to be a more cosmopolitan species. Interestingly, I'm also detecting the residue of brands of oils and soaps associated with the extremely rich on his skin."

"Who is he, anyway?" Laranth asked. "He looks familiar."

"He should," the Sullustan said. "He's Prince Xizor of House Sizhran. Rumors are that he's an up-and-coming player in Black Sun. Falleen rarely leave their homeworld; he's one of the few exceptions."

Silence reigned for a few minutes. If Black Sun was involved, then things had indeed taken an unexpected—and potentially nasty—turn.

"He's about half a kilometer ahead," I-Five said. "And he's signaling the local port to have his ship ready."

"Impressive," Nick said. "Your video and audio reception must be as good as your olfactory detector."

"It's much simpler, actually: radar and an all-band transmission receiver."

"I believe the latter is illegal for a protocol droid to possess," Jax remarked.

"I believe you're right."

"If he lifts, how are we going to follow him?" Dhur asked. "Even your nose can't track a scent in vacuum."

"Not to worry," Nick said. "I've got a ship. We'll be right behind him."

Jax said nothing more. This entire affair seemed to be mushrooming out of control. He'd set out on a solo mission to redeem his Master's honor and fulfill his last request, and now he had a most unlikely posse helping him. A posse that he didn't seem to be even leading anymore; that position had somehow been usurped. By a *droid*.

He wasn't sure what to do about it. Worse, he wasn't even sure he should do anything about it. The mission was the important thing, after all.

But it was becoming harder and harder to remember that.

thirty-four

Kaird had been conscious during the events of the last few minutes; conscious, but unable to move. The stun blasts had zapped him quite thoroughly, and it wasn't until they'd arrived at the staging platform that he started to feel the tingle of returning circulation.

Xizor stood over him, cool and calm, and said, "We'll take your ship. I came down in a shuttle, but I've always fancied that vessel of yours. Very nice lines."

Kaird glared at him, seething with rage and fury, but still unable to so much as twitch a muscle. On top of all the other indignities he'd been forced to suffer in the last hour, now the reptile man was going to steal the *Stinger*? This was an outrage! The modified Surronian Conqueror assault ship had a cluster of top-of-the-line sublight ion drives and a Class One hyperdrive, not to mention two fire-linked ion cannons. It was one of his most prized possessions. He would *not* lose it to Xizor. After all, he'd stolen it first.

Prince Xizor rattled off the proper docking code to the tower; how he'd gotten it, Kaird had no idea, though he suspected slicing into personal databases might have had something to do with it. They transferred from the skimmer into the sleek vessel and were airborne ten minutes later, Xizor having claimed royal privilege to bypass the launch queue.

By then, the uncomfortable sensations of paresthesia were occupying Kaird. Strapped into his seat, he tried not to writhe in discomfort as the nerve paralysis caused by the stun blasts wore off. Within a few minutes, the *Stinger* eased into low planetary orbit.

Xizor, in the pilot's seat, ran his hands over the recessed bank of controls. From where he was sitting, Kaird could hear the muted pinging of the threshold monitors and level indicators, and see the pulsing color bar graphs, VU meters, and LED status lights. "Quite a ship," Xizor said in a satisfied tone. "You have taste, Kaird."

The Nediji did not reply. In the seat beside him, the droid 10-4TO sat ramrod-straight. Beyond it, through the vessel's view-port, Kaird could see the untwinkling stars and the cresting arc of the planet below. He stared out at the infinite. Somewhere out there was the planet of his birth. Was this the closest he would ever get to it?

Nearly an hour passed. Kaird's circulation had returned to normal long ago. He tested his bonds again, even though he knew it was futile. He gave up; perhaps he would get a chance to escape once Xizor reached his destination . . .

Come to think of it, just what *was* the Falleen's destination?

Kaird had assumed that Xizor would be heading back to Sinharan T'sau and the hidden labyrinth of Midnight Hall. But now that he thought about it, that didn't make any sense. Xizor must have figured out why Kaird had been stalking him, and his questions earlier proved that the probability of this being an official assignment had already occurred to him. After all, the Nediji wouldn't attempt such a bold move as assassinating a Falleen prince without being sanctioned to do so by the Underlord. Knowing that, for Xizor to deliberately put himself back in harm's way would be foolish, to say the least. Obviously, then, he had another destination.

But where?

Even as he was wondering, Kaird heard the slight change in the purr of the engines, and saw the starscape outside shift in response. They were leaving orbit. He craned his neck, saw the bright curvature of golden, scintillating light that was Coruscant, and the approaching terminator line. They were going into the night.

A few minutes later, he realized Xizor's destination: the Antipodes. The area of the globe diametrically opposite to Imperial City.

The area known as the Factory District.

A chill ran the down on his arms and neck. The Factory District was, according to all accounts, one of the most dangerous places on the entire planet. Centuries ago, it had been a thriving industrial center that sprawled over most of the northeastern quadrisphere, near the equator. But economic downturns and the streamlining of production techniques on Metellos, Brentaal, Duro, and other Core worlds, together with the lifting of trade sanctions and political lobbying in the Galactic Senate, had resulted in most of the manufacturing and engineering contracts being moved offworld. As a result, except for isolated areas where automated minimal production of some goods still took place, thousands of square kilometers had become forgotten, and eventually cut off from utilities, supplies, and communications. The area was a wasteland now, more lawless and dangerous even than areas like the Southern Underground or the Invisible Sector. By day, primitive tribes of humans and other species roamed the dilapidated structures; by night the ruins were prowled by Cthons, stratts, and, some averred, by nameless horrors unknown on any other world.

Kaird had heard the tales, and had assumed that, for the most part, they were at best 1 percent truth to 99 percent bantha fodder. But as the *Stinger*'s trajectory brought her lower, and he was able to see the blighted landscape, he began to wonder.

The Factory District looked nothing at all like the underworld of metropolitan Coruscant. Two of the lesser moons were in the sky, bathing the entire scene in a radiance as silvery-cold and glistening as a Hutt's tears. The scene was one of urban decay and deterioration, stretching endlessly, it seemed, in all directions.

Very few buildings rose more than fifty stories, he estimated, not even qualifying for cloudcutter status. For the most part they spread horizontally, vast and wide. He saw factories, warehouses, landing fields, transport ramps and grids . . . all of it bleak and crumbling. Skeletal structural frames groped blindly toward the stars. The shattered remnants of huge, transparisteel transit tubes, which had arced and curved over and around buildings like fantastic ice formations, came to jagged ends, or lay in pieces on the ground below. As they drew closer, Kaird could see that some makeshift repairs had been attempted, with varying degrees of success: rope bridges made of cable and metal plating, crude open-air winch-and-tackle lifts, and the like. The streets were dotted with shanties, lean-tos, and other dwellings, constructed of cast-off materials. Kaird wondered what sorts of species were tough enough and/or desperate enough to call the Factory District home.

Xizor set the *Stinger* down in an open area, relatively clear of debris, near one of the larger buildings. The hum of the repulsorlifts died, and silence followed—a silence so profound that they could very well have been on the airless surface of one of the planet's satellites. It was 10-4TO who finally broke it.

"This isn't the location of the Whiplash." The droid's voice was unemotional, which was no great surprise, but there was something about its tone that suggested suspicion nonetheless. It leaned forward slightly.

Xizor stood, turned away from the cockpit and moved closer to it. He spoke two words that Kaird had never heard before: *"Zu woohama."* It sounded like a language other than Basic, but Kaird had no idea which one.

It made an impression on the droid, however. Ten-Four-Tee-Oh settled back. "What would you have me do?"

"Accompany me," Xizor said. "I'll show you where to download your data."

"Of course."

Kaird now recalled the significance of the cryptic phrase. According to Perhi, it was a code phrase that gave one control over the droid; Black Sun had learned it through its Palace contacts. It had been given to Xizor as part of his false mission.

Obviously, that had been a mistake.

Before they disembarked, Xizor carefully slipped a muzzle gag over Kaird's stubby beak-like mouth. "Just in case you feel a sudden urge to try the control phrase on our metallic friend." Then he moved past Kaird on his way to the aft hatch. The droid followed, as meek an automaton as Kaird had ever seen. There seemed to be no other choice, so Kaird rose and followed the droid.

It was just past dusk here, deepening into full night. As Kaird stepped from the hatch gangway onto the black, tarry ground, he was struck by the utter silence of the place. No breeze stirred; no insects or other night sounds were audible. But there was a tension to the night air, as if some massive, unseen creature held its breath while inspecting them. Without malevolence, or impatience, or even curiosity; rather with a clinical detachment, which was all the more frightening for its indifference.

Kaird shuddered. He had the worst feeling ever about this place.

thirty-five

As far as Den was concerned, everybody else in this little group had lost their minds. Even I-Five. *Especially* I-Five.

It was taking all his self-control to keep from yelling at the droid, *What are you, crazy?* Not content with finding the Jedi Pavan, now he—and, by extension, Den—was tagging along on a fool's quest after another droid. It was insane; and yet I-Five evidently had no intention of leaving Pavan's side, even though the Jedi had repeatedly demonstrated that he wasn't interested in the droid's help.

Den had had just about enough of this. He'd tried to be a good friend. Tried to be supportive of I-Five's quest, even though he'd privately thought it was verging on obsession. He'd tried not to let himself grow jealous over the droid's devotion to Lorn Pavan's son, even though he felt that he'd been tossed aside, his feelings neglected, his warnings unheeded. He'd tried to have an open mind about Jax Pavan, to believe there was a decent person buried somewhere beneath all that formal Jedi mopak.

And where had trying to be nice gotten him? On a dilapidated Corellian smuggler ship, headed who knew where . . . and, what's more, in pursuit of a ship that looked like it could make them eat cosmic dust without even kicking into hyperdrive. *Let's face it,* Den told himself, *this bucket isn't going to win any interstellar speed-setting trophies anytime soon.* In fact, he doubted it could come in third in a Tatooine Podrace.

All in all, it was hard to see how things could get any worse.

"He's headed for the Factory District," Nick Rostu announced.

It's worse, Den thought.

The Factory District, located on the opposite side of the planet from Imperial City, was reputed to be the most dangerous place on Coruscant: a nightmarish setting of blasted and demolished structures, prowled night and day by devolved members of various species, subterranean cannibalistic throwbacks using near-primitive technology, beasts that hunted in packs, and—possibly the worst of all, if even a fraction of the stories he'd heard were true—feral droids.

"We can't go there," he said.

No one answered. The *Far Ranger* began to descend, dropping out of the night sky.

It would be different if he were following a story. If he'd been hot on the trail of a good lead, he had no doubt that he'd be leading the pack—or at least somewhere in the middle. But he'd learned the folly of risking his favorite hide years ago if the stakes didn't warrant it. And following a droid, who was *maybe* carrying valuable information that *might* be of aid to a rebellion not even fully formed yet, seemed to him the longest of long shots. You couldn't give that story away.

"Listen to me," Den said. "If anyone here has any

higher brain functions still working, *think* about this. Why are we doing this?"

The silence continued. Then: "I have to fulfill my Master's last request," Pavan said. "I didn't ask the rest of you to come. Except for Laranth."

"Well, *I* don't recall volunteering for this," Den said. "And I especially don't recall wanting to go to a part of Coruscant that would scare the Red Guards white."

"It can't be that bad," Jax Pavan said.

Den looked at him. "You know what it's called if a tribe of Noghri moves in there? Gentrification."

"I agree with Den," Laranth said. "I understand your oath to avenge Even Piell, Jax. But if he were here, he'd be the first to tell you not to throw your life away."

"Then it's a good thing he's not here."

Nobody had any reply to that. Den stared gloomily through the viewport, watching as the ship dropped closer to the desolation below. "On top of everything else, there are the feral droids," he said. "Anyone thought about them?"

Laranth answered. "They may be apocryphal—"

"Let's hope," Den muttered. Supposedly the droids, which were mostly construction and wrecker units, had been left behind when the area was abandoned. The story was that they had gone bad; no one was sure just how. The most popular theory was some kind of worm or virus that had altered core programming and turned the droids into killers.

Rostu reached overhead and flipped a few switches. Den felt his stomach flip in response, along with the ship's landing gear extruding. A moment later the *Far Ranger* touched down, and Rostu cut the secondary lifts. "Let's hope we don't find out for ourselves how much truth there is to the stories," he said. He peered through the cockpit's blister. "There's their ship—but where are they?"

"A better question is, *Why are they here in the first place?*" Jax said.

"And an even better question is, *Why are we?*" Den added.

Rostu lowered the ramp. They started down it cautiously, the two Jedi first, then Rostu and I-Five flanking Den, who was the only one unarmed. Of course.

The buildings were dark, boxy geometric shapes under the leprous light of the moons. Centax 2 would rise soon as well, and their combined radiance would make the landscape almost as bright as day. *After all,* Den thought, *we wouldn't want the assorted monsters to have any trouble finding us, would we?*

"I've picked up the Falleen's scent again," said I-Five. "This way." He started toward an open entrance to one of the buildings that was as black as Rokko's heart.

"By the way," he added, "we shouldn't stay too long. According to my sensors, this entire place was powered by one of the old-style ion-neutrino reactors. I'm detecting some low-level radiation leakage."

Den shook his head. *It just keeps getting better.*

Kaird was between Xizor and 10-4TO as they moved through the dark interior of what had once been a droid-manufacturing plant. Xizor apparently knew the way by heart, because he led them through a maze of corridors, stairs, and chambers before they finally stopped. They were in a small room, coldly lit by moonlight through a grimy set of windows. Kaird saw no movement in the shadows, and felt slightly relieved. His sensitivity to light made the room more visible to him than to either of his comrades. There didn't seem to be an immediate threat, although he'd still feel a lot better with his hands uncuffed and his mouth ungagged.

The Falleen said, "I imagine you're curious about why I've brought you halfway around the planet to this forsaken place, Kaird. It's simple—I wanted you to meet someone." He set a portable sconce on a shelf and turned it on. Kaird looked at Xizor; the prince was smiling, and from long experience the Nediji had come to know that this was never a good sign.

The prince turned to 10-4TO and said, "Deactivate yourself for ten minutes."

The droid's photoreceptors winked out, and its body slumped slightly. Xizor waited a moment to make sure Bug-Eyes was inert, and then removed Kaird's muzzle. He gestured behind the Nediji.

"I'm sure no introductions are necessary," he said.

Kaird, with a mounting sense of dread, turned. Behind him, near one wall and formerly concealed in thick shadow, stood a man. A man whom Kaird recognized immediately, despite the utter impossibility of his being there. He stared in shock.

It was Underlord Dal Perhi.

thirty-six

Nick kept his hand on his holstered blaster as he, Laranth, Den Dhur, I-Five, and Jax moved toward the dark entrance. Jax and Laranth took point, and Nick brought up the rear.

It wasn't going to be difficult to find them—at least not as long as I-Five's olfactory sensors functioned. The droid's photoreceptors were on maximum brightness, so lack of illumination wasn't a problem, either. Nick's rudimentary connection with the Force sensed no immediate danger, although at the far fringes of his awareness he was fairly sure there lurked monsters.

And at least one lurks quite a bit closer, he thought. *That would be me.*

Time was running out. Nick knew he had to make a decision. He'd been putting it off, hoping against hope that something would happen to spare him from this terrible task.

There were a dozen different ways he could justify turning Jax over to Darth Vader. It wasn't like the Jedi was a close friend or relative. And he didn't know what fate Vader had planned for him—although, Vader being Vader, Nick felt it was safe to bet that he wasn't having

Jax brought back to Imperial City for spice tea and crumblebuns.

On the other hand, he knew all too well what would happen if he failed Vader: the jungle plateau that was home to his tribe would be reduced to incandescent slag.

Could Vader order it done? After all, Haruun Kal wasn't just another backreach dirtball. Despite its myriad diseases and pestilences and other forms of unpleasantness, it was the only source in the known galaxy for such necessities as lammas wood, thyssel bark, portaak leaf, and other botanical miracles. To eliminate even one tiny part of the arm of a galaxywide industry in what amounted to a fit of pique, well . . . it seemed ridiculous, on the face of it.

On the other hand . . .

No, there was no way out of this. He simply couldn't take the chance that Vader might carry out even part of his threat. It was an obvious case of the needs of the many outweighing the needs of the few—or, in this case, the one.

Nick wondered if he was trying to wring comfort and justification from the statistics. He shook his head in angry dismissal. He didn't need justification. He could see what had to be done, for the greater good. It wasn't *his* fault. Blame the tall, sinister man in the black mask.

And, after all, it wasn't like Nick hadn't fought the good fight. He'd fought plenty of good fights, and a lot of bad ones, too, on more war-torn worlds than he cared to count. When was it time for surcease? When did he get a little easement, a little peace? He'd accepted the fact that the luxury conapt, the wife and kids, the comfortable retirement, all were not part of his future. But being sealed up on a world like Despayre, knowing he'd been responsible for the destruction of hundreds of people, hadn't exactly been part of the job description, either.

He noticed Jax glance at him, and realized he'd forgotten to damp down his nervous system's reaction to his dilemma again; quite likely he was broadcasting his distress all over the Force's bandwidth, so to speak. He hastily shielded himself, hoping the Jedi wouldn't decide to directly probe his mind. Though Jax's power within the Force, from what Nick had sensed since he'd known the Jedi, wasn't nearly as powerful as Vader's, he knew that Jax could easily sweep aside any feeble mental defenses Nick might try to erect.

Fortunately, Jax did not attempt a direct probe. Instead he moved back to Nick's rear-guard position. "You okay?" he asked in a low voice.

"Yeah. Just—trying to keep things down to a simmer. I push too far out there, it starts to feel like something's pushing back."

"You sense a Force-user? Here?" Jax looked surprised and skeptical.

"No, not like that. But there's *something* out there on the fringes."

Jax frowned. He looked, for a moment, almost sad, Nick thought. And then, suddenly and seemingly out of nowhere, he got a flash through the Force about Jax. A realization that left him looking at the Jedi in astonishment. He couldn't have been more surprised if Jax had suddenly been revealed as a Clawdite changeling.

Jax Pavan was losing his connection with the Force.

He had no idea why his own less-than-optimal link had suddenly been given this startling revelation. It happened sometimes; there were no hard-and-fast rules, no discernible laws, by which the Force operated, although the more metaphysically inclined among the Jedi believed that all events were shaped and molded by its revelations. Toward what end it was not given to organic sentient life to understand. Nick had no idea whether this belief was true or utter grasser mopak; all he knew was that this particular datum was a certainty.

Jax's bond to the Force was sputtering.

Before he could stop staring, Jax looked at him, and it was obvious that he knew what was in Nick's mind; evidently his faltering link wasn't that bad. "Yes," he said, in a low voice. "It's true."

Nick had no idea how to respond to that. Even his relationship with the Force, dim as it was, was always there. It might not cast a light very far over the darkling plain of existence, but it always burned at a steady rate. He'd never heard of such a thing happening to anyone lucky enough to experience the connection in the first place.

"It's—intermittent," Jax continued. "Hasn't happened often, but when it does—I feel like I've been blown out of an air lock without a vac suit."

I'll bet, Nick thought. It occurred to him that this might work in his favor; it would be easier to keep his agenda hidden if Jax wasn't up to maximum thrust all the time. Immediately after having the thought, he felt a burst of self-loathing, which Jax apparently didn't notice.

"Have you told the Paladin?" Nick couldn't think of anything else to say.

"No—but I know she suspects. I'll have to tell her, for the same reason I'm telling you. If my connection fails at the wrong time, you and she have to be able to step in and complete the mission. Understand?"

"Absolutely," Nick said, the words tasting like ashes in his mouth. "We got your back."

After a labyrinthine journey through darksome corridors and chambers, they entered, through a broken door panel, what seemed to have once been a control room—there were banks of consoles, overhead monitor screens, walls of electrical paneling, and various pieces of equipment. One wall was a large, transparisteel panel that looked out over what seemed to be a vast, mass-production assembly line. Everything had a vaguely antiquated feeling to it. The only light came from dim sconces; they cast a cold cobalt sheen on everything and everybody.

The room had been trashed. Panels had been ripped out, exposing electronic entrails; monitors had been smashed; pieces of equipment had been shattered against the floor and walls. There was a spiderweb crack radiating from the center of the transparisteel panel.

The evidence of the destruction testified to its savagery. Whoever or whatever had done this had done it with passion and hatred, and it had taken enormous strength to crack the thick transparisteel. Jax watched Den Dhur pick up a panel facing from the floor and examine it. Then, wordlessly, he handed it to I-Five. Jax saw the droid reach for the facing. His metal fingers closed on one edge, fitting exactly the imprint of the four durasteel digits that had ripped it from its setting.

Laranth looked at the plate that the droid held. "Feral droids," she murmured.

—[PART III]—

FERAL CITY

thirty-seven

Nick was standing a meter away from the others, who were hotly debating the possible existence of the so-called feral droids. Jax, he noticed, still seemed resistant to any opinion or concept advanced by I-Five. Nick couldn't help but think that Jax was wound way too tight on this particular subject. Why was he so worked up over a droid? It was true that, if I-Five was claiming self-awareness and true sentience, it would certainly shake up some comfortable beliefs about machine intelligence. But Nick didn't see that it would rock his world too much. There were times when he thought a brain-damaged reek had more sentience than most so-called thinking beings.

He watched Jax, still finding it hard to believe that the latter's link with the Force was slowly eroding. It certainly added an extra wrinkle to his traitorous assignment. Turning Jax over to Vader with the former at the height of his powers would be bad enough; handing him to the Dark Lord this way was little better than ramming a lightsaber through him right now. In fact, thinking about it, the lightsaber route was probably the more humane way to go.

He was at the point of decision, he knew—past it, in

fact. He should have summoned Vader when they'd found Bug-Eyes in the Ugnaught slum, but things had happened too fast. Nick knew he couldn't stall any longer, however; if he really was carrying a tracker somewhere under his skin, then right now it was relaying the fact that he was halfway around the planet from where he was supposed to be. Of course, the droid Bug-Eyes was here, too; nevertheless, Nick didn't want to risk his ghôsh on the chance that Vader wouldn't think he was running from the job.

He had to face it: either he delivered Jax to Darth Vader, *now*—or he accepted and lived with the genocidal consequences.

The Dark Lord had told him he was not to attempt capturing the Jedi alone. He'd given him a comm device that was keyed into a special signal; all Nick had to do was activate it, and Vader would be alerted instantly. The device was a piece of smart fabric woven into his clothes, undetectable by any regulation scanning device. It was designed to recognize his DNA; a slight squeeze of the material between thumb and forefinger would be all that was necessary. Vader would know that Nick had found Jax Pavan, and the subcutaneous tracker would then lead him unerringly straight here.

Nick fingered the section of fabric lightly. Then he turned and, while everyone else was focused on the discussion, slipped quietly into the shadows and through a door.

Once he was out of their sight, he started walking swiftly. He wasn't sure where he was going, but it wouldn't be far. He just needed to be out of Jax's immediate vicinity, both to lessen the possibility of Jax sensing trouble, and because he knew he couldn't betray his friend while in the same room with him.

He wouldn't go far. He was aware that there could be various toothy dangers lurking in the shadows, but, even though he had only a nodding acquaintance with the Force, he still trusted it, and his hard-won battle skills and reflexes, to protect him long enough to do what he had to do. And if he was wrong—if something big enough and fast enough to turn him into a hot lunch before he could react came out of the dark . . . well, right now it was hard to see the downside to that scenario.

Kaird stared in disbelief. The Underlord of Black Sun was the last person he'd expected to see in a run-down, abandoned droid-manufacturing plant in the Factory District. But it was him, there was no disputing that. Kaird was standing less than two meters away, and he was quite familiar with disguises, bodysuits, and the like. He could spot someone so camouflaged far more easily than most could.

"Underlord Perhi," he said, grateful that he didn't stammer, at least. "Why are you here?"

Perhi scowled at him. "Isn't it obvious? I'm here to clean up the mess *you've* made of things. Prince Xizor informed me of the situation, and I came immediately."

Situation? What situation? Kaird was utterly confused. He was about to attempt a response when he noticed something very odd.

Kaird could see deeper into both the near infrared and ultraviolet than most species. He could see the heat waves that Perhi's body was shedding, and abruptly realized that they were cycling to extreme degrees between hot and cold. This was inexplicable. Perhi was standing still, and he obviously hadn't undertaken any strenuous activity or exercise recently; his respiration was normal for a human, and he wasn't sweating. Yet his skin temperature was rising and falling rhythmically, within the span of a single breath. Kaird estimated the cycle to be as much as fifteen degrees.

He walked over to Perhi and grabbed the human's upper arm to make sure, having to extend both force-cuffed hands to do so. No, it wasn't his imagination—he could feel the skin temperature rising and falling. This simply wasn't possible. There was no way Perhi could be standing there, conversing with him, if his internal thermostat was fluctuating to such peaks and valleys—

Kaird abruptly understood.

"Perhi" jerked his arm free of Kaird's grasp indignantly. "What are you doing? I'll have you—"

The thing imitating the Underlord suddenly stopped speaking. It shivered, then abruptly threw its head back, stiffening in an arc of agony. Kaird watched in horror as the simulacrum *melted*—its flesh blackened and shrank, then ran in a disgusting putrescence. Eyes and teeth, and a framework of metallic bones, gleamed for a moment in the dark foulness before dissolving as well, sloughing over organs that seemed part viscera and part electronics. A moment later, all that was left of the thing that had looked like Underlord Dal Perhi was a pool of black slime, in which the last fading sparks of circuitry sputtered and died.

Kaird stumbled back in horror. He stared at Xizor. "It—it was—some kind of *droid*?"

"A human replica droid," Xizor said. He seemed composed and unaffected by the horror they had both just witnessed. "The first real advancement in droid manufacturing in a dozen centuries. Cloned organic tissue melded with a cybernetic core and durasteel endoskeleton."

Kaird shook his head, perplexed. "I don't understand. Why manufacture a—a droid clone? Why not just use Kaminoan biotechnology to create a real one?"

"Because it takes a minimum of ten years to force-grow a blastocyst into a functioning individual. A replica droid can be produced much more cheaply, and in less than three standard months. And individual programming is easier, quicker to accomplish, and more comprehensive, in an artificial neural net."

Kaird's mind was whirling. "You're telling me you've underwritten a project halfway around the planet, in one of the most dangerous areas of Coruscant, to replace the Underlord with some kind of half droid, half clone? I thought you—" He stopped, but he could see that Xizor knew where his thought had been going.

The Falleen said, "You—and Perhi also, unless I'm very much mistaken—thought my goal was to gain the position of Underlord for myself. And you're right. That is my plan—but Black Sun isn't a clutch of Trandoshans, moving up the ranks by violence alone. I can't just walk into his chambers and blow him away. Some subtlety is called for."

Kaird glanced at the foul puddle at their feet. "This doesn't strike me as terribly subtle."

Xizor sighed. "It does appear that there is still trouble with the technology. These random fluctuations in temperature presage a deep-rooted problem. The droid brain seems to somehow become contaminated with the clone's genome. A strange hybrid virus develops—partly RNA from the cloned tissue, partly hardwired memetic algorithm from the substratum operating system. The droid is caught between two modalities of being; the sensorium circuitry overloads, and—" He shrugged. "You see the result."

"So why show me this?"

"Two reasons," the Prince said. "First, I was curious to see if the HRD was believable enough to fool someone who's familiar with the Underlord." Xizor stepped before the Nediji and smiled, most unpleasantly. "Second, I decided that, since a trained assassin has fallen into my hands, it would be foolish and wasteful not to use you. My scientists are second in technique only to the Emperor's in brainwashing. Simply killing Dal Perhi will not be nearly as effective, long-range, as replacing him with a puppet would be—but it'll be better than nothing. Especially since the evidence will establish that you acted on your own out of a desire to succeed him." He glanced at Bug-Eyes, as if making sure that the droid was still in deactivation mode. "I shall return to Midnight Hall in triumph, having found the droid carrying the precious data. You, on the other hand, will have failed, and your shame will drive you to a suicidal attack on the Underlord."

Kaird was thinking furiously, his mind questing this way and that for a way out. It didn't look good.

"Objections? No? Good." Xizor glanced at his wrist chrono, then at the deactivated droid. "I think we've chatted long enough, don't you?" He slipped the gag back over Kaird's mouth. A moment later, Kaird heard the almost subliminal sound of the droid powering back up.

Xizor gestured with his blaster. "Let's go meet my

people. They're going to give you a new reason to live—
and to die."

Rhinann left his conapt. He walked a short distance
down the hall and summoned a turbolift. He dropped
down seventy-three stories, walked perhaps a quarter
kilometer down another corridor, turned right, and
stopped before the fifth door on the left.

The entire trip had taken eight minutes and three seconds. It comforted him to be able to keep track of such
things.

Inside, the room was lined with cabinets; it was basically an all-purpose chamber, the latest function of
which was as a storeroom. Rhinann stood in the center
of the room and said, "Search Catalog Nineteen for
unidentified holocron."

Catalog Nineteen was a heterogeneous listing of various esoteric items that had come into the Empire's possession after the Clone Wars. In the cabinets, Rhinann
knew, were bits of esoterica like Tatooine flamegems, a
sphere of pure orichalc, a container of extremely rare so-
larbenite, and many other things.

A holodisplay of several different data storage cubes
appeared in midair. He asked for the most ancient, and
all faded out but one. Beneath that one the catalog code
blinked: SD41263.1: ANTIQUE HOLOCRON. He'd only
given the inventory a cursory inspection once, months
previously. He opened the cabinet that corresponded
with the listing, pulling one of the trays out. And there,
safely nestled in a molded cup of plastifoam, between a
Nikto totem icon and a Geonosian geode, was a cube,
about four centimeters on a side, with rounded corners.
It glowed a dull red. Illuminated on the cube's surfaces

by the roseate glow from within were ancient cuneiform markings—markings that Rhinann recognized immediately from his studies as the Sith language.

Gingerly, the Elomin picked it up, gripping it between thumb and middle finger, and held it up to look at it. All he had to do was replace it with another item, change the manifest accordingly, and it would be as if the holocron had never existed. Rhinann slipped the priceless artifact into his waistcoat, closed the cabinet, and returned it to its niche. He ordered the manifest display off. Then, before his nerve could fail him, he left the storeroom and strode, stiff-legged, back toward his conapt.

Before he got there, his comlink chimed. He activated it with a feeling of dread.

Lord Vader's voice said, "Come, Rhinann. We have a journey to take."

thirty-eight

After Laranth voiced the words they were all thinking, there was silence for a long moment. It was broken
by Den, who said, "Can we leave *now*?"

Jax Pavan shook his head stubbornly. "I have to complete Master Piell's—"

"Last mission, we know." Den raised his arms in a
gesture of mingled disgust and exasperation. "You, my
friend, are one crazy Jedi. Not to mention suicidal. I'm
just a reporter, but I'm thinking everybody in the immediate vicinity would be a whole lot better off if someone
took away your lightsaber, and anything else that's
sharp and pointy while they're at—"

"*Enough*, Den."

Den stopped in astonishment. Because it wasn't
Laranth or Pavan who had spoken. It was I-Five.

He'd just been *admonished*. By his friend, who had
never, as far as Den could remember, raised his voice in
anger to anyone before, not even to large, unfriendly
life-forms bent on doing the two of them serious harm.
Certainly not in Den's presence, anyway, and most certainly not to Den. He felt a cascade of emotions: hurt,
embarrassment, and—he had to admit it—anger.

Anger and indignation at being censured, by a *droid*.

Hot blood flushed through his face, out to the ridges of his ears. He stared at I-Five, who had turned back to Pavan.

"In that case," he said, "we'd best get to it. If there are such things as feral droids—and there does seem to be evidence to support it," he added, looking at the electronic carnage strewn about, "this looks like a place they might return to."

Pavan nodded. "I-Five, you and Laranth at the rear, while Nick and I—" He looked about, puzzled. "Where is Nick?"

Everyone glanced around. I-Five turned up his photoreceptors to maximum brightness, probing the shadows. Nick Rostu was nowhere to be seen.

"Something got him," Den said.

Laranth and Pavan both shook their heads. "No," the latter said. "Laranth or I would have felt it."

"Jax is right," Laranth said. "He left of his own free will."

"Yeah? To go where?" Den shivered and, despite his ambivalence, stepped closer to I-Five.

"Good question," Laranth said. "To go where—and do what?"

"Doesn't matter what he's planning," Den said. "He's going to wind up on the menu for the locals—if he hasn't already."

"He hasn't—yet. So let's find him before they do." Pavan closed his eyes for a moment. "I feel him," he said. "That way."

He pointed at one of the dark doorways. I-Five turned toward it, his photoreceptors at maximum. Even so, they illuminated the darkness only a short way.

Laranth gestured to Den. "I'll bring up the rear. You're safer in the middle."

It's nice to know someone cares, Den thought as he fell in behind Pavan and I-Five.

The downside to a self-aware droid, Den was coming to realize, was that self-awareness presupposed—demanded—flaws of which one must be aware. There was no need for a perfect being to know itself. Only in imperfection was there room to grow.

People make mistakes. I-Five makes mistakes. Therefore . . .

Den snorted. Syllogisms.

Kaird was thinking fast and hard. It was a prickly nest he'd dropped into, there was no denying it. The Falleen had a blaster trained on him. In and of itself, this wasn't a cause for worry—except for these blasted energy cuffs. In the past, Kaird had found ways to get the drop on opponents just as wary and skilled as Xizor. But there was zero chance of that with his wrists bound, especially since the droid had to be taken into account as well. Kaird didn't know how much control that cryptic phrase gave Xizor over 10-4TO, but he wasn't anxious to find out. He would have to wait until his hands were freed, and hope that it wasn't too late by then to do something.

Xizor kept them moving at a steady clip. Before long they rounded a corner and faced a set of double doors. Xizor raised a hand before an ID panel. The doors opened, revealing the interior. Xizor drew back, his skin flushing a deep orange of shock and rage.

The large laboratory within was a shambles. Equipment—electronic, medical, and chemical—had been destroyed with savage abandon and strewn about the chamber. Kaird saw broken beakers and test tubes, shattered bacta tanks, overturned diagnosters, and other destruction everywhere he looked.

But that wasn't the worst of it. There had been organic destruction as well. Xizor's team of doctors and scientists had been given the same treatment. The walls had been painted with the blood of various species, including the red of human hemoglobin and the blue-green of Aqualish hemocyanin. Kaird looked down at the mostly intact head of a Drall. Its furry face bore a look of horror.

It was fairly obvious that there would be no brain-washing done today—unless the term included cleaning splattered gray matter off the walls and floor.

Xizor was clearly furious. "The droids," Kaird heard him mutter. "The blasted feral droids. The Salissians told me they'd all been—"

"Someone's coming," 10-4TO said.

Xizor tensed slightly and dropped his hand to his holstered blaster.

Footsteps became audible, coming closer. A moment later a male human came into view around a corner. Kaird appraised him: lean, dressed like a spacer, but with the unmistakable aura of the military. He stopped when he saw them, and, after a moment of surprise, smiled pleasantly, as if they'd all run into one another on a leisurely stroll.

"Well," he said. "Prince Xizor." He glanced at the droid. "And the famous 10-4TO, aka Bug-Eyes. My, my, my . . . what *are* the odds?"

Rhinann hoped he didn't appear as frightened as he felt.

And who, really, could blame him if he did? Summoned by Vader with virtually no notice, to accompany the Sith Lord on a mysterious journey halfway around the planet, to a shunned and legendary area . . . could it be any more ominous? And his nerves weren't helped any by the fact that a small cohort of troops was accompanying them. Although, considering everything he'd heard about the Factory District, it was no doubt better to have them along. Rhinann had no problem with that; he had a problem with *him* going along. Just because he enjoyed stories of derring-do and high adventure didn't mean he had any desire whatsoever to participate in them. He was strictly the vicarious sort when it came to such things.

And yet here he was, standing on the bridge of Lord Vader's transport, watching the planet fall away beneath his feet. Vader had decided to stop waiting for Rostu's signal and was simply following the major's subcutaneous tracker. As the Sith Lord's primary aide-de-camp, it wasn't unusual for Rhinann to accompany Lord Vader on journeys, but that fact did little to ease his anxiety. It didn't help matters at all that he'd had no time to leave the holocron at his conapt, and so still carried it with him. He could feel it in his waistcoat pocket.

He knew nothing about the holocron save that it was ancient, and of Sith origin, judging by the inscriptions. It was in his possession because he had succumbed to an act of irrational desperation. He, Haninum Tyk Rhinann, who prided himself on never acting out of unconsidered or hasty judgment, had done the unthinkable for an Elomin: he had been rash. He had stolen the holocron in the purely illogical hope that there might be some knowledge in it that could somehow protect him from Darth Vader.

This was foolish on all sorts of levels, and he knew it. Just because the holocron *might* be of Sith origin didn't mean it contained anything that could be used against Vader. Yes, the man was a Sith, but as far as Rhinann knew the last representative of that ancient Order had lived thousands of years ago—there was no real reason to assume that any data the holocron carried would be pertinent now. For all he knew, it might contain nothing more than a list of long-forgotten recipes—and that was *if*, after all this time, the contents had remained intact. He wasn't even sure he could access whatever information might still be contained within it.

He knew all this. Yet still he had absconded with it; had stolen Imperial property, which in and of itself was a shocking abrogation of his own personal standards.

No, there was no excuse whatsoever for his action, save that of naked fear. And the mere fact that he was so desperate upset him almost as much as the desperation itself.

thirty-nine

"Something's coming," Laranth said.

Den rolled his eyes ceilingward. "Is anyone really surprised at this? Never mind," he added. "Rhetorical question."

"I feel them," Pavan said.

"So what are they?" Den asked. "Cthons? Stratts? Big, mutated stratts with four arms and enormous tusks?"

"It's not organic," the Jedi replied. "It's a droid. That's about all I can get at this point."

"More than one," I-Five corrected him. "I'm picking up tread vibrations, sonic pingers, and other indications. Based on the imaging data, I'd say they're either construction, maintenance, or worker droids. Estimating at least four, maybe more."

Den glanced around the operations center. "It looks like they were pretty cranky when they trashed this place," he said. "I'd say it's good odds their mood hasn't improved any."

"I think we'd better get out of here," Laranth said.

"I think it's too late for that," I-Five said. "My sensors indicate they're blocking the exits."

Den could hear the sound of something—a portal or a

partition—being knocked down. Judging by their reaction, the others heard it, too.

"Whatever we're going to do," I-Five said, "I suggest we hurry."

There was another crashing sound, this one closer. Laranth drew her blasters, aiming them at the door. I-Five followed suit with his finger lasers. Pavan lit his lightsaber. He glanced down at Den, then pulled a vibroknife from his belt and handed it to him.

Den crouched down, trying to shield as much of himself as possible behind an overturned cabinet. He looked at the weapon in his hand. *Terrific*, he thought. It was about twelve centimeters long, with a blade that vibrated fast enough to blur the edge when activated. A vicious and deadly weapon, if one were facing an organic foe. Against a pack of haywire automata, however . . . *Maybe I can cut my own head off before one of them gets a chance.*

He looked over at I-Five. The droid's earlier reprimand still stung, but this wasn't the time to be resentful. He didn't want to die estranged from his best friend.

The droid glanced at him. Den managed a grin. "Never thought I'd go out this way—up against a bunch of crazy droids," he said. He gave it a moment, then dropped the punch line: "I always figured it'd just be *one* crazy droid."

I-Five projected what Den knew constituted one of his rare smiles. "One isn't nearly enough in your case, Den."

It wasn't the most comforting battlefield farewell he'd ever heard of, but there was no time for anything further. Something smashed against the door, hard enough to shake the room. Then came another, harder crash, and the door flew apart in a shower of fragments—

While it wasn't exactly a big shock to run into Prince Xizor and the droid—and the bird man, who'd been unconscious the last time Nick had seen him—it was still a surprise, and not a particularly pleasant one. Nick kept both his eyes and the Force focused on Xizor. The droid wouldn't do anything unless told, he figured, and the bird man was an unknown quantity—although, given that he was cuffed and gagged, probably not much of a threat. The Falleen was, by far, the most dangerous of the three. It was rumored that he was affiliated with Black Sun. More to the immediate point, he held a blaster in his hand, and was also, from what Nick had heard, a master of various forms of unarmed combat. Not only that, but he controlled the droid—that much had been obvious back at the Ugnaught nest. All things considered, Prince Xizor was definitely someone to tread lightly around.

Of course, Nick knew the control phrase that would put Bug-Eyes on his team, but he also knew that by the time he'd barked it out and added some kind of instruction such as "Disarm him!" Xizor could have yanked his large intestine out and strangled him with it. Better, by far, to just play it cool.

"Who are you?" Xizor growled. "How do you know who I am? This place is deserted—how did you—?"

"I'm not from around here—same as you," Nick said, affecting what he hoped was an air of nonchalance while his brain lashed about frantically within his skull, trying to figure out a way to keep from being killed long enough to come up with a plan. He hadn't activated the beacon that would summon Vader yet. Might Xizor somehow be used as an ally against the Dark Lord? A way to save Jax's life—and his own—by distracting Vader? Unlikely; and even if it was possible, if it ended anywhere short of Vader's death, there was still the danger of part of Haruun Kal being decimated.

Nick figured he had about ten seconds before Xizor lost patience and shot him. He opened his mouth with no idea what he was going to say—only that he had to say *something*. What came out was: "I'm here to warn you. Lord Vader has sent a posse after you. They're tracking you, and they'll find you very soon."

Prince Xizor looked wary. "Are you referring to those fools who ran headlong into my droid's fusillade? I didn't think they could still stand, much less pursue me halfway around the world."

"Don't dismiss them," Nick said. "Two of them are rogue Jedi, and they're using the Force to track you."

"Again—why? What does Darth Vader want with—" Xizor glanced at 10-4TO and fell silent.

"Yes," Nick said. "He wants the data that the droid is carrying."

"And you came to warn me." The Falleen's tone was, to say the least, skeptical. "What's in it for you?"

Nick didn't need the Force to tell him that Xizor wasn't buying it. Still, there was no way he could back out now. "Black Sun sent me." It sounded absurd, even to his own ears, but it was all he could think of.

"Ah," Xizor said, his voice almost a purr. "Then you will, no doubt, be able to tell me the recognition phrase."

Nick felt various parts of his anatomy grow cold and shrink. If there was such a phrase, he had no way to guess it. There was only one slim chance now—he put everything he had into a Force probe, trying to read Xizor's emotional state and extrapolate from there. It wasn't easy; the prince kept his feelings and reactions closely guarded. Still, Nick could sense enough of his mood to feel reasonably confident in his reply.

"Phrase? What phrase?"

There was a long moment of silence; then, to his immeasurable relief, Nick felt the suspicion lessen slightly on Xizor's part.

"Very well," Xizor said. "You understand why I must be on guard."

"Of course."

"Where are these rogue Jedi? If they're planning an ambush, then obviously we want to be there first."

"I'll take you to them," Nick said, feeling relieved.

They started back down the dark corridor, Nick leading, Xizor directly behind him. Nick didn't need to look to know that Xizor's blaster was aimed at the small of his back.

So far, Nick thought, things weren't going badly at all, considering that he was playing this totally by ear. A plan was beginning to percolate, however. If he could find his way back to Jax and the others, and alert Jax through the Force that danger was approaching, they might be able to get the drop on Xizor. They'd have the droid and its data, at least, and Jax would have fulfilled his obligation to Master Piell. Then, he felt, he could tell Jax how Vader had conscripted him with the threat of destroying his homeworld. Working together, they might be able to figure a way out of all this . . .

But as he walked down the dark hallway, Nick, somewhat to his surprise, began to find the idea of turning on Xizor less appealing. Instead, he found himself thinking, perhaps it made more sense for them to find a way to join forces with Xizor. After all, the Falleen prince could be a powerful ally—and it was all about making the strongest alliances, after all, wasn't it?

The more he thought about it, the more Nick was amazed, and somewhat annoyed, that he hadn't sussed all this out before now. It made perfect sense. It was in all of their best interests for him to bring Prince Xizor to the others—but not so they could subdue Xizor. The prince could protect both him and his ghôsh against Vader—a sunstruck Gungan could see that. And he could, no doubt, help Jax hide from Vader as well.

Nick felt a wave of relief as these revelations tumbled through his head. Thank goodness he'd figured this out in time to prevent himself from making a terrible blunder. He glanced back at Prince Xizor. He would make a good and powerful ally, no question about that. Just the thought of it made him feel safer. Even as the feeling surged through him, Nick noticed that the Falleen's skin, previously as green as burning copper, had changed to a very pleasing shade of pink.

Three labor droids, of a design Jax wasn't familiar with, stalked into the control room. They were about two meters tall, wide and heavy, with standard extensible arms ending in three-pronged pincers.

"Bee-Ex-Ell-Ninety-nines," I-Five murmured. He didn't sound thrilled.

The droids stalked forward. They were all clicking, beeping, and whistling in Binary. Jax had no idea what they were saying, but it sounded somehow *wrong*.

There was something else odd about them: although they were the same model, the three droids didn't look the same. For one thing, they appeared to be covered with patches of rust. Then, as they came closer, Jax saw that they had been modified in bizarre ways. One had lengths of plasticene tubing snaking across its chest plate, through which circulated fluids of various colors. Another had blinking parity lights running up both arms in erratic patterns. The third sported two tall, thin terminal vanes on its head, with high-voltage electrical discharges climbing up between them. All three had various archaic pieces of electronic equipment, such as circuit boards and vacuum tubes, spot-welded to their heads and upper torsos, apparently at random.

All this registered in the space of only a few seconds. Then Jax Force-leapt, the threads catching him up in an invisible harness, manipulating him like a marionette, so that he executed a midair flip that landed him behind the droid with the discharge vanes. Before it could begin to turn, Jax swung his weapon at the no-neck junction between its head and shoulders.

But instead of decapitating it, the energy blade grew very bright for a moment, spat a sound like a hundred giant dynamos overloading, and vanished, leaving only the dead hilt and a stench of ozone. Jax stared in shock at his deactivated weapon, realizing too late that the droid with the parity patterns was reaching for him—

Twin particle blasts and laser beams, perfectly aimed, struck the vane droid and the parity droid in their circuit-link assemblies, disconnecting the robotic bodies from their CPUs. The two droids were effectively paralyzed. Jax reactivated his lightsaber and plunged it straight through the tube droid's thoracic subprocessor. In a shower of sparks the last BXL-99 was deactivated.

As he pulled the lightsaber from the droid's midsection, Jax looked closely at the chassis. What he saw made him shudder.

The patches he'd thought were rust weren't rust. They were blood.

There was a moment of silence, broken by the impact of something very hot and very fast against the transparisteel window. The center crack webbed outward.

Laranth stepped cautiously to where she could see out the window, her blasters ready. When she spoke, her voice was grimmer than usual.

"There're half a dozen droids down there on the assembly-line floor, maybe more," she said. "They keep milling about so that it's hard to count 'em. But," she added, "they definitely outnumber us."

Another ball of orange light struck the huge window, driving her back.

"And," she added, "one has a plasma gun."

"Terrific," Dhur said.

forty

Jax gripped his lightsaber and reached once more for the familiar lines of the Force. Another plasma burst would destroy the transparisteel panel, and then they would need all the help they could get to defeat the—

No, he thought. *Not again.*

As had happened before, there came what felt like a hesitancy, a stutter, in what was normally the smooth, nearly effortless connection. An uncertainty, a void where there was usually the familiar surge of the Force, the sense of power and confidence that had always filled him before.

It isn't there!

Jax fought panic. It was absurd, this flickering, on-again, off-again linkage. He'd used the Force to leap over the labor droid not five minutes ago, and it had worked fine then.

Well, it's not working now.

Another plasma bolt hit the panel, which exploded in half-molten fragments that sleeted into the room. Laranth deflected them, but shrapnel was the least of their worries. Jax looked back at the window in time to see another droid, obviously just as haywire as the previous ones, climbing over the edge.

It was an 8D8 smelting operator, a spindly humanoid droid designed to withstand the searing heat of blast furnaces and smelting pits. Its exoframe was made of a durasteel alloy that could withstand long exposure to extremely high temperatures. Normally the model was unarmed, but in this one's case, a heavy-duty blaster had been swivel-mounted to its left shoulder. And for some reason known only to its own psychotic processor, a strip of metal had been fastened around its head as a crude gag, covering its vocabulator.

The blaster began firing, sweeping the room, as soon as the 8D8's upper body cleared the edge. Jax knew he had only seconds in which to act. He couldn't trust his ability to anticipate and block the blasts, so he dived forward, body-surfing through shards of razor-sharp transparisteel fragments, his lightsaber extended before him. Before the crazed 8D8 could adjust, Jax was in front of it. He swung the energy blade in a short arc, neatly clipping the blaster from its mount. The blade hesitated at the droid's neck, but only for a moment; the frictionless shaft didn't have to burn through the durasteel column to sever it.

Because of his awkward position, Jax couldn't put his normal strength and speed into the blow. As a result, instead of cutting the head cleanly off, the incandescent blade resealed part of the inner conduits as it passed through them, while the impact turned the CPU partially around. The 8D8's head remained welded to its neck, only facing more or less backward.

The droid toppled, knocking off two others on the way down. There were two more climbing up, however: a Roche J9 drone and an asp droid. Jax pushed to his feet, part of his mind commenting ironically on the strange pairing of the two; the J9 was an exceedingly smart, if somewhat surly and intractable brand of droid, while the asp was little more than a walking calculator. Both seemed united in purpose here, however. Both had microchips, deactivated restraining bolts, and other impedimenta attached all over them. Both of them were chattering away in the same nonstop Binary babble the first three had been using. Only the "gagged" 8D8 had been silent.

Jax backed away warily, his lightsaber held before him. Sweat dripped into his eyes; at least, he thought it was sweat. When he blinked he realized by its viscosity that it was blood. The sharp fragments of the window panel had left a score of cuts on his face and hands. Blood from his lacerated hands also made it difficult to grip his weapon's hilt.

Keep it together, he commanded himself furiously. *You're a Jedi; these people are in your care. You cannot let them down!*

But how could he save them? Without a connection to the Force, he was blind, deaf, and lame. His fighting skills were weakened, his reflexes dulled . . . without the Force, he wasn't—

"Even without the Force, you are still a Jedi."

The memory hit him almost like a physical blow. It was something Master Piell had told him months before, back when he'd still been a Padawan. Jax's heart skipped a beat. In the midst of the chaos going on around him—Laranth coolly firing her blasters, I-Five just as coolly using his finger lasers—it was hard to believe such a still, small voice in his head could be heard at all, much less come through as clearly as it did. But there it was. He remembered the conversation, which had taken place in the Temple's training chamber, vividly:

"The Force aids a Jedi's power," Master Piell had told him. "It completes a Jedi's training. But the Force alone does not make a Jedi. That comes from a deeper place."

"But—the Force sets us apart, makes us unique," he had stammered. "Without it, how are the Jedi different?"

The Lannik's reply had been typically acerbic: "What, am I talking to myself here? Pay attention! The Force abets you. It doesn't define you. Before it laid claim to you, you were then who you are now; otherwise, it would not have chosen you as its vessel. Understand?"

A shadow fell over Jax from behind; he turned to see another droid looming. He wasn't even sure what type this one was; he just got an impression of machine bulk, tractor treads, two-pronged pincer hands—and grinning skulls of various species draped all over it. He ducked its first blow, then spun around and hamstrung it with his blade. Servomotors seizing and crackling, it stumbled toward the window and toppled through, carrying the J9 and the asp with it.

Without thinking, simply reacting, Jax spun again and brought his lightsaber up and over. The two halves of a maintenance droid, its interior power cells sparking and smoking, collapsed at his feet. He felt a moment of triumph, of elation—and then he was seized by a powerful grip from behind and lifted off his feet. Another jointed, extensible arm seized his right arm, holding it, and his lightsaber, still. The grip around his neck began to squeeze—

A laser beam drilled through the feral droid's thorax. It froze, and the holds on Jax's neck and arm relaxed.

He dropped and turned to see I-Five a meter away, index finger extended.

In the sudden, ringing silence, Jax massaged his neck. "Under certain circumstances," he said, "I could see thanking my nav computer."

I-Five nodded. "It can make for a safer trip."

Jax looked around. The floor was littered with still-smoking droids and droid components. Laranth and Den stood nearby. The Paladin holstered her blasters, and the Sullustan carefully deactivated the vibroblade he'd evidently been using to considerable effect.

"What were they saying?" Jax asked I-Five.

The droid shook his head. "Just incoherent nonsense. Word salad."

"Think that's all of 'em?" Dhur asked.

"For now," Laranth replied wearily. Then she suddenly stiffened in alarm. She reached for her weapons again, but before she could clear leather, cold blue fire enveloped them all.

forty-one

Kaird had known what was going to happen as soon as the human had opened that soft, fleshy mouth of his and spewed that babble about coming from Black Sun to warn Xizor. Even without Xizor knowing that Underlord Perhi, who had sent Kaird to kill the prince, wouldn't be overly concerned about Xizor's well-being, the human just didn't fit the part. He was hard, yes, no question of that, but he didn't have the ruthlessness, the certain type of emotional shielding, that marked one of the criminal elite. One didn't need a connection to the Force, or even to be marginally empathic, to see that. This human wasn't someone who enjoyed killing, as most of the enforcers did, particularly the human ones. There were exceptions, of course—Kaird liked to think he was one. But then, he wasn't human.

And it had played out just as Kaird had expected it to: Xizor had pretended to go along, and, as the human led them back to the others, he had subtly, oh so subtly, begun using his endocrine arsenal to influence him. Though Kaird was walking behind Xizor, he could see the Falleen's skin changing hue as he shed pheromones. And it didn't take long at all for the human to fall under the spell; his change in body language was obvious, even to a nonhuman.

Kaird remained unaffected by the mind-altering molecular mist. Whether his physiology was sufficiently different in this case to protect him, or Prince Xizor simply hadn't targeted him as well, the Nediji didn't know. Come to think of it, why hadn't Xizor simply mesmerized him back at the Ugnaught slum instead of having the droid zap him? Perhaps Xizor preferred the relative ease of using forcecuffs to constantly having to shed pheromones to keep Kaird under control. But Kaird thought the reason was much simpler—Xizor had liked seeing him suffer, and had wanted the avian in his right mind so as to fully appreciate it.

Prince Xizor now had two pawns—or at least, one automaton and someone favorably disposed toward him—and Kaird had none. The odds weren't looking good.

It didn't take very long for the human to lead them back to the rest of his party. Before they came within sight, Xizor bade them halt.

He turned to the droid and said, in a low voice that Kaird knew the human's feeble hearing would not detect, "Proceed by yourself. When you come within range, stun as many as you can. Don't kill them."

Kaird could see the logic behind this. The Jedi wouldn't, in all likelihood, be able to sense a droid's surreptitious approach until it was too late.

As 10-4TO headed off around the corridor's bend, the human said, "Why send the droid on ahead?" His tone was one of puzzled and polite interest, but no more. Xizor's mesmerizing sweat had done its work well.

As much as Kaird loathed the Falleen, he had to admire Xizor on one level, at least. The prince was always thinking, always working the odds. Even without those controlling body chemicals, he was a formidable adversary.

As the Jedi would soon discover.

The droid disappeared around a turn in the corridor. A few moments of silence ensued, followed by the sound of its arm-mounted weapon firing.

The human blinked at the sound, and Kaird could see reason return to his expression. "Hey!" he shouted. "What the kark—!" He turned to run down the corridor after the droid, but didn't get very far, due to the stun blast from Xizor's weapon that hit him squarely between the shoulder blades.

The attack had been sudden and devastating. Den had heard the whine of a blaster, or something pretty much like one, and then twilight-colored agony had struck every cell in his body. He wasn't sure how long he'd been out, but it had been more than just a few minutes, considering how thoroughly he'd been tied up. Whoever did it must've thought Sullustans were as strong as Wookiees. Laranth lay perhaps two meters away, also forcecuffed and still unconscious.

Den could hear voices. He looked about, located their source—and felt his insides drop into free fall. On the other side of the chamber, maybe six meters away, stood Prince Xizor, along with the bird man, who was still forcecuffed. Also present were the droid that had just zapped them all so thoroughly—that's how Den had it figured, anyway—and Nick Rostu. The droid—and judging by the size of its photoreceptors, it had to be Bug-Eyes—was holding Nick firmly by the arms.

This was all very bad, but Den's immediate concern was for Jax, who was standing, hands also forcecuffed, before Xizor. Den suppressed a gasp as the Jedi raised his head in response to one of Xizor's questions, giving Den a good look at his face. It was stitched with a score of cuts, some of which were still bleeding, from the transparisteel shards he'd dived through during the battle with the feral droids.

Xizor held Jax's lightsaber. As Den watched, the Falleen activated it. The glimmering blue blade extended. Den had a feeling that Jax would be getting the business end of the blade very soon.

Why doesn't he use the Force? Den could only assume that all the mopak Jax had been through in the last few hours had pretty much drained him. Whatever the reason, it was obvious that the Jedi had no mojo left to work.

He could save him.

Or, more accurately, I-Five could. During their pursuit of Xizor, I-Five had alluded to "further modifications" that he had made, with Den's help. One of them had been a programming change in the power-down module. In most protocol units, the activation switch was on the back of the droid's neck, making it easy for just about anyone taller than himself to turn the unit on or off. In the case of I-Five and other models of his line, the switch couldn't be removed completely—it was hardwired into his CPU as a fail-safe. But they'd been able to bypass the circuitry and add a password that could verbally reactivate him. It had to be spoken in Den's voice; once I-Five's audioreceptors registered it, his CPU would rekindle itself.

If he spoke the password now, I-Five would awaken

in time to stop whatever fate Xizor had in mind for Jax. If anyone could do it, the droid could, Den knew. It wasn't a sure thing, but it was, without question, the way to bet.

Still—if he waited, even only a few more seconds, there was an even better chance that Jax Pavan would be out of his hair forever. I-Five would grieve, but grief dies eventually. And Den would have his friend back.

He didn't hesitate. He leaned closer to the sprawled droid and whispered, "Bota."

I-Five's photoreceptors brightened slightly. He was looking at Xizor, who had his back turned. The prince raised the lightsaber over his head—

I-Five rose to his feet. Den realized what the droid was going to do, and had just enough time to realize also that he couldn't stick his bound fingers in his ears.

This is gonna hurt, he thought.

It did.

Standing near Xizor and Jax, with Bug-Eyes holding him in its unbreakable grasp, Nick Rostu realized that he'd been masterfully played. He'd heard of the influence the Falleen could exert over other species, how they could sway emotions, manipulate feelings, but he'd momentarily forgotten about it. Understandable, given all that had happened in the past few days, and Xizor had taken full advantage of his inattention. But there was no point in cursing Xizor's name now; the important thing was that the mesmerizing chemical triggers had worn off, no doubt due to Xizor's concentration on Jax.

"It's nothing personal, you understand," Xizor was saying to Jax. "But I've been looking for a way to establish an alliance of my own with Lord Vader. The information in this droid appears to be the key, and I have to make sure there are no entanglements that will impede my plan. Your friend here"—he nodded at Nick—"was kind enough to lead us to you." Nick saw Jax raise his eyes and look at him, and the look cut him to the heart—not anger, not even contempt; just weariness.

He had to do *something*. But what? Nick was a trained soldier, and he had no doubts of his ability to take down one, or even a couple or three opponents. But Xizor was a Falleen, trained in the martial arts and, at the moment, armed with a lightsaber. Not to mention having the whole pheromone thing going, as well as Bug-Eyes, armed and ready to zap anyone who got out of line. Nick still had his blaster holstered at his hip, but with the droid holding his arms, it wasn't going to do him much good. In fact, even if he could break free of the droid's grasp, it seemed the only advantage Nick might possibly have would be if Xizor was momentarily paralyzed by having to choose, among so many options, which way to take him out of the game.

The lightsaber's crackle sounded to Nick like the thrumming of a taut, vibrating cable. The prince raised the shimmering blade over Jax's head. "It's nothing personal," he said again. "It's just business."

There was no more time to wait for a miracle, and miracles weren't exactly regular occurrences in Nick's life anyway. He tensed. He had one card left to play, a bit of knowledge that Xizor didn't know he had, and a reasonable chance now of implementing it before the Fallen could, quite literally, hand him his head. If he could get the drop on Xizor for just a second, he might be able to delay the prince long enough for the rest of his plan to work. He doubted he'd get much more time than that; Falleen were much stronger than humans, and their reflexes much faster.

Well, no one said it would be easy.

"Zu woohama," he said quietly to the droid holding him. And then: "Release me."

The pressure of 10-4TO's grasp on Nick's arms vanished. Though he'd spoken softly, it was obvious that the prince heard him, even over the hiss and crackle of the lightsaber. Nick didn't hesitate; he leapt at the astonished Falleen, his target the upraised hand that held the lightsaber. As he did so, he shouted to Bug-Eyes, "Free the Jedi!"

He didn't know how close he'd come to grabbing the weapon's hilt, but it wasn't close enough. Even though taken by surprise, Xizor was able to backhand Nick away, knocking him across the chamber and against the far wall. He felt a searing pain in his chest as he fell—

And then, to his astonishment, there *was* a miracle.

Unfortunately, it, too, was very painful.

Kaird wasn't sure why he had been left alive. He'd figured on a life expectancy of maybe ten minutes after Xizor had realized his lab and its personnel had been destroyed—by what, Kaird didn't know, and didn't want to know. Xizor had muttered something about droids, but how could droids be responsible for such atrocities? Even battle droids were programmed for swift, clean kills—not so much out of humanitarian motives as simple expediency. Whatever had killed those scientists and their assistants had taken their time; they had *enjoyed* it.

He shuddered. If whatever had done this was still lurking about, then the only safe direction for them was straight up. But Xizor didn't seem to care. All his attention was focused on the Jedi.

"It's nothing personal, you understand," Xizor was telling the Jedi as he raised the latter's lightsaber. The prince's blaster was still in its holster; evidently Xizor favored the Jedi's own weapon for his execution. But then, Xizor had always been one for the dramatic gesture.

It's nothing personal. Kaird almost smiled. When you took another being's life, it was *always* personal. He'd looked into the eyes of too many sentients whose existences he'd terminated in the services of someone else's "business" to know otherwise.

His musings were interrupted by something surprising: two words, spoken in a low voice by the human who had tried to pose as a Black Sun operative. Two words that he had heard spoken for the first time only recently, by Prince Xizor, to 10-T40.

"Zu woohama." The code phrase to control the droid, followed by a quick, quiet command: "Release me."

Obviously Xizor's influence over the human had waned. Of course he didn't have a prayer of success, but, just possibly, the distraction might give Kaird a chance. His legs weren't bound; he could run, lose himself in the maze of corridors . . .

And get lost himself, no doubt. And then what? Wander around with his arms still cuffed until whatever tore through that lab like a rancor on synthoroot found him? His wrists were forcecuffed; they weren't bound with something like rope or plasticord that he might be able to cut on a jagged piece of metal. The only thing that would open them was the key, and Xizor had that.

Kaird gritted his teeth. He had no choice; unless a

miracle happened, his best option was to wait, and hope that Xizor gave him an opening once the forcecuffs were removed. And he knew from long experience that there were no such things as miracles.

Given that, he was very happy to be proved wrong—even with the pain the miracle brought.

forty-two

"It's just business," Xizor said as he raised the light-saber. And then Nick Rostu spoke the cryptic phrase that controlled Bug-Eyes, ordering him to "Free the Jedi!" as he leapt at Xizor. The prince, though obviously taken aback, was still quick enough to block Nick's attack and bat him away like an annoying insect. At the same time I-Five, whom Jax had thought had been deactivated by Xizor, rose to his feet and produced from his vocabulator a deafening, warbling screech that took everyone completely by surprise. It was unbelievably painful; Jax didn't know how loud it was, but it was definitely pitched much higher than the pain threshold of most sentient organics.

Of course, it had no effect on the other droid. Bug-Eyes moved quickly to Jax's side, intent on carrying out Nick's order to free him, but before it could, Xizor shouted, *"Zu woohama!"*

Ten-Four-Tee-Oh stopped in its tracks. Xizor, obviously in as much pain as the others, nevertheless managed to point at I-Five. The meaning was clear, even to a droid: *Stop him!*

Bug-Eyes spun about, aiming its arm cannon at I-Five. It fired, but I-Five, still screeching, pointed his right index finger at the other, aiming as precisely as only a droid could. The high-intensity light beam met the particle beam in midair.

Though the quantum states of the two beams were somewhat different, there was still a considerable amount of overlap. The intense energies battled for a moment, filling the chamber with blinding, pyrotechnic sparks.

Jax staggered back, momentarily blinded. Through dazzle-spots he saw Xizor, still obviously in pain from the droid's shriek. The Falleen clapped both hands to his ears, dropping the lightsaber as he did so, and sank to his knees. He had evidently thumbed the control to LOCK earlier, because the blade didn't vanish when the hilt left his hand. The weapon bounced once, sliced the corner off a metal cabinet, and came to rest with the hilt leaning against another piece of debris. The blade pointed upward at forty-five degrees, its hum cycling.

Just then the more powerful particle beam smashed through the ray of coherent light and struck I-Five full in the chest plate. The droid was hurled backward, hard enough to hit the wall. The screech from his vocabulator stopped as he sprawled on the floor.

"Five!" the Sullustan shouted, struggling with his bonds, which he had no chance at all of breaking. Jax could barely hear the cry. The air in the room seemed to be still shimmering with sound waves. He wondered if his ears were bleeding. He staggered toward his lightsaber and crouched before it, facing away from the blade. Cautiously, concentrating all his will on maintaining his balance, he extended his arms behind him, his wrists pulled as far apart as they would go. The lightsaber might sever the energy link that bound his wrists. Or it might resonate with the cuffs and fry him quicker than lightning. The only way to tell was—

There was a hissing sound nearly as loud as the droid's screech, a static discharge that made every hair stand on end, and he was hurled from the lightsaber to land sprawling a couple of meters away.

His hands were free.

As best he could, given the reverberating pain in his head, he assessed the situation. I-Five was beginning to get to his feet. Laranth and Den were still bound and lying against the far wall, although only Den was awake. Then he saw 10-4TO turning toward him, lining up its shot.

Jax pushed himself to his feet and thrust out both hands, hoping desperately that the Force would be there.

It wasn't.

He dived, tucked, and rolled to his feet behind a large piece of equipment as the energy bolt scorched the floor where he'd been standing.

The droid turned to fire again. Jax was momentarily safe behind the chunk of metal and circuitry, but for how long?

Once more he beseeched the Force, and once more he was denied. The droid stalked forward. It seized and hurled aside the shattered control bank behind which Jax was hiding—

And Jax lunged forward, one hand extended beneath the droid's extended arm cannon. He rammed the small dagger he'd pulled from the sheath hidden between his shoulder blades into the gap between the thoracic and ventral plates.

Bug-Eyes staggered backward. Jax glimpsed sparks

sizzling in the welter of wires and circuitry that constituted its innards. One foot struck a piece of debris, and
the droid fell against the transparisteel window. The material, already shattered and weakened, gave way, and
10-4TO dropped through it, disappearing from sight.
An instant later, a crash echoed from below.

Jax stood and turned, intending to go back and grab
his lightsaber's hilt; the blade had been extinguished,
along with the cuffs. But the hilt was no longer lying on
the floor. Desperately, Jax cast about for it.

"Looking for this?" The Falleen's silky voice came
from behind him. Jax turned, and saw that the lightsaber was in Xizor's hand. As Jax watched, the blade
again generated itself, with an ominous hum. Xizor,
grinning, started toward the unarmed Jedi. His skin
glowed on the cusp between green and orange. He evidently had recovered from the sound barrage's effects
much quicker than had Jax.

Jax snapped his right hand forward, palm-first, hoping to hurl the Force at Xizor. But there was only a
yawning emptiness as the Force refused him yet again.

Xizor stopped warily when Jax pantomimed the
blow; now he smiled and continued his advance. Before
he had moved farther than a couple more steps, however, a laser struck near his feet, and another flashed just
above his head. He turned with a startled shout, seeking
the source of the new attack.

I-Five stood nearby, aiming both fingers at the prince.
"Please shut off the lightsaber, Your Highness," the
droid said. "And toss those blasters aside as well."

Xizor snarled, his skin flaming with anger. I-Five's aim
did not waver. "I'm sure you're quite fast, Prince Xizor,

but not as fast as light." He shrugged. "Universal law
and all that."

The Falleen hesitated, then deactivated the energy
weapon and divested himself of both blasters. Jax
started forward, intending to claim his lightsaber from
him—but then he saw Nick Rostu, sprawled on his back
near one wall, with a bloody piece of transparisteel rising from his chest.

Nick was lying where Xizor's blow had tossed him,
his head propped up by debris. He could see the fragment of transparent metal protruding from just below
his rib cage, and almost smiled, because under his shirt
he knew the shard had bisected the old scar he'd gotten
back on Haruun Kal. The fresh wound bisecting the
previous one had no doubt marked an X across his
midriff—not that he needed such an obvious sign to tell
him he was done. He marveled that he wasn't feeling
any pain. *There's a lot to be said for shock.*

He realized that someone was leaning over him. It
was Jax.

Nick tried to tell him that he was sorry, that it hadn't
been him, that Vader had blackmailed him and Xizor
had manipulated him. He wasn't sure if he'd managed
to say all that, or, indeed, any of it, but Jax looked as if
he understood.

There was one more thing . . . what was it? Hard to
remember, it was like his mind was leaking away with
his blood. It seemed suddenly terribly important that he
tell Jax something. Again, he wasn't sure if he got it
across or not, but Jax nodded, smiling through the
crusted blood on his face. He also said something, but
Nick's hearing was about as useless as his legs after that

vocal solo from I-Five. He could see Jax going through the pockets of his greatcoat, looking for what Nick had told him was there, but he couldn't feel anything, either. He hoped there wasn't blood on his uniform. A soldier—particularly an officer—should try to look presentable, at least.

Still, Nick felt satisfied; he had managed to get through his debriefing. Very important; there was a war going on, and he had done his part. Now, finally, he could rest, which was good, because he was just too tired to try to talk anymore. And anyway, the fellow standing there—who had it been? Hard to see his face, what with all that light—had moved away to face another silhouette. Now the two were dancing around each other in slow motion, and there were flashing lights and faint, faraway buzzing sounds. Was one of them Mace Windu?

Nick didn't know. It really didn't matter anymore. It was time for him to leave. His new ship was waiting for him, its hyperdrive primed, ready to dust this world. He would lift in just a minute or so. Just as soon as he got his breath back. Just a moment, to rest. He'd earned that much, at least. The war was finally over. It was time to stand down.

The lights hurt Nick's eyes, so he closed them.

Jax rose and stepped away from Nick's body. Xizor stood a couple of meters away, still holding the lightsaber hilt. Jax was holding a hilt as well; one of the last things Nick had told him, in a barely audible whisper, had been about the enigmatic device the Korunnai had found in the *Far Ranger*. It was obviously a weapon; the only problem was, Jax had no idea what kind it was.

It looked to be something akin to a lightsaber, but lighter, and built for one hand. Nick had not had a chance to try it, and Jax didn't even know if it would work.

He didn't care.

He didn't care that Xizor had his lightsaber, or that the Falleen prince was a master of teräs käsi, a martial art designed centuries ago and refined through the ages to be particularly effective against Jedi. He didn't care that, for some reason he didn't understand, his connection to the Force had grown sporadic. None of it mattered now. It was in the past. The future was not his concern, either. What mattered was the present.

What mattered was *now*.

Jax glanced over at the others. The avian and Laranth were still forcecuffed, as was Den Dhur. Laranth was either dead or unconscious, but the fact that she was forcecuffed argued for the latter. The only one free was I-Five, who still stood a little way off, forming the third point of a triangle composed of himself, Jax, and Xizor. The droid was still covering Xizor.

"It isn't against my core programming to severely disable the enemy of my friend," he said to Jax. "If you want me to, that is."

"What I want," Jax said, "is for you to see what's happened to the other droid. It's still got the vital data stored within it."

"But—"

"No buts. Prince Xizor and I will settle this between ourselves."

I-Five hesitated, projecting concern, then nodded. He crossed to the transparisteel window, leapt nimbly through it, and dropped out of sight.

During the exchange with I-Five, Jax had kept one eye on Xizor. With a grin, the Falleen raised his free hand, palm-up, and beckoned. "Let's see what you've got," he said.

Jax thumbed the trigger button.

forty-three

From the weapon's hilt leapt a thin length of supple metal, immediately followed by the proscribed arc wave of an energy field, this one following the length of the flexible metallic cord.

It was a whip. An energy whip. Jax let its bright green length uncoil, then twirled his wrist. The lightwhip's end singed a larger, ragged circle into the floor in response. He snapped it experimentally, sending a running wave down its length. The tip made a satisfying *crack!*, louder than its wavering hum, as it broke the sound barrier. Jax couldn't even begin to imagine the complexity of the modulation circuitry within the handle.

As part of his training, he'd practiced with lightwhips, but not nearly as often as he'd used a lightsaber. He wasn't nearly as proficient with a whip as he was with a blade. And he wouldn't be getting used to it under the best of conditions.

"Very impressive," Xizor said. "But I think blade trumps whip. In any case, I'm sure you'll forgive me for not being chivalrous enough to let you practice a bit."

With that, Xizor jerked the lightsaber down in front of himself, brought his other hand over the handle, and aimed the tip of the blade at Jax's left eye as he attacked.

Jax backpedaled, trying to gain as much time as he could to get more familiar with this new weapon. It wasn't as elegant as an energy sword, or as powerful, or able to cut through as much. It did however, have the advantage of length—easily twice that of his lightsaber's blade at full extension. The metallic core's length was also elastic, he found, to a limited degree.

The Falleen brought the blade around and down in an attempt to sever the Jedi's wrist, but Jax blocked it with the thick part of the thong, near the hilt. Xizor recovered, twirling the lightsaber around his wrist.

Jax flicked the lightwhip again, sending a traveling wave down its length, snapping the tip with another supersonic *crack!* that warned Xizor to keep his distance.

It didn't matter how well versed the Falleen might be with a lightsaber, he told himself. No ordinary humanoid could contend with a Jedi one-on-one and expect to win. Even a true teräs käsi adept, harnessing his own inner energy and drawing on decades of honed skill, could hope, at best, for a draw, and there weren't more than a handful of those in all the galaxy.

The prince edged in, corkscrewing to his right, keeping the lightsaber before him. Jax turned slightly, reaching for the Force . . .

And, once again, he found nothing.

He kept his expression blank, but he could tell by the fierceness of Xizor's grin that the prince had somehow sensed his concern; smelled his fear sweat, most likely. And in that instant Jax realized what at least part of the problem was. All the months of hiding, of constant vigilance to avoid connecting to the Force in an active way, to avoid the possibility of alerting Vader to his presence, had become second nature. And now, in the extremity of his need, he found he *couldn't* connect.

Over the months he'd come to regard the Emperor's minions, especially Vader, as akin to carrion deathbirds, ever circling overhead, their sharp and cold vision catching the slightest movement below. Call on the Force and one of them would know, would swoop down and pluck Jax from the multitudes like a single fleek from a vast bevy of them. Even if he was wrong, even if Vader and his myrmidons weren't that constantly watchful, the effect was the same.

Whatever the reason, he could not let his inability undo him now. Jax slid his left foot back and turned almost ninety degrees aslant to Xizor. He raised his arm and rotated his wrist, whirling the lightwhip above his head in a circular pattern.

Xizor nodded, as if acknowledging the move. He turned to his left a bit and began to rotate the lightsaber over his wrist, nimbly switching hands at irregular intervals while moving forward. Jax tensed, waiting for the inevitable moment when his opponent would falter, when he could snap the energy braid forward and flick the blade from—

Suddenly Xizor ceased the almost hypnotic movement of the blade and leapt *over* him, tucking and somersaulting while slashing downward.

Jax wouldn't have thought anybody but a Jedi could pull a stunt like that. Frantically he struck up from the circle pattern, wrapping the energy braid around the lightsaber. Blue and green arc waves sparked and sang of conflict, searing the very atoms of the air around them, filling his nostrils with the tang of ozone.

But before he could follow through and yank the

lightsaber from Xizor's hand, the prince thumbed off the blade's power. The lightwhip's length dropped, and Jax had to dodge to avoid the deadly lash himself.

Xizor landed and reactivated the blade. From his crouch, Jax swung his arm back in a low arc, then back up and over his shoulder. The lightwhip sang through the air and wrapped again about the blade. Before Xizor could deactivate the lightsaber again, Jax yanked as hard as he could, pulling Xizor off-balance.

The sudden tug was enough to slow Xizor, but not enough to break his one-handed grip. He lunged after Jax as the lightwhip slipped free of the lightsaber, sending more sparks flying. Jax ducked, letting the luminous blade whistle by barely above his head, then dived into a roll as Xizor slashed again, missing him by a finger's breadth. He came up, half turned, and, while still moving, snapped his hand around at Xizor. The glowing whip lanced at the Falleen, almost as if it were a hurled spear.

Xizor ducked and spun in a full circle, dropping the blade to chest level as he moved, seeking to bisect Jax. But the Jedi was too fast—he was already in full back-pedal, snapping the lightwhip to cover his retreat. Xizor had to parry the flailing energy line to keep the tip from taking an arm off.

Once again Jax reached for the Force, and once again he found only cold vacuum. Evidently, understanding the problem wasn't the same as fixing it. And this was the worst possible situation in which to attempt a reconnection: in the midst of battle, overwrought and worried.

He should not have been so foolhardy as to challenge Prince Xizor. He should have simply had I-Five take him out; the Falleen was stronger than Jax, but little match for a laser-packing droid. Now it was starting to look like his macho posturing might have doomed them all. I-Five was occupied with 10-4TO, and Laranth was still out of the game.

He heard an odd noise behind him, but he could not afford to take his eyes off Xizor, who was pacing just outside the lightwhip's reach. The noise grew louder; a popping, tearing sound, which Jax recognized too late as the rending of the reinforced plasteel bolts on the other set of doors. He whirled about in time to see a wheel-mounted maintenance droid rolling at him, with pieces of jagged scrap metal welded to its chest, extruding like knives. It babbled in Binary, a nonstop cacophony of clicks, chirps, whistles, and trills, as it came directly at him. Jax sidestepped and brought the lightwhip up, over his head and out. The energy braid struck across the rounded dome of the droid's CPU and sizzled through it. Its brakes locked up, and Jax could smell the odor of burned silicone as the treads locked and skidded on the floor, the gyroscopes whining to keep it upright, but too little, too late. The glowing braid sheared through the droid's head and body at an angle, and, with a burst of electrical sparks and sputters, the droid collapsed, falling in two pieces.

Jax dropped flat onto the grimy floor, and not a heartbeat too soon—the energy blade hummed through the spot where he'd just stood. He rolled onto his back and came up, lightwhip describing a rapid circle in front of him.

The disadvantage of the lightwhip was that it took more time to recover from a committed stroke. Jax had to be careful lest Xizor spot him leaving an opening. He took a deep breath, allowed half of it to escape. *A connection with the Force would sure come in handy about now . . .*

"Jax! Look out!" Den cried.

He half turned, tried to duck, but too late. A chunk of debris, flung by yet another feral droid entering the shattered door, struck him a glancing blow on the head. Momentarily stunned, he dropped the lightwhip, which fizzled out as soon as it left his hand. He staggered back and caught a glimpse of the droid: an astromech, with a makeshift catapult-like contraption secured to its dome that hurled fist-sized pieces of metal and duracrete.

Jax was a dead man. Xizor had him; Jax knew it, and the prince knew he knew it.

The lightwhip was out of reach, and Xizor loomed over him, skin flushed crimson with the anticipation of the kill. Jax accepted the fact. Now he would join the Force, and perhaps all those unanswerable questions would be—

As if operated by some unknown puppeteer, his right hand shot out, palm forward. Xizor was hurled backward as if hit by a repulsor beam, to slam against the wall three meters away.

Jax felt the Force wrap itself around him, felt the familiar threads attach themselves to him once more. He let them move and manipulate him. He rose to his feet as if levitated. Another gesture, and the rock-tossing astromech flew back against the wall as well, hard enough to rupture its casing. Sparks flew and oil spewed. Its Binary echolalia dragged into low distortion as it ran down.

Xizor got to his feet, the shock on his face transmuting to anger. Jax held out his hand, and the lightsaber flew from where Xizor had dropped it into his grasp. As he activated it, he summoned the lightwhip with his left hand.

Behind him, he heard Den Dhur say, "*That's* what I call a comeback."

Jax understood what had happened. In the acceptance of his impending death, he had returned to the level of serenity needed to be one with the Force. It had not been a matter of him losing his connection to the Force; it had been a matter of the Force choosing him once more as a vessel.

Xizor's skin begin to shift, back to a warm shade of orange, and Jax guessed the Falleen was activating his pheromones. Jax gestured, felt the Force threads around him expand, driving the air currents back toward Xizor. The prince's expression turned to one of surprise.

"Yield," Jax said. Xizor had no choice; Jax had both weapons, and the Force.

Xizor laughed.

He leapt, covering the distance between them easily. The movement was fast, very fast. He flew toward Jax feetfirst, almost taking him completely by surprise. Even with his reawakened connection with the Force, it was hard to divine Xizor's purpose. The prince's mind was powerful, capable of concealing his intentions until the last second before he took action. His reflexes were far faster than those of a human, and his muscles strong enough to propel him almost as far as the Force could propel Jax. The Jedi dodged, then turned quickly, whip and blade both ready to kill, if need be.

Xizor's insane, he thought. *He has no hope of victory now, he—*

The Falleen landed nimbly on both feet, and Jax realized his intent—a moment too late. Lying on the floor nearby was Nick Rostu's body—and, within Xizor's reach, the major's blaster. Xizor scooped it up, whirled, and fired at Jax all in one smooth motion.

Jax blocked the bolt with his lightsaber. The glare of the two colliding energy fields was over almost instantly, but in that instant the scion of House Sizhran had vanished into the darkness of the corridor.

Jax felt no urge to follow. Prince Xizor was out of the picture; now he had to find 10-4TO and make sure the data were intact. He turned and started for the broken window where the droid had fallen.

Abruptly he experienced a sudden tingle that vibrated the lines of the Force—a plangent throb telling him that a new player was approaching the blasted landscape of the Factory District. Someone extremely strong in the Force—stronger than he'd ever encountered before. It could mean only one thing:

Darth Vader was coming.

forty-four

Jax felt himself grow cold with dread. He felt another tremor in the Force, a warmer, friendly one, and realized, even before he looked to confirm it, that Laranth was awake. He saw from her expression that she had also felt the vibration in the Force. She might not be able to identify it as quickly or as assuredly as he had, but she knew it was bad news.

"Stand up," he said to Den and Laranth, crossing to them. He brought his lightsaber in a quick, short chop, severing the forcecuffs binding Laranth. He was ready for the energy backlash that shorted out both cuffs and blade this time, and so it only drove him back a few steps instead of hurling him to the floor. It still packed a considerable punch, however. Laranth staggered back, then recovered, rubbing her arms.

"Ow," she said.

"Sorry," Jax replied. "Xizor had the only key, and I don't think he could be persuaded to give it up, even if we could find him."

He relit his lightsaber and turned toward Den. "Your turn."

"Hey, wait a minute," the Sullustan said. "Let's not be hasty. I'm sure there's another way to—*whoa!*"

The clash of the two fields knocked Den on his backside. He rose slowly, giving Jax a glare. "If I ever get a byline again, you, my friend, are in for some serious libel."

Jax turned away, clipping the weapon's hilt to his belt.

"Hey," the avian said. "What about me?"

"You can stay cuffed," Jax replied, "until we get to know you a little better."

The avian seemed about to protest, then closed his beak-like mouth with an annoyed click.

"Pretty amazing show," Den said, rubbing his posterior. "Can't say I was really all that glad to be ringside, though . . ."

Before anyone else could say anything, Jax, alerted by peripheral vision, looked over to the shattered transparisteel. I-Five was climbing up from below.

"Good news and bad news," he said, before anyone could speak. "The fall evidently immobilized 10-4TO, which was then set upon—I assume by feral droids. It was stripped of its appendages and CPU."

Jax went cold. "But that means the data are—"

"No longer in 10-4TO's possession, I'm afraid."

Silence for a moment. Then Den asked, "And the good news?"

"That *is* the good news. The bad news is that my sensors indicate that the radiation level is higher. You organics need to leave, and I'm not staying here by myself."

"It gets better," Jax said. "Vader's coming. He may already be here."

There was a moment of shocked silence, and then the avian said, "*Now* will someone please *get these fripping cuffs off me*?"

Jax unclipped the lightsaber's hilt again. They'd have to trust the bird man—they'd need all their speed and abilities, and the threads of Force emanating from him, while hard and ruthless, had no strands of possible betrayal interwoven.

He felt a wave of weariness wash over him. Even if they did escape, there was no guarantee that Vader would give up. For all Jax knew, the Sith Lord would pursue him across the galaxy. He'd already come halfway around the planet. Though Jax had no idea why Vader wanted him, it seemed pretty clear that he would not give up until he had either Jax or proof of his death.

Jax freed the avian—his name, he said, was Kaird—and powered up his weapon again. He looked at the glowing blade, nodded to himself, then turned to I-Five. "We need something big to cover our escape," he said. "And I think I know where to get one." Quickly he explained his plan to the droid.

I-Five projected surprise. "Are you willing to give up your weapon to do this?"

"I'm not happy about it, but I don't see another choice," Jax replied. "The only life-form readings that the freighter's scanners picked up in a five-hundred-kilometer radius were Xizor's and Kaird's. I don't mind sending a bunch of feral droids to the scrap heap, and maybe Vader as well. Are your sensors up to it?"

"Not a problem—the radiation signature is quite detectable."

Jax nodded, hesitated, then handed his lightsaber to I-Five. The droid took it and began to walk slowly around in the rubble-strewn chamber. He appeared to be looking for something.

Den and the avian joined Jax and Laranth. They

watched the droid with some perplexity. "What are you doing, Five?" Den asked. "We've got to get out of here."

"Agreed," the droid replied. "But as Jax has pointed out, simply leaving won't throw Vader off our trail. We need a distraction—a major distraction. Unless Vader is convinced Jax is dead, he'll never stop hunting him.

"Ah. Here it is." I-Five was standing near the remains of one of the destroyed feral droids. He locked the lightsaber's trigger button and held it out at arm's length, between two fingers, with the energy blade pointing straight down. Then he dropped it.

It struck the floor, point-first. The frictionless blade, hot enough to melt through a twenty-centimeter blast door, barely slowed down when it hit the duracrete. The sound it made dropped into a slightly lower register, but that was all. In a few seconds it had disappeared down the shaft it was melting.

I-Five turned and walked quickly back to the others. "Let's go," he said.

Den Dhur stared at him. "Have you flipped your chip? What was that all about?"

"It's about creating a major distraction, like he said," Jax replied. "Don't blame I-Five; it was my idea."

"It was a good one. I'll be happy to help you find a new lightsaber—if we get out of here alive."

"What about Rostu's body?" Den asked.

Jax turned and looked back at Nick's still form. He felt a pang of regret; Nick Rostu had died bravely, trying to save his friends and Master Piell's mission. He deserved a decent funeral, at least. "I-Five, can you bring him?" he asked quietly. "We can release him in orbit—he would have liked that, I think."

I-Five bent over Nick, started to lift him—then

stopped. He was quite still for a moment; then he said, "He's still alive."

"*What?*" Jax, Laranth, and Den spoke simultaneously. Only Kaird was silent, although he looked as amazed as they did.

"The transparisteel shard that skewered him passed through the lower abdominal cavity." As I-Five spoke, he used his finger laser to burn through the fragment near where it entered Nick's back. "It missed the spine and kidneys. I'm detecting some internal bleeding and the beginnings of systemic infection and peritonitis—but I believe it's reversible if he's treated within twenty-four hours."

Jax felt a surge of relief. "There should be a medpac on the freighter. Hurry!" He saw the droid carefully lift Nick, then turned and headed into the corridor, followed by the others.

"We've still got to get past Vader's transport to reach our own," Kaird pointed out. "Any ideas on how we accomplish that?"

"One or two," Jax replied. "Let's worry about getting out of here first."

"Will someone tell me just what we're running from?" Den asked as he hurried to keep up with the others.

"About ten meters beneath our feet is the reactor containment unit," I-Five said. "I mentioned before that it was unstable—in fact, long-term exposure to radiation leakage may be what drove the droids mad. In any event, I estimate that we have less than twenty-five minutes before the lightsaber burns its way through the impervium shielding and—"

"Gotcha," Den said. He doubled his speed, pushing past the others.

It might work, Jax told himself. The explosion would certainly be enough to remove Darth Vader as a problem from his life permanently. Even if Vader somehow survived, he would probably be convinced that Jax hadn't. Either way, this was a good chance to escape the Sith Lord's ominous shadow—if not for good, then at least for a considerable time.

They hurried through the dark corridors, I-Five carrying Nick Rostu and lighting the way. It appeared that he had a droid, Jax mused; not as property, but as a friend. An odd concept—but one he was getting used to.

It was good to have a friend.

forty-five

Lord Vader watched the bridge monitor, which was focused on the entrance. Rhinann watched as well, trying to divine the inscrutable thoughts going on behind the helmet and, as usual, failing.

Including Vader's transport, there were now three ships at rest before the decaying buildings. One was the Corellian freighter that had been given to Rostu. The other was an assault ship, graceful and sleek. Rhinann approved of the look. He wondered to whom it belonged.

Vader spoke to Captain Tanna. "When they come out, take Pavan alive. Kill whoever is with him. Take no chances; the Force is strong in him."

"Yes, my lord." Captain Tanna saluted. "But what of the droid? Was it not the reason for this journey?"

Vader waved a dismissive hand. "Don't worry about the droid. Pavan is more important."

"Understood," Captain Tanna said. He glanced at the monitor and reacted in surprise. "My lord—you will want to see this, I think."

The Dark Lord moved to look at the forward monitor. The movement gave Rhinann a momentary view of what the captain and Vader were looking at: a lone figure striding rapidly from the plant entrance toward the nearby assault ship. Rhinann immediately recognized the being's identity, and the surprise he felt was almost enough to make him forget, for an instant, his fear. Because certainly one of the last people he would have expected to see in this desolate place was Prince Xizor of House Sizhran.

The outside cam followed the prince as he crossed the rubble-strewn landscape toward the assault ship grounded nearby. "Shall I have him detained, my lord?"

"No, Captain Tanna," Vader replied. "As a member of Falleen royalty, Prince Xizor enjoys diplomatic immunity." He sounded slightly amused. "No doubt we'll understand his presence here better after we have questioned Pavan."

Rhinann watched Prince Xizor enter the assault ship. The prince did not so much as glance at the large *Lambda*-class shuttle, though he could not have failed to see the blazon of the Empire on its hull. After a few moments the repulsorlifts powered up and the sleek ship fell away from the ground, rising quickly until it was lost to view against the stars.

A young, ashen-faced lieutenant looked up from his station. "Lord Vader—Captain Tanna—sensors are detecting a buildup of intense heat and radioactivity directly below the droid plant. There's only one possible explanation—"

"The reactor core is overloading," Vader said, calmly. He stepped to the console panel and calibrated some instruments, then examined the resulting readouts. "Fourteen minutes until detonation. So much for taking Pavan alive. A pity there will be no opportunity for a second chance." He turned to Captain Tanna. "Take us up,

Captain. When we're out of harm's way, destroy that freighter."

"My lord, the Jedi Pavan has emerged from the building, along with the droid and several others."

"Excellent." Vader gave his attention again to the monitor. "We must strike quickly, while we have the element of surprise. A few warning shots should keep them occupied until our troopers take them." He looked closer. "Ready eight troopers, Captain—that should be enough."

Captain Tanna looked worried. "My lord," he blurted, "have you forgotten the reactor?"

Vader turned his expressionless visage toward Tanna. Rhinann shivered; he knew what looking into those black orbs felt like. "I forget nothing, Captain—including insubordination. Are we clear on that?"

Captain Tanna swallowed audibly and nodded.

Kaird was feeling considerably more optimistic. And why not? After all, his prospects for the future had improved immeasurably just in the last couple of hours. He'd gone from being a prisoner to freedom, and had apparently fallen in with a group of malcontents who, if not exactly friendly toward him, at least were not particularly disposed to let him die. Which was fine with Kaird; they didn't all have to be nest brothers. All he asked was that they let him come along until some outpost of civilization was reached; he could find his own way from there, thank you very much.

He had no intention of going back to Midnight Hall, however. He was done with Black Sun. He would never have a better chance to disappear from their crosshairs than now—assuming, of course, that he and present company could escape the imminent thermonuclear explosion. Even if Xizor somehow survived as well, there would be no reason for him to seek out Kaird, since he would not want any mention getting out about his plan to replace Underlord Perhi with a droid replica.

All of that, however, was in the future, which was an even riskier place to dwell than the past. Kaird knew that, if he didn't want his tail feathers singed in a really hot fire, he had best look to his present situation.

They rounded a corner and, much to Kaird's relief, saw the entrance in front of them. "How much time left?" he asked the droid.

"Twelve minutes, fourteen seconds."

"You don't sound happy," the Sullustan gasped, running hard to keep up.

"Prep time for the ship to lift is at least five minutes, and even at top atmospheric speed it'll take us another four or five to reach minimum safe distance," I-Five said. "We're cutting it very close."

Maybe too close, Kaird thought grimly. But here was the way out, finally. They emerged from the factory—and Kaird found himself staring into the muzzle of a blaster cannon, mounted on the underside of a *Lambda*-class shuttle not twenty meters away.

Jax saw the huge shuttle looming over them, saw one of the blaster cannons swivel toward them. No doubt Vader thought he'd won; he didn't know that in a few minutes they would all be incandescent dust, or he'd be gone by now.

"Laranth! I-Five! Buy some time!" he shouted. I-Five handed Nick's body to the avian, and immediately his lasers and the Paladin's blasters began firing at the targeting array. Jax knew that this would gain him only a few seconds before the computers implemented different vectors. He hoped it would be enough.

He leapt, letting the Force take him, letting it carry him across the intervening space between the plant entrance and the shuttle. He landed beneath the forward fuselage, and as his feet touched the ground he had the lightwhip in his hand. He lashed upward, extending the energized braid to its fullest length and slicing through the forward repulsorlift vanes.

One of the forward laser cannons lined up on him, but a particle beam bolt from Laranth's blaster fused the barrel to molten slag.

"Make for the freighter!" he shouted at the others. They didn't need to be told; they were already running full-out. Laranth and I-Five continued to give covering fire as they ran. Jax turned to follow—and found himself face-to-face with a tall, dark figure in a black cloak.

Vader—!

Captain Tanna shouted, "He's disabled the forward vanes! We can't lift!"

Time to go, Rhinann decided. This shuttle was doomed, and the other ship represented his only possible chance of survival. He had no idea what fate might await him if he deserted the shuttle for the freighter. He didn't even know whether Pavan and his cronies would make it to the freighter, or if they'd let him board. But once again he was doing a most uncharacteristic thing: acting on instinct. So, while Vader and the captain were occupied with the sudden emergency, the Elomin hurried off the bridge and down the corridors to the landing ramp.

It would take too long to lower the ramp, he knew. Fortunately there were also four emergency escape tubes on either side. He pulled the red release lever and stepped into the nearest tube.

The drop was only about ten meters; the landing, due to the repulsor cushion, barely hard enough to notice. Rhinann stepped out. He had only one chance for survival, he knew, and that was to convince Jax Pavan that he was not an enemy. He gathered up his robes, preparing to dash for the other ship—and, to his surprise, found himself in front of the very one he was seeking.

It wasn't Vader, Jax realized, after an instant's shock. He wasn't sure who it was; he recognized the species as an Elomin, but that was all.

"Listen to me," the Elomin said urgently. "You must take me with you! I have something—"

"Tell me later," Jax said. He grabbed the other's arm and ran for the freighter, half dragging the surprised Elomin with him.

They reached the ship and dashed up the ramp. At the top was the depressurized main air lock. Jax raised the ramp, watching it rise with agonizing slowness. Finally it closed; he slapped the comm switch and yelled, *"Lift!"*

He heard the muffled throb of the repulsorlift engines, and felt a g-force that nearly pulled him to his knees before the ship's gravity kicked in. He ran through the corridors that led to the cockpit, not looking to see if the Elomin was following.

The cockpit was crowded. I-Five was piloting, with the Paladin in the copilot's seat. Den stood behind them, watching tensely. The avian and Nick Rostu were nowhere to be seen. Outside the cockpit was the night sky, with one of the smaller moons in view. Jax peered over the droid's shoulders.

"Time?" he asked.

"Estimating one minute, forty-eight seconds to minimum safe distance," I-Five replied. "Approximately two minutes to detonation."

Jax gripped the back of the droid's chair. They could still make it—

The ship climbed at a steep angle. Jax studied the rearview monitor, which showed a magnified view of the Factory District. The Lambda shuttle was still floundering as the captain and crew tried frantically to bypass the damaged vanes. But it was already too late. He glanced at the chrono beside the monitor.

Five . . . four . . . three . . . two . . . one . . .

The monitor went white. After an instant polarization filters cut in, and the luminosity scaled down. Below them was a mushroom cloud, expanding and unfolding through colors of green, purple, and orange.

A moment later the shock wave hit them. The *Far Ranger* bucked, the view of the fireball bobbing crazily for a moment. The A-grav field held the internal environment steady, and they were already too high for the freighter to be thrown off-course.

I-Five checked the readouts. "Explosion yield was approximately twelve kilotons. No sign of hull damage; radiation levels minimal; shields holding."

"We made it," Laranth said. "With a whole ten seconds to spare."

"Do you always have to shave it so close, Five?" Den commented.

"Have you no sense of drama?"

Kaird entered. "Your friend's back in the crew's quarters," he said to Jax. "Still breathing, still unconscious."

I-Five stood. "I'll do what I can to stabilize him. If any of you know someone with access to a bacta tank, now would be a good time to call in a favor when we get to wherever we're going."

Jax slid into the pilot's seat that I-Five had just vacated. "I hope he knows enough medical procedure to help Nick."

"He does," Den said. "He spent six months in a Rimsoo, and he's a quick learner, as you've probably noticed."

"He's also raised an important point," Jax said. "Where are we going? Downlevel? Uplevel? Or offworld?"

There was a moment of silence as the others digested this. It was true; there was no real reason to return to the Yaam Sector. He had failed Master Piell's mission: he hadn't retrieved the data 10-4TO had been carrying.

Laranth was looking at a sensor readout. "The blast left a crater eighty meters across," she said. "I think we can assume that Vader is dead."

Jax shook his head. "No," he said. "He's not."

forty-six

They ultimately decided to head for a safe haven that the bird man knew of: a place used occasionally by Black Sun to hide beings toward whom other beings harbored ill will. The flight was taking several hours, due to the decision to avoid a suborbital trajectory in favor of flying low and cloaked. Den wasn't complaining; he was grateful for the chance to rest. The past twenty-four hours had been quite a ride—as intense as anything he'd experienced in the Clone Wars.

They'd acquired two new passengers: Kaird the Nediji and Haninum Tyk Rhinann, an Elomin. The latter said little, preferring to huddle by himself somewhat away from the others. Neither Jax nor Laranth could sense any clandestine motives from him, and so there was no reason not to believe his story that he had deserted Vader's ship at the last possible moment to escape the reactor explosion.

Ah, yes—Vader. At first, no one had believed Jax's conviction that the Sith Lord lived; the reactor core explosion had reduced a considerable amount of the Factory District to radioactive rubble. But Jax had brought up the playback of the last few moments before the blast, as recorded by the ship's rear cam. Just as the *Far*

Ranger had taken off, it was possible to see the blurred image of a life pod ejecting from the rear of the shuttle, heading in the opposite direction from the freighter.

"He's alive," Jax said. "I'm sure of it."

Den had been sorry to hear that. But the big question, as far as he was concerned, wasn't so much *What do we do about Darth Vader?* as *When do we space?* Because the only course that made any sense at all to him was to pile as many parsecs between them and the Core Worlds as possible.

The bird man, Kaird, understood that. His argument, which Den agreed with, was that they shouldn't even bother with the safe house; they should just haul back on the stick right now. Den was willing to wait long enough to be sure that Rostu would live, but after that his vote was for the same action, even though I-Five pointed out that such unauthorized flight plans tended to disrupt air and space traffic, which in turn tended to bring the system police, and usually not in the best of humor.

The Elomin was also anxious to leave Coruscant. He was hoping Jax could somehow help him accomplish that. Toward that end, he had given the Jedi something that he thought might be of use in some way, if Vader really had escaped the reactor explosion. He'd presented it to Jax just a little while ago . . .

Jax looked at the holocron in his hand, which Rhinann had just given him. He recognized the patterns marking it at once. "A Sith Holocron. Very ancient and valuable."

"And, perhaps, very useful to you, if Vader lives," Rhinann said.

I-Five took it and examined it. His photoreceoptors brightened in surprise. "If nothing else," he said, "it may serve as a piece of memorabilia."

Jax looked at him. "Memorabilia?"

"It's the same holocron your father tried to buy from Zippa the Toydarian," I-Five said. "I recognize it."

"Come on," Den said skeptically. "It's been twenty years, give or take a—"

I-Five just looked at him. Den made a gesture of defeat. "Right, you're a droid."

The droid continued, "Supposedly, it contains many lost secrets of the Sith. We had no way to find out, of course, since it can only be opened by someone who can use the Force."

Jax looked closer at it, turned it over, but made no attempt to open it. He looked at Rhinann. "And why are you giving it to me?"

The Elomin hesitated. "Because," he said at last, "I know that Vader, no matter what he says publicly about the Jedi no longer being a problem, wants you. He said that he had 'issues' with you. I know nothing more about that. Chance, however, always favors the prepared. As you said, only one who can touch the Force can open it. That leaves me out." The Elomin sounded surprisingly morose.

"Don't look so glum," Den said to Jax. "You're alive, and Vader most likely thinks you're dead. That sounds like a pretty happy ending to me."

"It might be—except that I failed to carry out Master Piell's last request," Jax said. "I didn't get the data from Ten-Four-Tee-Oh."

"There were no data," Rhinann said.

Jax turned slowly and looked at the Elomin. "What?"

"I don't know everything about Vader's plan," Rhinann said. "I was only told what was necessary. But I do know that the data that were supposedly so vital were, in fact, worthless. The droid was merely a decoy."

"Master Piell said—"

"The Lannik told you what he believed to be true. It had all been engineered by Vader toward one purpose."

"To flush *me* out? You can't be serious."

"Vader knew that word of Master Piell's death would eventually reach you through the Whiplash. That your friend Rostu was there when he died and brought you the news was pure serendipity."

It seemed absurd at first; and yet the more Jax thought about it, the more everything fell into place. The intervention of Prince Xizor and the avian Kaird had no doubt been unforeseen as well, and evidently had caused Vader a moment of concern. So he'd suborned someone already marginally in the game: Nick Rostu. Part of the confession Nick had whispered to Jax had been about the sword Vader had held over him—the threatened destruction of his people's home on Haruun Kal.

"Well," Den said, "if I were you, I wouldn't want to be within ten dimensions of anything having to do with the Sith. Maybe you can sell it once we get offworld."

Jax closed his hand around the holocron and slipped it into a pocket. Perhaps he would need the data someday. He hoped never to have to put it to the test, because he hoped never to encounter Darth Vader again.

Only a little more than two days ago, he'd been fully ready to leave—to take his berth on the Underground Mag-Lev and bid Coruscant farewell. No one would look at him askance, because he had earned it. He'd risked his life a score of times, saved people by hair-breadth escapes, gotten them on board freighters, transports, and other craft, barely in time for them to bid farewell to the bright hub of the galaxy, often leaving with little more than the clothes on their backs.

But now, somehow, it was different.

He looked up. "Sorry, Den," he said. "I'm not going."

"Ha-ha," Den said nervously. "What a kidder, huh?" He elbowed Rhinann in the ribs—or tried to. He wound up gouging the Elomin's knee.

I-Five looked at Jax. "Why?"

Jax took his time to answer. "I'm a Jedi," he said at last. "I'm sworn to help those in need, to uphold the Jedi Code. The Empire has decimated my Order—but they haven't won, and they *won't* win, as long as at least one Jedi remains. They drove me from the Temple, but they're not going to drive me off the planet. If Vader thinks I'm dead, well and good. I certainly won't go out of my way to attract his attention. But if he thinks otherwise, and is willing to expend this much time and energy on finding me—then somehow, someway, I'm a threat to him. And I'm not going to learn why or how I am, or how to use it against him, by hiding out in the Rift somewhere."

"If you plan on staying here," I-Five said, "I'm with you." The droid looked at Den, put a hand on his shoulder. "But as much as I want to stay, I'll only do so if Den agrees to stay as well. He and I have been through too much for me to abandon him now."

"No," Den said. He clutched his head with both hands. "No, no, no, this is *not* happening!" He faced the others. "I know I've asked this so often it hardly even qualifies as rhetorical, but—*are you all out of your minds?* I mean, we've got a *ship,* people—she doesn't look like much, but she's got hyperdrive and that's all we—" He stared at them, then sighed and spread his arms wide in a gesture of defeat. "I give up," he said. "Okay, Five—if you're crazy enough to stay here, I guess I'll have to be crazy enough to stay with you." He shook his head. "But it's gonna be broiled bloodrat and rankweed from now on, 'cause I'm out of gear to sell."

"As to that," Kaird said, "I might be able to help. I'm not without funds—most of them ill gotten, but even so . . . I need only enough to buy passage back to Nedij."

"You'd do that?" I-Five asked. "You might need it, someday—"

"The Empire's money is no good on my world. It's yours if you want it. It'll take a day or two for me to launder the funds, but—" The avian shrugged. "I've waited this long; one or two more days will make little difference."

Den winced. "Don't say things like that. You're just asking for trouble."

Jax sat in the pilot's chair and watched the dark cityscape race by beneath the *Far Ranger.* I-Five stood next to him. They passed the gigantic, box-like shape of a monad, its thousands of twinkling lights, each a window, bright against the structure's dark surface. "So many beings," Jax mused. "Am I doing the right thing in staying here? Or am I just delusional, thinking I can make any difference at all?"

"The Twi'lek philosopher Gar Gratius said, 'Even the humblest of beings contains within himself a universe of infinite diversity and wonder. Therefore, when you give aid and comfort to just one being, you are, for that moment, the deity of an entire cosmos.' "

Jax looked at I-Five. The droid was staring through the crystasteel cockpit shielding. His photoreceptors were bright, almost shining.

He thought about the sense of accomplishment and pride he'd felt when he'd received the mantle of Jedi Knighthood, created and tuned his first lightsaber, gone out on his first solo mission, during the last days of the Clone Wars. It had also been his last mission; a few weeks afterward the Temple had been attacked and the remaining Jedi, including himself, routed.

He shifted position, and something in one of the pockets of his coat dug into his side. He pulled out the reliquary, opened it, and looked at the jewel within. Exposed to the light once more, it began to glow, cycling from black through the spectrum to purest white.

Kaird noticed the effulgence and peered over Jax's shoulder. "Pyronium. I have never seen a sample that large and unflawed before. Where did you get it?"

"A gift," Jax said. "Years ago, from a fellow Padawan. Anakin Skywalker."

He stared at the glowing element, then closed the container and returned it to his pocket. Anakin, along with nearly all the rest of the Jedi, was gone now. The Order of the Jedi Knights, once a beacon of hope and justice, had been all but extinguished, save for a few fading sparks. But at least one of those sparks could still be fanned.

There is no emotion; there is peace.
There is no ignorance; there is knowledge.

There is no passion; there is serenity.
There is no death; there is the Force.

He had tried his utmost to adhere to these tenets, to make them the guideposts of his life. To be the best Jedi he could be. Toward this, he had disavowed any desire to know anything about his origins or his parents. They had renounced him, after all; given him to the Jedi. He, in turn, had smothered within himself any wish to learn who they had been, what they had been.

But to deny their memories was to deny himself. Jax could see that clearly now. Though the Jedi had shaped him and forged him, the raw material had been provided by Lorn and Siena Pavan.

Below them, the endless sprawl of the planetary city was coming to life. Traffic strata were beginning to build; towers, cloudcutters, and skytowers sparkled with light, and millions upon millions of beings, each and every one their own private cosmos, began their daily routines. The vast majority of those beings were respectable and honest. But deeper down, in the dark crevasses and rifts, those who were neither plied their trades as well.

Someone had to aid the ones who suffered. Someone had to find the ones who were lost. Someone had to stand and fight, for those who could not defend themselves.

Could a Jedi's work ever have been more clear?

Jax looked up. A golden gleam on the horizon; the *Far Ranger* was racing toward the dawn.

I-Five said, "Your father didn't think of himself as a great man. Yet when the situation arose in which he had to step up, he did. I wish I could tell you he succeeded.

It was a cruel and callous fate that made a mockery of his mission. But he tried. That's all, really, in the final analysis, that counts."

Jax stared at the coming dawn. "Tell me about my father," he said.

Turn the page for a preview
of the next *Coruscant Nights* novel
by Michael Reaves,
STREET OF SHADOWS

Planet Naboo
19 BBY

Padmé had never known how much he loved her.

She had died, as far as he knew, in a lonely, far-off place, on a planet which, if not the hell envisioned by the superstitious beliefs of sundry worlds, certainly came close. That was as far as he'd traced her final journey; to Mustafar, a globe still in the throes of creation, where rivers of fire and molten rock stitched across a landscape of basalt and obsidian, and where specially designed heat-resistant droids mined the lava flows for rare and precious minerals. A terrible place, a world of eternal darkness, of soot-filled skies and mephitic gasses. No one deserved to die in such a place, especially not Padmé. If she had to die, she should have spent her last hours on a world of sunlight and song, like their mutual homeworld of Naboo, a world of green and blue, not black and red.

But she had gone to Mustafar, gone after the Jedi Anakin Skywalker, on a mission so secret, she'd said, that not even her bodyguard could accompany her. And he, believing that she would be protected under the aegis of the Jedi, had let her go.

And had never seen her again—alive.

Captain Typho, once Head of Security for the Consular Branch of the Naboo Senate, castigated himself for his decision as he stood with the rest of the mourners, watching the flower-covered casket moving slowly down the esplanade. It had been his job as a soldier to protect Senator Amidala, to shield her from attacks by clandestine Separatist Agents. He had known there would be more attempts on her life. He had known it because there had been previous ones: the bombing of her starship on the very day of her arrival on Coruscant; the deadly kouhuns released into her sleeping chamber by a changeling assassin; her near execution in the Arena at Geonosis.

Even had he not loved her, he would have sacrificed his life to protect her without a second thought. That would have been his duty. His love for her only compounded his culpability. She had gone on her mysterious mission with Skywalker, and he had not gone with her. And now he had to live with the guilt of his survival, a curse infinitely harder than the relatively easy task of dying for her.

It was true that, had she lived, there still would have been no chance of his love for her being requited. Padmé had, after all, been a Senator, and before that the planetary Queen. He was but a soldier; the difference in caste had been far too great. But it hadn't stopped him from loving her. No power in the galaxy, not even the Force itself, could have done that.

After the funeral, Typho milled aimlessly about in the crowd, still stunned, still trying to wrap his mind around the fact of her death. Still reviewing, over and over, what he might have done differently, if he could possibly have persuaded her to reconsider that last journey . . .

Pointless. Fruitless. These self-flagellations served no purpose. Execrating his actions would not bring her back, nor would it honor her memory. Had she known how he had felt, had she known of his love for her, he knew Padmé would have wanted him to move on, to release her, to live instead of wallowing in despondency. And he was willing to do that.

But first, he told himself, *there is one last task that must be performed . . .*

Padmé Amidala must be avenged.

He had heard conflicting rumors, snatches of conversation during the chaos immediately after her death. Most of the government factotums and officials were caught up in dealing with larger issues; although to Typho there could be no greater concern than his personal feelings regarding Padmé's death. He knew that the diplomatic reverberations, especially in light of Naboo's already tenuous status of autonomy in the eyes of Palpatine's new regime, were gigantic. For the circumstances of the Senator's demise were, to put it bluntly, suspicious. There was evidence—compelling evidence—that she had died a violent death.

Of course, this was not meant to be known by the population at large. But rank did have certain privileges, and Captain Typho had learned some things about Padmé's last hours. There were conflicting reports, of course, but all the autopsy reports were in agreement on two things: that she had been strangled, and that the child had died with her.

But exactly how the former had been accomplished, no one was quite sure. The evidence of strangulation had been there, and obvious: the fractured hyoid bone, damage to the larynx, and compression of the trachea were all clear indications of fatal throttling.

But . . .

There were no signs of bruises on her neck, no scratches or signs of congestion . . . no indication of exterior trauma at all. Her throat had been pristine. It was as if she had somehow been choked to death *without* physical contact.

And there was only one power in the galaxy that Typho knew of that could accomplish such a thing.

The Force.

Padmé had gone to Mustafar to meet with the Jedi Knight Skywalker. And all evidence indicated that she had been killed through the Force.

It could not possibly be a coincidence. Even if Skywalker was not the murderer, he had to have been connected somehow. In any event, he was the best and only lead to follow.

Typho knew what he had to do.

He would go to Coruscant. He would find Anakin Skywalker. And, depending on what he learned, the Jedi would live or die.

And then, perhaps, Padmé would rest easier.

LEGACY OF THE FORCE

Read each book in the series

Book 1
Betrayal
by Aaron Allston
Hardcover • On sale 5/30/06
Paperback • On sale 5/1/07

Book 2
Bloodlines
by Karen Traviss
Paperback • On sale 8/29/06

Book 3
Tempest
by Troy Denning
Paperback • On sale 11/28/06

Book 4
Exile
by Aaron Allston
Paperback • On sale 2/27/07

Book 5
Sacrifice
by Karen Traviss
Hardcover • On sale 5/29/07
Paperback • On sale 4/29/08

Book 6
Inferno
by Troy Denning
Paperback • On sale 8/28/07

Book 7
Fury
by Aaron Allston
Paperback • On sale 11/27/07

Book 8
Revelation
by Karen Traviss
Paperback • On sale 2/26/08

Book 9
Invincible
by Troy Denning
Hardcover • On sale 5/20/08

   www.legacyoftheforce.com

Star Wars: New Jedi Order: Dark Journey

Elaine Cunnigham

The dazzling Star Wars space adventure continues in this latest instalment from *The New Jedi Order* series.

Following intense personal loss, Jaina Solo descends to the dark sode, determined to take her revenge on the Yuuzhan Vong. In the process, she learns something new about how to fight the alien invaders, but she must also remember that revenge is not the way of the Jedi – even when it seems the only way to fight the enemy.

arrow books

ALSO AVAILABLE IN ARROW

Star Wars: New Jedi Order: Rebel Stand

Aaron Alston

The bestselling series, *Star Wars: The New Jedi Order*, continues with the second book in the *Enemy Lines* duology of military and political action-adventure.

Luke Skywalker's daring mission to halt the Yuuzhan Vong's nefarious plot to overthrow the New Republic is struggling on all fronts. And time is slipping away for Han and Leia Organa Solo, trapped on a small planet whose rulers are about to yield to Yuuzhan Vong pressure to give up the Jedi rebels.

On Coruscant, Luke and Mara Jade Skywalker have made a shocking discovery that is preventing the Yuuzhan Vong from exerting complete control. But when the enemy tracks them down, Luke and Mara are thrust into a fierce battle for their lives. Suddenly, the chances of escaping appear nearly impossible. And in space, another battle rages, one that holds ominous consequences for the New Republic – and for the Jedi themselves.

arrow books

Star Wars: New Jedi Order: Shatterpoint

Matthew Stover

A must-read for everyone who saw *Star Wars: Attack of the Clones* and *Star Wars: Revenge of the Sith*! A special treat for fans of the Mace Windu character from the movie and for fans of Jedi action in general.

In the midst of the Clone Wars, Master Mace Windu returns from his separatist-occupied homeworld, where his former Padawan, Depa Billaba, has been working as an undercover agent. But Depa hasn't been reporting in lately, and Republic intelligence has been gathering disturbing hints of bloody ambushes and terror-strikes in the deep outback. Mace trained Depa – he knows that no-one but he can hope to even reach her, let alone save her from the darkness . . .

arrow books